Into the Terror

Book Eight of Rise of the Republic

By

James Rosone and Miranda Watson

****

Illustration © Tom Edwards
Tom EdwardsDesign.com

****

Published in conjunction with Front Line Publishing, Inc.

Manuscript Copyright Notice

ISBN: 978-1-957634-58-6
Sun City Center, Florida, United States of America
Library of Congress Control Number: 2022917263

Table of Contents

Prologue

Before the Zodark Attacks
Sumer, Qatana System

The Interstellar Marshal Service had been tracking a known member of the Mukhabarat for some time, collecting data about his contacts, places of business, and activities—whether he knew it or not, Odeh was a marked man. Every person he interacted with either became a mark in their own right or was quietly "disappeared" on the side, eliminated from the chessboard.

Kamran had been a part of the IMS contingent on Sumer since the service had begun incorporating Sumerians, and he *loved* a good stakeout. He had been following Odeh for weeks now, tracking his movements, learning his habits, and monitoring his communications. He knew when he went to bed, when he took a morning jog, how he took his coffee, and most importantly, what parts of his business were legitimate and which were not, and how he was furthering Mukhabarat activity. So, when a shipment arrived at the back of Odeh's restaurant on a Tuesday, late in the evening, Kamran knew something was up.

"We've got three small packages, about the size of a flower vase," Kamran announced over the comms.

"Any idea what they are?" asked his team lead.

Kamran was situated in a van in a parking garage nearby, looking at footage of the scene taken from various angles. He glanced at some of the monitors that held additional tools such as infrared and radiation imagery. He rubbed his eyes.

"I'm seeing an odd signature here, boss. I'm running it through our systems now…" Kamran swore. "This can't be real—"

"What? What is it?" pressed the team lead.

"It's—it's those energy bombs," Kamran stammered.

"You mean EMPs?"

"I think that's what you Terrans call them, but they don't work exactly the same. I think they're Zodark tech—anyway, that doesn't matter. We need to contain this!"

"Hold your horses there, Kamran," said the team lead. "If we take it all down now, we lose this gravy train we've got going."

Kamran took a deep breath and let it out slowly. He knew that was how the IMS operated, but he also knew what could happen if these things got out.

"We need to lock this down, boss. Put the best teams on it. You don't want to see the level of destruction these little jars can unleash."

"Don't get your panties in a wad, Kamran. Remember your training and just focus on your next task. Now, where exactly is Odeh putting these things?"

****

One Week Later
Office of the IMS Director
Jacksonville, Arkansas
Earth, Sol System

IMS Director Reinhard Gehlen was waiting for the agent in charge on the ground to call him with the news that they'd nabbed their HVI, but the call hadn't happened yet.

Last week on Sumer, they'd discovered three energy weapons that were Zodark technology, similar to EMPs—fortunately, two of those weapons had been captured before they'd left the planet, along with the Ani operatives that had been sent to collect them. Those Ani were now sitting in interrogation booths. However, the third operative had managed to evade the IMS personnel on Sumer, and he had slipped away into a freighter, lost in the wind—that was, until a few hours ago, when his biometrics had been flagged on the John Glenn.

He'd exited a freighter from Sumer and was now on his way down the space elevator, hopefully into the waiting arms of his agent in charge and the team Gehlen had hastily put together. Gehlen had had to suppress the urge to micromanage the hell out of that operation, but he'd settled for putting the fear of God in his people that this *must* be contained.

Gehlen's neurolink alerted him to an incoming call. "Yeah?" he asked, forgoing the more standard etiquette with voice conversations.

"Boss, I don't know what happened, but he's slipped past us. We've been scouring the area and scanning through the CCTV footage—he's just disappeared."

"Damn it!" Gehlen roared. "Keep searching—he has to be there, *somewhere*."

"Yes, boss. We'll exhaust all options."

The call disconnected.

Gehlen swore loudly. He picked up his coffee and threw it at the wall. The Republic-issued mug didn't break, but a huge mess remained. He sat back down and put his head in his hands.

His secretary must have heard the racket and cautiously walked in. "Sir, is everything OK?"

"No, it most certainly is not," he replied, calming himself down. "But unfortunately, I don't think there's anything you can do to help, other than help me clean up this coffee…sorry about that, by the way."

I can't believe they lost the Ani when he went down the space elevator, he thought. *Catching him at the bottom of the space elevator should have worked.* There were only so many entrances and exits there—but now that Ani was headed who knew where with some massively effective Zodark energy weapon. *Could this day get any worse?*

****

Two Days Later
Office of the IMS Director
Jacksonville, Arkansas
Earth, Sol System

Director Gehlen's neurolink alerted him to an incoming call from one of his agents in charge. "Gehlen," he said.

"Sir, we got a hit on that BOLO for the Ani from Sumer. His facial recognition popped up on a hyperloop."

Gehlen sat up straight as a board. "Where's that train going?" he pressed.

"It's going from Houston to Little Rock; my guess is he'll take the connection to the capital."

Gehlen blew some air forcefully out of his lips while he thought. "When is the train set to arrive?" he asked.

"In thirty-five minutes, sir."

"Let me look into something here," said Gehlen. "Give me one minute, and I'll get back to you."

"Yes, sir."

As soon as the call disconnected, another one came through. This time it was Drew Kanter from Republic Intelligence.

"Gehlen."

"This is Drew. I've been monitoring the same situation you have, and I know about the recent contact on the hyperloop," he said, cutting to the chase. "Does Republic Intelligence have your permission to act on this?"

"Yes. Please. I don't want to know about the how—just get this done."

"No problem, sir."

"I sure hope so."

******

Fort Banks, Arkansas
Earth, Sol System

The Kites had been on the base for some advanced Special Forces training. For these augmented supersoldiers, it had almost been like a vacation, with someone else cooking their food and no high-stakes activities to participate in. But that respite was about to be interrupted.

Drew reached out to them via neurolink. *Hey, team. I hope training has been going well, but duty calls and we've got an emergency on our hands. One that requires a team with the kinds of skills only you guys have. I'm sending you a data packet with more details on the mission and the target you're to take into custody or neutralize. It's time to put your war face on and go earn your pay. Do whatever you have to do, but get your asses up to the Little Rock hyperloop station before this operative is able to execute his mission. Drew out.*

Roger that, David replied.

The five of them stood simultaneously. Their instructor became incensed. "Where the hell do you think you're going?" he asked, hand on his hips.

"I'm sure you'll be receiving a message shortly," Catalina replied as they made their way out of the room.

"My apologies," they heard as they exited.

David tried not to laugh. Although he had technically died and then been revived to be a part of this secret group of soldiers, it was funny to think how his position in the world had gone upward in such a short period of time. Being a part of a clandestine unit for the Republic Intelligence had its benefits.

"All right, so how do we get there in time?" asked Somchai.

Amir pointed to an Osprey on station that had several soldiers near it. "Looks like we're going to have to interrupt a HALO jump," he said.

The Kites bounded over to the Osprey and were intercepted by the instructor and some of the armed soldiers who were getting ready to load up.

"Just what do you think you're doing?" the HALO instructor roared, making himself large as if he was trying to frighten off a bear.

"We need your ride," David announced.

The instructor scoffed as the soldiers moved their rifles to the low ready. The Kites flashed their credentials and the man's expression fell instantly. He held his arms up to the sides and dropped them, indicating that his students should lower their weapons.

"They're Republic Intelligence. We are to give them whatever they want," the instructor announced.

"What?" one of the soldiers asked, confused.

"Sorry boys, we're going to need you to give us your weapons!" Jess demanded. The students looked at their instructor in utter shock. "Give us your weapons *now*; this is bigger than you!"

"Hand 'em over," the instructor directed, pulling his own personal firearm from a holster on his leg and offering it up.

"You five—get in the bird," Catalina directed. "We're going to need your suits and we don't have time for you to undress out here."

They glanced back at the instructor one last time, but he just nodded and they dutifully climbed on in.

As soon as everyone was aboard, David flashed his credentials to the pilot. "Fly!" he yelled.

"Am I being kidnapped?" the pilot asked, confused.

"Just fly. We'll tell you on the way."

Seconds later, the Osprey was in the air, and the confused would-have-been HALO jumpers were peeling off their combat suits and forking them over.

Jess was the first to finish her quick change. She patted the armor on the shoulder. "This stuff is nice," she commented. "Not quite as good as our regular stuff, but it'll do."

"It's Dragon Skin," one of the soldiers replied defensively. "It's top-of-the-line."

"Oh, is it now?" Jess teased. "Well, you just go on thinking that, OK?"

"What the hell did we just get roped into?" one of the soldiers mumbled quietly.

"I don't know, but they're so freaking badass, I think I'm in love," another shot back.

"Sorry, boys, I don't have time for that," Jess replied with a wink, causing them both to blush.

David had received further instructions from Drew at that point, and he immediately attempted to patch into the operators at the central hyperloop switchboard in Little Rock. When he got through to someone with enough authority to handle his situation, he explained to the manager that they were moving to intercept the train arriving from Houston in thirty minutes, and that there was an individual aboard with an explosive device.

"Holy crap!" said the manager in disbelief.

"We're inbound to your position, but our time is going to be tight. Is there anything you can do to slow that train down?" David asked.

There was a two-second pause, but then the manager replied, "Yes, I can make that happen."

****

Five Minutes Later
Little Rock Hyperloop Station
Earth, Sol System

Kyla Jean tapped the monitor on her switchboard. "What the hell?" she croaked. "I've been a switchboard operator for almost twenty years, and I've never had a train run late."

She eyed her trainee, who was ten feet away, fixing him with a gaze that would have killed, if that were possible.

Damn intern, she thought. She was always having to fix his screwups. *Why'd they have to go and assign me a rookie?* she asked

9

herself angrily. *Just because I've been here for so long doesn't mean I want to train anyone.*

She straightened herself back up and turned her attention back to her station. "No matter. I'll fix this," she said to herself. She swiped her key card, typed in her override password, and reset the train speed so that it would arrive as scheduled.

When she finished, she looked over at her figurine of a Canadian Sphynx cat and smiled. "Now what would these people do without me?"

****

Twenty-Four Minutes Later
Osprey Inbound to Little Rock Hyperloop Station
Earth, Sol System

"Hey, bro, isn't that our train?" asked Somchai, pointing to a train that had just taken off.

"Crap! I thought the manager was going to be able to slow it down," said David. "I'm sure it's headed on to the capital now."

David yelled to the pilot, "I need you to get us to the station at the capital as soon as possible. Really put the pedal to the metal!"

"Changing course, but I gotta tell ya, I'm not going to be able to get you to a good landing zone there; it's not a big enough station for a helipad that supports Ospreys," the pilot explained.

"Just get us below a hundred feet over the station and open the back hatch. We'll take care of it."

For a second, the pilot looked at David like he'd lost his marbles, but given everything else that had already happened, he just replied, "If you say so, boss."

David went back into the bay. Everyone was all kitted out, and the soldiers that had been commandeered with the Osprey had answered any questions the Kites had about the equipment. Their HUDs showed them a map of the train station and they were patched into the CCTV there.

David updated Drew on the trajectory of the train and their new flight path, and he assured them that, just like before, IMS had been directed to stay out of their way.

The train would be arriving downtown, so there would be plenty of people there to witness their eventful entrance.

The Osprey continued at a breakneck pace until it suddenly came to a standstill in front of the entrance to the Jacksonville hyperloop station. The back hatch dropped and all five Kites dropped out of the sky without parachutes, their boots slowing their descent to the ground at the last second. They landed light as a feather and took off at inhuman speeds.

Women screamed and clutched at their children as if they were being invaded by a hostile army, but the Kites just kept sprinting forward. When they reached the biometric checkpoint, they leaped and flipped right over top of it, jumping higher than even a seasoned athlete could accomplish without the upgrades they'd had implanted. The crowd collectively gasped at the sight of these supersoldiers who'd come out of nowhere.

At the end of the hall, toward the trains, the Ani must have seen what was happening. He tossed a couple of grenades into the air so they'd explode over the crowd, creating mass chaos. A whole slew of people were hit with shrapnel, and there was mass hysteria and screaming.

The Ani raced up a nearby staircase, firing at the uniformed IMS agents as they ran, guns drawn. He hit several agents as they fired back, no match for the Ani, who was faster and more accurate.

The Kites were almost on him now. David saw him turn to go up another flight of stairs.

He's headed for the tram that goes straight to the Space Command headquarters, he announced to his group over neurolink. *Holy crap, if that thing goes off at the capital, just think of what an EMP would do there.*

We can't let that happen, Catalina insisted.

They were gaining on him, practically flying up the stairs two at a time. Then the Ani dropped another grenade behind him and it rolled toward the Kites.

Boom!

Shrapnel bits slammed against the armor of the Kites, bouncing ineffectually off the Dragon Skin armor like a snowball shattering harmlessly against a jacket.

The Ani ran and jumped onto the last car of the tram just before the doors started closing behind him.

David cursed as he lunged at the tram, somehow managing to get his hands between the doors before they closed all the way. He immediately pulled at the doors, using the additional strength of the suit to pry it open.

Amir had caught up to the train as the doors were closing, so he jumped directly on top of the car David was trying to get in. The other three were right behind him, in the process of leaping on top of the train when it suddenly lurched forward, dragging David along with it. Somchai and Jess fell flat on their faces and Amir nearly lost his footing and fell off as well, but he managed to recover. Catalina was just behind Somchai and Jess, so she saw the train moving and managed to readjust before she jumped at the back of the train.

I'm on, she announced. *I've got a handle back here.*

Somchai and Jess had jumped up at this point and started running after the train, but it was too late. Their screams to stop the train went unheard.

The train is not supposed to do that! Somchai exclaimed to the group. *Whenever there's a door open, a fail-safe keeps the trains from running.*

Unless someone overrides it, Jess suggested.

Meanwhile, David was struggling both to open the doors wide enough to get in and to keep himself from falling from the moving train. But even despite that, he managed to see the Ani push through the crowd, headed toward the front. David told his fellow Kites what he'd just seen.

I'll run forward from up here, then, before I break in from the sides, said Amir.

Is it just me, or is this train going faster than usual? asked Catalina from her precarious position.

No, I don't think you're wrong, Amir agreed as he continued forward.

David finally managed to pry his way into the car. The people inside were stunned by his presence—these poor folks were just on their commute, and they hadn't had their coffee yet. One woman screamed in sheer terror. But David didn't have time to comfort anyone. He took one deep recovery breath, told his team he was in the train, and then sprinted toward the front.

I'm in, said Amir, providing his own status update.

As David neared the first connecting door between the tram cars, he heard the sound of breaking glass behind him.

I'm in, Catalina announced. She must have found a way to swing her feet at the back window. David was glad she was all right.

After going through a few of the cars, David spotted Amir ahead of him through the windows in the doors. There were a few flashes of light and then Amir fell backward.

You all right, brother? David asked.

I'll be fine, Amir groaned. *The suit absorbed the blaster shots, but I can't move yet.*

Damn.

When David hit the car where the Ani had stopped, he entered at a blinding pace and rapidly fired his rifle.

Pop, pop, pop.

The Ani ducked down behind one of the rows of seats and held his gun up over his head, firing indiscriminately toward the center of the train.

"Get down!" David yelled over the panicked screams of the crowd. At least two people had been hit by the Ani's rapid fire already, although David's split-second assessment was that the wounds were treatable so far.

Knowing that even if he got hit, he wouldn't die, David continued to charge at the guy, firing sometimes up and sometimes down toward the leg of the seat. At least one of his shots hit something, because he heard a loud metallic ping.

Then David was right on top of him. As he prepared to fire point-blank, he realized in horror that while the Ani had been shooting at the crowd, he'd shoved one hand into his backpack and was manipulating the weapon within.

The Ani smiled. "You're too late," he declared, and then he pushed a button with glee.

David zapped him with his blaster, and the Ani slumped to the floor, dead.

And then nothing happened. David was sure that the device had been fully primed and ready to go, but there was only silence.

As the tram pulled into the station, soldiers immediately boarded. A bomb squad took possession of their mysterious EMP-like weapon and removed it from the tram in a special type of shield, to avoid any accidents in transit.

After a few minutes on the platform, one of the bomb techs brought the device over to David.

"I thought I'd show you why this thing didn't detonate," he said, showing a burnt-out panel in one spot of the device. "This right here—this was the golden shot."

Somehow, some way, David had gotten lucky while firing at the Ani. He could barely believe it.

****

One Hour Later

Admiral Bailey had requested to meet with Drew and his team directly, to which Drew had agreed. When the admiral seemed offended that they were keeping their helmets on, Drew had firmly replied, "With all due respect, Admiral, I plan on maintaining the anonymity of my action team."

"I guess I can't argue with that," Bailey had replied.

After the admiral had asked the team several questions about what they had observed, he turned to Drew and asked to speak with him privately.

"Guys, why don't you go get a coffee or something for a few minutes, all right? I mean, I think you've earned yourself a snack at least," Drew said jovially, shooing the Kites out of the room.

When they'd closed the door, Admiral Bailey leaned forward in his chair and lowered his voice. "You know, they wouldn't be trying to disrupt the electronics at Space Command headquarters if something bigger wasn't about to happen," the old admiral told the senior spook.

"Now you're thinking the way I do," Drew agreed.

The two men talked for a while before Drew said he needed to get his team on the road.

"Whoa, wait up there," said Bailey, holding up his hands. "We still have a lot of questions about what just went down, and we need to interview your people further."

Drew snorted. "Sir, you'll want to keep my team on the field right now."

"OK, look, at least leave me the guy who shot the device and disabled it," Bailey countered.

Drew started to say no, but instead he agreed to let David, who he referred to as "Smith" in front of the admiral, stay behind for now.

As Drew walked away from that meeting, he couldn't help but go back to what Bailey had said to him.

Something big is about to happen...but what? he wondered.

Chapter One
Peeling Back the Onion

Lab Site X

Dr. Katō Sakura had barely left her desk for the entire day. For hours, she had been ferociously reading a file she had uncovered, only stopping to use the bathroom when absolutely necessary. The rest of the time, she kept herself fueled with a protein bar or another snack she had squirreled away in her bag and sips of water from her canteen. This discovery was huge.

In her ravenous studies, she had unearthed some of the history of the Humtars and the war they had fought against some of the ascended people. At the outset, she had simply found it historically fascinating, but then, as she continued reading, she realized that the Republic was going to have great interest in what she was learning. It turned out that some of the strategies they had employed in their conflict might very well help the Republic deal with the Collective once they eventually encountered them.

Ever since the Republic had learned of this enemy made of ascended beings that could embody mechanized warriors at will, there had been a healthy sense of trepidation about this potential adversary. These ascended beings could communicate with each other without barriers, and they were almost impossible to kill since they weren't tied to fleshly bodies. And they seemed hell-bent on a long game of taking over the universe, one soul at a time.

Sakura took another bite of her protein bar as she continued to read. She was starting to understand the Humtar language without much translation at this point. She already knew that when the Humtars had had a similar movement to ascension, which they called "the stripping," a large faction of the Humtars had objected to this movement, but now she found that they had discovered a way to inhibit the communication between the "stripped" beings.

Viceroy Hunt is going to want to learn about this, she thought excitedly. *If we could stop the Collective from collaborating, it would remove their greatest strength.*

There were some dangers to this method, apparently. The device they designed to interfere with the stripped beings' communication could *absolutely* not be pointed at a live human being. She saw a photo of the deadly results and shuddered.

Thwump!

Something slammed against the wall outside of the lab where Sakura had been researching.

"What the hell was that?" she exclaimed.

Another colleague of hers stood up from her station and looked back at Sakura, confused and visibly frightened.

Thunk! Bam!

Sakura motioned to her fellow researcher, and they cautiously approached the door. There seemed to be a raucous crowd forming, because she could hear shouting.

"Get him!" someone yelled.

When Sakura reached the door, she carefully stood to the side and then pressed the button to open it.

Two soldiers who were engaged in a violent physical struggle fell to the ground right in front of the doorway. Sakura recognized them as Privates Rowan Connor and Dominic Brown.

Brown landed on top and took advantage of his newfound high ground, pinning Connor's arms below his knees before cocking his fist and connecting with Connor's face. Left, right, left, right— Brown whaled on him several times as he yelled out in a rage.

The crowd was getting louder and louder, taunting them to fight harder. Sakura was horrified. She caught the attention of her colleague and yelled, "Go get Captain Young!"

Her frightened friend nodded and managed to slip out through the throng that was gathered around. Sakura thought she even saw a few soldiers placing bets on the outcome of the fight.

"Stop!" Sakura yelled. "Stop it!" But no one responded to her calls.

Connor suddenly pushed every ounce of strength into lifting his arms, which threw Brown forward off him; Brown tried to roll to avoid landing smack-dab on his face.

"Please!" Sakura pleaded. "You have to stop!"

But whatever had started this fight in the first place apparently had them both seeing red. Both men stood to their feet. Connor wiped blood off his lip, and Brown positioned himself like a tiger about to pounce. With a wild-eyed expression on his face, he lunged at his fellow soldier.

At the last moment, a sergeant pulled Connor out of the way. "Fight's over!" he yelled.

Brown, who had been mid-jump, apparently didn't fully comprehend what had just happened and landed a haymaker right across the sergeant's jaw. The sergeant somehow took it in stride, barely losing his footing but rubbing his face.

The demeanor of the crowd changed drastically. A low "ooh" grumbled through the group, and a few people cussed quietly.

It was at that moment that Captain Aaron Young arrived. "What the hell is going on here?" he yelled.

"Nothing I couldn't have handled, sir," replied the young sergeant.

"Hmm, is that so?" asked Captain Young.

No one said a word for a moment. Connor had slumped to the floor, exhausted and bloody. A lot of the crowd quietly slunk away, back to whatever post they were supposed to be working on at the moment.

"Well, I think it's about time we get everyone some medical attention," Young announced. "And on the way, I want to hear about what exactly caused this little 'incident.'"

Young turned to Sakura, who had found herself frozen there. "Can you help me walk Private Connor over there to the medical bay?" he asked. She nodded grimly and pulled the young soldier up, putting his arm around her shoulder.

As the five of them walked down the hallway, Young asked, "So, what the hell was that all about?"

Private Brown clenched his teeth. "Connor's been banging my girlfriend," he hissed.

Connor snarled. "Carla was *my* girlfriend."

Sakura stepped a little further away from Brown and Young, concerned that they might decide to start the hostilities up again.

Young clicked his tongue. "All this over a woman?" he asked. "Hell, I don't know how many times I've told you guys that I don't care what you do in your personal lives, but it better not affect your mission."

Brown snickered. "Mission? Babysitting scientists?" he scoffed.

"You may not find it very important, but the intel being gathered here is going to be the breakthrough for the Republic," Captain Young shot back. "And if you want to hold that back, well, then, I have a brig I can throw you in."

Brown sobered up. "Yes, sir," he said quietly.

When they got to the medical bay, the medic on staff patched up their wounds. Captain Young assigned them to opposite shifts and scheduled a time with each man to formally review the consequences of what had happened. Then he thanked Sakura for her time and said something about going to meet up with Carla.

On her way back to the lab, Sakura's friend, Dr. Katherine Johnson, pulled her aside. "Sakura, do you have a minute?" she asked, putting her hand on her shoulder. "We need to talk."

"Oh?" Sakura replied.

Katherine glanced around. "This one needs to be in private."

Sakura followed her to one of the small conference rooms on site. When they'd closed the door and turned on the "do not disturb" option, Sakura grabbed a cup of tea from one of the replicators and plopped herself down in one of the chairs. "All right, Katherine, what is this about?"

"Have you ever heard the phrase, 'An idle mind is the devil's playground'?" asked Katherine as she sat down in another chair.

"No...what are you referring to?" Sakura grilled.

"Our military friends—well, some of them seem to have lost their minds, or at least their military bearings, due to boredom," she explained.

"Some of them seem very happily occupied," Sakura said with a wink, referring to Katherine's ongoing relationship with Captain Aaron Young.

Katherine covered her cheeks as if to hide her embarrassment. "Yeah, OK. I earned that one," she said with a laugh. "Truthfully, I'm not the only one in a relationship right now. That does seem to be keeping a few people out of trouble. Then there's the ones who are just hooking up—except the pool for random hookups is very limited here, and lovers scorned don't easily forget. You saw what just happened with Connor and Brown."

"Yeah," Sakura said sadly. "That was really messed up."

"OK, but honestly, there's been a lot more going on that hasn't resulted in the same level of discipline," Katherine explained. "*Tons* of pranks…so many, I don't think you want to listen to them all. But I hear about most of it because Aaron has to have someone to vent to."

"So, what are we talking about here?" asked Sakura. "I think you're going to need to spell it out for me."

"Right, so I guess some of the guys thought it would be funny to replicate a ton of what is the Humtars' closest equivalent to a lemon, and then a group of soldiers went through a sort of hazing to see who could eat the most wedges. There was no disciplinary action for this one because the resulting stomach cramps and diarrhea were their own punishment."

Sakura covered her mouth, trying to stifle a laugh. She was not successful.

"Yeah, that one is pretty funny," Katherine acknowledged, "but it also resulted in at least five soldiers being on sick leave for a day. It messed up the whole watch rotation."

"Yikes."

"Yeah, tell me about it. Oh, as if that's not enough, there's this junior officer, an ensign, if you can believe it—he's one of our Osprey pilots from the *Voyager*, call sign Spike. Some of the stuff he pulls is what you might expect from an enlisted sailor or soldier, but not from an officer. For example, he's been known to send young soldiers to the first sergeant to see if they can give them an ID-10-T evaluation so they can attend a training course."

Sakura almost spat her tea out in laughter before catching the stink eye from Katherine, who wasn't finished speaking.

Katherine cleared her throat. "As I was saying, this guy, Spike, sent a newly assigned spacer from the maintenance section in the hangar back to the *Voyager* to speak with the supply chief and ask for, get this, chem light batteries—"

Now Sakura doubled over in laughter. After regaining her ability to speak, she commented, "Oh, please tell me you're not serious. Are you? Did someone actually fall for that? I mean, who would possibly think that glow sticks need a battery?"

Katherine grunted. "Apparently, yes. Someone did take the bait."

Sakura laughed deeply from her belly. "I mean, honestly, that one is hilarious," she finally snorted.

Katherine shrugged. "On its own, maybe. But it's all adding up. There's a lieutenant above Spike who is, shall we say, a bit shorter in stature and whose last name just *happens* to be Shortman." She glared at Sakura before continuing, "The other day, he found a stool in the restroom by a urinal labeled 'For Lieutenant Shortman Only.' He doesn't have any proof it was Spike, but they *all* know who did it."

Sakura doubled over in fits of laughter, unable to contain herself anymore. The usually reserved scientist smacked at her knee while she laughed. "I can't..." She finally gasped for breath between tears and snorts of laughter.

Katherine frowned. "Sakura, I know you think it's funny and all. But I don't think you understand the seriousness of this," she insisted as she crossed her arms.

"Oh, lighten up," Sakura finally said, still chuckling. "Listen, these guys are stuck here. What do you expect them to do? Twiddle their thumbs in their time off?"

Katherine leaned back. "Humpf. Well, you may have a point there," she admitted. "Maybe we need to do a better job of creating ways for them to blow off steam. There's only so much time one can spend in the gym or training, and God knows they do a lot of that."

"I officially designate you the head of the social committee," Sakura said, feigning seriousness.

"Great...all that scientific education hard at work," Katherine replied.

"It's a tough job, but someone's got to do it," Sakura said with a smile. "So, is there something else on your mind?" she asked. "I've got a lot of work to do if I want to finish these reports for the next comms drone."

"No, that's fine," Katherine replied. "I guess I can take a little time out for a side project, as long as it keeps everyone moving forward."

Chapter Two
Back at the Capital

Waves
Emerald City, New Eden
Rhea System

Miles had been to a lot of restaurants over the years, but he and Lilly had already grown very fond of Waves. It was hard to go and try something new when he knew just how amazing his experience would be there. The seafood was fresh, the views stunning, the service impeccable—so when Lilly asked to eat out, this was the obvious choice.

As Miles took a bite of his shellfish dish, smothered in a sauce that involved a good deal of Andorran butter, he became lost in a world of culinary delight. Replicators did a decent enough job of keeping one fed and supplied with the appropriate vitamins and minerals—but they could never duplicate *this*. Real food made with real ingredients just had a level of flavor that no ship had ever attained. He breathed deeply, drinking in the steamy aroma of his food.

Lilly laughed. "You might want to wipe that drool off the corner of your mouth," she teased.

Miles pulled himself back to the conversation with his wife. "Heh, sorry about that," he replied. "Where were we?"

They bantered on for a little while, talking about the books they'd been reading and discussing where they'd like to travel to, if Miles's schedule would allow for an actual vacation at some point. When Lilly ordered a dessert and a coffee, Miles excused himself to the restroom.

As he stood at the urinal, relieving himself, the hairs on the back of his neck suddenly stood on edge. Gunther was standing next to him at another urinal—he hadn't seen the scientist in a while, and Miles wondered how he was progressing in his research into exploiting the Zodarks' weaknesses.

"We need to talk," Gunther announced as he casually took care of his own business. "We may have found something."

"Not here," Miles replied. "I have a meeting coming up with Liam and Riggins about the deposits of Bronkis5 on Éire. Get yourself placed on the list for that meeting." He zipped his pants and walked over to the sinks.

"Will do, sir," Gunther replied, zipping his own pants.

Why do we always do these things in the restroom? Miles asked himself. *There has to be a better way for us to pass messages off books.*

****

Viceroy's Office
Alliance City, New Eden
Rhea System

Viceroy Miles Hunt looked around the table at Liam Patrick, Cormac Riggins and Gunther Haas. Liam seemed especially agitated.

"Well, gentlemen, let's get this thing going, shall we?"

Liam didn't waste any time. He cracked his knuckles and leaned forward as he spoke. "Viceroy, I am *very* concerned about these reports I'm hearing about the alliance being on heightened alert. Are you expecting the Zodarks to attack again? Because we're all alone out there on Éire."

Miles shook his head. "Look, of all the potential targets the Zodarks could go after, I would have the absolute least concern about your corner of the universe. Our intel still indicates that the Zodarks don't have a full grasp of the value of Bronkis5, and they have much bigger fish to fry, quite frankly."

Liam folded his arms, obviously not entirely convinced.

"If it'll make you feel any better, I'll send a few more support ships your way for the short term," Miles conceded, to which Liam grunted. "I'm sure the Primords won't mind," he continued with a wink. "Anyway, the plans to beef up the security at the stargate are almost complete, are they not?"

Riggins interjected. "They are. The system will be quite state-of-the-art."

"Good," said Miles. "Because you aren't wrong about the threat the Zodarks impose—just about *where* they will attack. We're going to need a *lot* more Bronkis5."

Riggins held up a hand. "Whoa, hold up there. TOREC mining is absolutely maxed out at our current pace right now. We don't have enough manpower, Synths, or even machinery to go any faster."

"Ah, but if you had those things, it would be a different story, right?" asked Miles with a grin.

"What are you saying, exactly?" asked Liam.

"There are some benefits to meeting directly with the Viceroy," Miles chuckled. "The Galactic Empire would like to open up the floodgates of resources for you—essentially, if you can provide more Bronkis5, you have a blank check to make it happen."

Liam leaned back and looked over to Riggins. The two of them seemed to be sizing up whether the offer was genuine.

"I'm proposing that we build another naval shipyard in your system, to reduce transportation times for the Bronkis5 material and free up more of your ships to assist in the actual mining operations," Miles continued. "Musk Industries and Blue Origins are looking to create a joint venture to oversee their collective operations in your system. I've heard that the Terran Shipbuilders' Union would love to oversee the construction of the new shipyard."

The left corner of Liam's mouth crept upward, but Miles knew he was always a bit conflicted when it came to further involvement by the Republic in their new corner of the alliance.

"Go on," said Riggins, leaning forward.

"I believe that Kawasaki Inc. would make a great choice to build some large capital warships," said Miles. "And, Liam, if you're concerned about security—having some of these bad boys around you will certainly make you a less enticing target."

Liam tipped his head toward Miles. He wasn't fighting back on any of these suggestions so far.

"As for the support ships at the new shipyard, I think the new German-British merger, Babcock-Neptun, will be more than capable," Miles concluded. "So, what do you say—we'll feed the gravy train of supplies and labor, and you keep the gravy train of Bronkis5 rolling?"

Riggins stood and glanced over at Liam, who nodded slightly. Then he thrust his hand forward. "You have a deal, Viceroy," he said, shaking on it.

"Excellent. We can communicate more of the details by the standard methods, but I'm glad we could meet in person."

Liam also stood and offered his hand. "Viceroy," he said as a sort of farewell.

"You've got a great little haven over on Éire, Liam. I look forward to seeing where you take it."

Liam and Riggins left the room, leaving just Gunther behind.

"Well, that was a fun little show, Viceroy," Gunther remarked.

Miles chuckled. "I apologize for making you sit through that, but let's not waste any more time, shall we? What do you have for me?" he pressed.

Gunther interlocked his fingers in front of him. "We have it," he announced stoically.

"Have what, exactly?" asked Miles.

"We have been working on exploiting a specific weakness in the Zodarks' anatomy for some time," Gunther explained. "We began researching their respiratory systems because having four lungs is a unique genetic trait we have not observed in any of the other known species. While having four lungs might seem like an advantage in battle, they have a weakness in their linings at the points where their lungs meet. We've designed a virus that specifically exploits that vulnerability."

"How easy would it be for the Zodarks to isolate the infection and potentially treat it?" Miles asked.

"This virus has an extremely long incubation period," Gunther clarified. "A Zodark host will go for about a week without any symptoms, and all the while, they will be infecting anyone they come into contact with, and those new hosts will go on infecting others. When it does begin to manifest itself, it has about a sixty-five percent mortality rate."

"What about medical nanites and other advanced treatments that the Zodarks have available to them?" asked Miles.

"We've run this virus through several scenarios. Even in the best-case scenarios for the Zodarks, we would succeed in wiping out effectively half of their population," Gunther replied.

There was a heavy silence in the room.

"Should we start producing the virus to be placed in deliverable vehicles to infect the Zodarks?" Gunther asked after waiting for a beat.

Miles's stomach tightened. A big part of him wanted to get revenge on these giant blue beasts for all the savagery they had unleashed on his people and on the Sumerians.

But if we cross this line, we become like them, he realized. He didn't want to lose his humanity in order to achieve victory.

"Do what's necessary to make sure it can be rapidly built and deployed, but then shelve the project," Miles directed.

"Sir?" Gunther asked, very confused.

"We're going to keep this in our pocket for the moment. I believe we can defeat the Zodarks without taking things this far," Miles replied.

Gunther seemed deflated, but in the next breath, Miles thought he could see a sense of relief on his face.

"What do we do next?" Gunther asked.

"I actually do have something else I want you to work on," Miles offered. "I'd like you to team up with Dr. Katō Sakura, who's currently operating out at Lab Site X. They're discovering some very interesting things that may help us battle the Collective."

"Really?" Gunther asked, perking up at this information.

"There's a whole file I'm going to need you to read for context, but in a nutshell, the Humtars had discovered a way to inhibit the communication between ascended beings."

"And if we can translate that to the Collective, we will basically stop the right hand from knowing what the left is doing," Gunther summarized.

"Exactly," Miles replied with a nod. "If we can find a way to force the Collective to act individually, or to cut off one ship from another, they will have lost their greatest advantage. If they can't coordinate...let's just say it will be a much more even playing field."

"Well, I am intrigued," Gunther admitted. "All right, we will start on this right away."

Chapter Three
Feeling Green

Work had ended, and Ashurina headed to one of her favorite spots. This was her guilty pleasure; she would curl up with her Qpad, surrounded by greenery and flowers in overflowing abundance, and escape into a romantic novel. Back home in the Gurista society, such books would have been censored or outright banned, but here she was free to allow her thoughts to roam.

This had become her routine at least two to three days a week since her transfer to the new DARPA facility. Now that she didn't have to entertain a useful idiot, her time was more her own. It was something Ashurina had never experienced—control over her life.

After a few hours, she reached a natural stopping point in her story and decided to walk among the blossoms surrounding her. That was until she felt the barrel of a gun connect with the back of her hip.

"Just act normal and keep walking," whispered Dakkuri calmly as they strolled along.

"We weren't scheduled to meet today," Ashurina coolly stated. Her Watcher must have given him information on where to find her.

"We have worked together for years, Ashurina—nearly a decade at this point," Dakkuri hissed. "Either you were fed bad intel, or you intentionally fed me some bad info. So, I have to know—which is it?"

She had a split-second decision to make. "You're right, Dakkuri, we have worked together for years now. After all this time living among these people, surely you must know we are on the wrong side."

He stopped walking, so she stood still, bracing herself for her impending death. Then she dared to say, barely above a whisper, "Dakkuri, it's not too late to change sides."

"Change sides—I wouldn't even know how to do that," Dakkuri said hurriedly through gritted teeth.

Surprised by his frank response, she countered quickly, "I know, but I can arrange for that if you want."

The gun stopped pressing into her hip. Her heart quickened, unsure if that was a good sign. "If you want to speak to my handler, then come with me right now, back to my apartment," she pleaded. "But first, we need to take care of the Watcher—she'll report us."

Dakkuri grunted. "Stay here," he ordered. He walked away from her toward a woman she hadn't seen lurking in the shadows behind a trellis covered in vines about fifteen feet away.

As Ashurina watched him approach her Watcher, she could barely hear him, but she managed to make out the words, "She's compromised. Eliminate her."

Hearing those words sent a flood of adrenaline through her body as her heart began to race. *Should I run?* she wondered. Ashurina looked around for ways to escape, but her Watcher was between her and the closest exit.

Then the woman stepped out from behind the trellis and grabbed for her weapon, a compact pistol of some sort. But before she could raise the barrel, Dakkuri fired one shot to the back of her head. As her body began to fall to the ground, he reached out, grabbed her, and pulled her corpse backwards behind the trellis.

Ashurina stood there, frozen in shock. Dakkuri grabbed for some foliage and placed it over top of the Watcher's feet, covering her from all but the most astute observers. This was not how Ashurina had imagined her cover being blown, the severing of her connection to the Gurista society.

With the deed done, Dakkuri motioned toward the exit. "Lead the way," he commanded calmly as if nothing had happened.

As they walked out of the garden area, Ashurina shook herself back to reality. There was no sense standing near a dead body any longer than necessary. She began walking toward her apartment. On the outside, she was cool as a cucumber, but her pulse raced, and her palms were sweaty. She wasn't sure if she could trust that Dakkuri had just flipped or if he was playing her to get at her handler.

Is this just some trick to gain more access to the Republic? she wondered.

"I have to know…after all this time…why now?" she asked quietly. A couple with three young children chattered away as they made their way into the garden area they had just left.

"I don't know. I'm still rationalizing what I just did," he replied.

"Well, it's a little late to go back on that now. You're committed."

"Yeah, I suppose I am."

"So why now?" she pressed, not wanting to let him off the hook just yet.

"Look, Ashurina, I spent years on Sumer before the fall. There were years I spent on other assignments before that. I've seen things—I've done things…things I'm not proud of. But living here, being amongst these people…they live so freely, like they haven't a care in the world," Dakkuri explained. Then he added, "We can't destroy this."

She scrunched her eyebrows together. "What do you mean 'we can't destroy this'? What do you know that I don't?"

A low, gruff noise escaped Dakkuri's lips, and he stifled a laugh. "Oh, Ashurina. There is much you do not know, so much you have not been read in on."

"Yeah? Like what kinds of things?" she pressed, wanting to know more. She felt she needed to test him to make sure he was legitimate about wanting to flip and not just using her to lure her handler into the open before exposing her for the double agent she'd become.

"Not here. It's too public. All I can say is I need to talk to your handler, quickly," he replied.

"OK. Well, we're on our way to my apartment now. Why don't you try telling *me* about some of it while we walk?"

He released a frustrated sigh but explained, "You know there have been long-term plans to attack Sol. Hell, you've been a part of some of those plans."

"What are you saying? The attack is going to happen soon? I thought we were still years off," she stammered, suddenly sensing things might be in motion that she wasn't aware of.

A handful of people walked by, a young couple holding hands while the husband pushed a stroller. Then Dakkuri wrapped his arm around Ashurina's waist, leaning in closer to her as he whispered, "That invasion we've talked about…yeah…it's underway."

She tried not to gasp, playing it off as she smiled to another pair of ladies walking by and snuggled in closer to Dakkuri. "It's happening now—today?"

"Yes—I *need* to talk to your handler."

Hearing those words should have caused Ashurina to panic, but it didn't. She had known this day would eventually come. She'd just hoped she would have more warning. Still, something didn't sit right with her. She decided to try another approach. "OK, so it's today. You still haven't answered my question about why *now*—especially on the day this is supposed to happen."

There was an uncomfortable pause. Then he leaned in, his breath warm on her ear as he spoke, "Suppose the Zodarks succeed in their plan. Then what? They subjugate another society—use them like the Sumerians. What's to stop them from growing tired of us—our people—the Guristas? They've been using us just like they've been using the Sumerians. We're just cannon fodder to them. You've seen their birth rates. They can't replace their own population—not with the wars they've waged the last fifty dracmas.

"No, if the Zodarks succeed here—if they manage to beat the Republic…it's game over for us too. It's just a matter of time. I—I don't want this for our people. My loyalties to my familial bonds are much stronger than my loyalty to our blue-skinned 'patrons.'" He stopped in front of her door as she entered her access code to the habitat. Before she could go in, he grabbed her by the hand and turned her so she was facing him. "You were right when you said we are on the wrong side. I've known that for a while. I just didn't have the courage to do something about that until now."

Standing in the doorway, she studied his face, her eyes narrowing as they bored into his. He held her gaze, not looking away. Then she broke eye contact and led him into the hall that led to her apartment.

Once inside, Dakkuri moved to the windows and closed them as Ashurina followed her protocol to contact Drew. It took a few minutes, but then his image appeared as a 3-D hologram on her desk.

"Hey, you—I wasn't expecting to hear from you today, darling. Is everything all right?" Drew asked, flirtatiously in case she was under duress or someone else was in the room and she couldn't talk freely.

Ashurina smiled brightly. "Well, Drew, actually, there's been a development...," she said, and Dakkuri stepped beside her.

She saw Drew practically jump back in shock at the sudden appearance of her former handler. "Are you in danger?" he asked, his tone firm as his entire demeanor changed in the blink of an eye. Ashurina saw him study her carefully, waiting to see if she would give him the signal that she was OK.

Ashurina tried to suppress the urge to laugh at how strange this entire situation suddenly felt. She held her hands up in mock surrender, "It's OK, Drew, I'm bringing Dakkuri in," she began to explain. "In fact, he killed my Watcher, so there's no going back for him. He has to leave the Zodarks."

Drew crossed his arms. "Well, this certainly is interesting," he remarked. "But how do I know you aren't a double or triple agent?" he pressed, staring at Dakkuri.

"I suppose right now you don't. But here's the deal. We don't have a lot of time, so I'm going to be candid in the name of expedience. Let's just say I've realized that we Guristas are mere pawns in a bigger game that is much larger than all of us. While you may not believe me, I want my people to have a future that doesn't see them slaughtered as fodder for the Zodarks' wars or subjugated as slaves like the Sumerians."

Drew steepled his fingers. "Huh. OK, why now, then?"

"Because we are running out of time. If I'm going to try and help you survive what is about to happen next, then I needed to act and act now."

Drew lifted an eyebrow at his statement. "Really? How about you start telling me about these plans and what sort of things are about to happen. While you're speaking, I'll have my people start vetting what you're saying while a team's en route to your position."

Dakkuri shook his head and began to pace as he spoke. "We don't have time for this. There are plots and attacks by the Zodarks you can't even begin to imagine, and it's all about to happen...today."

Drew narrowed his eyes, examining Dakkuri's face skeptically.

"Today? So you're just going to flip sides, jump ship today—the day the Zodarks are supposed to invade—and I'm supposed to believe that?" As Dakkuri was about to protest, Drew interrupted. "Never mind. Let's say I believe you. Obviously, we're too late to stop it. So what's the value-added you're bringing to the table?"

"To be fair, Drew, I don't believe any of us could have stopped the storm that is about to occur," Dakkuri acknowledged. "However, should we all survive the coming days, there is a lot I can do to help you harm and even destroy the Zodarks from within."

Suddenly, alarms blared at Drew's office on Earth, then they began to sound at Ashurina's residence as well.

A look of panic washed over Drew's face. "You need to get to DARPA."

"Uh, sure, I can get in. But there's no way Dakkuri will," she reminded her handler.

Drew cursed and looked up at the ceiling, the alarm blaring in the background now intermixed with orders and shouts coming from outside his office. "Damn it, you're right. OK, here's what I'm going to do. I'm sending you coordinates of an underground safe house in the Gemini District," Drew instructed as he typed away on his Qpad. "You need to get there and hunker down. Lay low until I can send help. It may be a few days, maybe even a week. But I'll get you help and there should be plenty of food and supplies to last you a little while should you need it."

****

There was a sense of organized chaos throughout the biomes on Mars. Many people were running, but Ashurina felt that most of them didn't know where they were running *to*. A few Republic soldiers were busy throwing their body armor on and dashing to their assigned posts, but the average person was more than likely just trying to stay out of the way.

If we make it through this, I'm going to suggest that the Republic run quarterly drills, she thought. Some of the crowd was inadvertently causing more chaos through their confused movements.

Ashurina led Dakkuri to one of the underground trams that connected the Challenger District to the Gemini District. She hoped that whatever was coming down the pike wouldn't reach them before they exited this enclosed tube. She consciously slowed her breathing, taking care not to hyperventilate.

They reached the other end without incident, but as soon as they arrived at their destination, she heard a sound that made her blood curdle.

"I've never heard the Zodark war cry on this end before," Dakkuri commented uneasily.

"Come on, we need to hurry," Ashurina replied, grabbing his arm and leading him down a corridor, away from the Zodarks.

Fortunately, the four-armed blue beasts were coming into the biome down at the other end from where they now found themselves. However, they would have to get closer before finding their safe house.

They sprinted down alleys, slowing before each turn, weaving through the war zone like they were in a game of Pac-Man, avoiding the ghosts. As they continued their dangerous game of cat and mouse, the screams and howls grew louder.

At the next turn, they could see the Zodarks slaughtering unarmed citizens with impunity. Ashurina wanted to get in the fight, but she suppressed that urge as well as the desire to throw up in disgust. Dakkuri was suddenly frozen, watching the battle with his mouth agape. Ashurina grabbed him by the shoulders and pulled him down the street. They were almost to the entrance of the safe house now.

Dakkuri swore. "Babies, Ashurina…how can they call themselves warriors?" he bemoaned.

"I know. I don't understand why it took me so long to see it myself," she replied. Ashurina was still plagued with guilt over her role in the terrorist attacks on the people of the Republic. At least she'd never looked into the eyes of a child and murdered it—that was a line the Zodarks must have realized the Guristas wouldn't have had the stomach to cross.

Ashurina pulled Dakkuri into the basement of a casino and then unslung her "go bag" from her shoulder. She located Table 12, then slid her electronic key card along the dealer's spot. The floor below opened up, revealing a hatch.

"Ready to join the ranks of the Republic?" she asked with a grin.

Dakkuri nodded solemnly, eager to get to safety and away from the savages fighting outside.

They climbed down the ladder, and she secured the opening from within. Their surroundings were not exactly a five-star hotel, but they'd be able to survive there for some time. She thought Dakkuri would cry for a moment, but then he stood tall and set his jaw like flint. There was a fire in his eyes she'd never seen before.

"The Zodarks used to tell us that the Republic was full of barbarians. Well, now I have seen their true nature. And I will do everything in my power to destroy them."

Chapter Four
Potsdam Cookout

Moments Before the Invasion
Republic Trade Convention
Cecilienhof Palace
Potsdam, Germany
Earth, Sol System

Chancellor Alice Luca felt a sense of pride and accomplishment as she stared at the trade representatives from every member of the alliance. When she'd learned that a representative from the Gallentine Empire would also attend as they discussed ways to increase trade and economic activities between the alliance members, she had been beyond thrilled.

Until recently, the contingent of Gallentines living and working on Earth and across the Republic had been few in number and limited in scope. They'd largely functioned in more of an advisory role than as active participants in the affairs of the Republic or its internal development. That was, until Viceroy Hunt had somehow secured a deal with the Gallentines to build multiple Ring Stations throughout the Republic. Suddenly, there had been an influx of Gallentine specialists and engineers who'd rapidly gotten involved in constructing the stations over Earth, Mars, Alpha Centauri, and New Eden to accelerate the completion of these enormous projects.

As Alice beamed with excitement, observing the delegates speaking excitedly amongst each other, the stewards working the room diligently attended to the various drinks and hors d'oeuvres specially created for this event.

She couldn't help but marvel at the history of this room and the table they all sat at. In 1945, sitting at this very table were US President Harry Truman, British Prime Minister Winston Churchill, then Clement Attlee, his replacement, and last but not least, Joseph Stalin, the head of the Soviet Union. It was at this table, during those talks, that the fate of postwar Europe and Germany had been decided. Now, some one hundred and seventy years later, she was sitting at the same table with allied representatives from half a dozen alien species and planets. It was almost too much to wrap her mind around.

All of a sudden, something caught her eye. A member of Ambassador Zainou's security detail looked concerned as he approached the Gallentine. Then she felt a firm hand on her shoulder as the head of her security leaned in to tell her something.

"Ma'am, we just received a flash priority message from Space Command headquarters. They are reporting that a Zodark fleet has just entered Sol. Fleet Admiral Bailey ordered the Sentinels to go active and initiated the planetary defensive system. He has directed all tier-one government officials to seek refuge in the nearest Ark immediately," Agent Pierce explained. Her mind froze for a second as she tried to recall what he meant by seeking refuge in the Ark. Then Agent Pierce spoke more urgently. "Ma'am, this isn't a drill. This is happening. We need to move—right now!"

She looked Pierce in the eye, searching to ascertain the seriousness of his statement. "Yes, you're right," she replied. "We need to move."

Chancellor Luca stood, turning to her guests. "Um, can I please have everyone's attention?" she asked, speaking more tentatively than was usual for her. This caused everyone in the room to quiet down.

"I don't think there's an easy way to say this, so I'll just be blunt. Moments ago, I received word that a Zodark fleet has entered our system. Admiral Bailey activated the planetary defensive weapons system, and I'm sure that also means he'll be recalling the home guard fleet from a training exercise at the Joint Training Facility on Titan. While I don't have much information to share with you just yet, I want to assure you that we have several contingency plans in case of a situation just like this—"

"Excuse me, Chancellor," interrupted the Primord ambassador, Litnal Tolgfors. "Are we safe to stay here—or is there a more secure facility we should move to while we can?"

Alice looked briefly to her head of security, who nodded to the unspoken question. Turning back to Ambassador Tolgfors, she replied, "Yes, Ambassador, there is. Why don't we follow my head of security to the designated facility they have set aside for such a situation?"

****

318 Miles Away
Fleet Base Geilenkirchen

North Rhine–Westphalia, Germany

The alert klaxon had been sounding its warning for the past ten minutes, driving Captain Hosni nuts. *Yes, we know, the Zodarks are here...now turn the stupid thing off,* he thought to himself as he walked along the flight line towards the hangar where his team awaited him.

Looking at the activity swirling around the flight line, he saw the ground crews for the F-97 Orions working feverishly to get them armed and into the air before the base could be hit. Some crews were topping off the ammo canisters for the magrails while others finished attaching the new JATM missiles inside the craft's internal weapons bay.

He smiled approvingly as they loaded the bay with the Joint Advance Tactical Missile the pilots seemed to rave about. He'd heard one pilot explain to another how vastly superior these missiles were at blowing up enemy fighters, shuttlecraft, and orbital assault landers. Coming around the corner to where his guys were waiting, he saw them standing around gawking at the frenzied activity and not preparing their gear for the mission they'd just been handed.

"Eh! Enough staring at the flight line. That's not our mission, and it's not our fight. I want everyone suited up—full kits and a double combat load like the message I sent. We just got a mission, and it's a real ballbuster too," Hosni announced to his JSOC team.

"Ah, come on, Cap'n. You tellin' us playtime is over? We're done training these IMS SWAT teams?" Beaner joked halfheartedly. A few of the others chuckled at the comment, not realizing the gravity of the situation.

"That's right, Beaner, playtime is over. As I said, we got a real ballbuster of a mission. In case you forgot, we have a Zodark fleet moving into position up there"—Hosni pointed to the sky with his hand—"and God only knows how many of those giant blue beasts will be on their way to the surface or how long before they get here. So sit down, shut up, and let's get this brief done so we can load up in the Osprey and get on site before this invasion starts or the sky fills with Vultures looking to zap our ride before we even get there."

As the team made their way into the briefing room near the hangar, he heard a few NCOs scolding the team's newest member for trying to get smart with him. He nodded approvingly at how the NCOs handled the recent influx of new guys joining the Deltas and JSOC units of late. The older veterans quickly schooled the shake-and-bake Deltas to integrate them into the teams as quickly as possible.

In their case, Beaner was the newest shake-and-bake to the team. He was part of that new generation of operators who'd joined and gone straight into SF—skipping the traditional path that typically required you to have served some time in the conventional army before trying for SF. The operators who went through the traditional SF route tended not to like the shake-and-bakes, as they were often called. The pups lacked the experience often gained from serving in the conventional force. On the other hand, Hosni also recognized that the pups usually didn't come into the unit with bad habits that would have to be beaten out of them later. It was expected of soldiers who served in the conventional army to have learned some good and bad habits along the way. It was the bad habits that took the longest to unlearn.

Once they filed into the briefing room, an image of Colonel Jayden Hopper appeared on a secured comms puck sitting on the center of the table. A little icon near the bottom right of the screen showed he was broadcasting from somewhere in North America.

"Cut the chatter! We don't have much time, and I've got a priority mission to give you, so listen up before the Zodarks figure out how to jam our comms network," barked the commander of 4th Special Forces Group.

Hosni saw he had their full attention as they listened to what he had to say.

"I know I'm not part of JSOC and I'm not within your chain of command. General Reiker, however, just chopped your team over to me for this mission. Captain Hosni, the orders I just sent to you will verify what I just told you and will also have the details of your mission.

"Now that we have that settled—I don't know how the Zodarks opened a bridge to Sol, and frankly, I don't care. Right now, what matters is that I have a job, and your team is the closest team available until I can round up more SOF units and get them to Germany—hopefully before the Zodarks begin landing their troops. Right now my command is scattered to hell across Earth, Titan, and Mars. To top it off, Mars has gone dark. They reported being under attack, and we've lost comms with them since.

"Right now the Zodarks are battling it out with the Sentinel towers over Europe and North America. This is likely in preparation for an eventual ground assault, which they'll probably launch in the near future. While you may not have experienced any orbital bombardments yet, North America is beginning to get hit and hard. They hammered Space Command headquarters and the capital hard with orbital strikes. We suspect they'll send in fighters first, then landers once they feel they've secured the skies. Casualties are high, and I've been told the damage is pretty extensive, especially to orbital defense weapons—"

Then Hosni interrupted to ask, "Excuse me, sir. What about Fort Banks? Has it taken any hits? Iis it still operational?" He knew the base had several orbital defense cannons located on it.

Colonel Hopper grimaced at the mention of Fort Banks, home to Special Forces Command and its various training facilities. "It got hammered a few minutes before our briefing here. I don't know how bad it is, so don't ask. I just know it took close to a dozen strikes to the facilities and the base. I suspect it's been flattened. On a good note, it does look like we managed to get most of the units dispersed off the base before it was hit. Many units even deployed with their full kits, vehicles, and other gear, so it wasn't a total loss. Once we figure out where the Zodarks will start landing their forces, you can bet your ass we'll have a nice welcoming party waiting for 'em."

As the colonel spoke, some of Hosni's guys started whispering to each other about the loss of Fort Banks. Everyone knew someone there, and now they were wondering if their friends had made it out all right or were dead.

Hopper waved his M-111 Slayer in the air, trying to regain their attention. The man was already suited up for war, and his guys were jibber-jabbering on the side. Turning to his guys, Hosni snapped angrily, "For God's sake, shut up, everyone! He isn't done yet! Let the colonel finish before you start jaw-jacking to each other!" Returning his attention to the hologram, he said, "Sorry about that, Colonel. Seems a few of my guys misplaced their military bearings in the hangar. I can assure you they're ready to roll and start slaying Zodarks. This mission you have for us—what specifically do you need us to do?"

Hopper smiled approvingly at the impromptu ass-chewing before explaining, "It's all right, Captain. We're all on edge here. Back to the mission I've dumped on you guys—unfortunately, this one is going to be tough. Your team has just been tasked with protecting

Chancellor Alice Luca and the foreign trade delegation she was hosting until we can get them safely transferred to a more secure location."

Hopper paused for a moment, letting the gravity of what had been said sink in before continuing to explain, "The Chancellor has been hosting a trade summit at a facility called the Cecilienhof Palace in Potsdam. The Republic was playing host for an alliance-wide trade initiative or something when all this went down. The meeting was at the palace—eh, it's more like a large English Tudor house, looking at the pictures." The hologram showed a series of photos of the place and an overview map of its location. "Regardless of the location, this delegation is a big deal. The Chancellor has a representative in attendance from nearly every member of the alliance. To say this is now a security nightmare would be an understatement. It's obviously a high-value target if the Zodarks know about it; if they don't, it will be once they do.

"The Chancellor and the delegates' security details know we're under attack. The Secret Service has evacuated everyone to a nearby subterranean bunker beneath the Belvedere Castle on the Pfingstberg. It's part of a cleverly hidden network of underground bunker complexes designed to protect senior political and military leadership should an attack happen while they're nearby. That's the only details I have on the place other than it's considered a tier-two bunker system, meaning it's not part of the Ark network built specifically to stand up against orbital strikes.

"Your job is to haul ass over there—hopefully, before the Zodarks start landing forces on the planet or filling the skies with Vultures. Once you're on the ground, establish comms with the Secret Service and secure the area around the facility until they can be evacuated to an Ark. Should you encounter any Mukhabarat or Ani units in the area, clear 'em out and tell the security detail the site's been compromised. They'll likely want to relocate, which might be an added problem. But keeping the Chancellor and her HVIs alive is your number one priority.

"There are some nearby regular units in the area, but we're deliberately trying to keep them away from the place for the time being. We don't want to draw any undue attention to it if the Zodarks don't already know about it. Should you come under attack, Captain, do not hesitate to make contact with them and request assistance. Inside your orders is a special declaration order you can hand to any regular Army that will immediately place them under your command for as long as you feel you need their assistance. Use that sparingly, Captain—that's like a get-out-of-jail-free card. You only get to use it in a dire emergency. Now get the hell out of here and go protect our HVIs. I'm working my ass off to try and arrange more assets to get them moved to another facility— buy me the time I need. Hopper out," the colonel finished, and the hologram disappeared.

"Well, ain't that a giant turd they just gave us? What are we— babysitters for the ruling elites now or something? Doesn't Secret Service have a team that specializes in this kind of protection stuff?" chided one of the sergeants, not happy with a PSD assignment.

Before Hosni could say something, Sergeant Major Dickson leapt to his feet, his hand extended like a pointer as he unloaded on them in a fit of rage, sending spittle flying across the table. "What the bloody hell was wrong with you guys during that briefing? I cannot believe the behavior I just saw in that meeting from soldiers who are supposed to be a part of Joint Special Operations Command—the best of the best was *not* what I just saw! That was a *colonel* briefing us—not some junior NCO. I expect more from you dirtbags. You're JSOC, for God's sake— act like it! The brass gives the orders—and we execute. Without question, we execute the damn orders! Ya got me, Gibbs?" The sergeant major glared, just waiting for someone to say something stupid so he could tear 'em a new fourth point of contact.

The smirk Staff Sergeant Gibbs had had moments earlier was now absent as he held his hands up in mock surrender. He moved swiftly now to correct his error. "Yes, Sergeant Major, that was…wrong of me back there. It won't happen again."

Hosni saw the message was received. Now it was time to get them focused back on the mission and on being the ruthless killers they were. "Listen, everyone is under a lot of stress right now. The unimaginable is actually happening. Earth is under attack and likely to be invaded shortly. We all have a job to do, so let's just stick to what we're good at and get it done. Put the last thirty minutes out of your minds and let's move on," he said before turning back to his enforcer. "Sergeant Major, let's get the team to the Osprey and get our kit loaded. Tell the pilots I'll be out there shortly. I need to check in with the Ops Center before we head out."

As he left the briefing room, he made his way down the hall to the Ops Center, noticing a real sense of urgency from the soldiers coming and going from the room. As he entered, soldiers were already packing the place up like they were leaving.

He made his way over to Master Sergeant Leke, needing to get some answers before his team left, and apparently the Ops Center was looking to do the same.

As he approached the staff officer with the info he was after, the man looked up from his terminal. "Morning, Captain Hosni. I saw the briefing with Colonel Hopper ended. I suspect you have some questions; how can I help you?"

"Questions—that's one way to put it. Hell of a day, though, Master Sergeant. So I hate to pile on to your already full plate. But I suspect you know about my team's mission?"

Leke turned serious at the question, holding a hand up as he looked back to the computer monitor. After typing away for a moment, he looked up. "Sorry about that, sir. I wanted to pull up your orders and give them a quick read before you ask your questions so I can better answer them. Looks like you guys got a tough one here. Oh, and FYI, in case you didn't pick up the vibe around here, we're relocating the base to Ark Delta Two in the next ten or twenty minutes, so I don't have a whole lot of time, but I'll help if I can."

"Delta Two. Isn't that in Oberammergau?"

"That's the one, Captain."

"Geez, this really is an invasion, isn't it?"

Leke shrugged. "Who knows? They got the high ground for the moment, and that likely means they'll start hitting our facilities from orbit soon—hence our relocation to Delta Two. Hopefully, the Viceroy is able to get here with that ship of his, the *Freedom*, and the rest of the alliance."

Hosni sighed, knowing things were about to get ugly once the orbital strikes started up. "Eh, well, thanks for the update on your situation, Leke. But I need to know a bit more about this bunker the Chancellor is held up in. Am I really supposed to just sit around and wait for Colonel Hopper to somehow acquire us enough air assets to get everyone relocated to an Ark—like Delta Two? Can't we work some magic on our end here and just grab a few Scarabs and take care of it ourselves? I mean, we're talking about the Chancellor and numerous representatives from the alliance. That seems pretty damn important to me."

Leke nodded along with a mischievous look as he replied, "Captain, you and I both know that would make too much sense. Worse, the moment you suggest it, the Army and the Fleet will take that easy button sitting on their desk and place it in the drawer. Then they'll look at you with a smile as they summarily choose the hardest path they can, purely out of spite for daring to use that God-given brain between your ears."

Hosni laughed at the sarcasm-laden joke as it broke the moment's tension.

Then a new voice joined the conversation, and Hosni realized the joke might not have landed as humorously as they'd thought. The base commander, Brigadier General Jörg Gudera, offered his opinion, explaining, "The reason we don't have additional assets beyond that single Osprey Colonel Hopper convinced me to give you—right now we're trying to disperse as much of the Army and Fleet away from our bases as fast as possible.

"I'm sure Hopper told you about Fort Banks—nothing left of that place. It's just gone. Completely and utterly flattened. Whatever hit that place just wiped it out. They got lucky because someone there ordered the base to evacuate the moment the Zodarks showed up in the system. Had someone not made that call…well, I don't know how much of the SOF community we would have left right now. But Fort Banks, Captain, is why we can't spare the additional assets to help—not right now and not when the Chancellor and the others are still secured in a bunker the enemy doesn't know about."

Just as Hosni was about to say something, the general held a hand up, adding, "Before you tell me she's the Chancellor and that trumps dispersing our forces, I want you to know that she specifically ordered us *not* to divert assets away from defending the planet just to move them to another bunker. While this place isn't technically considered an Ark bunker, it also isn't some run-of-the-mill refuge. The place they're in now was an alternate command post for the Greater European Union back in the day. I can't say if it'll survive an orbital strike, but it won't be easily breached by a ground team either. My advice, Captain, is to get to the site and secure a perimeter until we can free up some additional assets to get everyone moved to an Ark. Understood?"

That was Hosni's cue for a quick reply and a chance to exit before he shoved his foot in his mouth any further. "Roger that, sir. We'll hold it—and you can count on us to make 'em pay should anyone try to get froggy around our perimeter."

The general smiled, seeming to like the response. "Excellent— now that we got that misunderstanding cleared up, get out of my office and get off my base. We'll get your Osprey some fighter escorts, but beyond that, you're on your own."

****

Forty Minutes Later

Hosni looked out the ramp, his mouth agape at what he saw. They had just passed Hannover on their way to Potsdam when a streak of light lit up the clouds over the city—getting brighter and brighter until an object emerged. He felt lost in the moment, powerless, as he saw what looked almost like the flaming finger of some deity reaching down from the heavens. Once the finger touched the center of the city, a giant flash occurred—replaced moments later with a glowing wall of red-and-orange flames expanding outward from where the finger had touched— consuming everything in its wake. A six-kilometer radius was turned into nothing but charred remains.

"Holy crap! What the hell was that?!" Beaner shouted in horror.

Yeah, Hosni thought to himself, not responding to the question.

"Reminds me of Alfheim. Back when the Fleet abandoned us— left us for dead for nearly half a year on that godforsaken frozen planet," Gibbs commented angrily.

Hosni knew Gibbs's Special Forces unit had nearly been wiped out during that campaign. It was a big driving reason he wanted to leave the military and try to start a new life—one far away from the memories that haunted him.

"Hang on back there. We got a Vulture trying to zero in on us," the pilot announced over the comms network.

"Oh, geez. Just what we needed. Fighters!"

"Stow it, Gibbs! Nothing we can do about it," snapped Sergeant Major Dickson.

"Give me a break, Sergeant Major. This is BS, and you know it. Where the hell are our escort fighters, for God's sake? Did we forget how to function as a military once the war ended?" Gibbs fired back in frustration.

The two NCOs had argued more since Gibbs had announced he wasn't reenlisting. When the promotion board Dickson sat on had passed him over for master sergeant, he'd decided that, between the nightmares of Alfheim haunting him and his lack of career progression, he was done with the Army.

Hosni cut into what looked like another argument about to start. "Sergeant Major, once we hit the ground, I want you to take Alpha Team, contact the Chancellor's security detail, and get us a sitrep. I'm going to take Bravo Team to check these towers out and see where else we might want to establish some defensive positions."

Dickson looked annoyed at the interruption for a moment, then acknowledged that what was really important was the mission—not his running beef Gibbs. "Roger that, sir. If I may, while you were at Ops, I looked at the map of this place and pulled up some archived satellite footage to get a better overview. If you agree, I recommend we establish a position here, here, and a spotter in this tower here, and in this position over here." He pointed to several different positions on the digital map displayed on their helmet HUDs.

Hosni looked them over and realized Dickson's suggestions were the best possible positions they could use given the size of their twelve-man team. He was thankful to have a sergeant major as his senior NCO in moments like this. With fifty-two years in the SOF community and thirty-eight of them in JSOC, Dickson was a legend in the unit despite being long in the tooth.

"Huh, OK, let's go with that. Good call on that tower for overwatch—I missed it somehow."

Dickson smiled. "Hey, that's what sergeant majors are for. To make you captains look good so they'll promote you out our hair and we can start training the next future general."

They laughed at the unspoken relationship often held between senior NCOs and the junior officers they gently guided into becoming competent and respected leaders whom their soldiers would follow to the gates of hell if required.

"Vulture! Six o'clock!" the crew chief yelled, alerting the pilot.

The Osprey banked hard to the right as it dove for the deck. The crew chief operating one of the guns engaged the fighter as a string of blaster shots zipped through the air after them, trying to knock them from the sky.

Hosni grabbed the straps holding him to his seat as he looked out the rear ramp to see if he could spot the fighter shooting at them. That was when he saw the Osprey fire off a burst of flares and chaff canisters as the onboard defensive system kicked in. *I hope that stuff works...*

No sooner had he thought the words than another stream of blaster bolts zipped around the Osprey. The pilot reacted fractions of a second faster than his Zodark counterpart as he banked to one side before shifting to another. *Hot damn, our pilot is good*, Hosni thought before chiding himself. They weren't out of the woods yet.

Flashes of light zipped around them—reminders that this guy wasn't giving up so easily. Looking towards the rear of the ramp, still lowered so they could see out, he swore he could see the pilot flying the fighter smile as he zeroed in for the kill. Then an object slammed into the Vulture—blowing it apart before he could fire his guns.

Cheers erupted as they realized they'd just been saved from certain death.

Then an F-97 Orion flew into view, wagging his wings twice as he took an escort position behind them. *Wow, cutting it a bit close, aren't you?* Hosni thought to himself.

"Five minutes, people! We're five minutes out!" shouted the crew chief.

"Equipment check!" barked the sergeant major. This snapped the operators back to the task at hand. They were moments away from hitting the objective.

Hosni felt the Osprey slow as it flew above the treetops. Soon the trees gave way to homes and businesses. Then the familiar landmarks of Potsdam—they were almost to the objective.

"Stand by. We're coming in hot. More Vultures inbound!" the pilot calmly announced.

Hosni surmised from his calmer demeanor that he must feel more confident now that they had some escorts. That or he'd found his groove and his prior combat experience had kicked in. The Osprey flared, the pilot shedding their speed to a hover before touching the ground.

"Go, go, go," Staff Sergeant Gibbs yelled from the edge of the ramp, leaping forward from his seat—rifle up and ready to fire as he raced into the unknown.

The others hit the quick release of their harnesses, bolting out the troop bay like the Osprey was about to blow, each of them now racing to their assigned positions, their HUD guiding them as they went.

The moment Hosni stepped off the Osprey, he felt a sick feeling in the pit of his stomach. He couldn't place what it was or what it meant. He just knew something wasn't right.

With the last of his team off the Osprey, it bolted skyward moments before a string of blaster bolts plowed into the dirt where it had just been. Hosni watched in shocked amazement as the Vulture came out of nowhere, briefly strafing the LZ as it tried to hit the Osprey on the ground, before it could get away.

Holy crap, that was a close one...

Pushing himself hard, Hosni raced from the LZ as the Vulture zoomed overhead in hot pursuit of their ride. By now, his HUD had identified his location in relation to the built-in map and began directing him toward a position near the bunker's entrance. Taking a knee behind some cover, he looked back into the sky near the LZ just in time to see another Orion crisscross the sky, its blaster firing away at the Vulture still pursuing the Osprey.

"Forget the dogfight, Captain. Your comms system should detect the bunkers once you get close enough to it," said the voice of Sergeant Major Dickson. It was a gentle nudge not to get lost in the events around them. He still had to make contact with the bunker to report in.

"Thanks, Dickson. Stay on the guys. Stay sharp. God only knows what's going to happen next."

As Hosni approached the hidden bunker, his comms system found their network and began the authentication process. Once the systems confirmed each other's identity, the security detail inside made contact.

"Thank God you guys arrived, Captain. Please tell me you've got a ride for the Chancellor and the delegates to Oberammergau—Ark Delta Two?"

Hosni's HUD identified the voice as that of Garret Sigmund, the Chancellor's head of security.

"Afraid not, sir. Air assets are limited right now. We're also contending with enemy fighters prowling the skies. Hell, our ride barely escaped the LZ when they strafed it during our insertion. The brass is still working on a plan to get you out of here, but in the meantime, we're going to keep the area secured and be ready to get your group on the move the moment they've got a plan ready to execute," responded Hosni, giving a quick rundown of the situation.

There was a momentary pause before another voice joined the conversation. "Captain, this is Chancellor Luca. If we have to hunker down while the Fleet tries to clear the skies, we can do that. Is there any word yet about the Zodarks landing ground forces?"

"Uh, hello, Chancellor. No, ma'am, we haven't yet received word about any ground forces. Our current concern is the possibility of Ani operatives working in the area that might try to coordinate some attack on this place should they discover you're here. Other than that, ma'am, they're trying to clear the skies before they land their ground force."

He paused for a moment, weighing if he should tell the Chancellor about Hannover. Deciding they had a right to know, he explained, "Ma'am, there's something else you need to know. On our way over here, we saw them hit the city of Hannover with an orbital strike...the city is gone. There was nothing left for miles in every direction. They may blast our cities from the high ground before launching a large ground invasion."

"Thank you, Captain. We had heard the city was destroyed a few minutes ago. Perhaps you're right; they'll bombard us for a while to soften us up before they invade. Should the Ani or Zodarks show up and attack this location, if it looks like too many of them for you to reasonably take on, then please, do not hesitate to fall back here, to the bunker. We'll take you in and move deeper into the bunker and the tunnels."

"Thanks for the offer, Chancellor. We'd probably decline if that happened. We aren't regular infantry grunts, and we aren't Delta. We're JSOC—the meanest bastards these Zodarks have ever encountered. And with this new Dragon Skin armor and our M-111 Slayers, these blue demons won't know what hit them. We'll be fine out here, ma'am," Hosni replied. His comment elicited a chuckle from Dickson, whom he'd asked to listen on the channel.

"OK, Captain. The offer still stands should you need it. Good luck, and Godspeed."

As the bunker signed off, an eerie silence enveloped the place. It was still daylight, the sun having passed its zenith just an hour earlier. Yet that same strange feeling was still there. Like they were watching someone or something.

As time ticked by, the sounds of aerial battles continued to rage, mixed with flashes, thunderous claps, and bangs in the heavens above. Hosni felt the hairs on the back of his neck rise as if something were about to happen. He took a knee, his rifle raised to a forty-five-degree angle—ready to engage when a threat materialized. Instead, he heard only the birds chirping and some squirrels moving about nearby. Then it happened. The first sign of enemy activity.

"One Alpha, Two Alpha. We got movement on the north side. I've spotted three UPs approaching the perimeter in a low crouch. How do you want me to respond?" came the calm, collected voice of Staff Sergeant Gibbs.

"Two Alpha, One Bravo. Can you verify if they're armed?" Sergeant Major Dickson asked, a hard edge to his voice at the sign of trouble.

"Two Alpha, still verifying weapons. Stand by."

"Oh, crap. I got movement," Beaner called out anxiously.

"Six Alpha, One Bravo. Say again and be more precise," Dickson snapped at the corporal, who had forgotten the basics of radio protocol.

Good grief. How did this cherry make it through selection onto my team? Hosni thought angrily. He hadn't been thrilled when they'd assigned him Beaner fresh out of selection. *I'm already missing my old unit—this never happened in TF Orange...*

"Um, One Alpha, Six Alpha. I have movement along the southern perimeter. I show nine UPs in what looks like a squad wedge formation—three hundred meters and closing," Beaner finally said, spitting out the more detailed callout they'd been waiting for.

There was a short pause after his call, the tension growing by the second. They weren't alone—someone was searching for them.

"One Alpha, One Bravo. Drones are up—sensors out. I'm not detecting any friendly IFFs coming from the unknown persons. Recommend reclassing UPs to hostiles. How copy?"

Hmm, that has to be a local Ani team, Hosni surmised.

"One Bravo, I think they're Ani—thoughts?"

"One Alpha, it's possible. They couldn't have been keeping tabs on the Chancellor's location when the invasion started. Maybe they spotted our insertion and want to stop us from moving the Chancellor before additional forces can arrive to assault the bunker."

Damnit, Dickson's probably right. They'll want to ensure she stays put until they can coordinate with the invasion force settling into orbit. We're gonna have to neutralize these guys...

"One Alpha, Two Alpha. My three UPs have turned into nine. They appear to be armed and now advancing in a wedge formation. I can't make out the weapons, but if I had to guess, they look like our M1s."

Ouch, those are a lot better than those garbage Zodark rifles they use. This complicates things...

"One Alpha, One Bravo. These are hostiles moving into our AO. What's the call, sir? Are we clear to engage?" Dickson asked, almost begging him to cut the team loose.

"One Bravo, I'm declaring them hostile. Alpha and Bravo Teams, we are clear to engage hostiles. Stand by for targets and hold fire until everyone is ready. Let's not blow our element of surprise," Hosni declared.

As the twelve-man team got ready to initiate contact, the targeting AI built into the HUDs began delineating and assigning targets based on which operator had the best chance to neutralize them. The process took less than a minute, and soon, they were ready to execute.

By now, the hostiles had closed the distance to nearly a hundred meters from their positions. The only concern Hosni had was the enemy's approach. They were closing in from opposite directions. It was going to place his team in an instant cross fire situation if the enemy was able to capitalize on it—something to be avoided if possible.

His HUD alerted him that his team was ready—he just needed to give the order. He took a breath in and peered through the optics of his rifle, zeroing in on the target he'd been assigned. He activated the comms, uttering the singular word "execute" as his finger squeezed the trigger—a blaster bolt flashing across the space between himself and the target.

He watched as the purplish flash of light careened into the man's face, his body dropping to the ground like a marionette with severed wires.

As the hostile went down, his targeting system had already identified the next target to engage. Moving swiftly from years of training and combat experience, Hosni transitioned the rifle to the next target, engaging as rapidly as possible, knowing his team was doing the same.

Twelve of the eighteen targets went down with single shots. The six remaining hostiles reacted to the ambush like a trained force—swiftly countering it with a barrage of magrail slugs from their Republic Army M1 rifles.

The high-velocity magnetic railgun projectiles zipped over Hosni's head as half a dozen pounded into the earthen berm he'd taken cover behind.

"Contact! West flank. I got twelve hostiles that are advancing quickly. Four Bravo is shifting fire to engage," one of Dickson's team members said as the newest threat materialized.

Dropping below the berm, Hosni moved and skittered along the side of it until he'd relocated to another firing position. As he poked his head above the ridge to find another target, a red light flashed on his HUD, alerting him to an immediate threat to his life. It guided him to the right until it lit up two figures closing the distance between him and Alpha Three's position.

Hosni aimed at the guy closest to him. He saw the man bounding forward, advancing like a trained operator, his rifle tucked in his shoulder as he fired aimed, accurate shots in the direction of Alpha Three while on the move.

Hosni squeezed the trigger, sending a few blaster bolts toward the man's center mass, hitting him several times across the side of his body.

While he'd been firing at the threat to Alpha Three, the man's comrade had taken a position next to a tree and knelt there for cover. In fractions of a second, he lobbed 20mm smart grenades in Hosni's direction, laying down suppressive fire for his comrade.

Remembering that the M1s carried six 20mm smart grenades, Hosni had an idea of what was heading his way as he ducked below the berm and sprinted further down the right flank of his position like he was racing for the Summer Olympics, desperate to put distance between him and those inbound grenades.

Boom...boom...boom...

Three smart grenades exploded near Alpha Three, who yelled out in pain.

Then, while Hosni was still running, he felt metal fragments hitting his own Dragon Skin armor long before his ears registered the concussive booms from the grenades exploding overhead. He winced at the sudden pain that tore through the joint section of the new combat suit between his left knee and thigh. As his leg momentarily gave out, he tried not to stumble, but his forward momentum was too much to overcome. As he tumbled, he tried to turn his fall into a haphazard combat roll to return fire at the shooter, who was likely chasing after him for a better shot.

As he came out of his rolling fall, he had his rifle up, firing at the guy still shooting at him. While the pain radiating from the shrapnel had burned a moment earlier, the suit's med kit had reacted to the injury and gone to work. A single nanobot shot had been shoved into his bloodstream and would begin healing the wound and deadening the pain.

Firing his rifle at the shooter as they both moved to new positions while blasting away at each other in the process, Hosni saw chunks of dirt and tree bark explode around him as magrail projectiles stabbed through the air around him. He cursed in frustration as he saw his shots barely miss the guy as he dove for cover, a momentary reprieve from the hail of fire around him. Hosni saw his chance, leaped to his feet, and took off after him as he continued to fire his rifle, looking to keep him pinned where he was.

While the pain in his leg hadn't fully subsided, it wasn't nearly as crippling as it had been just moments earlier. Closing in on where he'd seen his attacker dive for cover, he heard the high-velocity cracks of magrail slugs zipping around him, intermixed with the occasional flashes from the blasters of the M1s.

As he closed the distance between himself and the shooter, he saw the guy lying there injured—a nasty blaster wound to his stomach. He hadn't missed the guy after all.

When the Ani fighter saw him approach, he tried to reach for his rifle before Hosni could finish him off. *No way, you bastard—you ain't getting out of this so easy*, Hosni thought as he leaped on top of the guy, swatting his rifle away and landing a right cross to the side of the man's face. His eyes rolled into the back of his head, and his body went limp. *We're keeping you for interrogation*, he told himself as another barrage of slugs zipped over his head.

Briefly checking the status of his HUD, he saw three of his guys were down. Four others were injured but still fighting. The map now told him he had more than two dozen hostiles closing in on their position. They were in trouble, and he knew it.

Seeing one of the attackers approaching his position, he moved to the other side of the tree he was behind and caught the attacker by surprise before hammering him with a couple of shots to the chest and one to the face, then diving to his right and rolling behind a fallen log. The grenade his friend had tossed went off harmlessly away from him. Hosni leaped to his feet as he darted towards another tree—projectiles and blaster shots zipping around him as he moved.

Rounding the side of the tree as he searched for the guy still shooting at him, he spotted the guy moving, his rifle aimed where Hosni had been only moments earlier. The man must have sensed his presence as he tried to swing the weapon in his direction before their eyes met. Hosni saw the brief look of surprise and fear in the man's eyes as he fired first, reacting faster than the man could respond to the changing situation.

While Hosni moved to another position, his HUD alerted him to another one of his guys being killed. *Damn, we're down four now...*

It took him a moment to contact the Army unit he'd been told was operating in the vicinity. No sooner had he reached the commander than the guy told him they were five minutes out with a company of infantry and ten DF-12 Cougars. The news of the IFVs sent a surge of hope through his veins, giving him a renewed sense of purpose. *Five minutes and the cavalry arrives...*

He passed the news on as his team continued to fight off the remaining attackers. Frankly, he was surprised they hadn't found this particular Ani cell before now, given its size. Then again, they might have recruited some local help.

With the fighting still slowing as the remaining attackers continued to be picked off, Hosni doubled back to where he'd knocked one of the guys out. He wanted to keep this one alive and see what else he might know. As he approached the spot where he'd left him, he saw him starting to return to the land of the living.

Standing next to him, Hosni stared down at his would-be killer as the man's eyes briefly darted around, looking for his weapon—or any weapon he could use—but finding none within reach.

Then Hosni heard a new sound and smiled. It was the engine noise of the Cougar infantry fighter vehicles as they approached their positions. Hosni knew they had made it—the cavalry had arrived and not a moment too soon.

Keeping his helmet on, Hosni allowed his visor to reveal his face as he looked down at the wounded man, their eyes finally meeting. He stared at the man for a moment, almost feeling pity. Then a wave of anger and frustration washed over him as he knelt down next to the man. "You know I'm a Sumerian. I'm just like you. Only I was born as a slave to the family of a Zodark NOS. Can't you guys see you are on the wrong side of this war? The Zodarks are animals. They only use us humans as cannon fodder to serve their empire."

The wounded man looked at him, confused, hearing him speak and unsure what to make of it. Then his face hardened with a sudden cough that saw him spit some blood before he countered, "If you were born to the family of a NOS, then you know nothing can defeat the Great Lindow. He has given us this great victory today. We found the Chancellor of the Republic, the head of their government. Now she is dead at the hands of our team. Lindow will reward us greatly for our sacrifice to accomplish his will and purpose."

Hosni chuckled in amusement at the Ani's defiant attitude to the end. "Well, bud, I hate to break it to you, but your buddies are dead, and the Chancellor's still alive. You failed your mission, soldier. You're now my prisoner."

The wounded man snorted before coughing more blood. Then, with a shaking finger, the man pointed into the sky above them, laughing as he countered, "No, it is I who have won—you are too late, and now your time is over."

Hosni scrunched his eyebrows before looking into the sky. The moment he did, the man's comments suddenly made sense. He saw the glow in the clouds getting brighter and brighter, just like it had over Hannover. Then the Ani soldier said a quick prayer to Lindow as that same flaming finger of the gods pushed aside the cloud cover as if it was going to touch his very face.

Hosni closed his eyes, knowing nothing more could be done. While he'd survived more battles than he could count, he knew this was it. *You can't win them all.* This final thought ran through his mind before he felt a warm embrace and then everything went black, and suddenly— he felt nothing at all...

Chapter Five
Sky Towers

Sentinel 115
GEO Nagpur, India
Earth, Sol System

"Ah, damn it! That cruiser just got out of range again!" Corporal Corey roared in frustration.

"Forget the cruiser. That pair of corvettes is making another run on one-one-four," called out Master Sergeant Dayga, reminding them they weren't out of danger yet.

"Shifting fire to the corvettes now. Get ready on the PDGs, Lambrecht. They're lining up for another torpedo run," Lieutenant Rama Mahidol relayed to his crew.

"I'm on it, LT. By the way, if Fifth Platoon doesn't get their asses up here with that resupply soon, these PDGs are going to run dry. We're almost out of ammo," said Private Olaf Lambrecht. He'd been reminding them for hours about their ammo situation, which was growing more and more critical with each passing hour.

"Don't worry about it, Lambrecht. Let me and the LT do the worrying. Focus on keeping those torpedoes off our towers, and go easy on the guns if you can," countered Dayga.

"Sierra One-One-Five, Golf Charlie Actual. How copy?"

Ugh, you gotta be kidding me! Why does Major Dikksweed always seem to call during the middle of a fight? Rama thought to himself as he lined up the targeting reticle controlling the tower's double-barreled antiship turbo laser he was operating. Squeezing the trigger a couple of times in quick succession, he sent a controlled burst from the guns on the remaining six towers in the platoon. As soon he'd fired, he could tell they were going to miss. He'd failed to lead the target enough so the corvette would sail into the barrage.

He realigned for another shot, knowing they didn't have much time before the ship would fire its torpedoes. This was the eighth time they'd tried to take this tower out. He was determined to nail the buggers this time.

What is it they say...lucky eight? He smirked privately at his joke.

"One-One-Five, Golf Charlie Actual. Come in, over. I know you can hear me, Rama. I can see your face," Major Jules Dikksweed said impatiently through the video chat. The dour look on his face conveyed his annoyance.

"Golf Charlie Actual, go for One-One-Five."

"Fifth Platoon is sending another shuttle up to your position. They should arrive in seven mikes. Try and protect this one a little better than the last one, will you? There are more towers to supply than just your platoon, Rama."

What the hell, man? Is this guy for real?

The previous shuttle they'd tried to send a few hours back had blown up during a prior on Tower 113. The tower was ninety thousand kilometers from Tower 114—the tower under attack right now. He felt confident about this shuttle being the one to finally get through.

"Copy that, sir. We'll do our best to cover their approach to the tower. Might want to tell them to pick up the pace, however. We have another attack underway. This time they're going after one-one-four," he explained, making sure his boss was apprised of the situation.

"OK, that's a good copy. Try to keep those towers alive as long as you can. I know you're busy, Rama, but let me explain the situation to you. The enemy has regrouped their transports and landers overtop the South Pole for the time being. Our company is the only thing standing between the Zodarks and the Indian subcontinent. That means a lot is riding on protecting those towers that are still in the fight. Just keep at it, boys. Our unit is getting noticed in a good kind of way," came the rare bit of praise from the man they'd broadly mocked and ridiculed as an asshole commander. "Oh, and your next supply run is bringing in some fresh grub. Out."

It took Rama a moment to realize that Dikksweed had just paid them a high compliment. He briefly stammered in his response, thanking him for the brief update on the situation. They were like mushrooms up here, left in the dark and fed crap most of the time.

"Did I hear that right, LT? Was that Dikksweed complimenting us?" Dayga asked, the sarcasm obvious in his rhetorical question.

"It sounded like a compliment to me, Master Sergeant. Sounds like he's saying we're heroes up here—the line in the sand the enemy shall not cross! Hot damn!" hooted Corporal Garcetti over the sound of his turbo laser firing in the background.

"Stuff it, Corporal! Stay on those guns and take the bastard out already! This has to be the fifth time that corvette has eluded you, Garcetti! Stop dicking around and start being the hero you want the major to think you are," Dayga chided hotly, bursting his hero bubble.

Rama felt guilty for the ass-chewing given that he and Garcetti were shooting at the same corvette and still missing it. He struggled to hit the thing, despite his many attempts. Then he cursed as it evaded the volley he'd fired moments earlier.

Damn it, how can I expect to lead these guys when I can't even hit these ships?

Just as he was about to say something to Dayga, the corvette that had deftly evaded him moments earlier inadvertently flew into Garcetti's barrage. The half dozen or so laser shots tore into the vessel, ripping several gashes along its port side as the ship began to vent its atmosphere. Something happened internally, and suddenly it blew apart in a brilliant flash of light, and then it was gone. It was nothing more than broken pieces of debris that, given the speed of its reentry into the atmosphere, would start to burn up soon.

"Hot damn, Garcetti! You finally hit it! Now get his partner before they take our tower out!" Dayga praised him before redirecting all their attention to the other corvette still closing in.

Rama was about to congratulate his soldier when the other corvette must have gotten nervous and opted to release his torpedoes early. The captain must have seen his compatriot blow up and figured it was time to bug out. As the ship pulled away, probably trying to get out of Dodge, the targeting AI started to guide the reticle to his turbo laser up to the left by a forty-six-degree angle before turning from yellow to green, letting him know it was time to start firing.

He depressed the trigger close to a dozen times in seconds. His laser and the six others slaved to his terminal cut loose a barrage of eighty-four streaks of yellow light into the anticipated path of the retreating corvette. The pilot flying the corvette tried to evade Garcetti's shots, but he failed to adjust his flight path in time, flying into a hailstorm of laser fire that pelted the vessel from beam to stern. Moments later, the ship blew apart in a spectacular explosion.

"Whoa! Look at the LT getting in on the action!" Garcetti shouted excitedly.

They'd been trying to nail these corvettes for the better part of a few hours. Each time the enemy ships would swoop in to go after one of their towers, they'd come in from a different angle and hang around just long enough to line up their ships and pickle off a volley of torpedoes before bugging. By the time they figured out where this pair of corvettes was attacking from, they'd already be on their way out of the area before they could bring their turbo lasers to bear. It was frustrating as the nimbler Zodark vessels proved elusive and tough to take down.

"Don't celebrate yet, guys. We gotta take those torpedoes out before they convert to plasma," Rama reminded them. This fight wasn't over just yet.

Before he finished speaking, the point defense guns on Tower 114 came to life, spitting out a prodigious amount of proximity-fused slugs towards the incoming torpedoes. Until they converted into their final plasma state, the guidance system on the devices would continue to make course corrections until they reached a predetermined proximity to the target that would initiate the plasma conversion. At that point, each slug became an unguided plasma dart until it either plowed into its target or missed entirely.

Rama watched streams of laser shots zip around the incoming torpedoes, certain one of them was going to land the hit that would take it out. When the torpedo emerged through the barrage of fire, he cursed angrily, his frustration at their inability to protect these towers growing. Moments later, another volley of torpedoes flew into another string of fire, only this time, two of the four torpedoes blew apart. Then, as the final wave of defensive fire reached the final torpedoes, one of them blew up just as the fourth one converted into its plasma state before the blaster fire had a chance to stop it.

Master Sergeant Dayga shouted angrily. They'd missed the final torpedo while it was still vulnerable to destruction. Now they had to hope it'd miss the stationary tower, but the chances of that were slim, and they knew it. The towers didn't carry a large supply of fuel to their maneuver thrusts as they had never been expected to evade enemy fire for hours on end. What fuel they'd had had been used earlier in the fight.

Rama watched the torpedo like everyone else as it raced toward the tower. The distance between the tower and the flaming dart of plasma continued to shrink until the torpedo eventually careened into the midsection of the tower, splitting the structure in half. For a brief moment, the two segments drifted apart. There was a momentary puff of atmosphere that escaped from the inside—the crewed section of the tower if it wasn't being remotely operated. As the two parts continued to drift, they'd eventually burn up in the atmosphere in what Rama guessed might look like a shooting star to someone on the ground.

Rama keyed the mic to his headset. "OK, guys, that sucked. We lost another tower; nothing we can do about it. But you know what else we did? We bagged two more corvettes to add to the seven we'd already taken out, in addition to that freaking battleship we nailed at the outset of all of this. My point is, they're running out of corvettes and these smaller vessels we struggle to hit. That means they'll have to start sending in their cruisers and battleships. Stuff that's easier for our kind of weapons to engage. Let's put this loss out of our heads and continue to stay frosty, heads on a swivel—and let's not lose any more going forward. Oh, on a good note, before I forget—our resupply shuttle arrives in two minutes. They said they're bringing us a surprise, something about fresh food."

Rama heard a few cheers and excited comments. He knew they were exhausted, stressed, and unsure if they would live to see another hour, let another day. Something edible that wasn't the prepackaged dehydrated space garbage they called food was exactly what they needed.

I guess Major Dikksweed isn't a total douche after all, Rama thought privately of the special delivery he'd arranged for them.

Chapter Six
Bad News and a Message

High Council – Chamber of Decisions
Zinconia – Zodark Home World

Zon Utulf stared at the Groff Director, Vak'Atioth, unsure of what to think about what he had heard so far.

Councilman Tanhilff seethed with anger, his words dripping with venom and accusation. "Director Vak'Atioth! The Groff have been collecting intelligence on the Republic systems for many years. Yet somehow, during the planning phase leading up to the invasion, your spies failed to detect the redeployment of the Republic's home guard fleet—a fleet of warships consisting of more than forty vessels. This sudden disappearance was cause enough for concern that the Mavkah sought an emergency change to his orders to invade Sol instead of New Eden, which appeared likely to be a trap. How do you explain this failure of intelligence on the eve of an invasion that has been years in the making?"

The Groff Director stumbled at first in his response. Standing in the Circle of Truth, he knew he had to tread carefully. He couldn't hide the obvious reason for Otro's deviation from the plan. Taking a breath in, Vak'Atioth explained, "Councilman, intelligence is a fickle matter, one that can change rapidly. When my Laktish, NOS Heltet, received a message from his Karaff on Earth about the redeployment of the Republic's home guard fleet, he sent that information forward as he should have.

"The Karaff, however, broke protocol and secretly sent this information directly to Mavkah Otro as well," Vak'Atioth continued. "This deviation in protocol did not allow my agency the ability to vet and double-check that what was being provided was indeed accurate and not just another Republic ploy to distract us or lead us into a trap. This is why the Groff was unaware the Mavkah had deviated from the original plan to strike at the Rhea system—opting to carry out a multiday raiding operation against the Republic home world, Earth.

"With the invasion now underway, we have no idea what is happening beyond the fact that two warships managed to cross the *Nefantar*'s bridge before it mysteriously collapsed. My agency has attempted to find out what is going on, but as I said in my opening statement, the Malvari have prevented my people from questioning the ship's officers to find out exactly what is happening in Sol. Frankly, I would frock these insubordinate quants for their insolence and leave their fate up to the Great Lindow. We are still the Groff! Our authority to question these officers is unquestionable and must be respected."

Vak'Atioth stared daggers at Councilman Tanhilff before shifting his gaze to the chair where NOS Damavik sat, waiting to be called next.

Zon Utulf snorted at the interplay between the Groff and the Malvari—a love-hate relationship the Council often used to keep both sides off-balance. Utulf suspected Vak would personally frock Otro if he could, but frocking his chosen deputy while he was away in battle would send its own message—that despite how powerful the Malvari thought they were, it was the Groff who administered the disciplinary actions of the State—and sometimes the personal grievances of the Director or of his Laktish.

"Enough!" Zon Utulf declared as he slapped his hand hard on the desk in front of him. He took a moment to think while the chamber calmed, waiting for his next move. Utulf took in a deep breath, then exhaled as he spoke. "NOS Damavik! Come forward to the Circle of Truth so we may question you next!"

The Deputy Mavkah stood from his seat, then glared down at Vak'Atioth as they exchanged positions in the Circle. The beast of a NOS was a full head taller than even Vak, who was already tall in stature for a Zodark.

As the NOS walked into the Circle of Truth's center, he didn't flinch once as the blue flames briefly enveloped him. Utulf didn't know too much about Damavik, except that the man was a giant among Zodarks and was spoken of highly for his combat abilities. As he stood in the center of the Circle, Utulf began, "NOS Damavik, explain why you have defied the Groff and denied their right to speak to the officers aboard these warships."

The Deputy Mavkah lifted his chin proudly. "As you command, O great Zon. When the battleship *Chemosh* and the battlecruiser *Ashimmu* crossed the bridge, it collapsed behind them. No further ships were able to leave. Upon reentry into Tueblets, they immediately contacted the Malvari and relayed a message from Mavkah Otro directly to me with special instructions. After reviewing the message and verifying its authenticity, I honored the request from Otro, and I placed the ship and its crew under quarantine until I could bring you the message the Mavkah recorded himself to be played for you, Zon Utulf—"

"Wait a second, Damavik. Are you saying you have a message directly from Mavkah Otro with you right now?" interrupted Councilman Tanhilff before sharing a look of concern with Utulf.

"Yes, that is what I am saying. I have a message from the Mavkah himself. He has asked me to give it to Zon Utulf—and no one else."

The council members glanced at each other and then at Utulf. When the Zon looked at Vak'Atioth, he saw the Groff Director in shock, unsure of what this message contained or what it could imply. Judging by the look on Damavik's face, the message likely contained information that might not be so flattering to the Groff.

Before anyone else could say something further. Utulf stood, then declared, "Very well, we will call for a short break to listen to this message in private. This will not be part of the public record—at least not until we have first heard it ourselves to determine its contents. Let us break and speak in my study."

Utulf turned to head towards the door leading to his private study, with Damavik and Vak and the rest of the Council quickly following him out of the chamber.
****

Stepping into the Zon's private study, Vak'Atioth wasn't sure what would happen next. This revelation of a message from Otro to Zon Utulf had caught him off guard. What had he discovered that he didn't want the Groff to know? So many thoughts were swirling in his mind right now that he could hardly focus on the meeting that was currently underway.

"NOS Damavik, we are now in my private study. Please, go ahead and play this message from Mavkah Otro for us so that we may learn what has happened to our grand fleet," Zon Utulf directed.

Damavik pulled a small halo disc from his pocket and placed it on their table. He pressed play on the device, and a moment later an image of Mavkah Otro appeared before them.

"By the grace of Lindow, I pray this message has managed to reach you, O great Zon. Unfortunately, this message does not bring

Hintars of Glory. Rather, I bring forth news of a grand conspiracy. A conspiracy I fear has jeopardized the Malvari—and potentially the empire.

"You are already aware of the information provided by the Groff's Kafarr, One-One Alpha, that led to the decision to change our invasion from the Rhea system to Sol. What you are not aware of is that this new information was a deliberate, planned trap to lure my force into a carefully constructed ambush."

Vak'Atioth could hear the audible gasps and curses mumbled by those in the room. His gaze was still fixated on Otro as he continued to speak.

"Zon Utulf, I cannot say with certainty that the Groff did not intentionally mislead the Malvari with false information about the Republic's internal defense capabilities and their fleet's deployment. Or, Lindow forbid, the Groff themselves were played by the Republic's own intelligence service. Worse still, they may have been infiltrated by traitors. On a personal note, it would be more reassuring if they had been infiltrated than to believe someone within their ranks had deliberately lied to place myself and our fleet in grave danger of being overwhelmed—and destroyed.

"Let me give you an example of what I am speaking about. When we arrived in Sol, we used the encryption key provided to us by the Groff to disable the Sentinel towers above the Republic's colony on Mars and their orbital station. Instead of granting us access to the defensive network protecting the colony, the encryption key unleashed a cyberattack against my task force, disabling eight of the ten battleships before we could cut off the comms link networking our ships together. The cyberattack was so pernicious that it forced us to shut down and conduct a hard restart of the reactors and computer network to regain control of our vessels. During this reset, several battleships were destroyed by the Sentinel towers protecting the orbital station, the shipyard attached to it, and the colony itself.

"By the time our ships recovered control of their systems, we had a third of our ships involved in the Mars attack. Thankfully, we were able to abort using the Groff's encryption key when we attacked Earth, the orbital station, and shipyards. I wish I could say this was the only failing we encountered, but it was just the beginning.

"When we began to engage the Sentinel towers protecting Mars and Earth, it rapidly became apparent that these Sentinel towers were substantially stronger and more powerful than the Groff had indicated when they briefed us on their pre-invasion assessment. The weapon systems on them were incredibly powerful—numerous, too, compared to what the Groff had previously told us to expect.

"When my main force attacked these towers, we sustained heavy casualties and lost many additional battleships and cruisers to the planetary defensive network. The Sentinel towers in orbit and the ground-based ion cannons were incredibly powerful and completely unknown to us when we launched our attack and then began landing the invasion force.

"Shortly after the invasion got underway, we were surprised by not one fleet of Republic warships but two separate fleets, which appeared to have been lying in wait in different parts of the system— almost as if they knew we were coming, and they wanted to wait until we had become decisively engaged and couldn't withdraw.

"To add further insult to injury, the intelligence the Groff provided about the Republic's new star carrier and newly commissioned battleships did not match what we encountered. The star carriers are essentially identical in capability to the Altairian *Digimon* warships, and their battleships are on par with the Altairian *Berkimon* ships. This sudden appearance by two Republic fleets, the famed Republic home guard fleets, not only caught my forces by surprise, they began to inflict serious damage on the fleet and the *Nefantar*.

"When it became unclear whether the Republic had additional warships in the system or on the way to it, I issued the order to start withdrawing the ground forces we had just landed a few hours earlier. While I have questioned whether I should have put together a message like this sooner, I felt it prudent to do so now in hopes that should my force—should the *Nefantar* become trapped on this side of the bridge, at least the Malvari would have an account directly from me of what happened, what we encountered, and potentially how this befell our fleet. At this point, while I cannot confirm with a high degree of certainty, I would have to conclude the Groff's Karaff, One-One Alpha, has likely been turned and thus has been feeding false intelligence to the Groff. That or someone within the Groff had been turned and failed to make the proper assessments, but again, it is more likely that this Karaff has been turned and somehow the Groff failed to realize it had occurred and thus fed the Malvari and the Council useless intelligence and information for many dracmas.

"For now, it is my intention to evacuate my ground force from the planet below and draw my fleet back to Tueblets, where we can regroup and assess the damage we inflicted on the enemy and the damage sustained by the Malvari, then work to determine what happened with the Groff's pre-invasion intelligence. Before I end this message, Zon Utulf, should my vessel, the *Nefantar*, become trapped here in Sol, do not attempt to rescue us. The fate of the Empire is more important than the fate of the fleet and my warriors. Should this fate befall us, then I will order my vessels to fight until the end. I will order my ground forces to redeploy back to this planet and we shall wage a war of terror on their people and do our best to sacrifice as many of them as possible to Lindow in thanks for providing us with a Hintar's death. If this be our fate, O great Zon, endeavor to find out what happened—avenge us. Do not allow our deaths and sacrifice to go unavenged. My fleet has been betrayed— I have been betrayed—the Council has been betrayed—Lindow was betrayed."

Then the message ended, and for a moment everyone stood there, taking in what could be the final words of Otro. It was then that Vak'Atioth looked up to see the members of the Council glaring at him, unsure if they were in the presence of a traitor or if his organization was the reason for the disaster that appeared to be unfolding before their eyes.

"Zon Utulf, this is disturbing news from the Mavkah. An allegation like this must be addressed immediately. If a traitor has found their way into the Groff, then I will find this traitor, and we will deal with them—through Frocking," Vak said as he started to mount a defense.

Snorting loudly and disrespectfully towards him, Damavik hissed, "Everyone knows you despise the Mavkah. He is set to ascend to the Council at the end of the term. Should he not return from this expedition—this invasion—you are the one who is most likely to ascend in his stead."

The accusation hung there for a moment. It felt like a spear had been lunged into his gut as Vak stumbled for words to respond to this blatant lie and defilement of his character. He growled and snarled, curling his lip and exposing his teeth as he spat, "If we were not in the presence of the Zon, I would have you beaten for your insubordination.

You are an NOS! I am the Groff! You do not speak to me like that, you worthless quant!"

The two of them stared at each other, looking like they were ready to come to blows. Then Councilman Tanhilff interceded before matters could get out of hand. "Director Vak'Atioth, something is afoul with this Karaff and the information he has provided to your agency. This needs to be investigated and solved immediately. Unless the Zon would like to say something further, I recommend you leave immediately to return to your office and hunt down this traitor. You must find out what happened so we can fix this problem."

Vak looked to Utulf, almost hoping the Zon would want to speak with him, maybe in private so he could plead his case personally to him. But the Zon stared off blankly, still in shock at the news. Eventually, he nodded in agreement before walking towards the windows overlooking the expanse of the lands outside his study.

"Yes, of course, Councilman. You speak wisely. I will depart for Shwani immediately," Vak replied with as much confidence as he could muster.

As he made his way out of the study, his mind raced with thoughts of who could have betrayed him. The only name that came to mind was Heltet. But why? What could his Laktish gain by betraying him? *I guess I will have to find out…*
****

Once Vak'Atioth had left the room, Zon Utulf turned to face the other council members and NOS Damavik. Still gathering his thoughts, he pointed to the round table at the opposite end of his study. It was a table at which the Council had held private meetings when they'd wanted to discuss a sensitive subject outside the purview of the official scribes.

When everyone had taken their seats, he turned his attention to the Deputy Mavkah, Damavik. "What I need to know from you is the status of our fleet. If the Mavkah's fleet is lost, if it is gone—how bad of a position does that leave us in?"

Utulf observed the man weigh his answers carefully before giving them. He couldn't tell yet if he was unsure or afraid of speaking the truth.

"You are talking to the Zon, Damavik. Do not hesitate to answer me or attempt to give anything other than the truth. If the situation is bad—then it is bad. What say you, NOS Damavik?"

The giant Zodark lifted his chin, confidently replying, "The situation is grave. It is not unmanageable yet. If we have lost the Mavkah's fleet, then it will hurt our ability to protect our borderlands should we come under attack. If we were to be invaded, we might struggle against them—"

"But we could stop them, right? We are not entirely defenseless because of this tragedy, are we?" a councilman blurted out.

Damavik turned to the Zodark who had spoken. "It would depend on who is invading our territory and where they invade from. What concerned me and concerned the Mavkah was the Republic's Gallentine warship—the *Freedom*." The words dripped with venom as he spoke them. "That ship has a wormhole generator capable of opening a bridge from the Republic's territory to Zinconia."

A gasp came from several of the councilmen at the realization of just how vulnerable they were right now. They exchanged nervous glances and whispered conversations with each other.

Utulf raised his hand. "Shhh…be quiet," he whispered, hushing everyone in the room. *These warriors…these councilmen…they have grown soft in their old age. Otro was right—a younger generation of leaders must take the reins if our species is to survive this encounter with the Republic…*

Looking at Damavik, Utulf asked, "What is the status of the Gurgorra?"

The council members stared at him for a moment in silence. This was the first time anyone had mentioned them in more than ten dracmas. The question seemed to have caught Damavik off guard as he stumbled to find the words to respond to the question.

"Um, Zon Utulf…the Gurgorra are in the final steps to phase four."

"Phase four—so they are ready to begin the final phase, then?" Utulf pressed, wanting Damavik to give him the answer he was looking for.

The large Zodark stared at him for a moment. Then he seemed to catch his point as he slowly nodded his head in agreement. "Yes, Zon Utulf. They are ready to begin phase five. We could deploy a small percentage of them now. Let them gain some military experience in service to the empire."

Utulf smiled, then asked, "And the Guristas? Are they ready to step in and help fill this void until we figure out if it is possible to recover the Mavkah and his fleet?"

Now several of the council members were becoming uneasy with the questions being asked. The Council, under the great Zon Miyakzu, had first conceived of the idea of creating the Gurista and the Gurgorra societies. Miyakzu had believed that the empire could overcome its slow birth rate and high casualties from wars of conquest if it were to create a secondary society or caste that could act as the foot soldiers of their expansionist designs on the galaxy.

"Zon Utulf, it is true the Gurgorra have concluded phase four. The Guristas, however, have not. They have only just entered phase four. They are at least ten dracmas away from being ready to enter phase five," Damavik informed him.

Utulf took in a deep breath, holding it in deep for a moment before allowing it to slip past his nostrils. Looking at the NOS, who was the Mavkah unless they recovered Otro, he pressed, "If the Guristas are in phase four, then that means they can now operate their warships, does it not?"

"Yes, they do have the ability to operate their warships. However, their fleet is very small and would be ineffective to use with our fleets. Their warships, for the time being, have been designated for use as trainers. They have three battleships, five cruisers, five destroyers, eight frigates, and twelve corvettes. This is not a war-fighting fleet."

The news of the Gurista fleet had caused Utulf's temper to flare. He gripped the armrests of his seat, digging his talons into them. "Then the Guristas are out? Unable to assist us in this effort is what you are saying?"

"I wish I could give you better news, my Zon. But all I can give you is the truth. The Guristas are just not ready yet. The Gurgorra are barely ready—we could make a percentage of them ready immediately, but that does not mean they are operational yet and ready to be consistently used," Damavik relayed, making sure they knew the full situation, as grim as it might be.

Zon Utulf stood swiftly, kicking his chair out from behind him as he screamed in rage and pounded his four hands against the table's surface. After a moment to let his rage somewhat subside, he motioned for his chair to be brought back to him. Taking his seat, he surveyed the faces of the people around the table before making his decision.

"Given the situation at hand, I see no alternative other than to accept that the Mavkah and his entire fleet and ground forces have been lost—or we may seek assistance in launching a rescue operation to recover as many of our warships and warriors as possible from the Republic home system—Sol. I shall speak with the Orbots to see if they can assist us. NOS Damavik, I am ordering you to prepare a fleet to assist the Orbots should Lindow bestow favor upon my request to the cyborgs. I also want you to prepare five phalanxes of Gurgorra to accompany your fleet. We may need to deploy the Gurgorra and have them fight the Republic while we withdraw our warriors to their ships. If it comes to it, we can leave them behind to fight to the death and continue to wage war against the Terrans. But I want our warriors to have a chance at withdrawing to our ships and returning to the empire."

With the official orders given, NOS Damavik stood and left for his post immediately. The rest of the Council went about their duties and would do their best to pretend that nothing was wrong and the empire hadn't just suffered its greatest ever defeat and potentially left them wide open to invasion.

When Zon Utulf took his seat behind his desk, he picked up the communication device connecting him to the cyborg leader—Yarkeh— unsure of what might come next.

Chapter Seven
Unwrapping the Gift

Walburg Residential Retreat
Vail, Colorado
Earth, Sol System

Alan Walburg looked out the giant floor-to-ceiling windows of his study. This was his favorite room, and it was his favorite season; the leaves hadn't begun to change yet, and the tourists weren't yet overcrowding the downtown area, which was a mix of Bavaria and the Swiss Alps. Alan loved the calm, the pines and the spruce. It was why he had chosen this place—nothing better than idyllic surroundings to help you think.

Sam continued to make steady progress in unpacking "the Gift." At this rate, Alan was certain that he would find a way to unlock the final pathway before the end of the year. He was getting stumped on exactly how to facilitate that process, though.

Current events weren't helping anything. It was hard to work when he knew that Sol was under attack. His Qpad had lit up with notifications when the Sentinel towers in orbit had begun engaging enemy ships in space. He had lost at least an hour watching footage of the combat. But he had set that aside again, realizing it was all out of his control. He had an important mission to focus on, and he needed to think.

Ring, ring.

The noise startled Alan. He kept all notifications on silent when he was trying to work his way through a problem, but there was one phone that was authorized to break his concentration. On the other end of that line would be someone from the government.

"Alan Walburg," he said as he picked up the phone.

The military liaison to Walburg Industries answered. "I'm glad you picked up, Alan. This is serious. There's a group of Zodarks headed in your direction—it's not a small pack, either. There's at least two coming your way."

Alan scoffed. "Is that all?" he asked. "I'm not that worried. You do remember that I have two dozen C300s, right?"

His liaison was not amused. "Even your toasters have their limits," he retorted. "Look, we have reinforcements on the way, but they're about forty minutes out. I suggest you prepare to bunker down."

"All right, all right. I hear your concerns," Alan replied.

"Good. Stay safe."

Click.

"Is something wrong, Alan?" asked Sam from behind him.

Alan turned to face his creation and explained the situation.

"I will notify Holly," Sam replied.

Holly... Alan almost kicked himself. He'd practically forgotten that his granddaughter was still staying there. His son was still away on business, so at least there was one less piece on the chessboard to be concerned about.

Alan wanted to watch the action as it unfolded, but the more practical side of him took over. If the Zodarks managed to breach the doors of his property, he could retreat to one of two safe rooms, but there was plenty of damage they could do in terms of ruining some of his more recent research. He grabbed a duffel bag and started collecting hard drives and some of his old-fashioned chicken scratch notes. Despite all the advances in technology, he still found that something about writing things down on paper helped his mental process in solving problems.

Alan's Qpad vibrated. He picked it up. The Zodarks had made contact with the C300s he had stationed on the perimeter of his property, and he was instantly drawn into the footage from their built-in cameras. He wanted to watch how well his defenses held against a swarm of Zodarks.

There were six sentries in towers along Alan's fence line and another six that roved the grounds. The other dozen were stationed near the entrances of his home and inside his property. His house was a bit of a fortress—one doesn't become one of the top purveyors of military technology and leave one's residence wide open for attack. In fact, his grounds were a more modest version of Castle Hohenzollern in Germany. It was a walled compound. The glass of the windows near where he was sitting represented the latest in bulletproof and shatterproof technology. For the moment, he felt quite safe as he watched the C300s respond to the incoming horde.

Zip, zip, zap!

It was mesmerizing to see how the C300s could rapidly issue accurate fire, even while on the move. That Bronkis5 addition to their armor really made an enormous difference in their ability to take a hit too. The older C100s would have been easily overpowered by that much weaponry.

Some of the Zodarks ignored the sentries in the towers and rushed over the fence in search of an entrance. Even though the roving guards cut many of them down, the swarm was simply too great for the C300s to eliminate them all.

Alan watched with some amusement as a group of Zodarks tried unsuccessfully to pull apart one of his upgraded machines. That Bronkis5 armor was definitely doing its job. Frustrated, the vicious blue four-armed aliens eventually tossed the C300 aside. It immediately went back to combating the Zodarks that were closest to it.

A siren blared, pulling Alan out of his fascinated observance.

Damn! They've already reached the vehicle entrance, Alan realized.

At that moment, Sam showed up with Holly, who was looking quite disheveled and out of breath. She was carrying a duffel bag that had clothes shoved haphazardly into it—it wasn't even fully zipped up, and the contents threatened to spill onto the floor. Alan suddenly realized he hadn't finished packing his own bag and hurriedly shoved the rest of his paper notes in with his things.

"Alan, you don't have a lot of time," Sam warned. "You need to get to one of the safe rooms now. I will hold them off as long as I can, but my armor is no match for this many Zodarks. You need to go."

Alan knew his creation was right, even though he didn't want to hear it. "You're right," he acknowledged as he zipped up his bag. "Holly, come with me."

"Lead the way, Opa."

There were two panic rooms in Alan's home: one was attached to his bedroom, and the other adjoined the room he spent the most time in, his office. They started walking briskly to the corner.

Crunch!

Alan knew that the Zodarks had managed to overwhelm the C300s guarding the lower entrance to his home and shot their way in. Then he heard a noise he'd only read about but never experienced himself—the war cry of the Zodarks. The hair on the back of his neck stood up, and sweat beads formed on his forehead. He looked back sadly at Sam, realizing his favorite Synth was about to be torn apart.

"Run!" Sam ordered.

Adrenaline kicked in and Alan sprinted toward the entrance of his safe room. He used his key to move a bookcase and then began the biometric entry procedures.

"Hurry, Opa! They're coming!" Holly yelled.

There wasn't much Alan could do to go faster at this point. The authentication had to go through its cycle, checking his retina and performing facial recognition. There were options for him to open the door without biometrics in case he was horribly injured, but those methods took longer.

Zip! Zap!

Lasers were whipping through the air. One burst landed dangerously close to Alan. Finally, the door hissed open, and he shoved Holly through the opening ahead of him.

"Hey!" she cried, but Alan was too busy securing the door.

Through the last bit of opening, he could see Sam engaged in physical combat with the Zodarks. Without him, they likely wouldn't have made it inside the safe room in time.

Alan turned and leaned against the door, sliding down into a sitting position in relief.

Holly wandered around the room, inspecting their surroundings. She'd never been in one of the safe rooms before. The room was spartan but functional. A pair of bunk beds sat near a couple of couches. There was a desk set up with several computers and multiple monitors, which automatically turned on to the security feeds once the door to the room had closed.

She focused in on the food replicator in one of the corners. "I thought these were only available on the warships," Holly remarked.

"I have my connections," Alan replied with a smirk.

"I guess that's why you have all of those military-grade firearms in here, huh?"

"Maybe."

"Well, at least there's a functioning bathroom in here," Holly commented.

"It's hooked up to its own water source underground," Alan explained.

Holly flung herself down on one of the couches. "Opa, how long do you think we're going to be here?" she asked.

"I couldn't say for sure, Hollybear, but I believe a QRF is on its way here and should arrive within the next twenty minutes. How long it will take them to root out all the Zodark activity—I just don't know. They were a more formidable foe than I had anticipated."

"Anything is formidable when it comes in large enough numbers," Holly shot back.

"True enough," Alan acknowledged. He pulled himself up off the floor and walked over to the desk.

"Don't look, Opa," Holly chided.

"I have to see…" His voice trailed off as he watched the Zodarks tear one of Sam's arms off his torso and bend his legs backward in such a way that it was going to take days or weeks to repair.

Alan found himself overwhelmed by emotion. Tears flooded uncontrollably down his cheeks.

"He's just a Synth, Opa."

"Perhaps…but that Synth just saved our lives."

Holly pulled herself up out of the couch to give her grandfather a hug from behind. Their relationship had been a bit adversarial as of late, and the reminder that they were both still on the same team was welcome.

They settled in for a while. Holly even lay down for a short nap while they waited for things to clear up. Alan made himself a cup of coffee instead; he had a lot of data he wanted to analyze.

Eventually, he received word that his home had been cleared, and he woke up his granddaughter to give her the good news.

When they stepped outside of the panic room, Alan's stomach tightened. His office, which just hours before had been lined with beautiful printed books, was in tatters—papers and burnt scraps were strewn everywhere. The cleanup and replacement effort was going to take forever.

Then he found the remains of Sam, who was twisted like a pretzel and charred from laser burns. Alan rushed over to his creation.

"Sam, can you hear me?" he pleaded.

The light went back and forth on his face. "I'm here, Alan. I can't move, but my processors were not damaged."

Alan scooped Sam up like one would an injured child. "Oh, thank goodness you're still with us," he said.

Holly came up next to them. "Is he...?"

"He'll be all right, after repairs," Alan replied.

"Good," said Holly. She shifted uncomfortably as if debating with herself before she spat out, "Thank you for saving us, Sam."

This was not the first time Sam had gone against his programming in order to save someone, but clearly, his actions had had an effect on Holly.

"Why did you do it, Sam?" she asked. "Why did you sacrifice yourself?"

His light went back and forth a few times. "I am having a bit of difficulty explaining my actions," he replied. "I had this thought, this very strong thought that you might call a feeling, and the idea of losing you created this internal void that wouldn't go away. What do you call that?"

"That's love, Sam," Alan answered. "And you just unlocked the final piece of the Gift."

Chapter Eight
Get to the Bunker

Space Command
Jacksonville, Arkansas
Earth, Sol System

"Get down!" shouted Drew's mysterious supersoldier as he ducked beneath the frame of a blown-out window.

A thunderous boom erupted against the headquarters building of Space Command. The Zodarks followed the blast with another suicidal charge as they repeatedly tried to overwhelm the defenders. Bailey had already lost more than half of his PSD team since the Zodarks had started the orbital bombardment of the capital and this impromptu ground assault against his headquarters. The remaining security team seemed to have rallied around Smith as their de facto leader.

Fleet Admiral Bailey had barely had the presence of mind to open his mouth just as the concussive blast wave had washed over the room—throwing soldiers and civil servants across it like rag dolls amid a toddler's temper tantrums.

Somewhere in his subconscious, he had recalled an award ceremony. A soldier had mentioned how opening one's mouth helped equalize the pressure from a blast and reduce the likelihood of it causing internal damage.

With his body still against the overturned desk, Bailey had been shielded from the shards of glass and debris that had impaled the soft flesh of those not kitted out in body armor.

What the hell hit us this time?

Looking to his right, Admiral Bailey saw two soldiers kneeling on either side of a blown-out window. Both of them were firing their rifles in a downward position. That meant the enemy was close to the building—close to breaching the ground floor.

How much longer can those C300s continue to hold? This was a recurring thought with each explosion he heard.

Then a hand grabbed him by the shoulder and shook him. Bailey looked up at the man's helmet, and it bobbed a bit as if he were speaking, but Bailey couldn't hear a thing. He pointed to the sides of his head.

The supersoldier he'd been referring to as "Smith" nodded, asking, *Admiral, can you hear me now? Is your neurolink still working?*

Yes, Smith, it's working. Sorry, my ears are still ringing. They'll probably be fine in a moment. Have the Zodarks breached the building yet? Bailey asked.

No, not yet, Smith replied. *We still have a few C100s and C300s left on the ground floor, with a platoon of soldiers holding them at bay. They'll likely breach soon. We can't stay here, sir. We've got to relocate until the extraction team gets here.*

Bailey clenched his fist in frustration. *Has their ETA changed? Are they still coming?*

Smith paused, which told Bailey more than his answer. *Their ETA is still five minutes. Of course, that was ten minutes ago, so they likely got tangled up en route to our position too.*

The ringing in Bailey's ears subsided, and the sounds of the battle raging returned fiercely. "Well, here's some good news, Smith—I can hear again. But I think you're right, we need to get the hell out of here. Are we better off going to the roof while we wait on an exfil, or should we try for the bunker in the basement?"

Smith stared at him for a moment, likely weighing the options. "I don't like the bunker. It leaves us trapped. But the roof is also a risk. If the exfil fails to arrive…we're just as trapped up there as we would be in the bunker."

Then Bailey joked, "Yeah, but at least the bunker has food." Smith laughed. "It's a bunker—it's not exactly easy to break into. We can ride this out until help arrives if we must," Bailey continued, reminding him that being trapped wasn't necessarily bad.

Smith appeared distracted for a moment, like he might have been receiving an update. Then his face turned serious. "We're going to the bunker—*now!* The C300s are down. Zodarks are breaching the building. You know how to fire a rifle?"

A wave of fear washed over Bailey—the enemy was in the building. They were still coming for him.

"Rifle—you know how to use one, Admiral?" Smith asked again, more urgently this time.

"You point it at what you want to kill and pull the trigger. Is it more complicated than that?"

Smith snorted at the response. "I suppose not. Why don't you grab one, and let's go? We don't have much time."

Smith and the rest of the admiral's security detail led the way across the second floor until they reached one of the emergency exit stairwells leading to the basement. The soldiers entered, moving down to each landing with their rifles at the ready, hoping the Zodarks hadn't reached this part of the building.

When Bailey moved past the door that opened to the ground floor, he heard the sounds of blasters, then human voices shouting in anger and defiance. He also listened to the guttural howls and battle cries synonymous with the Zodarks. The hairs on his spine stood on end.

My God, this is what they sound like in real life...up close...

"Sir—we have to move," Bailey heard Smith say. He could sense the man's urgency and knew he was right. Looking at the faces of the two soldiers standing near the door, weapons aimed at it, he saw looks of fear, concern, and something else—rage in their eyes, knowing danger lurked beyond the other side. Yet, for some reason Bailey couldn't explain, he wanted to see a real-life Zodark and kill one himself.

"We're moving!" Bailey heard as he felt a firm grip tighten around his upper arm, and Smith moved him toward the stairs, hurriedly descending them to the basement.

Snapping himself out of whatever fixation had caused him to pause at the previous landing, Bailey apologized for delaying them, but Smith quickly brushed it off. This thing happening right now, and for the past hour or so, still felt so surreal, like a nightmare he'd wake from at any moment. But it wasn't a nightmare—he wasn't sleeping. The enemy was assaulting Space Command for a reason. They wanted *him*—and these soldiers were the only thing stopping them.

When they reached the bottom of the stairwell, the soldiers prepared to open the door leading into the hallway that would take them to the room with the hidden wall leading to the bunker's entrance.

When Smith gave the signal, the man standing next to the door turned the handle and pulled it open, allowing the first two soldiers to enter the hallway as they looked to clear a path to the room leading to the bunker.

Then, as the soldiers moved into the hallway, there was a loud crash and shouting from the floor above. A sharp bang filled the tightly confined space—a final booby trap left to cover their escape. When the grenade affixed above the door exploded seconds after it had been opened, the burst of shrapnel sliced through the flesh of the enemy, the shrieks and ghoulish howls that echoed within the confined space adding chaos, fear, and terror to the moment.

"They're in the stairwell!" shouted a soldier covering their position from the landing above.

The next thing Bailey heard was the rapid fire of the man's weapon. A primordial battle cry now drowned out the screams of the wounded as the enemy continued to rush after them—after *him*, Bailey corrected himself. He knew the intent of this insane pursuit.

"We gotta move now!" Smith yelled as he shoved Bailey through the doorway into the hall.

Bailey nearly fell to the ground as he tried not to trip from the sudden shove. "Get out of here, sir. We'll hold 'em off as long as we can," a soldier encouraged as he rigged a grenade to the door, the sounds of blaster fire and hideous shouts growing closer.

"You two!" Smith shouted to a pair of soldiers who'd reached the room they were headed to. "Prepare to defend the hallway. The admiral needs a few minutes to open the bunker. You think you can buy us some time?"

The pair nodded at each other before looking back at Smith, confidently assuring them, "We'll do our best to give 'em hell the moment they breach. Just hurry, sir, we'll hold out as long as we can."

Captain Smith nodded before leading Bailey into the room toward a door at the back labeled "Cleaning Supplies."

"There's a false wall in the closet. It leads into the room where we can access the control panel that opens the outer chamber leading to the bunker's entrance," Smith explained as he opened the closet, searching for the latch to open the wall that led to the next room. Finding it, he shoved the door open and pushed into the next room, revealing the control panel he needed to access. "Quick, in here. I need you to start the unlock sequence and get the door open so we can pile in before the bastards get here," Smith explained urgently, pointing in the direction of the control panel.

When Bailey saw the door to the outer chamber leading to the bunker's entrance, the memories of what to do next came flooding in. He declared to no one in particular, "The unlock sequence. I must start the process now, or it won't let us in!" He didn't wait for Smith to reply, just took off for the panel, knowing he didn't have long.

How long does the process take? He racked his brain while typing in his code to activate the biometric sensor that would scan his right iris, then his right palm print, then perform a vein recognition on the same hand before it would unlock the bunker's outer chamber.

BOOM!

An explosion erupted back in the hallway, followed by angry shouts in English and guttural yells by Zodarks. The roar of gunfire nearby was deafening as one of the soldiers cut loose with his weapon. The light-medium machine gun tore into what was probably a charging mass of giant blue-skinned aliens with blasters and short swords racing toward the two defenders protecting the door to the room opposite the control room they were now inside.

Come on, come on, open up, Bailey thought, willing the authentication process to move faster.

Then a light turned green—the door hissed—and the outer chamber opened.

Bailey rushed into the chamber, a room large enough for four people at a time. Reaching for the controls, he started the final sequence. The one that turned the bunker on, activating its systems and the power to open the last door that would usher them into the confines of the bunker known as Ark One Alpha—the primary command-and-control facility for the Republic.

After he entered the authentication codes he'd used just moments earlier, he ran through the biometric sequences once again. This time, he had to add one more layer to the process. A lancet built into the scanner would prick his thumb and obtain a drop of his blood for a DNA sample, a final safeguard to make sure the bunker was accessed only by those designated to use it.

While he was going through the sequences, the sounds of battle raging in the hallway spilled into the room opposite the outer chamber they were now in.

"It's now or never, Admiral. They're on the other side of this door," panted the soldier who'd just closed the armored door, sealing them off from the room connecting to the hallway.

Then, before he or Smith could respond, a terrifying noise startled them as the door shook violently. *Bang, bang, bang,* came the sound of fists and metal thudding against the door.

"We...are...coming...for...you...Bailey," growled a gravelly voice opposite them as the pounding grew in intensity.

"Hurry it up, Admiral. That door won't hold forever!" said Smith, his voice betraying a sense of panic.

Then a thud sounded against the wall next to the door frame as the wall began to splinter. "Oh God, they're going to try and tear through the wall to get inside!" the panicked soldier screeched in terror.

Come on, you bastard! Open up already! Bailey cursed as the control panel blinked the words *Authentication in process...* Just as he thought the Zodarks were about to break in, he saw the words *Authentication verified...*

Then the bunker unsealed—the door opened. With no time to delay and the Zodarks breaking through, they rushed into the bunker, hastily closing the door.

Then, to their shock and horror, a Zodark rammed the door with its shoulder, a loud thud echoing inside the room like a bell. The beast attempted to bust its way in before they sealed themselves in.

"You will not escape, Bailey!" the terrifying voice growled once more as the three of them pushed with all their might against the sheer strength and power of this beast still trying to kill them.

"Get ready!" Bailey heard Smith say as he saw the grenade in his hand. He tossed it between the Zodark's feet, then pushed for all his worth against the door, against the beast trying to get in.

BAM!

A guttural scream roared opposite the door as the Zodark pressing against it fell to the floor.

With their ears still ringing from the grenade blast, they shoved the door closed, Bailey slamming the locking mechanism with the palm of his hand—sealing the chamber at last.

Bailey turned to face Smith and the other soldier who'd made it into the bunker with them. "We did it. I don't know how, but we did." He paused for a moment before eyeing the young soldier, who looked visibly shaken. Placing a hand on the man's shoulder, he said, "Soldier, I am genuinely sorry more of your friends couldn't have made it into the bunker with us. Just know their deaths weren't in vain. They will be avenged—soon.

"Now, follow me. We need to get to the operations center to get the rest of the bunker turned on and see if any others have already arrived from one of the other entrances," Bailey declared, taking a breath before setting out to head deeper into the underground complex.
****

Lab Site X

Dr. Katherine Johnson hadn't spent years on end in universities and self-study to be the chairman of the social committee, but if they were going to be staying here for a while, and it certainly did look that way, then she realized they would all need sufficient activities to keep them occupied or else cabin fever was going to set in even more than it already had.

She solicited the input of all the people who had come to Lab Site X. There was a renewed interest in completing the planned greenhouse facilities, as well as the gymnasium. Although there were workout facilities in the actual lab, people were looking forward to having the running track, soccer field and basketball courts. And they threw in plans for a rock climbing wall and a pool as well.

This place is going to be pretty nice when we're done, Katherine thought.

In the meantime, they decided to put some creative thought into more immediate improvements. Lab Site X now boasted a dance club, an escape room with puzzles that changed each week, and a room where movies were played and trivia nights were held three times a week. Things had been a little quieter over the last few days, now that people had some more productive ways to entertain themselves.

Throughout the past few months of the expedition, Katherine's role had continued to morph. She was used to being a supervisor and a researcher, but she steadily became a mother hen, someone the younger spacers and soldiers began to confide in, almost like an aunt, or God forbid, a mother they could share openly with. It was a strange adjustment for someone who had been married to her work all her life— oddly, she was starting to like it.

Truthfully, Katherine did have a lot of sympathy for what the military personnel were going through, and not just because of her relationship with Captain Aaron Young. The days here all seemed to blend into one. Even the amazing discoveries they were making were so routine that it seemed like any other day—unless it was mail call day.

Every two weeks, the *Voyager* would receive their latest batch of communications from the Republic and they would send their own messages back to their loved ones. Although they were far removed from the day-to-day activities of the Republic, the Viceroy insisted on being kept informed of every little nuance and discovery made at Lab Site X, as did the extended research teams at DARPA.

It took five days of FTL travel for their comms drone to connect to the nearest stargate, then another two days of traveling the stargate network to connect to the far reaches of Republic space and the battlenet comms network. Each time the drone connected, it would deliver its data dump and then receive its newest packet of information for the *Voyager* and the scientific team. While these drones certainly weren't delivering real-time message traffic, they did allow sailors, soldiers, and scientists to stay in touch with family and colleagues. They would share what they could and live vicariously through the videos, pictures, and messages from afar.

Having never served in the armed forces, Katherine found it entertaining to see how everyone reacted to the biweekly message traffic. Some of the sailors and soldiers were giddy like small children unwrapping presents on Christmas morning. Then, when everyone was done with their shifts, they would record responses to their loved ones before the next drone was sent back to the Republic with their replies and the latest intelligence findings.

Usually, there would be an "all hands on deck" meeting when the newest comms dump came in. Then Sakura or Katherine would read all of the unclassified updates to the group, like a news anchor bringing them up-to-date on the happenings of the day. Katherine had to remind herself that not everyone had a neurolink, the convenient little way of passing along information with those who were at the facility but not necessarily in the same room. The neurolinks were still considered a luxury, mainly restricted to the senior ranks with the Fleet and the Army and those with a special need for such a device.

The most recent series of messages that had come in had contained a series of news bulletins about some peacekeeping operation the Republic was participating in near a border region with an alien species Katherine had never heard of.

Sakura cleared her throat as she began. "Peacekeeping operations continue in the Tully system Serpentis and the lone habitable planet known as Serpentis-6. After months of heavier-than-expected resistance, the Dominion-allied species known as the Pharaonis suffered a military defeat during Operation Kittash, breaking Pharaonis resistance in the capital city of Tutuna."

The crowd cheered. She let the military members expend some of their emotional energy before continuing, "There was a greater number of casualties than expected, but the Republic and her allies, the Tully and Altairians, were victorious. Commodore Amy Dobbs and Major General Vernon Crow have concluded combat operations on the planet and in the system. Admiral Pandolly, the head of the peacekeeping mission, has handed control of the system back to the Tully. The Republic portion of the mission will return to Sol for a hero's welcome while Admiral Pandolly redeploys his Altairian fleet to the Rhea system to await their next assignment."

Captain Aaron Young interjected, "I'm sorry, did you say Major General Crow—VC's crew?"

"Yes, I did," Sakura confirmed.

"Huh. I had no idea they'd deployed on this peacekeeping mission," he replied. "I have a younger brother in the Screaming Eagles." Aaron laughed. "He tells me Crow is a psychopath of a general, but he's a soldier's soldier and knows how to get the job done."

Sakura just nodded. There wasn't much to say. She clearly felt bad for Aaron. He wouldn't know if his brother had survived the hostilities with the Pharaonis for a couple of weeks, and that was *if* they released the information in time to make the next comms package.

****

Lab Site X
Dr. Katherine Johnson's Private Quarters

Aaron sat in one of the more comfortable chairs, halfway reading something on his Qpad, but not really paying attention. Katherine came up behind him and wrapped her arms around his shoulders, giving him a hug.

"You OK?" she asked.

"Yeah, I'm all right. I *am* a little upset I didn't hear from Logan before he went off to battle the Pharaonis, but it won't do me any good to spin my wheels. I just have to wait until I get the facts."

"Such a practical assessment," Katherine half-teased. "However, if you need to talk, I'm here for you."

"Thanks...babe."

They both laughed. The two of them weren't exactly a secret at this point, but they kept all the pet names and PDA in private. It was a running joke between them to use as many terms of endearment as possible when alone.

Aaron gave Katherine a kiss on the cheek, and she pulled her arms away and stood up.

"I'm going to go hit the gym and give you a little time to yourself, OK?"

"Sounds good. I'll send you a message when I'm done recording a video for Logan."

"All right."

The door closed. Aaron was alone with his thoughts.

Am I really OK? he asked himself. The message they had received didn't say much about the number of casualties. There was a distinct possibility that his brother was dead, and he just hadn't been informed yet. Aaron wasn't sure if it was luck, but he had caught the tail end of the last war with the Zodarks. Granted, Alfheim had been no picnic—but he hadn't had to slog through fourteen years of war like many of the more senior officers and NCOs he knew had. Losing friends and family as the conflict dragged on was a brutal way to live. Ultimately, Aaron knew he couldn't dwell on what might be; he'd focus on what he knew until told otherwise.

Opening his Qpad, he started a message to his brother, addressing it to 327th OAR, Demon Company, First Platoon. "Hey there, little brother. What's the deal, bro? Your division deploys on a mission along the borderlands, and you don't send your big brother a little heads-up? Had to find out about it on the news. Well, I hear congrats are in order, Mr. War Hero. The news said they're giving your unit a parade or something when you get back to Sol. Must be nice." He snickered.

"You know, I was honestly irate when I got sent to this sandbox of a planet to babysit a bunch of scientists while you get to go out there and be a big hero. Part of me is still a bit jealous, truthfully. But…well, since everyone here knows, I guess I should tell you. I met a woman; we've been seeing each other for a while now. It started as a fun fling, but, Logan—I'm actually in love."

He paused. He hadn't said that out loud to anyone yet. The words felt surreal as they left his lips, but he knew that he meant them.

"So, yeah…you may be getting some medals to decorate your chest, but I think I'm probably the real winner here. Besides, I've got enough medals from the last war—time to let you earn a few. Just come back. Mom still isn't over Rachael. You being the baby of the family, I'm not sure she could take the loss of another kid."

Unsure of how else to tie off the conversation or how much he should say about the age difference between him and Katherine, Aaron finally concluded, "Take care of yourself, little brother. Talk soon."

Chapter Nine
This Might Work

Second Fleet – JTF2
RNS *George Washington*
Battle Line between RN Shipyard and Earth

"Admiral, the Zodarks are disengaging. They appear to be pulling back," announced Captain Reginald Birtwistle from his position in the section just off the bridge commonly known as the CIC or combat information center.

"Very well, Captain," replied Admiral Fran McKee. "That was outstanding work back there, XO. Your people found us a ship in trouble and pointed our gunners toward where to land the next hit to push it over the edge. We removed a capital ship from the battle due to the constant battle analysis from the CIC. Actions like this, Captain, will lead us to victory and push these bastards out of our system.

"Now, tell your people to find me a way around that battle line so we can get at those transports to the rear of that fleet. We must take 'em out before they fully deploy their ground force to our cities below. The more warriors they land, the more civilians will die. So set your people to tasks, and make some magic to find a way around that freaking battle line!" McKee was relieved to have survived another battle, yet frustrated at their inability to get at those transports still delivering wave after wave of the enemy to the surface.

Birtwistle blushed at the compliment. He'd done an outstanding job filling in for Commander Bonhauf, who'd been severely injured shortly after they'd joined the battle. He lifted his chin. "Thank you for the kind words, Admiral. I've got my best people looking for paths around the flanks. If there's a way, we'll find it," he assured her.

McKee smiled at his confidence and calm demeanor. She liked that about him now. He'd come a long way since he'd first reported aboard her ship, a royal pain in the ass sent to spy on her by Admiral Halsey. In time, he'd grown into the position he'd had no right or proper training to fill. But as the flagship of the Second Fleet had joined their Primord allies in invading the Sirius system and the ice planet Alfheim, they had come to an understanding of sorts, and he had transferred his allegiance and loyalties from the patron who'd endangered him with an assignment above his station to McKee. Having received the proper training and mentorship he'd desperately needed, Birtwistle had grown into a competent officer, ready for his own command. Had they not emerged from slip space amid a Zodark invasion, she had planned to advocate personally for him to be given command of the next available warship.

As McKee looked around the bridge, noting the damage to the CIC and that tactical action officer station, she admired how Birtwistle and her TAO, Commander Arnold, had the groups working hand in glove, hitting targets where the CIC's battle damage assessor pointed his gunners to hit. The collaborative effort between the two groups had yielded results far beyond what she thought they might have otherwise achieved. Then, as Birtwistle had leveraged this ad hoc arrangement the CIC and the TAO had with the other warships in the Fleet, namely the battleships, they'd started pummeling the enemy ships with a level of accuracy and volume of fire that had started to devastate the Zodark fleet despite their superior numbers. Although her fleet was outnumbered and outclassed, with more than half of her warships dating back to the years before they'd discovered New Eden and the Zodarks, this impromptu means of focusing the main guns' fire on a singular target had cost the Zodarks ship after ship as the volume of fire overwhelmed the ship being targeted. This strategy had now thwarted the enemy's multiple attempts to bulldoze their way through her fleet in hopes of ravaging the lunar colonies, wrecking the naval shipyard, and further destroying the settlements on Mars.

As McKee looked at the bridge monitor, observing the Zodark vessel limp away from another beatdown, she was reminded of their baptism by fire in this apparent restarting of the Zodark war. Her fleet had cut short their planned port call at Intus, opting instead to return home a few days ahead of their scheduled arrival. Then, as her fleet had emerged from slip space into Sol, she'd hoped to surprise Space Ops with their early return once they had connected to the Fleet's battlenet, the systemwide data link on which Republic forces operated. Instead of receiving a welcome home greeting from Space Ops, they had emerged near the middle of a massive cluster of Zodark warships, perhaps larger than the final battle she'd fought some twelve years ago that should have ended the war between their people.

By the time the sensors and communication systems aboard the *George Washington* had readjusted to Sol, they had seen the *Ark Royal* covered from stem to stern in flames from the gashes along its armor.

Having just entered the system and not understanding what was happening around them, McKee and the others on the bridge had watched the Navy's newest ship initiate its FTL drive while apparently aimed at a giant warship she assumed was Zodark. When the Republic ship had careened into the front quarter of this giant ship, it had blown a hole through the giant vessel, shattering the Republic ship into millions of fragments while severing the front quarter of the Zodark vessel from the rest of the ship.

What McKee hadn't known at the time of impact was that not only had Admiral Halsey been aboard the ship, it had been her order to ram the vessel before it could activate what McKee had learned later was a wormhole generator aboard the vessel. With the realization that Admiral Halsey was dead and having received no further communications from Space Command or Space Ops, McKee hadn't hesitated to assume command of the remaining ships battling the Zodarks. She'd folded them into her fleet and ordered a withdrawal from the battle to establish a new line of defense between the enemy fleet and the sprawling Republic Naval Shipyard. She'd focused on reorganizing the remains of what she'd come to understand were multiple separate fleets into a semblance of a cohesive defensive line. Somehow, through the on-again, off-again battles that raged, her force had managed to hold the line, though for how long was anyone's guess.

Shaking her head, she brought her mind back to the reality at hand and heard the raised voices of Captain Birtwistle and Commander Arnold disagreeing about something. She walked over from her chair to see what they were arguing about, hoping it wasn't anything of note.

"I get it, Captain. But you need to understand, there isn't any more we can do now. Half the main guns are down, a third of secondary guns are down, and nine of the twelve pulse beam turrets are melted slag. We're out of ship-to-ship missiles, and maybe ten percent of our torpedoes are left. What more do you want me to do?" Commander Arnold threw his hands up in frustration.

Captain Birtwistle leaned in closer to him. "I want you to figure it out, Commander," he replied through gritted teeth. "Find a way to get more of our guns back online so we can get back in the fight. We've got people dying on the planet! The more warriors those transports can land, the more people will die. Figure it out and get it done!"

McKee stepped in before either of them lost their cool further than they already had. "Whoa, wait a second there, you two. We're on the same side, just so you know. Let's try to remember that and tone things down. In fact, Birtwistle, it looks like we have a reprieve. I have to circle back with the fleet captains and see if I can't try and reestablish comms with Space Command. I need you to head down to engineering and see firsthand how the repairs are coming along. Once you've done that, then stop by the medbay, check in on our wounded spacers, and see how they're doing. When you return to the bridge, I'd like a no-holds-barred report from you on how things are looking. You think you can handle that for me?"

Birtwistle stared at Commander Arnold for a moment before acknowledging the order. He then turned on his heel and headed for the lift connecting him to the ship's internal tram system that would ferry him to engineering towards the ship's rear.

With Birtwistle gone, McKee motioned for Arnold to follow her to the map table so they could talk privately. With no ears to listen nearby, she asked, "What the hell was that, Commander? Why are you two at each other's throats after working like a well-oiled machine most of the day?"

Commander Arnold's shoulders slumped at the question. McKee could see the stress and exhaustion had taken their toll on him. *We have to do a better job of cycling people through crew rest. They can only survive for so long on stimulants and no sleep...*

"You're right, Admiral. I lost my temper back there. I'm sorry about that. Captain Birtwistle doesn't get it. The guns are bust. We've been slugging it out with these Zodarks from the moment we dropped out of slip space. There comes a point in a battle where you have to withdraw from the field to make repairs or risk losing the ship—"

"Hang on there. Are you implying we should abandon Earth? We just up and leave or something?" she interrupted, not liking where he was going with this.

Arnold shook his head. "No, not at all, Admiral. That's not an option here. At the same time, though, we can't fight if we don't have guns. Maybe with the shipyard not far behind us, we might be able to see if we can get them to send us some repair crews. Suppose we could have one of those expeditionary salvage ships and an ammo tender link up with us? In that case, we might get our ship-to-ship missile pods reloaded and a few turrets repaired or replaced. It would give us a better punch against the enemy than we have now, which is less than forty percent of our guns."

McKee bit her lower lip as he explained the predicament they were in. She knew the ship was in bad shape. She also didn't have the luxury of withdrawing from the battlefield to head off to a repair depot. Each attempt to break through the enemy line had cost her ships. They'd snipe at each other or try and make a push to get at those transports, only to be pushed back each time. They were undoubtedly destroying enemy warships with each attempt. But she was also losing ships she couldn't readily replace until reinforcements arrived from somewhere.

Taking a breath in, she tried to respond. "Commander, I know the situation is grim. We've seen grim before and found a way to snatch victory from the jaws of defeat. We can do it again here. That was a good suggestion you had about the shipyard. Let me reach out to them and see what they can do to help us. In the meantime, do what you can to get more guns back online and ready for action. I'll also see if we can't get an ammo tender to give us a reload on those Havoc-2 missiles you brought up. That's a good idea."

He thanked her for hearing him out, returning to his station to see what could be done to get a few more guns returned to action before the next fight.

Sitting in her command chair, McKee contacted the remaining ship captains to get an update on how they were faring. Some ships were in better shape than others. A few were too damaged to continue fighting until substantial repairs were made. She'd ordered those ships to head to the naval yard to see if they could render assistance and potentially get them back in the fight. The yard manager, for his part, had dispatched dozens of repair ships loaded with engineering and construction synthetics to render what help they could. When she looked at an image of the naval yard, she lamented the sight of twelve partially finished battleships. At least five of the ships looked ready for battle, if only they had a crew and munitions aboard for their guns. Near the center of the naval yard was at least one carrier that looked ready to be commissioned. *If only we could use those battleships and that carrier right now…it just might make the difference in defeating the remains of this invasion force once and for all.*

In many ways, she found it ironic that Second Fleet was being recalled from Primord space to begin phasing out her wildly outdated ships. Judging by what she saw sitting in the naval yard, McKee wagered most of those ships were slated for Second Fleet.

In terms of battleships, she had several older *Ryan*-class battlewagons still operational. She also had the last remaining *Rook*-class battlecruisers among some of the older heavy cruisers from the pre-Republic days. Her fleet was long past due for an upgrade to the newer warships. If that upgrade had occurred a few weeks or months earlier, the outcome of this battle might already have been settled. Instead, her fleet and the Zodarks would continue to dance, like two prize fighters slugging it out, round after round, to see who would outlast the other or land that one lucky punch that turned the lights out on the other guy.

"Excuse me, Admiral, I think I have an idea on how we can get at those transports," announced Captain Anatoly Kornukov. He was her commander, flight operations or C-FLO, the person who oversaw the starfighter wings aboard the *GW*.

When McKee turned to face Captain Kornukov, he had a determined, confident look about him. Seeing that look made her believe he just might have found something.

"Oh yeah? Okay, let's hear it. Whatcha got, Captain?"

"OK, this ship was only recently fielded with the Fleet, so bear with me for a moment. One of my analysts reached out to the C-FLO aboard the *Lexington*. That's the other star carrier in Admiral Halsey's Seventh Fleet—" Bonhauf explained when she interrupted.

"Wait up there, Captain. What ship are you talking about? We've been gone a very long time. I'm sure the Fleet has updated a lot of ships in our absence, so please, be a little more precise about what you're talking about."

Kornukov blushed at the interruption, realizing he'd skipped over an important detail about this idea he was about to share. "Um, yes, you're right. Let me explain."

McKee smiled, then nodded for him to proceed. He breathed in.

"Admiral, as you know, the Zodark and Orbot ships have continued to be susceptible to our electronic jamming and spoofing capabilities. A key weapon during the war and, in particular, some of our major ship battles was a missile known as the SM-98C or Casper missile. These are missiles typically fired from our remotely piloted bombers, the B-99 Raider, our newest manned bomber, the B-11 Valkyrie, and any of our current and past warships—"

"Wait, aren't these the electronic jamming missiles typically fired in conjunction with a missile swarm attack so it can better jam the enemies' defenses as the missiles close in on their targets?" interrupted McKee.

"Yes, that's right. When used correctly, they can greatly increase the number of missiles scoring hits against their targets. One of my pilots brought something up while we were spitballing some ideas on how to get around that Zodark flank so we could get at those transports. In the past few months, the Fleet began augmenting their fighter and bomber squadrons with a new electronic-attack ship to better support and assist them during combat operations," Kornukov explained while bringing up the specs and some images of the ship.

When McKee saw the image of this new electronic-attack ship, a memory flashed in her mind about a briefing Fleet Operations had sent a while back. The ship in question was going to be called the EA-12 Phantom. It was a fully upgraded, modernized version of the AT-70 Osprey assault transport. The Osprey was used on just about every warship in the Fleet. It was a mainstay in deploying ground forces during a planetary invasion or hostile landing zone. It could also conduct hostile ship takeovers and assaults in space and while on the move. The shipbuilder, Textron Defense Spacecraft, had partnered with DARPA to create a separate, fully independent electronic-attack spacecraft with a built-in suite of advanced electronic warfare equipment. Utilizing the latest technology in electronic spoofing, the Phantom could project its electronic signature to mimic the much larger Type 001 frigate. By masking its actual signature with that of a Republic frigate, it would force the enemy to react to what it believed was a frigate, not the less capable Osprey troop assault transport.

"This right here, Admiral, is the game changer beyond the Phantom itself," he continued to explain as her mind had momentarily gotten distracted while she recalled the briefing about this new spacecraft, the Phantom. "Orbital ATK, the original designer and manufacturer of the SM-98C, had recently created a new variant specifically for use with the EA-12 Phantoms and the B-11 Valkyries.

The new missile is a G-model instead of the C-variant. The G-model, or Ghost as they call it, carries out two specific purposes. The first task it performs is jamming. Once fired at its target, the EW cone in the nose of the missile will begin to jam the enemy's targeting sensors. The second task gives it its Ghost name. Affixed to the side of the body of the missile are these five slightly smaller variants of it. These submissiles, as they call them, are ejected from the primary missile once it has acquired its target and is moving toward it. These submissiles will, likewise, acquire the same target and begin racing towards it. The difference, however, is that the main missile is focused on jamming the enemy's sensors and spoofing their targeting radars. At the same time, these submissiles can be programmed to mimic the presence of the much larger, more dangerous Havoc-2 antiship missiles or spoof the signature of a B-11 Valkyrie. In either case, it forces the enemy to engage and react to an electronic ghost while the real attack is underway," Kornukov explained before going over the scenarios the pilots had cooked up.

The more she heard about this idea, the more she thought it might work. By the time Kornukov had finished explaining their plan, she had a real sense that it could succeed.

"Captain, I hope I'm not jinxing this when I say you may have just found a way for us to get at those transports and finally take those bastards out. Let's get on comms with the captain of the *Lexington* and explain this idea to him. It's ultimately his people who will have to execute this. If we propose sending them on a mission, they likely won't return. So we owe it to him to see if he thinks his people can accomplish it before we order them to do it."

Chapter Ten
The Plan

Aboard RNS *Lexington*
Near Luna, Sol

Captain Ethan Hunt had spent the past few hours working with the crew chiefs, getting damaged fighters ready to fly again, checking in on his exhausted pilots, and doing what he could to get them some rest between sorties. As if he wasn't busy enough, the captain sent a message requesting his presence on the bridge.

As he left the flight line to head to the command deck, he saw a swarm of repair Synths moving about the hallways and the damaged sections of the ship. If it wasn't for an army of synthetic humanoid workers—androids—they probably would have lost the ship by now, he thought to himself as he approached the turbo lift that would take him up to the command deck in the center of the ship. He verified it was working before summoning it. The emergency stairwell was a few feet away. He could have used that. Lord knew his legs could probably have used the workout. Mentally, though, his brain was checked out.

Stepping onto the command deck, Hunt made his way over to the bridge, noticing two Republic soldiers standing guard near the entrance, flanked by four C100 combat synthetics. It was a subtle reminder that the battle wasn't over and the danger had not passed.

He walked onto the *Lexington*'s bridge, noting that it was in better shape than the first time he had seen it a handful of hours ago. The repair Synths had managed to get the ceiling tiles and HVAC pipes repaired, and shredded wiring and cables that had hung loosely from the ceiling had been repaired and hidden behind their appropriate panels once more. The damage to the bridge was still apparent, but at least now it looked functional. Thinking back to the battle that had nearly destroyed the *Lexy*, he still couldn't believe she'd survived after taking so many hits from that Zodark superweapon. He could see the occasional blood splatter against the floor or, in some cases, a workstation where a crewman had been injured or killed.

With his own ship, the *Ark Royal*, gone, that meant that *Lexington* was going to be their new home for the time being. After a brief conversation with the ship's captain, a man by the name of Frank

Mitscher, call sign Props, Hunt made a point of assuring his new commander that his people would do their best to assist the *Lexington* and execute the orders he issued. With the remaining fighters of CVW-3 Battle Axes and *Lexington*'s own CVW-2 For Liberty, the ship could field a hundred and forty percent of its flight capacity. That meant the flight deck was constantly at capacity, particularly during the launch and recovery phases, when they had to swap out the combat space patrols around the remnants of the fleet they now shepherded and the naval yard they hoped to protect.

Hearing a loud conversation between the voice he knew to be the captain's and another voice he was unsure of, Hunt began looking around the bridge to see where they were. Taking a couple of steps further into the bridge, he spotted the captain in a heated debate in the CIC. This was the section of the ship where the Fleet's big brains worked in conjunction with the ship's AI.

As he headed towards them, he saw them arguing over something displayed on the TAM board next to them. Hunt hadn't known Mitscher before today. What little he did know was by reputation and word of mouth. He knew his call sign, Props, was due to the man's hobby back on Earth. He wasn't sure how he'd acquired not just one ancient turboprop warbird from a bygone era but two of them. The man owned a fully functional North American Aviation P-51 Mustang and a Douglas A-1 Skyraider he kept in a hangar on some family land of his. Props was an old-school aviator who'd earned his wings in the days before they'd had manned space fighters. He was also known for looking out for his people and going to bat for them if he thought they were getting the short end of the stick or being railroaded.

When Hunt got within earshot of the conversation, he finally recognized the other person he was talking to. Her nametape read "Commander Heidi Cartwright." He hadn't met her personally, but others said she was the queen bee in the CIC and on the bridge. She ran the place with an efficiency that put many officers to shame.

"Hold up there, Heidi. Someone on the *GW* seems to think we have an operational squadron of these birds. They say they can pull off the mission with five of them. But heck, I don't know if we have that many operational for a mission like this."

Phantoms...is he talking about those electronic-attack craft? Huh, Hunt thought to himself as he approached the TAM table but chose to remain silent while they talked.

Commander Cartwright looked down at her tablet for a moment. Then, looking up, she explained, "Well, you're right about not having a squadron of them. We've lost a few of them going in on that attack run with the Rawhides and the Tridents. They were supporting that cruiser, the *Toronto*, when they attacked that battleship a few hours back. That said, we do have five we could make ready. I guess the question now is, do you think it'll work, and do you think it'll be worth the cost?"

Mitscher grunted at the question but seemed deep in thought about this mission. Hunt cleared his throat to announce his presence. He didn't feel he should stand on the sideline listening without being invited into the conversation.

Turning around to see him, the captain smiled, then motioned for him to stand next to him at the TAM. "Captain Hunt, the man of the hour. Sorry to have to pull you up here to the bridge. Some conversations are best done in person, so I'll cut to the chase and give it to you straight. What I need from you, though, is a no-BS assessment on whether this harebrained idea from the *GW* could actually work."

"OK, sir, explain away. If I can make it work, I'll be the first to say so. If we can't...well, it depends on how badly you need us to succeed and how many pilots you're willing to lose to make it happen."

"Fair enough, Captain. Now that I have you here, let me explain the situation we find ourselves in. Then we can go over this plan from the admiral, and you can give me a better assessment," Mitscher explained before walking him through the situation around Earth and why this particular plan had to succeed.

When the Zodarks had first invaded, they'd thought taking out the orbital sentries would be a walk in the park. They'd also assumed the operational defensive weapons on the Ring Station and the weapons on the John Glenn Orbital Station would be easy to neutralize. Once the guns had been taken offline, that was when the stations could be boarded and seized. This would also pave the way for the orbital invasion once the Sentinel towers had been taken down. Of course, that had been the Zodarks' plan—until reality had punched them in the face.

Instead of the cakewalk they had anticipated, their ships had been rapidly torn apart by the Sentinel towers as they'd haphazardly approached them, thinking they would be easy picking. After sustaining heavy losses to cut through a chunk of the planetary defense system, the first wave of the ground assault had finally gotten underway. They had managed to land an initial force on the surface—mainly in the southern hemisphere. Then they'd received a recall order to withdraw to their ships and rejoin the fleet. Turned out they were getting cold feet, and it looked like they were going to prepare an exit out of Sol before additional Republic reinforcements could arrive.

As Hunt stood there, taking the information in, it started to fill in many holes about what had been going on the last twenty-four hours. He had been baffled by their decision to recall their ground force after finally breaching the defenses. As Mitscher continued to explain, he now understood why—they didn't want to become trapped in Sol should their giant supership and its wormhole generator get damaged.

"As you can see, Hunt, when Admiral Halsey plowed the *Ark* into that giant ship of theirs, it apparently destroyed whatever wormhole generator technology they had and collapsed the bridge they were opening. In that instant, their entire fleet became trapped. Like a cornered animal, they lashed out and tried to cause as much death and destruction in our world as possible. But this right here"—Mitscher pointed to a cluster of Sentinel towers over the Northern Hemisphere, particularly the Indian subcontinent and the Middle East—"this cluster of towers is positioned at just the right angle to keep most of the Zodark transports and landers localized to entering Earth's atmosphere from the southern axis of the planet.

"When this cluster is added to another nine Sentinels over the equator in Central America, it limits their ability to use their heavy transports across large swaths of the planet without getting shot up and destroyed by those Sentinels on the way in. If they do use them to drop large numbers of soldiers and equipment, they're dropping them geographically in the wrong place, not where they're needed. Now try as we may to pretend these Zodarks are idiots, they have come up with a workaround until they can finally finish off those remaining Sentinel towers—"

"Let me guess. They're using those smaller troop landers to evade the Sentinels," Hunt interrupted.

"Ding, ding, ding. See? I told Heidi you were a smart cookie. Unfortunately, the Zodarks haven't exactly given up on taking those remaining Sentinels out. In fact, they've managed to take out three of the eight left over Central America and two more from that cluster over India. They're doing their best to hold out. But they aren't going to last much longer. That's where this plan from Admiral McKee comes in."

Mitscher turned to his CIC chief. "Heidi, why don't you go ahead and explain the mission the *GW* sent over and let's see what he thinks?"

The more Hunt heard about this mission, the more he felt his earlier assessment was correct. It was a suicide mission. Worse, it had little hope of even accomplishing its stated goal. *No...we cannot throw away resources like this on something that has no hope of working. We need something better...*

"Judging by the look on your face, Hunt, I suspect you don't particularly like this mission."

Shaking his head side to side, Hunt replied, "I don't mind a tough mission, sir. Even missions where the risk is high that we may not come home. But this mission is asking us to die for no reason. There is simply too much distance to cross, and no way those Phantoms will be able to buy us even a fraction of the time we'll need to do it and get at those transports."

Mitscher bunched his eyebrows together in frustration before countering, "I understand it'll be a tough mission. But here's the deal. We're giving you five of those new EA-12 Phantoms for EW and ECM support. With them tagging along to help, you don't think that'll be enough to get you around the flank of their battle line, or at least get some missiles off towards those transports?"

Hunt bit his lip. He needed to think for a moment. If he and his pilots were going to have a chance at being alive twelve hours from now, then he needed to figure out how he would buy his pilots the time and position necessary to get around this battle line between him and those transports. Turning back to the TAM, he looked at the remnants of ships from the Second and Seventh Fleets. Some frigates, a few cruisers, then a couple of older *Ryan*-class battleships were what they had left. He stared at the battleships for a moment, noting the name of one of them— *Berlin*. Then a smile spread across his face as he looked at Mitscher.

"Actually, if you'll hear me out, I think I found a way to make this work and legitimately give us the time we'll need to get around the enemy flank and tear into those transports."

Mitscher and Cartwright exchanged looks for a moment before staring back at him. "OK, Hunt, if you've got something better, that'll work. Let's hear it."

Chapter Eleven
Welcome Home

Task Force Five
RNS *Vanguard*

"Ma'am, we are approaching system 33X-TY7 in ten minutes," announced helmsman Ensign Godley as the ship continued to move through slip space.

"Thank you, Ensign Godley. Once we've exited, go ahead and plot us a course to link up with the *Digimon* and get us in position to jump once they open the wormhole to Sol," replied Commodore Amy Dobbs.

"Aye, ma'am."

"You think they'll throw us a party when we return?" asked Commander Joe Wright as he walked up next to her.

They were staring at the monitor as the strands of light whipped around the ship. She found herself almost lost in the swirling motion of the multicolored strands of lights that seemed to dance around them as they were squeezed through slip space from one point to the next.

"Maybe. I guess it depends on what's transpired since we left," Dobbs replied, then turned to face him before adding, "When we get to port, I want you to know I'm requesting that Space Operations give you your command as soon as possible. I think you've earned it, and you more than proved you can handle the *Vanguard* during a fight."

"I appreciate that, ma'am—"

"Hey, none of that ma'am stuff when it's us, Joe. Just call me Amy. No reason to get fancy. Besides, they'll need more captains to field all these new warships in the coming months. Last I heard, they have a dozen more battleships coming out of the yard soon and at least a few dozen cruisers. We're supposed to be retiring the last of the *Ryan*-class battleships and the few remaining *Rook*s floating about."

"Wow, crazy to think those were top-of-the-line warships when we first set out for New Eden all those years ago. Now look at what the shipyards are building," Wright commented, reminiscing about a time long ago. A time before the Zodarks, a time before the decades-long war.

"It's all the more reason we need good captains commanding these new warships. You've seen how this works in battle. Suppose you don't have bold risk-takers. Captains willing to risk the lives of their crew and ships. Then how can we continue to defeat the enemy if we allow ourselves to become paralyzed by fear? During the battle over Serpentis-6, you didn't shy away from making the tough calls. You had the *Vanguard* stand its ground and hold firm when the Pharaonis attempted to rally their fleet for a final battle. In the end, we defeated a force we had never encountered before. We trusted our ship, our people, our training, and our superior tactics, and it worked. If Space Command is going to leave me as commodore or one day promote me to fleet commander, I'll need more ship captains, Joe. That's just the God's honest truth. So do me a favor. When they offer you a command to be the captain of a vessel, don't overthink it. Just take the command, excel in it, and look for ways to continue to advance."

The two stood there momentarily, silently looking at the monitor. It had been a long deployment, and the spacers aboard the ships returning home were tired. They needed a reprieve, a chance to unwind and reconnect with family and loved ones. What should have been a peacekeeping mission had turned into a campaign to liberate an allied planet from a species of aliens they had never encountered before. The Pharaonis, as it turned out, were ferocious adversaries. The bastards had fought like hell on the surface, giving the orbital assault division a real run for its money.

Her task force had left with forty-two ships and some seventy-five thousand soldiers to recapture the system. She'd lost five warships, a cruiser, the RNS *Westminster*, and the frigates RNS *Daring*, *Kent*, *Chennai*, and *Kora*. The frigates *Somerset* and *Hessen* had taken light damage, and so had the cruiser *Dragon* and her warship—the *Vanguard*. But the battleship *Rheinland* and the cruiser *Delhi* had both sustained medium damage. It would take more than a simple fix while underway. They would require some time in a repair yard before deploying again.

Despite the losses she'd taken, they paled compared to what Major General Vernon "VC" Crow's force had sustained. His troops had encountered stiff resistance in trying to root out the Pharaonis, who had dug themselves in for a long fight. The Pharaonis were nasty fighters, too, aside from appearing like some demonic-looking ants that stood about a meter and a half tall. The bastards fought like devils, rarely surrendering, which meant the general's soldiers had had to hunt them down. Dobbs was glad she didn't participate in that kind of fighting. She preferred her battles in the vacuum of space rather than down on the surface of a planet. It would be relatively quick if she died up here in space. On the surface of a planet, death could be swift—but it could also be long, brutal, and painful.

"We're coming out of slip space, ma'am," Ensign Godley announced as the ship's alarm blared throughout the vessel, alerting the crew to the pending exit.

Dobbs had returned to her seat a few minutes before the slip space warning and already had her belt fastened while they waited for the ship to exit back into regular space.

She was looking at the bow of the *Vanguard* on the main display. The strands of colorful lights swirling about the ship started to change. They no longer danced about in a collage of colors but had changed to more solid strands that seemed to blanket the vessel moments before a flash of multicolored lights dumped them back into the blackness of regular space.

The moment the *Vanguard* exited the bubble, the Altairian fleet came into view. The Altairian fleet, led by Admiral Pandolly aboard the battleship *Berkimon*, was gathered around the giant supercarrier, the *Digimon*. These enormous vessels were the ones that housed the wormhole generators the Altairians used to ferry their fleets across the great distances of alliance space and beyond.

Dobbs saw the Altairian ships arrayed around the star carrier. She furrowed her brow when she realized they weren't lining up to make the jump. They had deployed in a defensive posture one would expect along the neutral zone—not leading into the territory of the Viceroy's people.

Something must have spooked them, she thought pensively, unsure what it could be.

"Commodore, we're being hailed by Admiral Pandolly. He's asking to speak to you on a private comms channel," announced Lieutenant Waldman, her comms specialist.

"Put him through," Dobbs replied calmly as she waited to hear his voice via the small earbud communicator.

"Commodore, we need to speak. Something has happened in Sol," announced Pandolly urgently, in a show of emotion rarely displayed by an Altairian.

Bunching her eyebrows together at the stress in his voice, she countered, "What do you mean something happened? Did you send a warship to scout the system?"

Pandolly nodded, then added, "Yes, I dispatched one of my frigates to cross into Sol and establish contact with your…battlenet. I need to see if there is a message for my fleet, a change to our orders before we make our journ—"

"What happened? What did you find?" she blurted out, cutting him off before he could continue.

"Amy." Pandolly dropped the formality as he began to explain, "We are unsure how long this has been going on or even how it started. But the Zodarks—they have invaded Sol."

Dobbs gasped at the news, her hand involuntarily rising to her mouth in shock. *How could the Zodarks have slipped past our forces in the Rhea system?*

Almost as if he had read her mind, Pandolly explained, "I am sure you may be asking how they slipped past the stargate in the Rhea system or if the Orbots had somehow found a way to increase the range of their wormhole generator. If I can, I need to inform you of some basic information we have acquired before you or your people chase questions down a path with no answers. My people are still going through the reports your Space Command sent to the alliance military command center and what it all means. We can confidently say that this appears to be a Zodark operation that did not include the Orbots using their wormhole technology to aid in the invasion of Sol. This means the Zodarks have found a way to create wormhole-generating technology beyond that of even the Orbots. If this technology is more advanced than that of their Orbot masters, it means it must have come from—"

"The Humtars," interrupted Dobbs, adding, "Something that even the Orbots wouldn't have but would desperately want."

Pandolly wasn't fazed by the interruption but took a moment to consider its implications. He added, "Yes, the Orbots would want to ensure that their technical ability always remained above that of their client state. What is more plausible and likely what happened is that the Zodarks came across a derelict craft or relic site that had this device present and they somehow figured out to get it working again, or how to rebuild it themselves. While I am sure these are important questions that will need to be solved in the future, a Zodark fleet is still battling outnumbered Republic forces that are desperately waiting for reinforcements to arrive.

"Before you recommend we charge into Sol, there is more we need to discuss so we may formulate a plan for how our fleet can better assist Republic forces still in battle near Earth. When our scout connected to the Republic battlenet, we received the communication and activity log of what had transpired in Sol since the Zodarks arrived. Your people have delivered a severe blow against the enemy fleet these past forty-eight hours. Near as we can ascertain from the logs, that appears to be when the sensors detected the wormhole formation in Sol. That is when Space Command sent their first message concerning the invasion to the Rhea system. Given the distances between Earth and New Eden, it would have taken three days for this message to have arrived. If I had to guess, upon hearing this news, the Viceroy would likely leave immediately, leveraging the *Freedom* to create a bridge between the systems and bringing the bulk of the alliance fleet with him to destroy the Zodark force before they could try to escape," Pandolly explained as he attempted to bring her up to speed on what they had discovered since arriving a short while ago.

For a brief moment, Dobbs sat there, just taking the news in as she tried to comprehend what it all meant. *The Zodarks are attacking Earth...they are attacking our home world...*

The shocked look on her face was the only outward sign to those around her that something terrible had just happened. She knew the crew needed to know—the Fleet needed to know.

Returning her gaze to the Altairian, she replied, "Admiral, you're right about us needing to formulate a plan before rushing in. While I'm not sure how or why the Zodarks haven't used this new wormhole technology to leave before our reinforcements can arrive, I'm not going to offer them strategic military advice either. We will seize on their apparent overconfidence and use it our advantage."

"That would be most wise, Commodore. I, too, am puzzled as to why they have not used this technology to leave the system just yet. It appears there is some sort of enormous vessel near Earth surrounded by a large debris field. I cannot say what it means or what has happened, but I am sure we will learn more once we enter the system. Do you have a plan you would like to offer before I formulate one myself?"

Dobbs smiled at his approvingly at the question. Before this last campaign, she wasn't sure he would have cared what her thoughts about his plan were, but she had proven adept at space warfare and appeared to have earned his respect.

"Actually, I do. Once we enter Sol, I propose we move our force to the Joint Military Training Facility at Titan, assuming it hasn't already been wrecked. This will allow us time to establish contact with whoever's still in command of the Fleet while we're en route to Titan. In addition to being a training facility, it's also one of the key munition hubs for the Fleet. Stopping here will give my ships a chance to take on munitions while we devise a plan to coordinate our actions with the Republic forces still in system. Before we get things moving, Admiral, I do have one request," she said, explaining her plan before prepping her next question.

Seeing Pandolly nod expectantly, she continued, "When we arrive at Titan, I would like to request that you detail some of your cruisers and frigates to help protect my fleet of transports and orbital assault ships. These are not warships and do not belong near a hostile force we intend to engage. Can I rely on you to help protect my charges so I may lead my squadron in battle?"

The Altairian stared at her as he considered her proposal and her request. The longer he looked at her without responding, the more unease she felt. The Altairians, unlike the humans, Primords, or even the Gallentines, didn't have eyelids. While she had worked with Altairians during the last war and extensively during the Serpentis campaign, she found this one of the alien biological features that were the most challenging to get past.

Then, coming to a decision, he acknowledged, "You continue to surprise and impress, Commodore. This is a sound proposal—and I agree with it. Our forces will bridge into the system and move to this Titan facility you mentioned. You will leave two of your frigates to aid my detachment in better understanding what forces we may still encounter in Sol that are considered friendly. Upon establishing communications with the senior ranking officer and remaining Republic warships in the system, we will merge our fleets with theirs and look to finish the remains of this enemy force. Come now, we have much to prepare and much to go over. Advise your captains that our fleets will bridge into the system in sixty of your minutes."

Chapter Twelve
Another Plot

Outside the Office of the Viceroy
Alliance City, New Eden
Rhea System

Emad felt his pulse pounding as his hand closed around the trigger of his suicide vest.

Not yet, he reminded himself. If he triggered his explosives too early, he would not accomplish his goal of flushing the Viceroy out of the building. He wanted his death to mean something. He hadn't trained all his life to become an Ani to throw it all away when it mattered most.

Emad nervously checked the countdown on his watch. Everyone else on the team would be approaching their positions now, and he didn't want to be the one to screw this up.

He emerged from his waiting spot inside a service vehicle and started walking toward the entrance. Despite the adrenaline coursing through his veins, he had reached a Zen-like state; this was all happening as planned. This was his destiny.

O Great Lindow, he silently prayed. Each step took him one step closer to glory. He braced himself for the explosions he knew were about to come.

****

Bilal was conscientious about maintaining his distance limit from his partner, Firas, who carefully followed the route they'd practiced in his truck. Their NIPs or neuro-integrated processors allowed them to communicate with each other in a manner similar to how the Republic's neurolink implant worked. But unlike the Republic's device, the range was definitely not as great as they would have liked—their vehicles didn't need to be precisely within line of sight, but a city block was about the extent of their parameters.

Traffic patterns in Alliance City could vary widely depending on the day. Although construction projects moved quickly, a new one was always cropping up. The capital was evolving at a blinding pace. Bilal hoped to change that.

They wouldn't be able to stop for too long without drawing suspicion, and they couldn't keep circling the block for the same reason, so this dance had to be perfectly timed.

Bilal checked his countdown. Less than a minute out. Soon they would unleash the full power of the explosives stowed away in the cargo holds of their shipping trucks.

As they drove closer to his final destination, Bilal imagined the blaze of glory that would be his end. The glass encasing the building that housed the Viceroy would shatter on impact, the blast force transforming the tiny shards of glass into indiscriminate shrapnel projectiles that would injure many more inside the building. It would create the kind of mass chaos they were looking to achieve. Then, as the bloodied and screaming individuals tried to escape from the wreckage, Emad would enter the crowd, initially pretending to be a first responder looking to provide aid to those in need. As he moved within the crowd, he'd find the right moment and location to maximize his contribution to the chaos they would have unleashed—exploding his suicide vest at just the right moment. Then, as the Viceroy's security reacted to the explosion across the front of the building, they would rush the alliance's leader to the shuttle pad on the roof, where his long-awaited meeting with the great god Lindow would finally take place.

Everything in Bilal's life had led to this moment. All the years of training, separation from his family, and all the suffering he had endured would all have meaning.

Finally, that wicked tyrant will be taken out once and for all…
****

Senior Agent Mason Matthews had perched in a parking garage for several minutes with his specially designed rifle trained on the unsuspecting sniper a few hundred meters away. The target, in this case, was a member of an Ani assassination squad, attempting to carry out a plot to assassinate the Viceroy.

Shifting his position ever so softly, he finally heard the words he'd been waiting to hear over the neurolink.

All agents stand by to simultaneously engage the targets on my mark, came the voice of the head IMS agent over the neurolink. *Three…two…one…mark.*

Matthews squeezed the trigger when he heard the voice say "mark." The projectile hurtled down the barrel, slamming into the target almost as fast as he'd pulled the trigger.

One is down, he announced calmly, waiting to hear the others.

Two is down, said Agent Amelia Wilds. Then Agents Asher Nichols and Nolan Arnold confirmed that targets three and four were down.

All targets down, Head Agent Mia Soto concluded, affirming her role as on-site commander.

Whew, that was close. Another cell neutralized before it could act, Matthews thought as he blew some air through his lips, relieved that they had stopped the assassination attempt without incident. They had been tracking this Ani cell for days, and the hard work had just paid off.

Suddenly, Matthews felt like he was being watched as the hair stood up on his neck. Then his instincts took over, and he rolled to his left just as a laser bolt impacted against the surface of the parking garage. The sudden impact of the laser splintered the concrete mixed with coral-like biomaterial, blowing chunks of the substance into the air around him. As Matthews rolled once, then a second time while looking for cover, he felt the left side of his face being slapped with flying debris.

Damn it! Matthews exclaimed over the neurolink as he jumped to his feet and sprinted as fast as possible away from where the last shot had just impacted. *Where did that come from?*

What the hell? Soto shouted over the neurolink. *Was that a Zodark laser? I'm converging on your position now,* she exclaimed.

Matthews ran full-out, pushing his body to the edge of its limits. Suddenly, he realized something. *If we have a human using a Zodark device, we must be dealing with a Watcher,* he told the group.

I've spotted someone on the balcony of the apartment building on Third Street, said Soto. *They must have been using one of those Zodark cloaking devices—but I can see him now. He can't fire that laser and stay hidden.*

WHAP!

Another laser blast struck right behind him, throwing chunks of the hybrid concrete up to nip at his legs. It stung fiercely, but he couldn't allow the pain to slow him down. He sprinted forward until a laser blast landed right in front of him. He had no time to stop his forward momentum, so he jumped up as high as possible, coming up and over most of the flying debris. He tucked and rolled, then kept racing toward cover. He was way too exposed where he was.

Nichols and I are entering the ground floor of the apartment building, Arnold announced. Heading up the stairwell, he directed, *Soto, we need your eyes. What floor is he on?*

The bastard is up on the tenth floor, she replied. *Matthews, I'm headed that way to provide covering fire!*

Hang on, I'm still on the way! Wilds shouted. *Don't let me miss out on all the fun.*

Another laser blast reached out toward Matthews. This time it met its mark. He couldn't move or scream—an unintelligible gurgle came out of his mouth. And then his world went dark.

****

Matthews? pleaded Soto, hoping he was still alive. There was no answer.

She had just reached a decent vantage point to fire on their nemesis. She cursed and fired her weapon, suppressing the primal urge to scream in rage. Her anger was channeled into killing the man who had taken down her teammate.

Her shot narrowly missed the side of the Watcher's face. Soto wondered if her emotions had gotten the best of her and decreased her accuracy. Regardless, the Watcher shifted positions and now trained his weapon on Soto's position, forcing her to duck behind cover.

When there was a pause, and he hadn't fired at her, she felt like he might have moved to another location, so she peered around the corner, looking to where she'd last seen the Watcher—he was gone.

I think he went back into the building. Nichols and Arnold—be on the lookout! Wilds, Matthews is hurt, maybe worse. It would help if you got to him up in the parking garage.

Everyone acknowledged her message, and Soto raced toward the apartment building. She flung open the door to the stairwell just in time to hear Arnold cry out in agony.

Bastard! Soto thought as she bounded up the stairs, weapon raised. There was a series of blasts. An unknown voice groaned. Then she reached what had turned into a scene of horrific carnage.

Nichols and Arnold were mortally wounded, with laser burns to their chests and abdomens. Intestines and other organs that belonged inside the body were on gory display. But they hadn't gone down without landing a few hits.

The Watcher lay there, one arm and upper shoulder completely severed, bleeding profusely from the hole where his appendage had been. He gasped for breath.

"Shooting you would be too merciful," Soto declared. Instead, she pressed her foot down on the man's open wound and watched him writhe in pain, too anemic to scream, until he passed out.

She turned her attention back to Nichols and Arnold, but there was nothing left to do but to mourn their loss.

I just hope Wilds can salvage Matthews, she thought.

The higher-ups at the IMS were certainly not going to like this.

****

Office of the Viceroy
Alliance City, New Eden
Rhea System

"Viceroy, where is this grand invasion? Three weeks have gone by, and still nothing—"

"I would not call the terrorist attacks across the alliance nothing. The families of those killed deserve more than just a dismissive hand gesture from the senator," interrupted the Primord senator, Aguard.

Miles watched the two senators argue for a moment. The Altairian senator, Jandolly, had a knack for making enemies amongst friends and seemed to revel in his ability to make people dislike him. For the life of him, he could not understand why Admiral Grigdolly, the previous Viceroy and the Altairian King, kept this insufferable man on the Alliance Council.

Miles interrupted them before they could dive into another topic to argue and disagree about. "The intelligence is conclusive, Jandolly. A Zodark operation is already underway. The Mukhabarat launched operations across Republic, Primord, and Altairian space. Yesterday's thwarted attack just outside this very building proves their operation is underway. More than a dozen of these Ani cells, as they call them, have been apprehended across the alliance. These are precursors to an invasion—"

"Yes, your security forces were enough to stop their attack. You have baited the Zodarks to invade the Qatana or the Rhea system for months, yet it has not happened. We cannot keep our forces in our highest states of readiness indefinitely. At some point, the ship crews need to rest and the ships be maintained. When will you acknowledge that this plan has failed so we can—"

"Enough, Jandolly," Admiral Grigdolly interrupted. "You have spoken your piece. Your point was made. The Viceroy and all of us have heard it. Stop before you find yourself pushing the issue too far," the elder statesmen rebuked, his patience expended.

Miles saw the old man give him a slight nod like he was apologizing for Jandolly. At least he finally saw that his underling was beginning to cross the proverbial line of no return in questioning his authority.

Regaining their attention, Miles explained, "We will maintain the fleet's readiness for another seventy-two hours. If there's no further movement by the Zodarks or the rest of the Dominion, I will issue a phased stand-down order to the fleet, and we will return to a state of readiness, but not one of imminent war. We will maintain our standard ready reserve force and quick reaction forces along the alliance control points near the border zones. We will reconvene in seventy-two hours to confirm the stand-down if the enemy hasn't arrived. That is the end of the discussion, and I will speak with the council in three days. That will be all," Miles declared as he stood and then made for the nearby door to his office.

****

Miles walked into his office after another frustrating meeting with the council. He was about to pour himself a drink and prepare to get back to working on another project when the outer door opened, and Admiral Wiyrkomi walked in.

"Pardon the interruption, Viceroy. I have received an urgent communiqué from my people on Earth. The attack—it is happening—Earth is being invaded!"

It took Miles a moment to take in what Wiyrkomi had just said. Sol was outside the Orbots' ability to bridge; last he knew, the Zodarks hadn't possessed the technology either. *The Collective...could it be the Collective?* Almost reading his very thoughts, Wiyrkomi added, "It is the Zodarks that are attacking. They invaded Sol. No one else. No assistance from the Orbots, nor the Collective. They must have found some Humtar technology, perhaps a wormhole generator on a derelict ship they are now exploiting. What are your orders, Viceroy?"

Exploiting a derelict Humtar ship... His mind raced with thoughts of what else could have been found aboard a Humtar vessel long abandoned when he realized he'd been asked a question and hadn't responded.

"Viceroy, Earth is under attack. What are your orders?"

Miles felt himself involuntarily standing almost at attention as he defiantly replied, "Admiral Wiyrkomi, order the fleet to battle stations. Recall all personnel to their assigned ships and units. Inform the fleet we depart for Sol before the end of the day. It's time to finish this fight—to finish the Zodarks once and for all."

Chapter Thirteen
Where Have You Been?

Lab Site X

"Wait, rewind. Someone actually turned the *engines* of the Humtar ship on?" asked Sakura incredulously.

"Yeah, I know," replied Jack. "And here's the kicker…it was Spike."

"Are you serious?" she replied. "I've got to see this."

She raced over to the ship, Jack chasing after her.

Oh, this will certainly make our Republic friends happy, she thought with a smile.

Sakura approached the ship. The entrance along the lower section of the fuselage was wide open. She hadn't really spent too much time with the ship since the engineers had found a way to turn the ship on and they had unloaded and cataloged all the contents in the cargo hold, so everything still felt very novel. The ramp was made of some kind of material she had never seen before, and the way that appeared to pour out of the ship like a liquid made her question again whether it was safe. But as she took one step and then another, she confirmed that her footing was quite sturdy.

The lights had already turned on, and as she approached the cockpit, she felt a surge of excitement. When she opened the door, she saw Spike seated in the pilot's chair, his feet kicked up on the seat next to him. He had a Humtar tablet in his hands and acted as though he was reading it and understanding what it said.

"Did you really turn on the engines?" Sakura questioned, unsure if she had underestimated the troublemaker.

Spike placed the tablet on his lap, and a cocky grin spread across his face. "I did," he replied. "Guess I'm not a total screw-up, am I?"

Sakura just stared at him for a moment before exchanging a glance with Jack. She was completely unsure of how to respond.

"How did you do that?" Jack asked. "I mean, the lights came on automatically before, but no one has been able to gain access to the more complex functions of the ship."

Spike's brash smile turned serious. "Dr. Sakura, as you probably already know, I'm an Osprey pilot assigned to the *Voyager*. No one up there wants to live down here, but I volunteered. It gives me a chance to get off the ship and spread my wings, so to speak—"

"How about we cut to the chase," Jack interrupted, in a tone that was more brusque than Sakura was used to.

Undeterred, Spike continued to explain. "As I was saying, while the Fleet deemed me fit to fly assault transports instead of fighters, what people don't know about me is that prior to being drafted at the end of the war, I used to be an engineer for Textron Spacecraft. Call me young and dumb, but I had a knack for flying and hyperactive reflexes that they said made me an ideal test pilot. Of course, Space Command had to draft me just as my career was finally taking off—no pun intended.

"Once we got settled on the surface and started exploring this place, I got one of your nerdy friends to let me look around the ship. I wasn't sure at first, but the more time I spent looking it over and digging through any files I could find about Humtar ships, or this ship in particular, the more I noticed some parallels between this ship and a few of the ones I had flown prior to being drafted. In fact, once I was able to gain entry to the cockpit, I realized something. I can probably fly this thing."

Sakura's left eyebrow rose at the statement. "Whoa, wait a second, Spike. Are you serious?"

"Ma'am, I fired her up, and I am quite sure."

"Hmm. Well, maybe we should slow this down a tiny bit," offered Jack. "Is there anything you can show us before you actually fly this bird that would demonstrate you aren't just going to crash it?"

Spike pulled his feet off the chair and frowned a little. "Well, that won't be as fun, but I guess we probably should make sure it doesn't have any problems. I mean, it *has* sat here a *long* time, buried in sand for who knows how many years until we came along."

He turned around to face the control panel and tapped various buttons that eventually brought up a menu. "Don't tell any of the guys, but I've been studying the Humtar language pretty hard the past few months."

"Really? Why wouldn't you want anyone to know that?" asked Sakura, genuinely curious.

Spike shrugged. "You know, I have two and a half years left before I'm finally able to leave the Fleet. The last thing I need is for Space Command to find out I'm special and decide they want to keep me around awhile longer."

"Huh, well, I don't know about that, Spike," Jack replied. "Frankly, I'm kind of surprised they haven't already separated you from the Fleet. Typically, someone is an ensign for at most three years, not seven and a half. If an officer or enlisted can't get promoted or keeps getting in trouble, they usually separate them from the service."

"Yeah, that's what they told me too. Yet here I am, an ensign, seven and half years into this ten-year draft requirement," Spike responded humorously as his fingers continued to dance across the control panel. "All right, here's all the systems checks," he explained. He ran through a description of what each one was and showed that the status of everything on board was up to snuff.

Jack visibly relaxed and seemed to accept at this point that Spike did indeed understand the inner workings of this ship.

"Oh, and there's one more thing I wanted to show you," said Spike.

"What's that?" asked Sakura.

"You see, when you all accessed the travel logs before, you only found *part* of the information."

"What do you mean?" asked Jack.

"Well, you saw all the travel between this place and Alpha Centauri, and you even figured out that this ship has a wormhole generator, which is so awesome—I can't believe that they miniaturized the technology that much. Anyway, you missed some of the more confidential locations this bad boy went," Spike explained.

"How in the world did you figure that out?" asked Sakura. "Are you some kind of cryptologist now too?"

Spike laughed. "Naw…believe it or not, I actually do have a friend or two here. I explained what I knew to one of your scientist friends and he went to work cracking the code…here you go."

A three-dimensional star map populated above the control panel, with a list of explanations below. Sakura and Jack studied the screen and then looked at each other to see their reactions.

"This thing went to Earth?" asked Sakura.

"Yep."

"What's this one?" asked Jack, pointing to a location that was far removed from the rest of the map.

"That, I don't know," Spike admitted. "It's a stargate way out in the middle of nowhere. I can't find any information about it."

"Maybe we should go check it out," said Sakura excitedly.

Jack laughed. "Maybe. We should probably talk to Katherine first. But don't you think we should fire this thing up and make sure Spike can really fly it first?" he asked with a wink.

"Well, no time like the present," she answered.

"Normally, you'd be the one reminding *me* of protocol, but don't you think you should bring Katherine in on this one?"

She sighed. "I guess you're right. Let me get her over here."

****

A few flight engineers and technical staff outside observed the ship from afar before coming near to examine it more closely. Sakura wanted Spike to fly them right on out of there and give this thing a go—Katherine, on the other hand, wanted to allow the engineers outside enough time to gather the data they needed before the joyride began.

Sakura hardly felt the ship move as it seemed to glide effortlessly from the flight deck into the late-afternoon sky.

When Spike had turned the engines on, she hadn't been sure what to expect. The ship had been lying dormant for untold thousands of years, buried under sediment, sand, and time. But when the engines had powered up, the vessel had levitated just above the ground—barely a noise to be heard.

After a while, Spike announced, "*Voyager* says they're ready when we are. They've got their tracking radars and equipment ready to monitor us the entire way."

A sense of excitement and adventure coursed through Sakura's veins. The hairs on her arm rose in goose bumps.

"OK, Spike. Let's run her through those tests we talked about," Katherine said. Judging by the look on her face, Sakura guessed she was nervous about testing a ship while she was still aboard.

"Ah, come on, Katherine. Spike's a former test pilot and racer. Cut 'im loose and let's see what this can do!" Jack chimed in, giving Spike a wink.

Sakura glanced over at her fiancé in surprise. She had never seen this side of him before—throwing caution to the wind in an untested ship they knew virtually nothing about. The left corner of her mouth curled up in a half-smile, thoughts beginning to race through her mind of what their plans might be once they returned to the base later that night.

The next thing she knew, Sakura was on the ride of her life. Spike had placed the ship at a downward angle, accelerating at blazing speeds toward the ground before pulling up, only to roll the ship down into a valley she hadn't even seen them approaching. Now they were sprinting through the valley, the ground nothing more than a blur.

As Spike ran through a series of terrifying maneuvers, Jack excitedly egged him on as he hooted and hollered with excitement. As adrenaline flooded her system, Sakura wondered if this was what the soldiers experienced when they assaulted a planet from orbit—but even this probably didn't compare to a terrifying journey to a planet's surface while taking enemy fire the entire way down. She felt like her life flashed before her eyes more than once. But as she started to breathe into the turns and wild maneuvers, Sakura realized Spike really knew what he was doing.

This guy's a damn good pilot…

Then, just like that, the maneuvers and crazy flying were done. They'd done the series of tests and appeared to be headed back to the landing zone.

"So…I don't know about you guys, but who's up for taking a longer ride and seeing what's at the end of that stargate?" Spike asked casually. He was cool as a cucumber, not a bead of sweat on his forehead.

"Definitely, count me in," Sakura suddenly found herself saying.

Jack grinned, apparently amused by her eagerness to continue flying with this daredevil.

Katherine was a bit less convinced. "We don't know what's on the other side of that thing," she rationalized. "Could be a Collective trap for all we know."

"Well, what if we don't go through the other side?" asked Sakura. "It wouldn't hurt to just check it out. No one in the alliance even knows this place exists. Who knows what we will find out there?"

Katherine looked at her friend for a long time. "Well, I guess that's why we're out here, isn't it? To make discoveries?"

She turned to Spike. "I guess I'm going to have to talk to your commanding officer and get your schedule cleared for tomorrow," she said with a smile. "Looks like the Republic might have an extra duty for you."

Chapter Fourteen
Phantoms in the Night

CVW-3 Battle Axe

Captain Ethan Hunt was betting the lives of every pilot in his wing on this harebrained idea of his working. If it didn't...well, at least he wouldn't be around to stand before a board of inquiry.

As his Gripen continued to hug the side of the *Berlin*, he hoped the old warrior would be able to deliver one more victory for the Republic before she met her demise or was finally retired to the mothball fleet. She was among the few *Ryan*-class battleships still left in service, and he was glad as hell they had her, or this might not have worked.

Looking out his cockpit window, he saw his pilots maintaining their intervals and doing their best to stay as close to the battleship as they could without accidentally hitting each other.

When he'd shared the idea with Commander Mikhail "Flattop" Pushkin, his lone surviving senior commanding officer, his friend had stared at him for a moment, not sure if he was being serious or joking around. Once he'd explained the situation on Earth, his plan to slip past the Zodark battle line had finally come into focus as the only viable option if they wanted to get at those enemy transports.

The plan was audacious, maybe even suicidal. But every Zodark transport and landing ship destroyed took out thousands of Zodarks who wouldn't reach the surface to wreak havoc on their home world. Like it or not, this was their best shot.

"So far so good, right, Paladin?"

"Yeah, so far. Don't jinx it, though. The *Berlin* is about to make her turn and go to full power. Once she does that...it won't take them long to figure out what she's up to."

The plan called for the *Berlin* to begin turning past the edge of McKee's battle line. Then the old warship would take a downward angle as she turned hard before accelerating to maximum burn. The low tilt and hard turn for the enemy's flank would place the battleship out of alignment with the Zodarks and the rest of the Republic fleet. It was Hunt's belief that once the Zodarks saw what the *Berlin* was doing, they'd have to adjust their flank, or the *Berlin* would slide past them before they could move to intercept.

"Yeah, I suppose you're right. But like you said, once the Zodarks do that, that's when our Phantoms will go to work. This was a hell of a plan you put together, Paladin. I think we have a real shot at making this work," his friend encouraged.

"Thanks, Flattop. You have no idea how much I needed to hear that right now. We have a lot of things that need to still break our way before this is over. Oh, and lest you think I forgot, buddy, you still owe me two hundred credits for the stomping my Buccaneers gave your Eagles last week."

Last week was the NFL division playoffs. Just one more game to determine who would play in the Super Bowl.

They laughed at the reminder of the bet, which helped ease the moment's tension as they continued to fly on in silence. Hunt tried to busy himself by checking in periodically with his squadron commanders via the peer-to-peer comms network, ensuring their pilots were doing all right and no problems had appeared requiring his attention. He watched the time to their next move steadily hack to zero; they were about to make their first significant turn.

Traveling along the battle line between the opposing forces, one could see the lasers, missiles, and projectiles being hurled between the two sides as the battle continued to ebb and flow. At times the fighting picked up with great intensity, only to peter out a short time later as the two sides struggled to separate themselves before any significant damage was done.

As Ethan thought about how this battle was being fought, he was reminded of a boxing match his grandfather had taken him to before he died. Ethan was nearly eighteen, getting ready to leave for the Space Academy. One day his grandfather had wanted to spend some time with him before he left, so he'd arranged for them to see a boxing match. The fight had been exhilarating to watch during the early rounds, much like the initial battle had started around Earth. The fighters had fought like savages, landing blow after blow, bloodying each other up. But as the fight dragged on and they became exhausted, the match seemed to transform itself into a battle of wills—a standoff between the two sides that saw neither one strong enough to knock out the other but both unwilling to give up the fight. With each successive round, one fighter or the other would lunge forward into the clinch position. It was a defensive technique where an attacker leaned into their opponent and wrapped their arms around them; the haphazard embrace and occasional jabs to the gut would eventually be separated by the referee. But the match his grandfather had taken him to was different. After the two boxers were briefly separated, one of the fighters began to circle the other. Hunt watched on curiously to try and decipher what the boxer was doing. That was when his granddad told him to watch what happened next.

After being circled a couple of times, the fighter who looked exhausted, bloodied, and like he was about to pass out suddenly lunged at his opponent with more speed and zeal than Ethan had thought possible. The man landed not one or two solid blows, but a series of punches to his opponent's head and face, causing the defender to raise his arms up to defend himself. Once his opponent's abdomen was unprotected, the boxer landed a hard punch to the gut, causing the man to almost double over. When the guy fell forward from the blow, the boxer landed an uppercut that knocked the other man clean off his feet and flat on his back.

Hunt smiled at the memory of that day. His granddad had jumped out of his seat, hooting and hollering in excitement over the sudden turn of events. "That, Ethan, is how you lull your opponent into thinking you're weaker than you are. Once you've sold the deception, that's when you strike," his grandfather had said.

If we can convince the Zodarks to take the bait...we'll land our own uppercut and knock 'em on their asses...

"Battle Axe Actual, Berlin Actual. We're about to execute our turn and go to full power on the engines. We'll do our best to get you as close to the transports as possible and keep the guns off your back. Good luck, boys. Have a beer for us when this is over. Berlin out."

As the connection to *Berlin* ended, Hunt felt he should say something, anything, in response to the man and his crew. But he knew he couldn't. If he transmitted now, there was a chance the enemy might figure out that *Berlin* wasn't alone out here after all. Using their peer-to-peer comms system when near each other was one thing. It was another thing to generate a power source strong enough for a warship.

Watching the time and speed of their travel continue to move at what felt like a snail's pace, Ethan could feel his inner fighter pilot dying just a little with each passing minute. Speed was life in the fighter world, and while the Gripen was no Hellcat, she could still run circles around a Zodark Vulture and certainly this battleship they were hugging.

Just a little longer…just have to get a little closer before we can make our move, he kept telling himself.

The minutes ticked by, and then the situation around *Berlin* changed in the blink of an eye. A singular brilliant streak of light zipped overtop the giant warship in a warning that the calm they had experienced to this point had just ended.

Soon, dozens of tiny flashes of light were swirling around the giant warship as the helmsman aggressively maneuvered the lumbering giant as best he could. Ethan figured that for every flash he saw harmlessly miss the *Berlin*, dozens more hammered the other side. At first, he could tell it was the corvettes, frigates, and cruisers shooting at them by the width of their lasers. But when he saw flashes as thick as his Gripen, he knew the battleships were now getting in on the action. It wouldn't be long before they had the *Berlin* zeroed. Its life expectancy now measured in minutes.

With the battleships focusing on them, Hunt activated the comms, sending a message to Lieutenant Commander Rojas that it was time. His flight of Phantoms was cleared hot to unleash their electronic wizardry and go to town on the warships laying into the *Berlin*.

After relaying the order, he stayed on the channel, wanting to listen in and see how the Phantoms performed. This was his first time flying with the electronic-attack birds, and he was eager to see how they worked.

"Shadowhawks, we're a go for mission—it's wizard time! Prepare to cut engines to ten percent on my mark…three…two…one…mark…"

I like this guy already, Hunt thought as he watched their ships fall behind the strike group and the Berlin shielding. The Phantoms were still new; even the *Royal* hadn't received their squadron of them just yet. Space Command had just started fielding them to the operational carriers first, then would begin integrating them into the rest of the space wings aboard the battleships.

Rojas continued, "Okay, we're past the *Berlin*. It's time to earn that hazard duty pay my lovely wife spent on her new Tesla Model H."

"Whoa, tell me that's a bad joke, boss. Those things aren't cheap," commented Shadow Four.

"What can I say, guys? She's a material girl in a material world," Rojas joked with his pilots before things got serious.

Hunt found himself laughing with his pilots. He could remember a song with those lyrics, although the singer's name was escaping his memory.

Damn it, Rojas. I'm going to have that song stuck in my head now...

While he didn't know a whole lot about these electronic-attack birds, he knew they were modeled on the newly redesigned Osprey attack shuttles. Any existing Osprey pilots wanting to cross over into the new craft were being rewarded with a bonus based on the entirety of their previous year's pay in addition to a twenty-five percent pay bump if they flew with an operational squadron.

Continuing to watch the group fall further behind, he saw his sensors momentarily scramble before returning to normal. When they did, the five shuttles were now showing as Republic frigates.

Hunt smiled, knowing the sudden appearance of not one or two but five of the vaunted Altairian-Human hybrid frigates was sure to get the attention of the Zodarks. While they'd love nothing more than to keep hammering *Berlin*, he knew they couldn't ignore the threat five frigates posed to their battleships.

With the frigates falling further behind the battleships, they turned towards the Zodark battle line and accelerated to full power. The bait had been laid—the trap set.

As Hunt watched the Phantoms continue to race in the opposite direction of the *Berlin* towards the enemy lines from an upward angle, he had to hope this move created the quandary necessary to split their attention and get *Berlin* and thus his strike package that much closer to the main target.

Having started his career as a navigator on an earlier version of Republic frigates, Hunt understood better than most the fear these torpedoes and missile boats stirred in the captains of the battleships. These fast, nimble warships could rapidly close the distance between themselves and the enemy ships before unloading a barrage of plasma torpedoes and swarms of missiles designed to overwhelm their point defense weapons.

Monitoring the Phantoms' progress on his display, he waited anxiously, hoping and praying the enemy would take the bait and shift their fire from the *Berlin* to engage the more immediate threat.

"Paladin, I'm starting to get nervous. Do you think it's possible they sniffed out our trap? The *Berlin* is still taking a hell of a pounding," Flattop asked nervously.

As if on cue to highlight the problem, he saw streaks of lights flash in front of the *Berlin* while a few others passed below.

"Give it time, my friend. They just went active with their ECM and EW equipment. Once they fire those Ghost missiles, they'll realize they've got a frigate problem," Hunt replied, trying to sound more confident than he felt.

"Yeah, I suppose that's true. If seeing a swarm of missiles racing towards your base stars and battleships doesn't get your attention, I'm not sure what will."

"Just keep your ships tight. Now's not the time to slip up. We're almost there."

"I hear ya, boss. We're tight back here. I'm making sure we don't have any stragglers. Whoa, speak of the devil. Looks like they just fired their 98s. I'd give it a few minutes and we should have an idea if this ruse is going to work or not."

"It'll work, Flattop. You wait and see," Hunt replied confidently, his earlier doubts beginning to wash away.

Within seconds of being fired, the 98G or Ghost missiles began releasing the ten smaller variants that would rapidly accelerate toward their intended targets. With their own ECM module spoofing the enemy sensors into thinking they were the much larger Havoc-2 missiles, the five missiles fired at the battle line had transformed into a swarm of fifty new contacts.

Now you'll have something to react to..., Hunt thought to himself. Then a smile crept across his face as he remembered that the final missile was about to join the fray. Soon the enemy would have a hundred tracks to contend with. If this worked like the admiral had said it would, they'd be too distracted to realize how close the *Berlin* would have gotten to the transports they were supposed to be protecting.

But time wasn't on their side. Hunt knew the enemy would eventually burn through the electronic ruse. You could spoof and blind their sensors for a while, but eventually, they'd see through the trickery, and the jig would be up. For now, all he cared about was getting closer to the target before they'd have to reveal their part in this grand plan the admiral had cooked up.

As the minutes ticked by and the volume of laser fire around the *Berlin* hadn't changed, his nerves were beginning to fray. *Come on...take the bait...take the bait*, he thought, willing the enemy to cooperate. Then, like a switch had been flipped, the flashes of lasers and strings of projectiles swirling about them suddenly stopped.

Yes...they've taken the bait...this is gonna work!

The admiral had bet the lives of Rojas's pilots to draw the enemy off while he'd bet the lives of those on the *Berlin* to shield his strike group to get him closer to the transports. He felt terrible for the sacrifice he was asking of *Berlin*. But he knew as the admiral did that each transport they destroyed saved the lives of untold thousands on Earth.

As the plan started to work, he could feel a sense of excitement take hold. Then Flattop chimed in, "I'll be damned, Paladin. The admiral was right. They're taking the bait."

"Yeah, so far, so good. But it's not over yet. We have to hope they buy the *Berlin* at least another five to ten minutes, then, if we're lucky, the *Berlin* may get us another ten more before we break cover and make our move. Then it's game on for us. Just promise me one thing, Flattop. If my fighter goes down, you won't hesitate to take charge and finish the fight. God only knows how many warriors they cram into those transports. But every one we take out—it's more lives we save."

"Of course, you can count on me. But you aren't going anywhere. You're the best damn pilot in the Fleet!"

Hunt laughed at the comment but didn't reply. His attention was now totally focused on the battle between the Phantoms, their electronic wizardry, and their attempt to flank the Zodark line so his strike force could get at those transports. With the swarm of missiles barreling down on their positions, several of the cruisers hanging back began to advance past their battleships.

The cruisers appeared to be on an intercept course with the Phantoms pretending to be frigates. While the cruisers gave chase and closed the gap, a handful of enemy frigates and corvettes moved into a blocking position between themselves and the path of the incoming missiles. They were preparing to intercept them or, if all else failed, place themselves in their path so they didn't hit the capital ships.

While the battle continued to unfold, the gunners aboard the *Berlin* were doing their best to hurl copious amounts of magrail slugs into the paths of the frigates and corvettes. If they wanted to play bodyguard and stand in the way of an assassin's bullet, they were happy to send a few thousand for them to absorb.

As he watched the tactical display, he saw the frigates and corvettes position themselves in front of the battleships, acting as a shield. Strings of projectiles steadily merged with the would-be bodyguards, and the occasional frigate or corvette blew apart. Each time he saw one blotted from his scanner, he knew it was one less warship that would eventually be shooting at his pilots when it came to their turn to sprint around the *Berlin* and begin their attack run on the transports.

Glancing briefly at the blue triangle icons representing the Phantoms, Hunt saw one flash for a moment before fading to a subdued blue. He felt his stomach tighten, knowing what it meant—they'd lost one. Then, moments later, two more flashed briefly before fading into the background.

The enemy cruisers had closed the distance. The ruse had been discovered—revenge exacted. Then the final pair of Phantoms flashed like the previous trio, joining their comrades on a patrol without end.

Seven minutes...hallelujah, they managed to get us seven minutes, Hunt thought to himself as he calculated the distance between the transports and their current position. They'd massively closed the gap, putting them almost in striking distance. They just needed a little more.

Then his comms came to life as a message from *Berlin* came in.

"Battle Axe, Berlin. The Phantoms are down. Our sensors show that the Zodarks are refocusing their efforts on us. Once their main guns start laying into us, I can't guarantee how long we're going to—"

"Berlin, Battle Axe. We understand the situation and we're eternally grateful for what you have done. No need to explain things further—you've done your part. The *Berlin* and its crew have served with honor and distinction beyond what should have been asked of you. Now it's our turn to end this fight—we'll take it from here," Hunt interrupted the captain, not allowing him to disconnect before he could reply.

There was a short pause. Then the voice resumed, the sound of alarm bells blaring in the background. "Before we're done, Paladin, there's a pair of frigates and four corvettes racing ahead of us. I think they'll set a blocking position to protect the transports. I'd launch your force now. Don't wait—"

The comms channel went dead before the captain could finish. The last thing Hunt was able to hear was the sound of alarms, loud shouting in the background, then an explosion that ended the connection.

"Paladin, we need to get out of here! It looks like *Berlin*'s going down," came an urgent warning from one of the other squad leaders.

Going active with their normal comms channel, Hunt needed to make sure everyone heard the message before it was too late.

"All Battle Axe elements, *Berlin* is going down. Now it's our time to carry on the fight. Squadron commanders—take charge of your elements and execute! Let's go kill us some transports!"

"Hell yeah!"

"That's right, it's time to Roll Bama Roll us some Zodarks!"

"Time to shake and bake some blue bastards!" hollered another pilot excitedly as a raucous cheer went up before the squadron commanders chimed in to regain control. The hours of silence were over. The time to fight was now.

With the tensions of the moment broken as quickly as their formation against the side of the battleship, the fighters were now peeling away from the warship rapidly being consumed by flames burning from multiple gashes to her hull.

As the distance between themselves and the warship continued to grow, the various squadrons were hastily coming together into their attack formations. Some of the guns on *Berlin* were still blazing away as the ship continued to burn. The Zodarks remained focused on finishing them off—oblivious to what was happening on the other side of the dying battleship.

Keying the comms, Hunt loudly declared so even the Zodarks could hear him, "All Battle Axe squadrons—commence your attacks. It's time to rock and roll and get this party started!" Then, in complete disregard of naval regulations, he momentarily blared his favorite song he liked to listen to as he flew into battle—AC/DC's "Highway to Hell."

Looking out the window of his cockpit with a smile from ear to ear as he blasted his fight music, he saw the remaining seventy-six fighters across his twelve squadrons start to race towards their primary targets—the enemy still not responding to their presence.

Then he spotted the first sign of trouble. A pair of corvettes and a frigate attempted to race ahead and place themselves in front of the transports. Then a squadron of Gripens broke off from the main force along with four of his Valkyries, who looked to be lining up for an attack run on the corvettes.

While he wanted nothing more than to assist one of his squadron commanders, he had to remind himself that he had an entire wing he needed to lead. Gripping his controls tightly, he accelerated to maximum power as he and his pilots pushed their fighters to their maximum capabilities. No longer did he feel a sense of dread or uncertainty. All he felt now was the adrenaline coursing through his veins as he finally caught sight of the prize they had lost so much to reach.

"Paladin, Flattop. We got Vultures inbound. Count is now forty-two. I'm going to lead Rampagers, Swamp Foxes, and Wildcats to intercept them. We'll do our best to cover your attack on the transports. It's on you, Paladin. You got this! Good luck, and I'll see you on the other side."

With no time to think about it or question what his friend had just done, Hunt simply moved on to the task at hand. Connecting to the squadrons still racing towards the transports, he said, "Gunslingers, Swordsmen, on me. Target your JATMs on the landers. We got the best chance at taking those down with them. Screwtops, Zappers, Dusty Dogs, you got the transports. Make your missiles and attack runs count. It's just us now. We're all that's left to take 'em out. You all can do this. I trust you. I believe in you. Now let's go get 'em!"

A few pilots from the Dusty Dogs squadron barked and howled in excitement as the attack got underway. Hunt had a few moments before he'd be in range to begin his own attack. He watched as one of the Dogs angled in for a shot on a large transport. A couple of guns opened fire—stabs of light shot through the darkness attempting to blot the Valkyrie before it could unload its torpedoes.

The pilot deftly maneuvered the bomber from side to side, jinking back and forth to throw off the gunner's aim. As the bomber closed in on its prey, a pair of torpedoes emerged from its belly. Once they acquired the target, they shot off like shooting stars.

The pilot flying the B-11 pulled away as he applied more power to his engines. Like the seasoned veteran he was, he'd already realigned for the next transports as he dodged the crisscrossing of enemy fire shooting at him now from half a dozen transports and landers that were fully aware they were under attack.

The pilot was cool as a cucumber, releasing another pair of torpedoes moments after acquiring his second target. Having fired off two pairs of torpedoes, he veered off into the blackness to realign for another run.

While that had been taking place, two more Valkyries had gone in for their attack runs. Within minutes, the space around this particular cluster of ships had come alive with defensive fire from the transports. Hunt smiled as he saw one torpedo after another complete the plasma transition, becoming flaming darts as they sped through the blackness of space, impacting against the transports.

As the torpedoes tore gashes across the superstructures and fuselages of the Zodark vessels, giant plumes of flame, atmosphere and fluids ejected themselves from the newly created holes in the ship. While he couldn't see the physical bodies of Zodarks being sucked out into the vacuum of space, he suspected this was happening. The thought of them choking, suffocating from lack of atmosphere, somehow made him feel good inside. He wanted them to suffer. To die slow, agonizing deaths if possible. These invaders had killed God knew how many of his people.

We just wanted peace...to be left alone...to grow...to prosper...to make babies and expand our species across the stars. Now we have to destroy you...to remove you as a threat once and for all...

"Paladin, Gypsy Six. We got runners. I'm tracking twelve landers attempting to break orbit and make a run down to the surface. How copy?" asked Lieutenant Callier.

He had just assigned Callier to be the acting squadron commander for the Fighting Swordsmen eight hours earlier. Lieutenant Commander Puck had been shot down shortly after the *Ark Royal* had arrived in the middle of the enemy fleet.

"Six, Paladin. That's a good copy. You're free to engage. Follow 'em, but don't enter the atmosphere. If you can nail them before they do, go for it. Otherwise, break off your attack and get back up here with the rest of us. How copy?"

The last thing Hunt wanted was for his limited number of Gripens and Valkyries to start scattering themselves. Their strength lay in their ability to cover each other while fighting as a team. That only worked if they stayed together.

"That's a good copy. We'll be back."

Missile Warning—Missile Warning—

The alarm sent a jolt of adrenaline through his body. The missile was closing fast. Approaching from the right rear sector of his current attack vector.

Damn it, I'm finally closing in on that group of landers. Now I have to deal with this missile, he thought angrily. Cursing under his breath, he activated his ECM and jinked hard to the left as he pulled up on his controls, creating a large space where his Gripen had been moments earlier.

He saw the Vulture's missile sail through space he'd just occupied before detonating harmlessly out of reach of him. Cutting his power in half, he flipped his Gripen 180 degrees in the opposite direction to face the projected flight path his sensors said the Vulture was about to cross.

Just then, the targeting reticle to his guns had gone from yellow to briefly green as the fighter flew across the path of his guns. He mashed the trigger, sending a burst of fire that stitched the side of the Vulture as it flew into the path of his guns. The fighter exploded in a brilliant flash before the blackness swallowed it up.

With the immediate threat neutralized, he applied more power to his engines and returned his attention to the group of landers he had his sights on as he continued to close the distance. His sensors told him there was a dozen of the medium-sized troop landers, all appearing to close ranks and try to maximize their defensive weapons. The pilots looked like they were going to attempt to land on the planet's surface as a group before he could take them out. "You're too late, little piggies," he muttered to himself, a smile spreading from ear to ear.

The color denoting the eight JATM missiles tucked away in the weapons bay had gone from yellow to green. They'd acquired their targets—they were ready to hunt. Depressing the pickle button with his thumb, he sent missile after missile toward their assigned targets until he had released them all.

Then he jinked to the right just as a flash of blue light zipped right past his cockpit. He swore he could have touched it if he had reached his hand out. Applying more power to his engines, he changed trajectories every few seconds, moving up and to one side only to change angles moments later. Flashes of light continued to chase him despite his aggressive maneuvering.

As he continued to evade the Vulture still shooting at him, his missiles had finally reached the landers, scoring hit after hit. One by one the ships were either blown apart or left adrift from the damage they took. He smiled for a second before an alarm shouted in his ear.

Warning Eject—Warning Eject—

Suddenly his body was momentarily crushed against the seat as the Gripen's self-contained cockpit ejected from the body of his fighter. The shock of suddenly being thrown from the craft lasted for a moment before he caught sight of a missile as it plowed into his baby. It blew apart in a brilliant flash before the blackness returned and he found himself floating helplessly in the ejected cockpit.

What the hell just happened? was the only thought he managed to have before his world went black, the cockpit's life support system injecting him with a shot that knocked him unconscious.

With the drug having put his body into a deep sleep, he now consumed half the oxygen he would have staying awake. Slowing the heart rate and breathing of the pilot added hours to the life support system, giving the pilot more time to be recovered before their air ran out. While he slept, the emergency beacon would transmit until a recovery craft eventually found him. Until then, he'd remain asleep, consuming as little oxygen as possible, or pass away in blissful ignorance.

Chapter Fifteen
Taking Flight

Lab Site X

Sakura's hands were sweating in nervous anticipation, and she felt her heart beating faster in her chest. All the same, the butterflies in her stomach were not entirely unpleasant. Her recent ride on the Humtar ship had been one of the biggest adrenaline rushes of her lifetime, and she wasn't sure anything else could top it.

As soon as they strapped in, Jack gave Sakura's hand a little squeeze. "You ready to see how far the journey down the rabbit hole goes?" he asked with a wink.

She was starting to understand more of his references to American culture. This one from *Alice in Wonderland* seemed especially apt. She'd been in a ship that had wormhole technology before, but never one this small—it could be a wild ride. And she had no idea what awaited them on the other end.

I just hope we aren't traveling into some sort of trap, she thought. *Spike's pretty sure this thing has weapons, but I sure don't want to test that theory on our maiden voyage.*

Just like their last ride, the ship glided into the air so smoothly, Sakura could barely tell that it had even moved. Spike maneuvered it out of the orbit of the planet in a relatively short amount of time, and then he was talking out loud as he performed his own personal checklist before engaging the wormhole technology.

"Hold on to your seats," Spike announced. "Engaging wormhole in three, two, one…"

Whoa, thought Sakura, half panicked and half filled with wonder. The space around the ship became like a cloud of swirling sunsets; it was beautiful and awe-inspiring, and so close she felt like she could touch it. She felt like she took a single step forward, and then it was gone.

"What just happened?" she asked. "Didn't it work?"

"Oh, it worked all right," Spike answered. "Take a look around."

Sakura couldn't believe her eyes. This was definitely not the same system they were in just a moment ago. She was dumbfounded.

The last time she had traveled in a ship with wormhole technology, it had felt like she was being pulled through time and space in a strange motion, as though she was being rolled out in a pasta machine. This time, she had barely even noticed they had crossed over. This Humtar technology was even more advanced than what the Gallentines had.

"Status report," Katherine ordered. Spike might be the pilot, but he was definitely not in charge.

He fiddled around with some instruments on the ship before he announced, "There's really nothing out here except for this stargate. There are no planets, no stars, no signs of life of any kind…this really is out in the middle of nowhere."

"What did you hide out here?" Sakura wondered aloud, thinking about the Humtars who had put this here. She was filled with awe that it had remained undiscovered, at least by all the species she had knowledge of.

"Can we move in a little closer now?" Spike asked.

"Go ahead," Katherine assented.

Spike moved the ship ahead at a steady pace. There was nothing but blackness out here. Sakura had never seen anything like it—what stars were visible seemed extremely far away, faded points of light in a distant part of the universe.

As soon as she saw it, Sakura knew this gate was different. All stargates had markings on them, fragments of the Humtar language mixed with artwork, but this ring was ornate, made of multiple colors of metal, at some points woven together in a filigree pattern. Even the bolts were decorative.

"It's…beautiful," said Katherine.

Sakura agreed. The craftsmanship was superb. And unlike other stargates she had approached in the past, she could see through the center of it like looking through a fish tank. On the other side lay at least one planet, and a string of brightly colored nebulas behind it.

"What is this place?" asked Jack.

"I don't know," Sakura answered, "but I sure wish we could find out."

Suddenly, an alarm on the ship sounded, and a window popped up on Spike's control screen.

"What's going on?" Katherine pressed.

"Hang on, I'm reading the message," Spike said, waving away further questions with his arm. "It...they're asking for a password."

"A password?" asked Sakura incredulously. "Katherine, none of the other stargates have ever required a code, right?"

"Not that I'm aware of."

There was a moment of strained silence as they processed what was happening.

"So, if we do want to enter this gate, how are we getting in?" Sakura finally asked.

Spike shushed her and pushed his hands down, multiplying his request for quiet. Sakura felt offended, but she also felt that Spike had earned some respect at this point.

Finally, he spoke. "Do you see this symbol here?" he asked, pointing.

The three passengers squinted and focused on what he was highlighting. "Yeah. What is it?" asked Katherine.

"I don't know exactly, but I know I've seen this before back at Lab Site X," Spike replied. "Jack, can you take a picture of this?" he asked. "I'm sure if we head back, I could find it. Maybe there's a clue there."

"All right," said Katherine. "Let's gather whatever data we can here and head back then, I guess. I'm sure the Viceroy will want to know about this."

****

When the ship came to a halt, they'd barely gotten off the vessel when they received an urgent message from the captain aboard the *Voyager*.

Opening the message, Sakura only managed to see the headline before she felt Jack's hand grasp hers. *The Republic is under attack—the Zodarks have invaded Sol...*

The mood was somber. They had no idea what was going on back on Earth and Mars, and everyone had at least *some* family or friends back in Sol.

After they'd had a few minutes to process what they'd just learned, Katherine spoke. "All right, it's time to stop sulking," she announced. "All our communications out here are severely delayed, so for all we know, the Zodarks may have been wiped out by now. Either way, it won't help our loved ones for us to sit here and feel sorry for ourselves."

Sakura nodded slowly. Her friend was right.

"Spike, I want you to look for that symbol," said Katherine. "Who knows what we'll discover behind that stargate, but maybe we will find the missing key to save Earth."

"Yes, ma'am," replied Spike, with more respect than he usually mustered. Then he walked off in the direction of the library.

Katherine, Sakura, and Jack followed quietly behind. When Spike opened the door, a soldier inside looked up from a holographic scroll and snickered.

"You read?" he asked Spike pointedly.

"Shut up," Spike replied.

"Beat it," said Jack sternly.

The soldier seemed a bit confused, but seeing as how he was outnumbered, he got out of the way and left the room.

With a bit of finagling, Spike managed to enter the picture that Jack had taken into the lab's internal search engine. They were directed to one of the physical books present in the library.

Sakura had been so busy with the extensive databases in the labs that she actually hadn't spent too much time in this room. Studying the history of the Humtar people had taken a back seat to finding new information about things that had real-world applications for the Republic, like the extremely efficient food replicators or the air purification systems that were going to revolutionize future ship design. But here they were, and Sakura felt that this mystery was different.

I sure hope this helps Sol, she thought to herself.

Spike located the book and pulled it off the shelf. Sakura still hadn't figured out what materials these books were made of—possibly fabric, but it was unlike any textile she had ever felt. In any case, it didn't take long for Spike to locate the symbol, in the very beginning of the book.

"Here—look," he exclaimed excitedly. Then his expression soured. "This looks like only part of a code," he said glumly.

"How do you know?" asked Katherine.

"The code they asked for back at the stargate had twelve characters—this is only six."

The group thought about what to do for a moment before Katherine suggested, "Sakura, we should put this into the database that Dr. Audrey Lancaster created from the Alpha Centauri site. I mean, that ship went from here to Alpha frequently—maybe there's something there."

"It's certainly worth a try," Sakura acknowledged.

Within a few minutes, they were at her personal workstation, and she was entering the image into a search.

Ding.

"We have a hit," she replied excitedly.

"And...?" asked Spike.

"And...it looks like we have the rest of our code," said Sakura.

Chapter Sixteen
First Blood

Task Force Five
RNS *Vanguard*

"Commodore, the task force is now underway—the ships are in position and following our lead," Ensign Godley announced as the *Vanguard* approached the wormhole.

"Thank you, Ensign," Dobbs replied before turning to look for Lieutenant Commander Dildine, who ran the ship's combat information center. "CIC, we need the TAM operational when we cross into Sol. Get us a picture of our immediate surroundings and identify any potential threats. Then I need your team to see if the battlenet is still operational since the last time the Altairian scout ship tapped into it. If by some miracle the Zodarks still haven't taken it down, see if you can establish comms with whatever Republic forces and facilities are still on the net. Particularly the facility at Titan. Then I need your people to assess the status of any Republic warships still in the system and what kind of hostile force remains."

"Yes, Commodore. Do you want us to transmit the findings and our reports to the *Berkimon* once Admiral Pandolly's fleet arrives in the system or run it past you first?" Commander Dildine tried to clarify.

Dobbs paused for a second as she thought about that. Part of her wanted to look it over before it was sent. *What's the point? It's not like we can hide what's happening...* Looking back to CIC, she replied, "No, if they arrive in the system before I've had a chance to review it, go ahead and send it. Got it?"

"Yes, ma'am."

Dobbs nodded approvingly, then turned to her Flight Ops section of the bridge. "Commander Mitsu, that brings me to you. The moment we cross into Sol, I want our fighters scrambled ASAP. Get us a combat patrol up and running to protect the transports and make sure to send out some patrols with their suite of sensors active. We'll let them act as pickets and screen for the Fleet until Pandolly's fleet has finished crossing the bridge. Let's also make sure to have our bombers ready to launch should we encounter any hostile ships in the vicinity."

"Aye-aye, ma'am. Our fighters are armed and in the tubes—ready to launch the moment we exit. My counterpart on the *Rheinland* and I have already coordinated our scouts and squadron rotations for the combat patrols over the fleet. We got this, Commodore. You can count on us," he confidently assured her.

"Now this is what I'm talking about, Mitsu! Out-freaking-standing taking the initiative like that!" she praised her fighter boss. During the last campaign, he had demonstrated how effective the Fleet's new space wings could be when properly trained and led into battle.

She smiled a moment longer, observing how efficiently he'd trained the nonflight crews who aided in the operations that kept the fighters deployed and in good working order. Knowing he had things well under control, she turned to her tactical officer next, zeroing in on Commander Little. "TAO, the moment we're across the bridge, I want our guns spun up and be ready to engage whatever we may encounter. God forbid we land near an enemy formation and they get a jump on us the moment we enter regular space. I want to be as ready as possible for it. It's going to be incumbent on your people to rapidly counter the ambush the moment we're able. Got it?"

"Aye, Captain. We'll be ready," Commander Little confidently replied. Her gun crews had more than earned their pay against the Pharaonis, smashing ship after ship during several battles for control of the system. Now they'd have to repeat that performance against a numerically superior Zodark fleet.

Dobbs took a moment to breathe and accept that the crew she'd trained and mentored the last few years was ready to fight. Commander Wright joined her as the ship began to near the wormhole connecting them to home.

"The crew's ready, Captain. You've done a good job training them, and the Serpentis campaign gave them a taste of what to expect with the Zodarks. They've got this," he assured her. His confidence rubbed off on her as she felt a renewed sense of purpose. She'd led her task force to victory during the last campaign. Now she would lead them into an even greater battle with larger stakes: the battle for Sol—for the heart of the Republic.

"I know, XO. You're right—they're ready for whatever comes next. I just hope I'm as ready as they are," she confided quietly.

Wright smiled warmly. "Captain, this is my third assignment with you. In each tour, you led us from victory to victory. You are an exceptional commander, and we have the utmost confidence that your winning streak will continue."

"Huh. Well, thanks for the vote of confidence, XO. Just don't jinx us with it." They shared a brief laugh before Godley announced they were twenty seconds out from entering the wormhole.

"Guess it's time to buckle up and put our war faces on, as the grunts like to say."

"Damn right, Captain," he said with a devilish smile as they returned to their seats.

She liked that about Joe. He was confident without being cocky, and he was decisive when needed. He wasn't the kind of officer who looked for a fight to prove himself. But when a fight had to happen, he was a vicious killer and wouldn't think twice about ordering his ship to its death if that was what it took to win. He had that fighting instinct that not all captains shared.

As she strapped herself into the plush leather captain's chair, Godley announced, "We're entering the bridge."

No sooner had he said the words than, just like that, the light from the nearby sun and the twinkling stars disappeared into the blackness of the void that drew them into the wormhole.

Despite having traveled through dozens if not hundreds of such wormholes and stargates these past twenty years, she still marveled at how they could cross the vastness of space in mere seconds or minutes via these seemingly unknown trapdoors that somehow tied space and time. When she had worked in the R&D department some years back, she'd asked if someone could explain it like they were talking to their golden retriever. One of the eggheads had snickered at her analogy before giving her the easiest way to understand how the basic concept worked.

The wormhole technology aboard the few ships that had it basically held down the point in space the ship currently occupied. With its anchor point known, some gobbledygook within the machine then found the shortest path between their present location and that of their destination. She was told to think of it like folding two separate points on a piece of paper until they touched. Folding the paper was essentially bending space and time, connecting two impossibly far-off locations almost instantly. Then it was a matter of just crossing the bridge, and bam, you'd just traveled thirty or even sixty light-years in the blink of an eye.

The one limiting factor she'd been told the Altairians and the Orbots still hadn't solved was how to increase the range generator unit—a mystery she had no desire or intellectual ability to solve. As a ship captain, all she cared about was that it worked and got her ships to where they were needed most.

As the *Vanguard* entered the wormhole, it troubled her that the Zodarks had somehow managed to do what their Orbot masters had not yet figured out—increase the range of the generator unit. The limiting factor in the range had more or less allowed both alliances to know what systems each other could jump into and which ones were out of range. Armed with this knowledge, the two sides reinforced those specific systems or gateways into each other's territory. Some of these systems sat astride the stargate network while others could place you in a nearby star system, but easily within FTL range to converge on the gate and gain entry to the network. Admiral Pandolly had shared with her how this limiting factor to the wormhole generator had created a détente of sorts, in that it focused the war on specific border regions instead of leaving vulnerable the entirety of the alliance core worlds and habitable systems.

If the Zodarks have this technology… this will change how war will be fought…and not in a good way.

Before she could drift too far into her thoughts, the voice of Ensign Godley snapped her back to reality. "All stations—we are approaching the exit. Stand by for normal space in three…two…one…we're out."

Dobbs looked at the monitor still showing the blackness of the wormhole when suddenly they emerged from the darkness, now bathed in the light of the sun. The stars of the Milky Way and the occasional glow of the planets of Sol refracted the sun's light. They were home.

Then Commander Wright got to his feet—taking charge for the moment as he kicked the crew into action with rapid-fire orders. With her XO riding the crew of the bridge, she entered her captain's code into the battlenet's command channel and hoped it was still operational.

The BC2, as it was called, was a captains-only system channel for ship captains to converse amongst themselves away from the prying eyes of their crew and subordinate officers. The private channel gave them the freedom to talk openly amongst their peers and instantly know what Republic warships were in the system. Unless the ship operated under some sort of special order or permission, it would automatically show up in the BC2 channel regardless of whether the captain had logged in. It had become an incredibly useful tool since its implementation shortly after the war had ended.

Dobbs stared at the screen, waiting for the ship to detect the battlenet—praying it would tell her there were still ships in the fight. That the Zodarks hadn't prevailed just yet.

Then Commander Dildine announced excitedly, "Captain, we're picking up a signal from the battlenet—it's still up. The Altairians were right. The Zodarks either don't know about it or haven't gone after it yet."

Oh, thank God. The battlenet is still up...the battle hasn't been lost yet, she thought pensively, hope rising within her.

"Authentication verified. We are now connected to the system. New data is beginning to populate our libraries. My people will need a few minutes to sift through the incoming data, but we should have a systemwide status update report ready for you shortly."

Hearing the update sent a wave of emotions through her, and judging by the faces of those around her, the others felt it too. The Zodarks hadn't won yet. The battle was still undecided.

Rising to her feet, she took command of the situation. "All right, people. This confirms it. Our people are still fighting, which means we have work to do. The battle isn't over, and we still have foxes raiding the henhouse. Right now I need everyone to stay focused on the task at hand and not get ahead of themselves. We still need to figure out the fleet's status and where the enemy's at. Ensign Godley, set a course for Titan Station, and get us on the move again. I want impulse engines to ten percent until the Altairians have joined us."

"Aye-aye, Captain," came the quick reply as the ship got underway. The engines powering the vessel surged the ship forward into what might soon become the final battle to save the Republic.

With the ship on the move, the officers across the *Vanguard* began issuing orders to their sections—preparing the ship for battle. Having just completed a combat deployment to the Serpentis system, her crew had become a well-oiled machine, ready to wage war and to lay waste to the enemies of the Republic.

"Captain, we have established comms with the task force. All ships report green status and are now underway," Lieutenant Waldman announced.

Dobbs turned to her comms officer. "Thank you, Lieutenant. Send a message to *Delhi* telling them to form a forward picket line with the frigates *Duncan*, *Somerset*, *Bremen*, and *Hessen* as we head toward Titan. Then order the *Rheinland* to come abreast to our port side as we take lead ahead of Fleet support vessels and assault ships."

"Aye-aye, Captain. Do you still want the cruisers *Dragon* and *Hamburg* to cover the flanks towards the rear of the formation?" Waldman asked before transmitting the next round of orders.

"Yes, keep them on the flanks. Tell them if we run into the enemy, we're going to call them forward to join our battle line."

With her task force on the move, it wouldn't be long before the Altairian fleet began entering the system and their two forces would merge. Once they secured the noncombatant ships at the Titan facility, Dobbs was certain Admiral Pandolly would order the warships of the fleet to advance on the enemy. She just hoped they weren't too late.

Then she saw an alert flash on her terminal next to her chair. The message was letting her know the battlenet had finally synced with *Vanguard. I have to check on this before the rumor mill starts.* Looking to Commander Wright, she said, "XO, you have the bridge. Let me know if you need anything."

"Aye, Captain. XO has the bridge," Wright announced as he took command of the ship.

With the XO running the ship, her attention shifted to the terminal attached to the side of her chair. She synced the feed to her neurolink before scrolling through the ship's registry. She could now access the BC2 channel without anyone seeing what she was looking at. She set a filter to show all the vessels that had stayed in or passed through Sol during a twenty-four-hour window from before the invasion had happened until the moment they'd arrived.

With the filter in place, she started her search, noting the names of warships, transports, and orbital assault ships she had friends on. She continued to review the names of the ships in Sol at the time of the attack. More and more names of the ships were being highlighted in red, far more than what she had hoped to find—gray or green. *My God...how could we have lost so many ships? Whoa, we lost the Ark Royal,* she thought before learning the fate of Admiral Abigail Halsey, who had apparently, despite being gravely injured, stayed aboard the carrier as she rammed it into some previously unknown Zodark supership no one had seen before.

Dozens of Republic ships—many with friends she'd known her entire career—were now highlighted in red. Lost to enemy action. Seeing the enormity of the loss only fueled the burning rage for revenge steadily building within. She was angry. Frustrated beyond belief that while her task force had been deployed to the Serpentis system, the Zodarks had been plotting this entire time to restart the old war by invading Sol and smashing the heart of the Republic to pieces before they had a chance to organize a defense.

Staring at the registry at the number of ships highlighted in gray—ones that had left the system—and the ones highlighted in green—still operational—her mind pieced together the losses the Republic had likely sustained thus far. *My goodness...we've probably lost north of ten percent of the warships in the entire fleet.*

The staggering loss of ships during a single battle or campaign was beyond mind-numbing. Feeling her emotions wanting to take the lead, likely to do something stupid, she calmly closed her eyes, taking a breath as she focused on clearing her mind and emotions. *I am a warrior of the Republic, an officer, and the captain of the* Vanguard—*I control my mind, my emotions, my actions*, she told herself, reciting her morning and nightly incantations.

When she opened her eyes, she saw a glimmer of hope—the status of the warship *George Washington* was still showing green. *What—the* GW*...that's Second Fleet...that means Admiral McKee must be in system...*

Selecting the ship, she opened a private channel to the admiral and waited for the chat box to respond. She crafted a message giving a brief summary of the ships she had with her, along with the news that Admiral Pandolly and an Altairian fleet would be joining her momentarily. Hitting send on the message and not knowing how long it might take for a response, she looked for the most recently transmitted significant activity or SIGACT reports in hopes that reading some of them over might help get her up to speed on what was happening across the system and where the heaviest fighting was still taking place.

As she looked at the reports, a particular headline caught her attention, and she scanned its synopsis. It read that the Ark bunker near Oberammergau had reported that multiple orbital strikes by Zodark warships had devastated several cities across the European continent. What caught her attention, though, was the mention that it appeared likely that Chancellor Luca, along with members from an alliance trade delegation, had perished in a strike on the city of Potsdam, near Berlin. It also mentioned the presence of Zodark fighters prowling the skies over parts of Europe as elements of a Zodark ground invasion that appeared to have begun.

Unsure if she should believe the report about the Chancellor's death, she looked for any possible reports out of Space Command. With Admiral Halsey having died aboard the *Ark Royal*, Admiral Bailey was probably the only person left trying to run Space Command. Then she found the report she'd hoped she'd see. Admiral Bailey had been secured in the command facility beneath Space Command.

He had transmitted a series of messages to the people of Earth, assuring them that help was on the way. While temporarily entombed in a command center under the debris of Space Command headquarters and the city of Fayetteville, he had continued to encourage the remaining warships in the system to fight where they could and for the Army to give the enemy hell wherever they landed forces on the planet.

Not wanting to focus further on that report, Dobbs was about to open another when the chat box flashed—the admiral had replied. When she opened the chat, it automatically connected a video call request from the admiral. A moment later, the image of Fran McKee appeared on her screen. "Well, if it isn't Amy Dobbs. Damn, it's good to see you. I just read your message. Are you telling me you have thirty-seven ships in your task force and an Altairian fleet about to join you?"

Dobbs smiled when she saw her friend. It had been years since they'd seen each other, but that seemed to melt away when they started talking. "It's good to see you too, Admiral. Um, yes, I do have thirty-seven ships in my task force. But just so you're aware, only nine are actually warships. The rest are orbital assault ships, troop transports, and my fleet support ships. My task force was returning from an alliance peacekeeping operation in the Serpentis system when one of Pandolly's scout ships learned of the Zodark attack.

"Right now our plan called for us to head to Titan to take on munitions and rearm while we tried to figure out who was still in charge. We figured we'd try to link up and coordinate how best to utilize our force. But, hey, since I've got you on the line, what do you think, Admiral? Can you plug us in somewhere to help finish the bastards off?"

McKee flashed a broad toothy grin in response to her question. "Amy, I can't tell you how happy and relieved I am to see you right now and hear the words you just spoke. My God, we might save the Republic before they torch it all. You shared the strength of your vessels. Tell me this Altairian fleet is packing a bigger punch than your nine warships are. No offense, of course. We're just incredibly overwhelmed right now."

"None taken, Admiral. As to the Altairians, it's Admiral Pandolly's fleet. He actually has a pretty substantial force with him. Some forty-six warships and another twenty-two support vessels. He's loaded for bear. Two *Digimon* supercarriers and fourteen *Berkimon* battleships, with the rest of his fleet split between cruisers and frigates. Together we're a pretty heavy force. What exactly are you guys still facing and where are they?" Dobbs asked, starved for news and actionable intel on the situation.

Just as McKee was about to speak, the voice of Lieutenant Waldman broke into Dobbs's thoughts. "Sorry to interrupt, Captain. The Altairians have just bridged into the system. Admiral Pandolly is requesting to speak with you immediately."

"Thank you, Lieutenant. I'm in a comms channel with Admiral McKee right now. Can you patch Admiral Pandolly into our call? He's going to want to talk with the admiral so we can figure out what our next moves should be."

There was a momentary pause, then the comms channel split to show McKee and Pandolly now in the same channel.

"Admiral Pandolly, it is good to see you, my friend. I suppose you heard about this little party the Zodarks decided to bring to Earth?" McKee said as she added a little levity to the seriousness of things.

Pandolly cocked his head to the side slightly, then countered, "Oh, I see now. You are attempting to use humor to make light of a bad situation. Yes?"

Dobbs tried to contain her smile and keep a straight face, but it was proving impossible when McKee busted out laughing, causing her to join in. Thankfully she'd switched out of her neurolink connection to the group, or the crew might think she'd gone mad, laughing to herself.

"That's right, Admiral. Us humans are notorious for adding humor to what would otherwise be a terrible situation. It helps us to mentally and physically get through the stress, tension, and sometimes despair of the moment by laughing at it. That probably doesn't make much sense, I get that, but it's one of those quirky little things about us humans you're probably still trying to figure out," McKee explained before her face turned serious again. "Admiral, I'm not going to lie or sugarcoat the situation here. We're in dire straits, and the situation is not good. I'm having my staff send both of you the most current breakdown of the situation in Sol as it currently stands.

"If you'll indulge me for a moment, I feel a brief understanding of how the situation unfolded and my fleet's interaction since our arrival may help you better understand what's happened and what we're still up against," she offered, waiting for confirmation from the Altairian before she began.

"Second Fleet, my command, had been stationed with the Primord fleet at Kita for over a decade. This means most of the ships under my command are among the oldest warships still active in the Fleet. Once the drawdown began in the region following the withdrawal from Alfheim, Space Command was going to use the opportunity to have my command undergo a multiyear stand-down while my oldest warships were retired and new ones were commissioned.

"I feel I need to share that point, Admiral, to highlight the fact that when my fleet arrived in Sol, I wasn't exactly bringing the Republic's most powerful warships to the fight. By the time we realized what happening, that Earth was under attack by the Zodarks, and we were able to join the fight, Admiral Halsey's fleet had already sustained catastrophic losses in ships and personnel. When my fleet could link up with Halsey's, this strange unknown warship we hadn't encountered before suddenly appeared to have opened a wormhole bridge just like we've seen by your *Digimon* ships or the *Freedom* in the past.

"That's when Admiral Halsey made her move—you should have seen it, Pandolly. The *Ark Royal*, which at this point was a flaming wreck, aligned itself to point at this mystery ship when suddenly it opened a bridge between Zodark-controlled space and Sol. A couple of Zodark ships moved across, but before further ships could join—or worse, new ones crossed over—Halsey engaged her ship's FTL drive. One moment the *Royal* was there. Then the next moment it was completely obliterated as it collided with whatever this new Zodark ship was," McKee explained as Dobbs and Pandolly listened with rapt attention.

"Admiral McKee, when the ships collided, did this collapse the bridge between the system, or is this vessel still operational?" Pandolly pressed for more information.

She nodded at the question, then explained, "When the *Royal* collided, it collapsed the bridge instantly. It appears to have caused catastrophic and unrecoverable damage to whatever this new ship is. With the entire forward section of the vessel missing, it's not just exposed to the vacuum of space. It's now exposing whatever is left of its crew to lethal levels of solar radiation, and other harmful rays a ship's hull would typically protect you against. For better or worse, what's left or still operational of that ship is stranded at this point. We plan to take it out at some point so it'll no longer pose a continued threat or, God forbid, their engineers figure out how to jerry-rig some sort of repairs to get it back underway. Right now we're trying to figure out how to get at the enemy landers and troop transports before they can land more of their ground force on Earth."

"Hmm," Pandolly grunted as he listened to her recount what had happened. Then he explained, "Admiral McKee, this is your home system, and your home world is under assault. If you want to assert command of alliance forces until the Viceroy arrives in the system, then I will submit my command to your authority. If I may, however, offer a suggestion?"

McKee nodded for him to continue as Dobbs watched the interplay continue.

"The ships of your command, they largely consist of the oldest warships in the Fleet. You have also lost more than half of your vessels during the past few days of battle. I believe in this situation, given the disparity in capability, it would be better and more efficient at this point if the alliance forces were to fall under my command until the Viceroy arrives on the scene. Would you or the remainder of Republic forces be opposed to allowing me to command your forces until his arrival?"

McKee didn't hesitate for a second—she readily agreed to place her command and the remainder of the Fleet under his command until the Viceroy arrived to assume control of the situation. With the lines of authority now clearly identified, Pandolly ordered Dobbs to make haste to Titan Military Complex so her ships could reload their munition stocks and prepare for the next battle. Pandolly would leave a minimal escort to protect the orbital assault ships and the fleet support vessels they would leave behind at Titan, out of harm's way until they were needed. Then Dobbs would merge the nine warships of her command with Admiral McKee. While her ships would reinforce McKee, Pandolly's force would angle in to hit the enemy formation from two more vectors of attack— forcing the enemy to further split dwindling resources in an increasingly futile fight. With a relatively easy plan to execute now underway, they prepared for the coming battle to decide Earth's fate and the Republic's future.

****

Twelve Hours Later
Vicinity of Republic Naval Shipyard
RNS *Vanguard*

Commodore Dobbs was now overseeing a squadron of warships after Admiral McKee had assigned another six warships to her command. Commander Wright found himself in the command seat of the *Vanguard* as they prepared for the biggest battle they'd have fought in yet.

Listening intently to the modifications being made to their attack formation, he hoped the Altairian admiral knew what he was doing. The enemy force, while technically trapped in Sol, still outnumbered their combined force. Despite the loss the Zodark fleet had already sustained, there were still nearly two hundred warships of various classes still clustering tightly around the massive warship—the one Admiral Halsey had rammed during the first day of the battle. He'd been told this was the vessel that had generated the bridge that connected their territories. With the forward section of the vessel missing, the enemy had lost their ability to escape and return to friendly lines.

"Commander Wright. Did you copy that?"

Wait, did I miss something? he questioned when Dobbs singled him out.

"My apologies, Commodore. Can you clarify that?" he responded as he hoped to cover his momentary distraction.

"OK, let me give everyone a little more detail about what's about to happen. Admiral McKee has a clever attack underway along the left flank of the Zodark line. Apparently, it involves an older *Ryan*-class battleship acting as a shield for a strike package of fighters and bombers from the *Lexington* and the remnants of the *Ark Royal*'s space wings. The battleship is hiding the strike package in the dead space of its shadow on the opposite side of the enemy fleet. Once it's gotten the fighters in close to the transports or it ends up going down itself, then the plan calls for the fighters to reveal themselves and initiate their attack on the transports. When that happens, when those fighters launch their attack, that's when Admiral McKee wants us to micro-jump using our FTL drive to the coordinates I sent to each of your helmsmen.

"The *Vanguard*, *Sumer*, and *Intus* will move into a blocking position, placing their vessels between the rear of the Zodark formation and the rest of our squadron. Then it's a race to take out as many troopships and transports as our cruisers and frigates can before the enemy can try and interdict our little raiding party inside their rearguard. You can bet the Zodarks will shift their firepower against our battleships pretty quickly, so our cruisers and frigates will need to act fast. At some point, they'll force our battleships to withdraw before we take on too much damage and find ourselves unable to withdraw. Is that a little clearer for everyone now? Everyone understands the plan now?"

"Yes, Commodore. Loud and clear," Wright acknowledged with the others.

"OK, then. Everyone stand by and we'll wait for the signal—don't jump out of sequence. You'll alert the enemy before it's time."

This is freaking nuts. We should be sniping at the enemy's flanks, not risking the bulk of our warships in a direct head-on melee like this..., he thought privately. He'd learned early on in his career—if you valued your next promotion, keep your opinions to yourself unless asked.

He obviously wasn't privy to the plan the admiral had cooked up. Like his little brother serving in the Army, he just had to nod along and do his best to implement the orders of those above him until one day he was the person giving such orders. Still, what troubled him was the knowledge that reinforcements were likely to arrive in twelve to twenty-four hours. Why risk so many of their ships in a battle like this when in the near future they'd have an overwhelming force that would be able to crush this enemy fleet without risking the remaining force they had?

"Lieutenant Waldman, see if the bridge camera can pick up that battleship *Berlin*. Let's watch how the attack unfolds."

"Aye, Commander. One second," Waldman announced as his fingers danced across the console.

A moment later, the bridge monitor was showing an image of the RNS *Berlin*, which looked to have already crossed nearly half the distance between the Zodark and Republic lines. He watched with rapt attention as the older *Ryan*-class battleship did its best to slip past and around the enemy lines on an intercept course to a cluster of transports his own ship was going to attack.

Come on, guys...you can do this. Like the others on the bridge, he found himself rooting for them to go unnoticed just a little longer. He knew it was unlikely the enemy wouldn't detect them. They were too big, and right now they were burning their thrusters, which only further attracted attention. Yet with each passing moment, he felt strangely confident that the *Berlin* would pull it off.

"Lieutenant Waldman, let's go ahead and split the bridge screen and get the *George Washington* set up on the right side and the *Berlin* on the left. TAO, I want you to keep an eye on the volume of fire being directed at Admiral McKee's ships as they move forward. Try to figure out which enemy warships will likely be the closest ones to us after we initiate our jump. Watch to see how those warships to the rear of their formation react as the admirals advance and the *Berlin* continues to creep along on the left flank," Commander Wright directed, wanting to get his people ready to react to actions of the battle that was now starting to heat up.

In moments, he had the two screens set up the way he wanted. Now it was a matter of waiting and watching as the battle unfolded.

Watching and waiting for things to start once the plan had been put into motion was among the toughest aspects of space warfare. Beyond the great distances across which these battles could sometimes take place, they often stretched across multiple axes of attack while sometimes forcing one to deal with various types of threats. Some you might see coming at a slow enough speed that you could maneuver out of their way. Other times they traveled at the speed of light, often slamming into your vessel before you had a chance to react.

Combat in space was weird like that. The action happened quickly, with little time to react, or it moved at the pace of a snail crawling on a salt lick. It wasn't uncommon for battles to last for hours, sometimes even days, as ships or groups of ships tried to maneuver around each other or searched for a better angle to initiate their attack. If your ship moved too fast toward an adversary or failed to decelerate at the right time, you could end up sailing past the enemy ship or simply miss any effective means of using your weapons in anything more than harassing fire.

As Wright briefly stared at the enlarged image of the *George Washington*, the ship's superweapon—the giant plasma cannon that to this day was still the most powerful cannon in the Republic arsenal—began to move. When the giant four-meter-wide barrel fired, it hurled a plasma projectile at near-light speed to slam into whatever its gunners had aimed for. If the Republic hadn't encountered the Altairians when they had, they likely would have more of these weapons on their warships than just the single one on the *GW*.

Suddenly the screen showing the giant warship of the *GW* flickered and whited out before returning to its earlier image. The momentary flash marked the moment that the plasma cannon had fired. It was a signature mark when it did—the flash happening when the superheated plasma was hurled from the barrel into the coldness of space. In that brief moment, as it left the barrel, it produced a temporary outer casing as the plasma around the edges cooled, forming a loosely crafted slug filled with superheated plasma before slamming into its intended target—often boring a hole through the vessel it had just hit.

Once the screen's resolution returned after the flash, he and the others watched what looked like a vapor trail stretching the distance between the *GW* and the Zodark ship he knew was one of their base stars or supercarriers.

Reaching for the controls on his console, he rapidly enhanced the magnification of the vessel the *GW* had just hit. The crew on the bridge looked on at the detailed resolution of the enemy warship, in awe at the level of damage the giant cannon had just delivered. The plasma slug had torn a gash that looked to stretch nearly a hundred meters in length across the forward starboard side of the ship—ripping it open to the vacuum of space.

An instant later, all hell broke loose between the two sides as the Zodark vessels started engaging the warships closing in on their positions. Soon the blackness of the void was being filled with streaks of orange, blue, and red lights crossing back and forth between the opposing warships shortly after the two sides engaged with lasers. Waves of thirty-six-inch, twenty-four-inch, and sixteen-inch projectiles were hurled at the enemy vessels in volleys designed to place as many slugs as possible in the estimated location where the two would most likely cross. If the gun crew was good and knew how to effectively use its targeting AI to blanket an area the enemy vessel had to cross, they could land dozens of armored-tipped high-explosive projectiles across the enemy ship, causing enormous damage when they tore through the outer hull and armor to explode inside the guts of the warship.

He continued to watch the two sides advancing steadily toward each other, knowing that in a few moments, the admiral would order the ships of the line to begin their turn to one side, bringing to bear both the main and now the secondary turrets on the enemy vessels. With the full weight of all the battleship guns able to bear in on their opponents, the volume of magrail projectiles being hurled at the enemy line would be almost impossible to miss.

While this main battle continued to unfold, Wright pulled himself away from the fleet battle to focus back on the *Berlin*—the part of this operation tied most closely to his own.

By now the Zodark warships nearest the *Berlin* seemed to have caught on to what it was trying to do. Several of the battleships and cruisers began firing at the older warship. A handful of cruisers, frigates, and corvettes appeared to change course and looked like they were now on an intercept path. That was when he saw something unusual occur.

"Hey, Quinn, do those look like Ospreys falling away from the dark side of the *Berlin*?"

Commander Quinn Dildine canted his head to the side with a puzzled look on his face. Then a look of realization took its place. "Actually, Joe, if I'm not mistaken, I think those might be those electronic-attack craft the Fleet started deploying just as we left for Serpentis. I think they're those EA-12 Phantoms."

Huh, OK. Let's see how they work…

"Attention, all ship captains! Attention, all ship captains!" Commodore Dobbs's voice broke into his conversation as he held a hand up to forestall his friend from continuing. Dobbs then ordered, "All ships, prepare to execute maneuver Yankee Five-Five—acknowledge now."

Oh man, here we go. This better work. The thought raced through his mind as he listened to several of the captains acknowledge the order. He waited a moment longer until it had reached his turn to respond.

"*Vanguard* acknowledges, standing by to execute."

Taking a breath in as he steeled his resolve, he looked to the helmsman position, declaring loudly, "Helm, prepare to execute Yankee Five-Five on my mark."

"Affirmative, Yankee Five-Five—standing by to execute," Ensign Godley acknowledged. Wright saw a bead of sweat run down the side of his face before his hand could stop it.

Turning to Commander Little, he said, "TAO, your section ready? We good to go?" He knew the success or failure of this attack was going to come down to the accuracy of their gunners and the speed of the crews to keep 'em firing.

"XO, weapons ready—all turrets showing status green," she replied confidently, holding her chin up in pride, knowing her gun crews and the spacers that manned them were among the best in the fleet.

He smiled at her confidence, nodding as he did. He knew she ran a tight crew. Her chiefs practiced and drilled the ship's gunners' mates until their weapon scores were nearly perfect. They were accurate as hell and swift on the trigger when it counted—two things critical to slinging lead at your opponent and taking them down before they could do the same to you.

He returned his gaze to the *Berlin* while he waited to hear the final order that would start their role in this growing battle. Watching the older battleship, he saw that the volume of enemy fire around it had gone from a few loosely aimed shots to a hailstorm of laser fire intermixed with missile streaks racing towards them and the occasional haphazardly spread of plasma torpedoes looking to rely more on luck than actual skill to score a hit.

Then a flash occurred near the *Berlin*'s midsection, the explosion's size and brightness catching him off guard. It looked to have shaken violently from the blast. Then several of its engines appeared to go offline simultaneously with most of its weapon systems. That was when he saw a swarm of tiny little dots racing away from the ship's far side. His brain told him this was the strike force, the combined space wings of the two supercarriers, *Lexington* and *Ark Royal*, now hurling themselves toward the enemy transports and troopships before the enemy could react to this sudden turn of events.

"XO, here come the Altairians," Commander Little announced as the bridge monitor focused on the *George Washington* began to zoom out and reframe the image to display the broader battlefield now unfolding.

Commander Wright looked at the broader image on the monitor as he spotted dozens of tiny flashes now appearing along the enemy's right flank—opposite where the *Berlin* had been before the flames had consumed its atmosphere and choked the life from it.

While he wasn't counting the flashes denoting the ship's arrival as it exited slip space, he knew the Altairians were still bringing forty-plus ships to the fight, many of them battleships and a couple of supercarriers. This was even after leaving some ships behind to help defend Titan Station and the growing number of noncombatant ships continuing to arrive from across the system.

His gaze returned to *George Washington*, noting the intensity of laser fire stabbing relentlessly into her armored shell. Then Commodore Dobbs shouted excitedly across the command channel the words he'd been waiting to hear—"All ships! Execute Yankee Five-Five *now!*"

OK, this is it. Time to see if this little maneuver is going to work...

"Helm, XO, mission's a go. Execute Yankee Five-Five on my mark. Three...two...one...mark," exclaimed Wright as he braced for what was about to happen.

The ship lurched forward as the FTL drive catapulted the ship from behind the naval shipyard to a position behind the Zodark battle lines. In fractions of a second, the micro-use of the FTL drive had allowed them to travel several million kilometers as they appeared to have skipped overtop the enemy position like a flat sandstone rock across the surface of the water.

As the *Vanguard* came out of slip space faster than it was squeezed through it, his mind raced with the realization: *Hoooollllyyyy crap! That worked...* Until the ship's forward camera came back into focus, and he saw the enemy ships. *My God...look at the size of that fleet...*

Shaking the thoughts from his mind, he jumped to his feet, not wasting a second as he rattled off orders to the crew, knowing time was not on their side.

"CIC, where's the TAM? We need that operational *now!*" he barked hotly at them for not having the tactical action map already up and running the moment they exited slip space.

"Helm, set us a course that'll bring our starboard guns to bear on the enemy and give us the best chance to run cover for our frigates and cruisers. Keep impulse engines at twenty percent and relay to engineering to be ready in case we need to jump to one hundred percent should we need more maneuverability."

Commander Wright then turned to face the part of the bridge controlling the vaunted weapons of the *Vanguard* as he began to rapid-fire his next set of orders.

"TAO, the moment the TAM is up, I want those starboard guns to zero in on the closest battleship and two of their cruisers. Start laying into them hard with everything we got. I want speed of action right now, and hammer those ships as hard as we can, as fast as we can.

"Then tell your gunners on the port side they're free to engage the transports and troop landers as the opportunity presents itself. Ensure they're watching out for our frigates and cruisers as they begin their attack runs on the same targets. I don't want to hear about any friendly fire incidents—God forbid we nail a few of our own ships in the process," Wright explained, making sure she knew the parameters to pass on to the gun crews.

Then Commander Mitsu interrupted before he continued with his next round of orders. "XO, I just released the dogs from the kennel. Both Gripen squadrons have launched and are moving to engage the Vultures still mixing it up with the earlier strike force. The rest of the 20th Fighter Group will be ready to launch in the next five minutes."

He smiled at the news and the initiative taken by the *Vanguard*'s top pilot. "That's outstanding, Commander. The moment the rest of the pit bulls are ready to get in the fight, I want you to cut the muzzle and take the leash off and sic 'em at the battleship the TAO tagged for today's gunnery practice. It's time to feed the dogs some Vultures and Glaives for lunch."

Mitsu and those on the bridge broke out in laughter at his humorous reply. The levity of the moment seemed to have tempered the anxiety steadily building on the bridge. From the moment they had come out of slip and gotten their first view of the enemy fleet, he'd seen the faces and eyes of those on the bridge—looks of fear, uncertainty, and doubt about how they would overcome the sheer size of the enemy fleet. When he saw what remained, particularly against the backdrop of the still partially operational Zodark supership, he felt compelled to try and work in some humorous motivation to keep their minds from slipping into despair or feeling like the situation was hopeless.

We can win this...they can be defeated...I just have to keep them focused on that...

With the actions to fight the ships now fully put into motion, Wright circled the bridge, checking with each department chief and lending support when and where it was needed. After his initial check to see how they were doing, he was drawn to the holographic display map the ship's CIC managed and oversaw.

Standing next to the real-time three-dimensional rendering of the battle happening around them, he became transfixed by what he saw. Then, sensing someone approaching him, he turned to see Master Chief Abe Ellis nearing the terminal next to the map. Typing as he spoke, he commented, "It can be overwhelming if you try to take in the entire battlespace at once."

Overwhelmed by the data was exactly how he felt. He was still getting used to these three-dimensional holographic renderings of the battlespace. Throw in hundreds of tiny icons representing friendly, allied, and enemy warships on different planes and axes of attack, and it became overwhelming.

"I'm changing the center of the map. This should make it easier to see what's happening around us," Chief Ellis explained as the hologram momentarily disappeared, then reappeared. Now an image of the *Vanguard* was anchored in the center of the hologram. To one side were the transports and landers their squadron was attacking while on the other side were a handful of cruisers and a pair of battleships trying to stop them. While slow to respond initially, they were now reacting with a vengeance against those trying to cull the flock they were charged with protecting.

Too late now. The fox is in the henhouse and he's hungry...

Wright furrowed his brow, then pointed. "Zoom in on this battleship if you can. I want to check something."

"OK, one second."

A moment later, the battleship came into focus, much larger than before. Now the details of the giant ship were visible, with the kind of clarity only the TAM could give. The closer high-resolution image showed flashes of crisp blue light from the turbo lasers of the *Vanguard* intermixed with volleys of magrail slugs scoring hits against the vessel while some volleys of fire missed and sailed by harmlessly. Then his eye caught what he was looking for. Smiling, he pointed excitedly. "Right there, Chief. That spot on the battleship. Get it highlighted and sent to the gunners. I want them to focus their efforts on hitting that spot with everything they've got!"

Ellis bunched his eyebrows as he looked at it. Then a smile appeared. "Aye, sir. Good catch. Gonna have to scold the kids for not spotting that sooner."

"Eh, they're learning. Just point it out and make sure they're looking for it on the other ships. We don't get many chances like this, so we can't miss 'em when they happen."

BOOM!

A loud explosion rocked the ship. Alarm bells blared and shouts erupted near his engineering officer. Then a second explosion rocked the ship, causing him to grab for something—anything to keep from falling to the floor.

"Eng, what the hell happened? Give me a damage report now!" Wright shouted, catching a glance from Commodore Dobbs, her eyes betraying her concern.

"XO, we took a hit to the starboard replenishment dock. It shot through the blast door and caused a rapid depressurization of hangar six and warehouses six, seven, and eight," Lieutenant Hinkel replied from his station.

"OK, how about finishing the report, Lieutenant? Is it contained? What happened with the second explosion? Don't leave us hanging with an incomplete report like that," he rebuked softly, annoyed at having to ask the obvious follow-up questions that the engineering officer should have anticipated.

Damn it, Tinker. You had to send me a bridge replacement who isn't ready for the job, he cursed silently at his senior engineering officer for not sending him a better substitute for Herricks when he'd injured his hand in the weight room.

"Um, XO, sorry about that. The decompression has been contained and stopped at the adjacent rooms and corridors surrounding the damaged areas. The second explosion occurred when a Havoc missile exploded in one of the VLS pods. It caused the two other missiles in the pod to detonate, which caused a blowback into the deck below, causing a decompression event to happen. That led to six other rooms venting atmosphere before the areas were sealed off. Casualties are still coming in. Should have them shortly," the baby-faced lieutenant replied, making sure to cover all the details this time.

Dobbs walked up to him. "Everything OK, XO?"

She had a look of concern on her face but hadn't resumed command of the ship just yet.

"It is now, Captain. Minor decompression event and a missile cook-off in a VLS pod."

Grunting at the reply, she replied, "Is that it?" The smile on her face told him he'd handled the situation correctly, the way she would have.

"XO, TAO, gunners are laying into that spot you found on the battleship. They've breached it! We're getting multiple secondary explosions from the surrounding areas. It just might work!"

"What did you find?" asked Dobbs, her curiosity up.

"He found a golden BB, Captain. A blown-out laser turret right behind Section Nine-Charlie. Just like the intel weenies told us about," Chief Ellis chimed in proudly.

"Really? Well, I guess we'll see in a minute if that actually works, won't we? Seem you got it under control. I need to get back to the squadron. You know where to find me if you need me," commented Dobbs before returning to her station.

"XO, TAO, I think the battleship is gonna blow. We're spotting secondary explosions rippling across the rear of the ship. Then its engines went out and it appears to be dead in the water."

Looking to the bridge monitor, he saw the battleship prominently displayed, flames arcing into the void from gashes along its port side as it vented atmosphere and fluids in a fiery mix. With its guns silent, the *Vanguard* continued to pummel the dying ship until a giant explosion erupted—splitting the rear of the warship from the rest of it.

One battleship down...one more to go, Commander Wright thought ruefully, having scored the squadron's first victory.

Chapter Seventeen
You Got a Mission

Task Force Silver Fox
Titan Military Complex

"I still can't believe the bastards got past the Altairians and the Sentinel towers like that," bemoaned Major Hiro quietly as he stood next to Colonel Royce, the two of them staring out the floor-to-ceiling windows in the briefing room next to the Ops Center.

"Our ships never stood a chance, Colonel. Once those corvettes got inside the fleet..." His voice trailed off for a moment. "Well, assault ships and transports aren't battleships no matter how large and tough looking they are. They can't shrug off hits from plasma torpedoes and volleys of missiles like they're a warship or something. I still can't believe those Altairians fell for that ruse and chased after that cruiser, leaving our ships exposed like that."

Then the booming voice of Major General Vernon "VC" Crow unexpectedly joined the conversation. "I'm angry about the situation too, Major, but some things are outside our control, and this happens to be one of them. So let's put this out of our minds for now and focus on the task at hand. Once these bastards have been thrown out of our system, we can properly mourn the dead and pay our respects. But the dying ain't done yet. So until it is, let's keep our war faces on and make the enemy pay for what they've done. Hooah?"

Royce snickered at the proverbial Army saying for anything and everything except the word *no*. "He'll be all right, sir. We knew some of the units on the *Crystal City*, that's all," Royce interceded for Hiro.

The general nodded, holding his tongue before explaining in a softer tone, "Colonel Ty Johnson and I were good friends. We went to the war college together, the command course, and for a time he worked as my aide-de-camp before he pinned his eagles and took command of the regiment. His loss is personal, Major. So I get where you're coming from. You need to get this sadness, this frustration, out of your system here. Once the briefing starts and I hand out the new assignments, I don't want to hear any whining from the officers. Our mission just started, and I want you focused on killing Zodarks—we good?"

"We're good, General, and I agree. It's time to refocus the mind on the task at hand—killing Zodarks," Hiro replied with an edge to his voice. Royce saw the general smile approvingly at the quick change in attitude. He knew his friend had won some respect from the general, and that wasn't a bad thing to have.

A handful of minutes passed, giving them a moment to clear their minds before the briefing started. Soon the room began to fill as a crowd of officers and senior NCOs filled the room, taking a seat with an uncomfortable view that stirred the emotions of anyone with half a heart.

Beyond the floor-to-ceiling windows of the briefing room overlooking Range Two was the wreckage of the RNS *Crystal City*. The giant second-gen orbital assault ship had come under attack by a swarm of enemy corvettes. When three out of the five Altairian frigates had gotten lured away from the fleet, the enemy had pounced before anyone knew what was happening. The *Crystal City*, *Canberra*, and *Dixmude* had been pummeled by multiple barrages of plasma torpedoes fired at almost point-blank range, leaving little to no opportunity to evade. What made the loss of the orbital assault ships sting the most was how fast they'd blown apart or crashed into the moon, leaving no time for the crew and the soldiers aboard to escape before it was too late.

"Listen up, soldiers!" the general's voice boomed loudly throughout the room. Colonel Royce observed the chattering soldiers quiet down as the general got things underway.

"I want to acknowledge the elephant in the room before we get going," VC declared as he waved a hand in the direction of the *Crystal City*. "They sucker punched us. No way around it. Sometimes it's pure luck how you end up being the one to survive, and others don't. I can't change what happened and neither can you. I won't lie and say it's not hard to accept the loss of six regiments like this—it freaking bites. But right now we're still alive and are being charged with a new mission— killing Zodarks. Something I know all of you bastards are good at doing.

"About an hour ago I received an updated SIGACT report from an Ark located in Oberammergau near the Bavarian Alps. I also received an update from Admiral McKee on the battle taking place near Earth, and unfortunately, I have to be the bearer of more bad news on top of it all. So let's rip the band-aid off and get the bad news out of the way first," the general said before he began to look uncomfortable.

He took a breath in before he continued. "There's no easy way to say this, so I'm just gonna say it. The Chancellor, Alice Luca—she's dead—gone. The Zodarks killed her and a JSOC team sent to beef up her security prior to moving her to Oberammergau," VC explained, holding a hand up to quiet the room so he could continue.

"Unfortunately, the rest of the news I have to deliver isn't good either, so let's just get it through it," he stated before signaling to an aide to bring up the slides to the briefing. "As it stands right now, six battleships and eight cruisers continue to fly over our cities in low Earth orbit. With each trip around the globe, these bastards continue to pummel our cities from the high ground. When this initially began, Space Command headquarters, the Senate, and the Chancery were among the first targets to be hit via an orbital strike.

"Admiral Bailey is currently secured in the command bunker underneath Space Command. So he's safe, but he also stuck as the Zodarks recently began landing ground forces near the capital—Jacksonville, Little Rock to the southwest, and Memphis to the east. We also got word that Fort Banks was hit. Actually, according to the report, the place has been flattened. Nothing left. That said, it does appear that most of the units at the Special Forces base were able to disperse to the field prior to the base being hit," the general explained succinctly, then looked to Royce, explaining, "I wish I could give everyone more information about the disposition of our forces and those of the enemy, but I can't.

"We haven't received additional information about what's happening on the ground, which, obviously, is going to make the actions I'm about to order next risky to say the least. But I'll be damned if we're gonna sit on our asses on the sidelines and wait for better intelligence before we act. Every hour we delay, every minute that goes by, is just giving the enemy more time to spread out across our home world, killing our people for sport. Well, I ain't allowing that to happen so long as I have soldiers to fight with and ships to get us into that fight. So here's what we're going to do next," the general explained.

As his aide scrolled through the slide deck, Royce heard some excited chatter from the officers and senior NCOs when a few slides appeared with detailed maps outlining a series of orbital assaults. The more maps he saw, the more he realized this wasn't going to be a standard drop like they'd done on many a hostile planet. This plan called for a series of swift engagements designed to close with and destroy the enemy before loading back into the dropships to reset and prepare to do it all over again.

Well, I guess this is typical VC...crazy like a fox. I think this crazy plan just might work...guess it's time to get the team ready...
****

Task Force Silver Fox
RNS *Wasp*

The sound of engines continued to grow as Colonel Brian Royce neared the entrance to the flight deck. Then the engines cut out just as he exited to get his first look at the fleet's newest dropship. Since arriving on Titan nearly a day ago, the *Wasp* and the other orbital assault ships from the Serpentis campaign had begun taking on some of the new dropships, knowing they'd be used in battle in the coming days. Now that he saw one in person, however, he was impressed. Looking it over from a distance, he figured it had to be close to twice the size of an Osprey and at least three times as deadly. They had kitted this bird out with more weapons, missiles, and rockets than he cared to count. Standing there, hands on hips, he surmised privately, *'Bout time they gave us a bird that'll clear a DZ in the middle of a fight...* It wasn't that he didn't like the Ospreys. They were a tried and tested vehicle, but they were also pushing past forty years of service. They had modernized to a B-model a few decades back. He'd also heard the new C-models were finally being phased in. *I guess we'll see what these Ospreys look like in a few hours too...*

"Pretty wicked looking, isn't it?" commented Command Sergeant Major Lou Bossi as he stood next to him.

Royce grunted at the obvious. The ship was loaded for bear. Turning to Bossi, he answered, "Yeah, I think this will work, Sergeant Major. What are they calling it again?"

Bossi reached for his Qpad and then commented, "Found it—the spec sheet I was looking for. OK, so they're officially calling this the 'AHT-12 Scarab.' That stands for Assault Heavy Transport, kind of like the AT or assault transports the Ospreys are technically called."

"Scarab, huh? Interesting. You know what the other name for a scarab is?"

The sergeant major bunched his eyebrows before slowly shaking his head.

"It stands for Scarabaeoidea. You know what that means, Sergeant Major?" Royce asked, barely able to contain the smile spreading from ear to ear. "It means dung beetle. Think about that for a second. They named our newest dropship after a beetle that feeds and rolls around in feces. That's right, what they say they built this to be able to do is roll around in the crap, survive, and come out on top."

They had a good laugh at the name but were glad someone had finally gotten around to developing a platform to deploy their Cougars into a hot DZ without getting blown apart.

"Colonel, if we have to leave Sol to go on more of these quote-unquote peacekeeping missions for them to come up with something useful like this while we're gone, then perhaps we should volunteer for more of these so-called peacekeeping missions," Bossi joked halfheartedly.

"Oh man, don't give them any more ideas than they already have, Sergeant Major. Besides, I didn't mind deploying all that much when I was a single man. Now I've got a wife I haven't seen in nearly two years, a six-year-old who hasn't seen me since she was four, and a two-year-old I've never met. If I thought the Zodark threat was gone, I'd retire tomorrow and spend the rest of my days with my family and not miss this job. So back to this Scarab—aside from laying waste to a DZ, what else can they do?"

Bossi turned serious as he listened to him. Everyone in the SF community knew who Brian Royce was and what he had done and gone through during the last war. He was a legend in the Deltas, a legend that had only grown when he'd led Task Force Orange in the counterintelligence effort to hunt down and eliminate the Mukhabarat's direct action teams known as Anis. But once an operator got married and started a family, they either got divorced relatively early in the marriage or they tended to get out. Few actually made it work.

"I hear ya on the family, boss. That's why I'm waiting until I'm ready to hang it up. Seeing as the war is back—guess that's gonna be a little while. So if I'm reading the Scarab spec sheet right, it says it can carry two fully loaded DF-12 Cougars straight off the ramp into battle. I'll believe that when I see it," Bossi muttered before adding, "They also say it can be reconfigured to carry a Cougar and a single platoon, or two platoons and some mixed cargo. That's, eh, actually not bad, sir. Might have been nice to have on the Serpentis campaign, but hey, they're going to let us use 'em now, so I guess that's good."

While Bossi steadily explained the rest of the Scarab's details, Royce walked towards the giant machine and surveyed the exterior. *Hot damn. They finally gave us something that can fly into a hornet's nest and stick around to fight alongside us—and it can carry not one but two Cougars directly into the fight. 'Bout damn time...*

As they talked and got a quick tour of the inside from a crew member, Royce got a message from the ship's captain to come see him. Letting the captain know he was on the way, he told the sergeant major to make sure the teams were ready. He had a feeling it wouldn't be long now before they were sent in to recover the fleet admiral and get him aboard a ship where he could take proper command of the fleet—from the bridge of a battleship or carrier, not hiding in a bunker.
****

RNS *Wasp* CIC

Captain Pritchard saw the Delta commander walk onto the bridge and waved to get his attention, gesturing for him to come join them in the CIC section.

As the Army colonel approached, Pritchard was glad he was on their side. Something about these augmented supersoldiers kind of unnerved him. He knew about Colonel Royce's exploits during the war—hell, everyone did. The man was a savage killing machine in battle. But Pritchard knew something else about the man that few knew—something that had only been shared in confidence one drunken evening during a card game on their way back to Sol.

Beneath the facade of a Special Forces warrior was a man struggling with deep regrets and pain from a loss so strong he wasn't sure how the guy hadn't offed himself yet. He talked about his new wife and kids, how he had a new baby that had been born while they were gone. He suspected it was his wife and kids that had kept him going. After that evening, the two of them had gotten along better than at any other time during the deployment.

Walking up to the holograph table, the Army colonel didn't mince words, asking, "Captain, I assume from your request for me to see you on the bridge that we've been given the green light to proceed?"

"That we have, Colonel. Seems the battle over Earth has turned in our favor. Reports have it the remaining Zodark fleet has relocated to Ceres—that's one of the dwarf planets in the asteroid belt between the orbits of Mars and Jupiter," Pritchard explained before adding, "Now that their fleet, or at least what's left of it, is gone, Admiral McKee wants us to recover Admiral Bailey from the bunker beneath Space Command and bring him aboard the *Wasp*. I'm sure once the Viceroy arrives with the *Freedom*, he'll transfer his flag there.

"In the meantime, the enemy fleet had held the high ground for several days. They've taken that time to deploy a substantial ground force to the surface while hitting many of our installations with orbital strikes flattening much of our military infrastructure. What's interesting to note about this deployment, however, is that they appear to have scattered their forces around the planet, creating smaller defensive pockets rather than trying to consolidate into any sort of large force. The Zodarks seem to be coalescing around these roving bands that look to attack nearby cities and population centers.

"This is where you guys come in. General Crow wants your Deltas to recover Admiral Bailey from the command bunker beneath Space Command, then recover General Ridgeway, who was vacationing in Lisbon, Portugal. I don't have an exact location on him just yet, but we should once we arrive in orbit above Earth—"

"Sorry to interrupt, Captain, but aside from the few ODA teams for this deployment and the single battalion from the Rangers, have any other ground assets been given to us to use?"

"Colonel, that sounds like a question for General Crow. If you'd like to take a moment to send him a quick note, we can take a short pause before continuing?"

The soldier shook his head and motioned for him to continue.

"As you're aware, Colonel, a few upgrades the fleet has been working on appear to have finally made their way into operational status. I assume you saw some of those new Scarabs on the flight deck? Well, we're also taking on some upgraded Ospreys too. We should have everything aboard the *Wasp* in the next half hour. Once we do, the fleet will rally together, and then we'll jump to Earth and arrive as a group.

From there, we'll await orders from Admiral McKee telling us we're clear to begin landing operations. In the meantime, If you need anything else from my end. Don't hesitate to ask," Pritchard finished, doing his best to ensure everyone was playing the same sheet of music.

"I think we got it, Captain. Thank you for your help, and the ride. Just ensure our air assets are available when we need them, and we'll take care of things on the ground."

Pritchard didn't envy the task ahead of Colonel Royce's men. His people sat aboard starships. Occasionally they fired the ships' weapons. But those Deltas, on the other hand, they had the toughest job in the service. Killing Zodarks on the field of battle—up close and in person.

I'll make sure you have all the CAS we can offer...that's my promise to you, Colonel.

Chapter Eighteen
Let Me Show You, Son

FMT-161 "Greyhawks"
Approaching Jacksonville, Arkansas
Earth, Sol System

Packed in the troop bay of the Osprey, Colonel Royce had no idea what to expect as they approached the city that had once been the capital of the Republic. Looking at the faces of his fellow operators, he saw the same questions, concerns, and uncertainty he was feeling.

"Captain Yoder, your guys set?" Royce asked over the neurolink. He wanted a candid response. Asking in private was a sure way to get it.

"They're a little nervous, sir. Their training will kick in, and they'll do fine, though."

"We're all a little nervous, so that's OK. Once we're down, Yoder, 914 needs to keep the quad clear. We can't have the place become bracketed by enemy fire. It'll be tough to get a ride out of here," Royce explained. He'd placed ODA 914 in charge of clearing the quad; that was what they called the giant parade field opposite the headquarters building. Surrounding the quad were six-story buildings with glass siding, all part of Space Command.

"They know the urgency of the situation, sir. We will get it cleared, and we'll keep it cleared."

"Captain Canty, once we're on the ground, 915 needs to bum-rush the headquarters building before the Zodarks can react to our sudden appearance. I'm going to tag along with your team, but we must push hard and fast to get to the bunker. The admiral knows we're coming for him, so he'll be waiting. But you can bet your ass once the shooting starts, the Zodarks are going to react, and they'll likely call for reinforcements," Royce explained softly, the Osprey jostling them a bit as they continued their descent toward the city.

"Roger that, sir—915 knows the deal. They know what they have to do, and they'll do it. No worries on this end, sir. We got it. And it'll be a pleasure having you with us. Everyone loves having the 'Beast' with them," replied Canty, using the unofficial call sign by which most operators had come to know Royce.

Speaking over the comms for the sake of everyone listening, Royce directed, "Sergeant Major Tanner, the moment we're off the bird, I want those LMGs set up and ready to rock. When those Zodarks decide to die a martyr's death, I want to ensure we're ready to give it to them."

"Hooah, Colonel! Nothing like killing Zodarks to start your day off on the right foot. We'll be up and running before 915 reaches the stairs to the building," the sergeant major confidently declared. Then the six gunners manning the light-medium machine gun shouted their own battle cry of excitement.

Good, everyone is about as ready as they're going to be...now we just have to land.

Tapping into the Osprey's exterior cameras, he saw they were through the clouds and rapidly approaching the city. A few moments went by as they continued their descent, now dropping below three thousand feet. The closer they got to the capital, the more his heart tightened at what he saw.

The once-beautiful city was gone. While it was still a relatively new city—most of it having been built from scratch once the Altairians had forced Earth's governments to unite under one banner—it had grown exponentially once the planners had set their minds to getting it built.

Soon they'd had buildings going up in record time. An army of synthetic engineers and construction Synths working around the clock could accomplish the impossible if given the task and resources to make it happen. Within a few years of starting work on the new city, buildings had stretched high into the heavens, reaching upwards of two hundred and eighty levels at the tallest points. Most buildings were connected at various points to one another by the many hyperloop tubes that tied the city so effortlessly together. Now, as Royce stared at the city—ruins were all he saw.

Many of the tall buildings had vanished, consumed by the flames and intense heat that had vaporized much of the city. Occasionally, though, the charred ruins of a partial skyscraper still remained. A grim reminder of the life that had ebbed and flowed from the city before the arrival of the Zodarks.

It angered him that this had happened. It wasn't supposed to be like this. They'd fought the enemy away from Sol to keep this from happening. Somehow, they had failed. They had let the people of Earth down, and the consequences were being felt by each destroyed city.

"Stand by, Colonel, we're lining up for the final approach to the city," Commander Luke "Scooby" Dueu announced, interrupting his thoughts and alerting him to their pending arrival.

"Thanks, Scooby. Once you spot the HQ building, you think you might be able to set us down as close to the entrance as you can?"

The pilot took a moment to respond, then replied, "We'll give it a look, Colonel. If we can do it without jeopardizing the bird, consider it done. Oh, FYI, I got a message from the Scarab flight lead. He wanted to pass along that they're going to land in the four corners of the quad to offload the IFVs. It was a last-minute request by the infantry commander. He wanted me to pass it along to you."

"OK, Scooby, sounds good. Thanks again for the ride. We'll call a taxi when we're ready to boogie out."

"Copy that, Colonel. I'll have your ride ready and waiting. Good luck—and get off my bird the moment we touch down. I have a feeling this is going to be a hot one," Scooby joked before signing off to focus on flying.

The plan called for diving the Osprey into the city and using the charred remains to cover the approach to the target. As they zipped over top of deserted city streets and jagged and torn buildings, Royce felt a wave of anger growing within. He wanted to punch something—to hurt something. This wasn't supposed to happen. The whole reason to fight afar was to keep the enemy out there—away from home…

Then he spotted the first sign of enemy activity. A string of red lights shot into the air, reaching out for the Osprey that dared to violate its newly claimed territory. The further they flew into the city, the more tracer fire they encountered. Soon, six different positions were throwing blaster fire into the flight path of their bird, in hopes of swatting them from the sky.

"Stand by, Colonel. We're now on the final approach to the LZ—and it's going to be hot. As we come into the area, we're gonna give it a strafe on the way in. See if we can't take a few of 'em out for you on our way in. Then we're gonna give you a swift kick at the last minute to get you off the bird so we can get out of here," Scooby said, half-joking, half-serious about not sticking around longer than he needed to.

"Hang tight, people! It's going to be a hot landing. Everyone off the bird the moment they say go. Then eyes up, guns up, and let's hit our targets fast and catch a ride on the way back to get us out of here," Royce said, explaining the last-minute change in the situation around them.

"Hooah," came the obligatory response, letting him know they were ready to roll. Ready to get off this ride and on with the mission.

While he was talking, the Osprey started taking enemy fire from the nearby buildings. That was when Scooby hooked the Osprey hard to the right. It looked and felt more like it was drifting through the air as he slowly spun the Osprey's nose into a 360-degree turn.

With the pace of enemy fire steadily picking up, Scooby engaged the hostiles with the Osprey's forward guns while his copilot worked the turret mounted below the chin of the aircraft. In moments, the two of them had laid waste to a dozen or more Zodarks shooting out of blown-out windows and torn-apart walls from the buildings lining the parade ground opposite the headquarters building.

By the time Scooby had completed a full turn of the Osprey, the crew chiefs normally seated behind the pilot had made their way into the troop bay and lowered the rear ramp as the pilot rapidly approached the ground. When the pilot gave the signal, the crew chief shouted, "Everyone out! Get off the bird and start shooting those bastards!"

"You heard the man. Get off the bird now!" roared Sergeant Major Tanner as he hit the quick release to the harness. Then he was on his feet, yelling at the operators around him to get the Osprey like it would blow any moment.

After hitting his own quick release, Royce was on his feet— moving to the ramp as the operators emptied off the Osprey faster than he had thought possible.

As he approached the ramp, getting ready to jump a couple of feet to the ground below, he finally saw the parade field and knew they were in trouble before they'd even arrived. Crisscrossing the LZ at a dizzying pace were flashes of red tracers. Some were angled down. Blaster shots kicked up dirt and debris around the feet of the operators already engaging them. Other streaks of blaster fire zipped across the parade ground at chest and head height from shooters firing from the ground level of the various buildings around the parade field.

Taking his eyes off the enemy for a moment, Royce studied the ground, then jumped as the Osprey began to lift away, looking to gain some altitude and get out of the firing range into which the parade field had quickly devolved.

Keeping his knees bent at a slight angle as he landed, he didn't even grunt as the Dragon Skin's improved exoskeleton system absorbed the impact his knees, hips, and back would have absorbed in the old suits.

With his feet on the ground, the Dragon's targeting system built into the HUD started tagging targets for him to engage while quickly denoting the friendlies around him. Turning in the direction of the headquarters building, he saw the operators of ODA 915 bolting with blinding speeds towards the building's main entrance.

Royce took off at a sprint after them, doing his best to ignore the HUD's targeting system as it highlighted hostile after hostile for him to engage. Under any other circumstance, he would have some cover and could work his way through the targets. But he couldn't allow himself to get bogged down in a shoot-out. Clearing a path to the basement in the headquarters building and extracting the fleet admiral was the only thing that mattered.

Then a barrage of blue tracer fire tore into the headquarters' second and third floors, followed quickly by a handful of missiles. Fiery explosions laden with shrapnel exploded across the second and third floors of the building. Then streams of red lights stretched from multiple points across the ground floor of the building to slam into several of the operators who had nearly closed the gap on the building's main entrance.

As the soldiers tumbled from the hits to their Dragon Skin, Royce had his rifle up—sighted on the first target his HUD had identified. Squeezing the trigger as he continued to move forward, he sent a string of purple blaster fire into the face and upper torso of the Zodark he had aimed at.

Coming up on one of the soldiers who'd been knocked to the ground by enemy fire, he reached down, grabbed the guy by a strap sewn to the back of his body armor, and dragged him behind some cover. Looking down at the man, whose nametape said Sergeant Danes, he asked, "You all right, Danes?"

The sergeant looked up through gritted teeth. "I will be in a few seconds. The drugs are about to hit. Once they do, you want to lead the way, Colonel, or follow me in?"

Royce laughed at the fearless bravado of Sergeant Danes. While the Dragon Skin armor provided a huge level of protection that their older suits never could, the physical impact of being hit by blaster shots still jostled the body inside the armor. If it wasn't for the built-in med kit that injected the wearer with small doses of pain meds to numb the injury while medical nanites healed the body, jumping back into the fight might have been easier said than done.

Reaching a hand down to help him, Royce said, "Follow me, Sergeant. I'll show you how it's done."

The man laughed, then nodded in agreement as he readied his rifle.

"Watch and learn how us old dogs get 'er done," Royce said with a bit of a southern twang.

Grabbing for a grenade, Royce pulled the pin, activating the charge, and gave it a good toss into the entrance of the building. Then he leaped to his feet, rifle tucked in his shoulder, blasting away as he ran towards the entrance, counting down as he did. He'd reached the bottom of the stairs leading up the entrance when the grenade went off.

Then a horrible screech like that of a wounded animal tore through the air—assaulting their ears with another terrifying sound to contend with. No noise on the battlefield was more terrifying than the hideous sound of a severely wounded Zodark.

"That's our cue, Deltas! Let's roll!" Royce shouted over the team's comms as he bounded up the stairs, taking them three at a time.

When he reached the landing to the shattered entrance, he leaned against the side of the wall as Danes stacked up behind him. As he grabbed for another grenade, several more soldiers had raced up the stairs and taken a position on the opposite side of the entrance. The operator closest to the door gave him a nod to let him know they were ready.

Pulling the pin and activating the charge, Royce twisted around the corner just far enough to toss the grenade down the hall. Then a flash zipped across his visor, barely missing him as he pulled himself back. When the grenade went off moments later, Royce looked to the others. "Kill 'em *all*!" he shouted sadistically, and he and Danes jumped around the corner, guns blazing.

****

Circling Above the LZ
FMT-161 "Greyhawks"

"Hawk One, Condor Three. How copy?"

Scooby pulled the Osprey a little higher, out of the reach of the blaster fire stabbing blindly through the air to find him.

"Condor Three, Hawk One. Go for traffic."

He sounds a lot calmer than I would be flying in that soup down there, Scooby thought to himself. Those new Scarabs were flying tanks, armored like a turtle and loaded for bear. He liked the Fleet's newest heavy attack transport. It was a beast of a machine and sorely lacking during the last war.

"Condor, it's looking a little tough down there. You want to clear it out yourself, or do you want me to bring in the Bulldogs?"

As the flight commander for the operation, Commander Luke "Scooby" Dueu was in charge of not just his flight of Ospreys but also the flight of Scarabs and a flight of RPCs from FAS-223. This was the Fleet Attack Squadron 223, the Bulldogs stationed aboard the *Wasp*. The pilots flying the remotely piloted crafts or RPCs operated the newly upgraded Charlie models of the AS-90 Reaper. It was perhaps the quintessential close-air support fighter of the Zodark war. It had made the difference between victory and defeat in battles too numerous to count.

"Hawk, do we really have to call in the RPCs? I think I got this," Condor Three opined.

There was a bit of a rivalry between the crewed fighters and transports versus the remotely piloted ones. Both sides claimed to be pilots, but one flew outside the ship while the other pretended to fly in a VR tank akin to Fighter Aces 10 in the Metaverse game.

"It's your funeral, man. But you know what the old man will say if you crash one of his new birds on your first mission."

There was a momentary pause before the Scarab acknowledged, "OK, point taken. Call the Bulldogs. I guess we can throw 'em a bone."

They laughed at the joke, which helped break the moment's tension. Scooby placed the call, throwing a bone for the RPCs to chew on.

"Doggy One, Hawk One. I hear you have a Zodark problem. How can I help?"

Scooby shook his head dismissively at their call sign. Lieutenant Laney Hansen had embraced the nickname of the Bulldogs, only she liked to use whatever fluffy dog names she could come up with for their missions. It drove some of the pilots nuts having to use terms like doggy, fluffy, and poodle—but she had her allies, and she ruled the roost.

I wonder if the four guys in her squadron are lucky bastards or just tortured souls...

"Doggy One, see if you can establish comms with ODA 992. Tell 'em you gotta expand the perimeter and regain control over the LZ. It's gotten too hot for their taxis to swoop in for pickup. See if they can help guide you. How copy?"

"That's a good copy. Dogs out."

Go get 'em, Bulldogs...

****

"Frag out!" Royce shouted as he gave the grenade a good toss down the hallway.

BOOM.

"Moving!" Sergeant Danes shouted as he leaped into the hallway.

Royce followed after him as the two of them moved rapidly down the hallway, taking advantage of the momentary confusion the blast of the grenade in the confined space had likely caused.

Danes spotted movement just inside the door Royce was approaching. Dropping to a knee, he aimed his rifle at the door while Royce reached for another grenade. They'd learned the hard way, fighting to the basement, that it was better to clear the rooms with a grenade than to try doing it with a rifle or pistol. People sometimes forgot how strong a Zodark was. With four arms, they could wrap you up quickly. Then they'd knife you with a free hand, or one of their nearby friends would. Dragon Skin was tough, but even it had its limits, particularly at the seams.

With the grenade in hand, Royce was about to toss it in the room when, further down the hall, he saw a Zodark emerge from the room that led to the bunker entrance. Momentarily surprised by its sudden appearance, Royce shifted positions as he threw the grenade hard and fast at its face. The Zodark guarding the room seemed surprised and alarmed at how close he and Danes were.

The grenade drilled the Zodark like an errant pitch hitting a surprised batter during a ball game. The hit to the face caused it to stumble, taking a step back. Then it shocked Royce by having the presence of mind to kick the grenade right back at him while firing its blaster blindly from the hip.

Royce juked to the left like a halfback dodging a tackle. The unaimed blaster shots zipped around him just as the grenade exploded moments after the Zodark had kicked it. The blast in the confined space of the hallway slapped his body like a brick, throwing him backward off his feet. As his body thudded against the ground, his HUD reported shrapnel hits across much of his suit. His medical icon turned red, then flashed green three times. The suit's internal med kit flooded his body with medical nanites and painkillers that numbed the searing pain he felt in his left leg, right arm, and abdomen. Then the med kit's adrenaline kicked in, pushing the sense of shock from his mind, returning his focus to the fight he was still in.

While dealing with his own part in this desperate fight, Danes fired his rifle, sending a short burst into the Zodark's chest before the grenade went off. When it did, the explosion blew the Zodark's leg apart while the shrapnel from the close-proximity explosion eviscerated its lower extremities.

As Royce lay on his back, sprawled across the floor in the center of the hallway while the drugs and nanites went to work, he lifted his head just enough to see a figure emerge from the room his grenade had originally been meant for. As the smoky haze swirled about the Zodark, Royce saw the figure turn to the left, likely drawn by his comrade's agonizing screams. The wounded Zodark thrashed about in pain, its legs absolutely shredded.

Then the beast turned to look in his direction—their eyes momentarily locked on each other. In that brief moment as Royce stared into the eyes of his adversary, he saw a fiery look of enmity, hate, and pure murderous rage burning within those yellowish catlike eyes of theirs.

Royce watched its eyes narrow as it sprang into action, lurching forward with astonishing speeds he hadn't expected from the large muscular beast. Royce barely had time to roll to the side before blaster shots crashed into the floor where he had just been.

As Royce scrambled to get out of its way, Danes lowered his shoulder and lunged into the side of the charging Zodark. The sudden hit from the side had momentarily caught it off guard as they collided with the wall. Before it could react to Danes, he'd shoved the blade from his trench knife into the side of its upper chest cavity before twisting it hard to the side, causing the Zodark to shout in pain and shock.

With the blade still buried inside, he leveraged the added strength of the Dragon Skin's armor, pulling the knife down as it sliced through bone and muscle tissue before the Zodark could react. Then it swung its left arm in a flailing motion like a backhanded slap that crashed into Danes's chest and helmet.

Royce came out of his roll into a kneeling position, rifle at the ready. He caught sight of Danes just as the Zodark's arm slammed into him, hurling him off his feet to slam against the wall. As his body went limp and crumpled to the floor, he pulled the trigger, sending a burst of shots into the chest of the Zodark just meters away.

Standing upright as the Zodark went down, Royce looked at the beast, its legs twitching, its fingers tapping aimlessly before going limp. Hearing a final gasp from the beast, he double-tapped it with a couple of shots to its face, ensuring it was dead. Moving past its body, he approached the Zodark the grenade had gravely wounded. Bluish blood had pooled around its missing leg, with more still oozing from its tears and gashes across its lower extremities. Aiming the rifle, he put the beast out of its misery, ending its ghoulish howls and cries of pain.

"Did we get 'em all, Colonel? 'Cause I don't think I can go another round with these bastards," Sergeant Danes asked, slowly getting to his feet.

Royce looked around the hallway as he motioned for them to move into the final room where the entrance to the bunker was. "I think so. But you never know with Zodarks. The bastards don't know the word *quit*. They'll keep coming at you until they're dead, or you are." He paused as they caught their breath before adding, "This is the last room. It leads to a fake wall. Behind it is the entrance to the bunker. Once I've contacted the admiral inside, I'll need you to watch the hallway until he's out and we're ready to move. Alpha Team should still be protecting the stairwell leading to us. Unless they tell us otherwise, we shouldn't have any more visitors."

Sergeant Danes grinned as he nodded along in agreement. "Sounds good to me, sir. The sooner we get him out of here, the better. We've been on target for twenty-two minutes now. That's seven minutes longer than you said we should be."

Grunting at the reminder, Royce knew they were on borrowed time—hell, the enemy could have reinforcements on the way. *Maybe I was overly optimistic about how long it would take to reach the bunker…*

"Yeah, let's just finish this."

Royce entered the room, seeing the fake wall had already been destroyed. Making his way to the control panel, he typed a series of numbers he'd been given and waited to see what would happen next.

Then a voice spoke, and a question was asked. "Soldier, what does napalm in the morning smell like?"

Stifling a chuckle at the challenge phrase, Royce felt a renewed respect for Fleet Admiral Chester Bailey, who just so happened to be a fan of what Royce thought was arguably the most amazing film ever made. While the phrase wasn't an exact quote from *Apocalypse Now*, he recognized it just the same and would have known the counterphrase even if he hadn't been given it earlier.

"Victory… it smells like…victory," Royce countered as he tried to use his best Lieutenant Colonel Kilgore accent.

A laugh came from the speaker. "They didn't tell me who they sent to get me out of here. But I'm glad it's you, Colonel Royce. By the way, that's the best Robert Duvall accent I've heard. Let me open this door, and let's get out."

Chapter Nineteen
The Freedom Fleet

The Freedom Fleet
RNS *Freedom*
Sol System

When the RNS *Freedom* crossed the bridge into Sol, Miles wished he could say he felt like he was coming home. A soldier on leave after spending too much time away from family and friends while he stood watch along the perimeter, protecting the society to which he had sworn fealty. But that was not the reason why they had returned.

The arrival of the RNS *Freedom* and the fleet of warships he led should have received cheers of excitement, gratitude, and joy as the defenders of the Republic. Instead, their return resulted from their failure to protect the Republic from an adversary they had defeated once but which had somehow grown strong enough to strike back. As a warrior and leader, he'd failed in his most fundamental duty—protection.

When the bridge had been opened, connecting Rhea to Sol, the *Freedom* connected to the local battlenet, allowing it to receive the most recent reports of the battles still occurring throughout the system. It was the first time his analysts had been able to study the full breadth of what had happened since the arrival of the Zodarks. While very little time had elapsed since their invasion, the enormity of activity across the system was overwhelming. Battles and skirmishes had been fought near Mars, Luna, the orbital station near Venus, and various mining operations throughout the semiautonomous regions of the Belt. As the ships of his fleet began to cross into Sol, the heart of the Republic, Miles had tasked his analysts with sifting through the reports and data available from any ship or station since the first day of the invasion. He needed a better understanding of what had happened, how the local forces had reacted, and what kind of enemy forces were still in the system.

As the reports arrived in his inbox, he wanted to read each description of the day's actions, but his time was limited as the convoy of warships he'd assembled would soon require his full attention. While he had wanted to bring a more extensive fleet, the kind of numbers that would leave no doubt as to who would win this final battle, he felt compelled to leave a substantial force behind in the Rhea system to guard against a possible follow-on invasion should this be part of a grander scheme.

"Excuse me, Viceroy. We completed the BLUF report of what's transpired in the system up until the moment we connected to the battlenet, just as you requested. I just sent it to your tablet for review," said Captain Heidi Leon before waffling on what she was trying to say next. "While I haven't been able to review all of the information myself, it gives a grim assessment of what happened during the first day of the invasion."

Miles grunted at her hesitation before placing a hand on her shoulder. "It's OK, Heidi; it's expected to be pretty rough those first few days. Why don't you give me a rundown on the more critical actions we may need to handle sooner rather than later?"

She nodded, seeming to feel better after his comments. Looking at her data pad, she highlighted something that correspondently linked to his. "This one here is a big deal. The MOS went dark shortly after the invasion. There's been a communication blackout from the facility since their last transmission. You can see from the report I highlighted that shortly after the arrival of Admiral McKee's Second Fleet, she dispatched a frigate to the MOS to see what had happened. You can see the highlighted portions of their report—it paints a pretty bleak picture."

Miles scanned it swiftly, taking the information in so his mind could formulate an opinion.

My God...they breached the habitat domes. What—how could they do that...?

The more he read, the angrier he got. Pausing to ask a question, he said, "Heidi, this report says they found survivors, even contacting them. Are there any reports of what happened next? Was Admiral McKee able to dispatch a rescue force or try to aid this group that spoke with them?"

Her head shook softly in response. "Unfortunately, no. As you can see from the third point we highlighted, her fleet has been under constant attack since they arrived in Sol. Just a few hours ago, the remainder of the enemy force had only recently disengaged and jumped away. It took an hour or so for the listening posts throughout the system to triangulate where they had gone. The fleet was found near the Neptunian moon Triton. The admiral highlighted the key findings in her recent post-battle report, noting specifically that for the time being, she focused on saving the warships she could and getting the damaged ones repaired and ready to fight should the enemy return, which is why her force hasn't pursued the Zodark fleet to Triton."

Miles shook his head, frustrated by how things had played out. While he had been twiddling his thumbs on New Eden waiting for a Zodark invasion, one he had carefully planned to be an ambush, the Zodarks had somehow circumvented his carefully laid plans. They'd delivered a blow that would send untold shockwaves not just through the Republic but through the alliance that he tenuously led. He wondered if he had been played—if, somehow, he'd gotten outwitted by the Mukhabarat and the Zodark intelligence service.

How did they manage to outfox me like this? Could our Mukhabarat spies have carefully been playing us this whole time?

"Viceroy, the bridge is complete. All warships are present, all comms have been established, and the TacNet is ready to assume control of the fleet's weapons," Lieutenant David Rowe announced from the comms stations.

"Thank you, Heidi, for having your people complete this report as quickly as they did. If you can spare a few people, perhaps you can assign someone to look into what led the Zodarks to invade Sol and not the Rhea or Qatana systems, as we carefully designed for them to do. Something isn't adding up. It could be that we have a leak in our organization, or maybe something else is at play. But this shouldn't have happened the way it did. I've got to get back to running the fleet for now. But keep me apprised if anything comes up," Miles directed.

Then Miles returned to his role as the fleet commander. He turned to his comms section. "Lieutenant Rowe, have we established comms with Admiral McKee yet? If we can't connect directly, we should be able to piggyback on the battlenet."

The lieutenant's fingers danced across his station before he responded to Miles's question. Pausing from what he was doing, he looked up. "We're connected now, Viceroy. I can open a channel and send it to your chair if you'd like?"

"Yeah, go ahead and send it."

Miles walked to his chair and took a seat. He pulled the retractable half desk towards his body while opening the comms app. The channel flashed green a couple of times, then the image of Fran McKee appeared.

"Ah, there you are. Greetings, Viceroy. I was beginning to wonder when the *Freedom* would make its grand entrance," McKee joked as she greeted him with a smile and a look of relief.

She'd been his TAO aboard the *Rook* and then his XO aboard the *GW* before he'd been taken in by the Altairians and later the Gallentines. They had a twenty-year history together, much of it earned through the crucible of war and combat.

"It's good to see you too, Fran. I wish we could have gotten here the day they arrived. We're lucky that the Gallentine scout was able to FTL to Rhea when it did," Miles replied as he momentarily looked off camera. Looking back at the screen, he went on, "Fran, what's the disposition of the enemy fleet? I saw from the reports that it's been found near Triton. But how many warships are we still looking at, and how badly mauled is your force right now?"

McKee grimaced at the question, and Miles felt bad for being so blunt.

"We got mauled bad, Miles," she explained. "Half my original fleet is gone. Of the remaining half, a third took severe damage—the kind that means I wouldn't want to depend on them in a fight if given a choice. If we do, they'll go down fast once the shooting starts.

"That brings me to the second set of ships with light to medium damage. These are the ships I've been trying to keep in the fight as best I can by prioritizing their repairs. With the shipyard's repair depot nearby, I figured I'd try to leverage them and see if they could help keep us in the fight until help arrives or the enemy pulls back. I've been working with them to carry out emergency repairs to the most critical systems when possible during lulls in the fighting. That leaves my third set of ships, the ones I've come to call my lucky thirteen. I don't know how or why it's shaken out like this, but these ships hardly have a scratch on them. That said, they don't have much firepower to them either, so their contribution to a fight like this isn't great," she explained, then paused for a moment before continuing.

"Viceroy, the Second Fleet has been forward deployed for more than ten years. Our ships, as you know, are almost exclusively first-gen warships. They're survivors and veterans of the Sirius campaign and the battle for Intus, Alfheim, and the Primord worlds. They're also old and outdated ships. I have the fleet's final remaining *Ryan*-class battleships still in service. Don't get me wrong, they're tanks in a fight, and we've used that to our advantage in this battle. But their weapon loadout can't compete with the newer battleships replacing them.

"To answer your earlier question, Viceroy, I can confidently say the warships from my original fleet that are ready to fight are a single *Ryan*-class battleship, four cruisers, four frigates, and two old torpedo destroyers. However, now that Commodore Dobbs has returned with Task Force Five, I can add two *Victory*-class battleships, two cruisers, and three frigates. During this last engagement, her command lost a cruiser and frigate. Her flagship, the *Vanguard*, sustained some damage, but she assures me they're still more than capable of holding their own should the Zodarks return. I wish I could offer more help, but if you want to assemble more combat power into your fleet, then I would get in touch with Admiral Pandolly. If I had to guess where he is, his fleet is likely engaging what's left of the Zodark fleet around Triton. He's got a substantial force, Viceroy. They really saved our bacon here," McKee explained, painting him a better picture of the current situation.

Miles shook his head slightly as he listened to her recount everything. *I can't believe how this happened...and her fleet...and the home guard fleet...both fleets were nearly wiped out...*

Miles looked around the bridge, making sure no one was nearby. "Thank you for the update, Fran. Your fleet fought valiantly against an overwhelming force. For that, the Republic and the alliance owe you a debt of gratitude." Looking off camera again, he squirmed uncomfortably in his chair, then asked, "Fran, there's something else—"

"It's OK, Miles. He's safe. A recovery ship from the *Vanguard* was nearby where his fighter was shot down. They recovered him and another thirty-eight pilots floating amongst the debris field in their life pods. Last I heard from Amy, he was doing well and in good spirits," interrupted McKee, reading his mind.

Oh, thank God...that boy's got more lives than a cat. Miles breathed a sigh of relief, a hand quickly rubbing his eye in time to catch a tear that almost escaped to run down his cheek.

This was the part of being a commander and a father to a child in the service that he found hardest to deal with. It was one thing to know that his orders could result in the death of dozens, hundreds, and even tens of thousands or more. But that decision became very hard to accept when his son was one of those possible casualties. He could have worked his contacts and put Ethan aside to a staff position or his command. Lilly had made that request when he'd graduated from the Academy. However, in the end, he couldn't do that to his son—not after all he had gone through in pursuing his desire to become a naval officer.

Maybe it's time for me to stunt his military career with an extended staff position at Alliance Headquarters, he found himself thinking again. But then he realized once more, *He'd never forgive me if I did that to him...*

"Thank you for looking into that and letting me know, Fran. Given all the losses we've taken the last few days, I wasn't sure how to ask if my son was OK. It feels selfish to care about my boy while many other parents and children have just lost theirs."

"It's all right, Miles, to want to check on your son. That's a normal response as a father. I can't imagine what it must be like to order your children into battle, knowing they may die. I don't know how I could live with that decision—you're a stronger person than me, Miles," McKee offered, reassuring him that he hadn't asked for anything inappropriate or out of the norm.

Interrupting the conversation, Captain Leon walked over to him from the CIC with a smile and a determined look on her face. "Excuse me, Viceroy, sorry to interrupt. We just got a priority message from the RNS *Wasp*. It's classified, and I don't have the clearance to access it— it's directed for your eyes only," she explained while sending the electronic report to his tablet to read.

Miles scrunched his eyebrows as he thought about the report and what it likely meant if the classification was beyond what his CIC chief could access. Next to him, the skipper, and a few intel personnel, the CIC chief usually held the highest security clearance on the ship.

"Fran, I need to let you go. I have a situation on this end that I need to focus on. Now that I understand your situation better and what Admiral Pandolly is likely doing, I'll have my fleet, which I've aptly named the Freedom Fleet, relocate to your position around the naval yard. In the meantime, I want to get my ground contingent deployed to Earth to assist in putting down whatever Zodarks managed to deploy," Miles explained as he motioned for Admiral Wiyrkomi to start issuing some of the orders and getting the *Freedom* on the move.

"Fran, before I end the call, it sounds like we may have a Zodark problem on Mars. If I'm not mistaken, Dobbs's task force had two orbital assault divisions assigned to it. I've got one division of OADs with me, but my ground contingent is primarily regular Army divisions, except for the Ranger division we grabbed on our way here. Do you happen to know the location of Dobbs's ground force?"

McKee looked off camera for a moment, then replied, "Actually, I do. The *Wasp* is home to the SF contingent. They're being led by Colonel Brian Royce and a JSOC element he's in charge of. They also have a battalion of Rangers with them. The task force ground contingent consists of two orbital assault divisions, as you mentioned. They're led by Major General Vernon 'VC' Crow—"

"VC—that's the Screaming Eagles CG, right?"

McKee nodded. "That's the one, 101st OAD. He's also got the Red Devils with him, the 6th OAD. I have their ships still tucked away at Titan for the time being. When the Zodarks withdrew to Triton, I ordered the JSOC bubbas to figure out how to retrieve Admiral Bailey from the bunker he's been hunkering down in beneath Space Command. He's been able to stay in comms with the other bunkers and command centers across the planet, but I wanted to get him aboard a starship just in case something else happens here in Sol and we need to fall back to Rhea suddenly.

"My thinking was that once I got him aboard one of our ships, I'd let him determine where and how he wanted to deploy those specific divisions. I mean, technically, they've got enough forces on Earth to handle this, but then again, dropping an OAD on top of an enemy force couldn't hurt. Whatcha thinking, sir?"

"I think I need to read this report that just came in from Admiral Bailey now that he's aboard the *Wasp*. Let me get back to you, Fran. *Freedom* out," Miles hastily replied before he cut the connection. He liked Fran and had enjoyed their many conversations over the years. He also knew she had a way of keeping you on a call longer than you intended. Right now, he needed to see why Bailey had just sent him an "eyes only" report even his CIC and intel chief couldn't access.

"Admiral Wiyrkomi, I'll be in my office if you need me," Miles announced as he got up and left the bridge.

Making his way to the office just outside the ship's nerve center, he took a seat, preparing himself for whatever he was about to discover that Admiral Bailey felt only he could be trusted with. Once he pulled up the report and submitted his biometrics and authorization code to unlock it, the cover sheet materialized into the text of what was, apparently, a closely guarded secret.

He made it a couple of sentences into the report when his stomach tightened. The more he read, the sicker he felt. He wasn't sure if it was the betrayal of trust that made him want to vomit or the sense of being used. As he reached the end of the report, one thing was certain. A come-to-Jesus meeting was in order. When he got to the bottom of this, heads would roll.

Chapter Twenty
The Meeting

Zinconia – Zodark Home World

Zon Utulf looked at Yarkeh, the leader of the Orbots, with a bit of uncertainty. He found it difficult to read the body language of the half-mechanical, half-biological cyborgs. Something about them seemed unnatural, bizarre. It bothered him that any creature would willingly give up portions of its body to become a mechanical abomination.

"Zon Utulf, when one examines this request of yours—it does not make rational sense. You are proposing to risk a substantial amount of resources and expend an enormous amount of effort to recover a single Zodark, one you have admitted may not even be alive when we reach Sol. What is so valuable about this particular individual that you would ask us to risk so much to retrieve them?" questioned Yarkeh, speaking flawlessly in the language of the Zodarks.

Utulf didn't try to butcher the Orbots' native tongue. "You ask a wise and reasonable question, Yarkeh," he replied, "one I shall try to answer to your satisfaction.

"In our society, members are chosen to serve upon what we call our High Council for a period of time. When our term on the Council comes to an end, a replacement is chosen who then succeeds us and continues to administer and lead society. The leader of the Council, and thus of our people, is chosen among the nine members of the Council. For more than two hundred dracmas, I have mentored, groomed, and trained the man who will one day take my place on the Council and who will one day become the Zon, the leader of our people as I have been the leader these past thirty-nine dracmas. The person I seek to recover is the person I speak of."

The Orbots didn't exactly grunt, but Yarkeh made a sort of strange clicking noise that indicated he understood the significance of what Utulf had just said.

"Mavkah Otro is not just the head of our military council and of our military—he is my chosen replacement on the Council, the man who will become the Zon and leader to our people. This is why it is imperative that we attempt to recover him from Sol if at all possible," Utulf concluded. In sharing this, the Zon was more open and transparent than he would typically be amongst his own people, especially considering the presence of his compatriot, NOS Damavik. However, just like when standing in the Circle of Truth, nothing less than complete transparency in the presence of Yarkeh would be tolerated. The cyborgs had no use for emotions and made decisions based on logic and necessity.

Yarkeh looked at Utulf for an uncomfortable amount of time, then turned to his companion. "Garkeh, you have heard the request of the Zodark leader. What do you think? Is this something your forces could accomplish?"

Utulf looked to Garkeh, knowing the response of the senior Orbot admiral would determine the fate of Otro's recovery effort if one was to happen.

"It is not a matter of whether it could be accomplished. It is a matter of whether this would be a valued expenditure of resources," Garkeh began. "An operation like this, especially to the home world of the Republic after a failed invasion by the Zodarks, will almost certainly mean that the system will have been substantially reinforced by their alliance. One can almost certainly expect that Gallentine Titan, the ship they call *Freedom*, to be there in the system. That ship alone could cause significant problems for us.

"On the other hand, this failed invasion may give us a unique opportunity we otherwise might not have had. Namely, it is a chance for us to deliver a devastating blow against the Galactic Empire by destroying or severely damaging this Gallentine warship. Without knowing where it is in advance, attempting to coordinate an ambush of this warship is almost impossible; however, we can almost be assured it will be present in Sol as it responds to this botched invasion by the Zodarks," Garkeh concluded.

If he hadn't needed the Orbots' help so much, Utulf would definitely have had some choice words for Garkeh's insistence on calling it a "failed invasion."

It was never supposed to be *an invasion, you cyborg quant!*

"Garkeh speaks the truth," Utulf said, suppressing his more primal desires. "The Gallentine ship—*Freedom*, it will most assuredly be present. The *Tikiona* could bridge our force into Sol. While we look to establish communications with Otro to find and recover him, your ships could engage the *Freedom*, inflict the damage you desire and then exit the system having severely damaged or, by the grace of Lindow, destroyed it."

For a few moments, no one said anything. Utulf would bet the two were communicating privately between themselves, intentionally leaving him out of the conversation.

"Utulf, we have considered your request," Yarkeh announced. "We would not agree to do this for the sole purpose of recovering your chosen replacement—that would be foolish. But the opportunity to ambush, to destroy or inflict severe damage on the one ship that poses the gravest threat to our alliance, to the success of our future endeavors—that is an opportunity worth seizing with both hands.

"We will support your request. We provide the necessary bridge to reach Sol, to ferry in your forces necessary to find and extract this Mavkah Otro of yours. All we ask in return is that you stand ready to assist us in the destruction of this warship called *Freedom* when the time comes. For now, prepare your forces. We leave within four dridals. If your force is not ready, then we will leave without you and not recover your man," Yarkeh declared, then stood and made for the door without giving Utulf a chance to respond or even thank him.

As the cyborgs left the room, Utulf turned to NOS Damavik. "It would appear we have convinced our Orbot partners to agree to our plan. Can your forces be ready in time to leave when their fleet will be ready?"

Damavik grunted unhappily at the question but didn't hesitate to give his response. "We have been given a time and place to have our forces ready. We shall do so and be ready to execute the plan the Zon has given us."

"And the Gurgorra? They'll be ready?"

"As ready as a species like them can be, yes."

"OK, NOS Damavik, you have your orders, then. Do not fail me; do not fail Lindow. He has spoken to me in my dreams—Otro is to become the Zon who will replace me, the Zon who will lead our people into a more prosperous future."

"As you wish, Zon Utulf. I shall not fail you, or Lindow. Now I must go; time is short and much needs to be done."

Chapter Twenty-One
A Mission to Mars

Wardroom
RNS *Freedom*

"What are you saying, Chester? This Karaff, Dakkuri, he wants to switch sides?" Miles pressed, not sure if he should trust the Mukhabarat spy chief further than he could throw him.

"This is what I was saying, Miles. This Dakkuri character, this could be the opportunity we've been waiting for—a chance to learn more about the inner workings of their organization, its plans, and who knows what else he could tell us about the Zodarks," Admiral Bailey defended, pointing to the opportunity of the moment.

Miles sighed, looking away for a moment. "It could be an opportunity. He could also be playing both sides or just trying to save his own skin until a more opportune time arrives for him to sell us out. Let's not forget this is the same bastard who's been spying for the Zodarks, who just invaded. Not to mention the mountains of fake Zodark intelligence he's fed our operatives via his own spies and what he's passed to this Ashurina character we flipped. God knows how many of our people he's killed or the deaths he's been responsible for."

"You're right, Viceroy. He's a spook. We should space him out an airlock the moment we get our hands on him. However, that's not how the espionage game works," Drew countered, catching a look of warning from Reinhard Gehlen. The Director of the Interstellar Marshals Service was eager to get his hands on the spymaster himself and didn't want to give the Viceroy any ideas.

Reinhard jumped in as Drew finished speaking, explaining, "I think what Drew is trying to say, Viceroy, is that the currency these operatives trade on is information. What's of value to me or you may not be of value to the Mukhabarat, the Primords, or the Zodarks. In this case, however, Dakkuri's value is his knowledge of how the organization works, what its vulnerabilities are, and where those vulnerabilities can be exploited for our gain. I don't like cutting a deal with a mass murderer like him either. But I think over the years, you've taught that sometimes the burden of command, as you like to say, requires us to make decisions we don't always agree with or want to make, but we make them because the ends justify the means."

My own words being quoted back to me. Miles had to stifle a chuckle at how far Reinhard had come in accepting the hard truths often associated with the spy world.

"If I may be allowed to comment, Viceroy," Admiral Wiyrkomi said, speaking for the first time since the meeting had started.

"Yes, of course, Wiyrkomi. You're always welcome to provide insight into whatever we're discussing," Miles assured, motioning for him to continue.

The Gallentine took a breath before saying, "During my years of service to the Emperor as his emissary and advisor to you, and the people of the Republic, I have come to understand that you humans are a most peculiar people. You struggle morally to make some decisions while others come with ease. You are by far the most vicious, cunning species I have ever seen. Your ability to adapt to an ever-changing situation continues to astound me, and the Gallentines the Emperor has tasked with aiding the Republic.

"I say this to you to tell you that you should, as you say, 'trust your gut' and go with your instincts. If you think this Kafarr is playing you—that this is just another ploy, another trap—then be done with him and move on. But do not dwell on this issue. There are still Zodarks to fight in system, on Earth and in your colony on Mars. Time is not on your side, and your force has been severely weakened. It will take time to repair your ships and rebuild what has been lost. Make a decision—then move on," Wiyrkomi commented, the sting of his simple response hitting Miles where it hurt—his pride.

Nodding slowly to himself, Miles stood, motioning for the others to stay seated. "Issue the orders. Go fetch this Kafarr and bring him to me. I want to see him face-to-face, then I'll be the judge of his intent. Oh, and bring Ashurina too. She's part of this, whether she realizes it or not."
****

327th OAR, 101st OAD
Regimental Ops Center
RNS *Intus*

Major Frank Pannachia stared at the image of the division commander, Major General Vernon "VC" Crow, on the holocom as he explained the new orders they'd just received. Instead of going in with the rest of the division to assault a series of Zodark positions around Central Africa, they'd been retasked to clear out the Zodark force on Mars and to support Task Force Silver Fox on the RNS *Wasp* with some kind of high-value mission.

"Come on, Frankie, don't look like I killed your puppy or something," VC commented. "You gotta view this as an opportunity here, a chance to really shine in front of the brass. This mission came down directly from the Viceroy himself. It's a big freaking deal. You still want to make colonel, right?"

"My apologies, General, you're right," replied Major Pannachia. "Sorry if I gave off the wrong impression. This is a big opportunity for the regiment. It just caught me off guard, that's all."

Damn, I hope I didn't just blow it in front of the general, he thought, chiding himself for not jumping at the opportunity to participate in a mission the Viceroy himself had ordered.

VC shrugged. "It's OK, Frankie. It's tough having to step in and take the place of another unit, especially one of our sister regiments. The 506 had been the regiment augmenting those JSOC freaks of nature. Now the 327th has to step in and take their place, something I'm more than sure you and your soldiers can handle."

The general paused for a second, looking off camera before locking eyes with him. "As the division commander, losing three out of the sixteen regiments to a single event is a kick to the balls. There's no other way to say it than it sucks. I've lost four thousand, six hundred and eighty-two soldiers because those bastards in Fleet couldn't protect our ships. That's a loss I gotta carry—not you, *me*. But those are the cards we've been dealt and we're gonna have to play the hand as best we can. When Colonel Royce speaks with you, he'll let you know how he wants to use your regiments. Just remember, they may be augmented supersoldiers, but they aren't invincible. They can bleed like us, and they can still die. But Royce...that dude's immortal and he scares the hell out of me. Just follow his lead, and his freaks will do the rest."

Then the connection ended, leaving Major Pannachia and his second-in-command, Captain Sophia Fern from Demon Company, wondering what the hell had just happened.

"Well, that wasn't what I was expecting when I came in to see if we had any orders," Captain Fern said. She'd been sitting to the side, just out of sight of the holocom device.

Pannachia blew some air past his lips as he shook his head. "Me neither. But like he said, it's an opportunity for us to shine and get in the fight faster than the rest of the division."

"So how do you want to handle this once this Colonel Royce contacts us?" Fern asked.

"Well, unless you have an objection, I figure I'll loan Demon Company to him. I'll keep the Baker Boys on deck to help you. What do you think?"

Fern gave him a mischievous smile. "Of course Demon Company can handle this. We're savages, remember?"

Pannachia rolled his eyes at the comment. First Platoon, under the command of Lieutenant Joseph Grubich, call sign Psycho, paired with Master Thorun, sometimes called Thor, had named the platoon *savages*, dating back to Thorun's first introduction of his tomahawks during the Intus campaign. It had taken a few years and additional campaigns, but eventually the tomahawks had spread to the rest of the company, and they'd fought like bastards since.

"Just keep an eye on Psycho and Thor, will you? This isn't the time to get embarrassed in front of the brass. You heard the general—this mission came from the Viceroy, and this Delta colonel—Royce...damn, if you don't know about him, best do some research. There's a reason even VC is nervous around him."

Fern snickered. "Ah, come on. You're telling me he's a scarier dude than Psycho, Thor, or Dread?"

Pannachia just smirked, shaking his head dismissively at her. "Girl, you don't know the half of it. That guy's been awarded two Medals of Honor, four Distinguished Service Crosses and five Silver Stars to go along with seven Purple Hearts. Guy's a damn killing machine—some kind of immortal freak of nature like the general said. Just get your people ready. I'll keep Baker on deck in case you guys screw it up or this colonel asks for additional help. Dismissed."

As Pannachia watched her leave, he thought he saw a look of concern on her face. *Good, you should be concerned about working with JSOC. We're going to be in the thick of it now...*
****

327th Regiment, Bastogne Bulldogs
Demon Company Troop Bay
RNS *Intus*

The room was abuzz with activity as soldiers double-checked loadouts, adding magazines, power cells, and grenades to their pouches and straps to their kits.

Grabbing another grenade for his vest, Master Sergeant Karl Thorun gave the setup a final once-over, satisfied with the loadout he'd chosen for the mission.

We're pulling perimeter security for JSOC—what a load of crap..., he thought to himself as he tightened a strap on his vest.

From an outside perspective, he should be excited about the mission. It was a chance for regular Army grunts to work with JSOC. That wasn't something the line units got to do very often. Inwardly, he chafed at the idea of orbital assault troops not being considered "good enough" to be on par with the ORDs who normally ran these kinds of security missions for Deltas. Hell, the two Orbital Ranger Divisions had originated from OADs to begin with.

He sighed. *Whatever. It's a chance to kill Zodarks and get some payback for what they've done...*

When he looked up and saw the mirror against the wall, he chuckled to himself at whoever had taken the liberty of adding a parody below the silly morale-boosting poster next to it.

He sighed, then stared at his reflection, giving himself a once-over before strapping his armor and the tools of their trade to his body. He looked cut, physically fit, in the best shape of his life. But his eyes told a different story. Staring back at him, he saw something he wasn't sure if he should hate, fear, or embrace. The image staring back was that of the Norse god Thor, wearing a gilded Viking helmet, hair stretching past his shoulders, his beard in braids and a pair of tomahawks in his hands. Part of his brain told him it wasn't real, but staring into those eyes—it was like looking into his soul. It was a strange feeling, an odd sensation that always seemed to visit him on the eve of battle. It was like a switch was flipped when the blaster fire started to fly and the fight was on. His inner god, or demon, or whatever it was—all he knew was that on the eve of battle, it demanded control, and Thorun gave it, allowing it to lead his men into battle and savage the enemy.

Blinking away his shadow, he stared back into those bluish-gray eyes—some found them intimidating, others charming. Except he knew the truth. He knew what lay behind those eyes and the chiseled physique he spent hours strengthening to carry his tools of the trade. Behind those eyes—buried deep in his mind churned battle after battle in a war he was steadily losing.

He snorted at the melancholy he'd momentarily allowed his mind to wander into, shaking it off and smirking at himself. He adjusted the gray beret sitting atop his closely cropped head, lost again in the moment. He imagined he must have looked similar to the paratroopers of old, the Sky Soldiers of a bygone era.

They might not jump from planes over enemy territory to dangle beneath the silk of a parachute while he invaded from space, but he hailed from these same legendary units of the past that now paved the way to what they were today. Like the elite of the infantry—the shock troops of the nations—he was proud to continue that legacy today as part of the orbital assault troops, specially trained infantry whose job was to assault a planet from the high ground of orbit. The OATs would land under fire and clear out the landing zones so that follow-on forces could begin the process of occupying the planet.

The Red Berets and Jump Wings of the Airborne had morphed into the Gray Berets and Globe and Winged Dagger of the OATs. While they weren't Special Forces, they were the first regular Army units to land dirtside on an enemy planet, and that meant something. There were certainly times when he'd thought he was going to try out for the Deltas, to insert days and sometimes weeks or even months ahead of an invasion force. The more he thought about what he wanted, though, the more he realized he just wanted to be in the action. Not sneaking around behind enemy lines or carrying out sabotage missions. He wanted the action. To be a shooter. It was why he'd turned down a promotion to command sergeant major not once but twice to stay at the platoon and company level. A promotion would end that—and it would end him if he lost the dopamine rush he got from the thrill of combat.

He'd almost crossed over to the Rangers, and likely would have if he hadn't gotten injured. Following his injury, he counted himself lucky to have kept his slot in the OATs.

"So how about that, Master Sergeant? We got our first mission to hit back at those blue demons. You excited?" asked Private Luka Rhodes, masking his fear with faux excitement.

Thorun finished tightening his vest before looking up at the kid. When he did, the young man's eyes told him all he needed to know. He was scared, nervous to fight the Zodarks—something the Republic hadn't done in nearly seven years.

"You'll do fine, Rhodes. Just remember your training and listen to Cannon. He's fought 'em before. He knows what he's doing."

The young soldier nodded and moved on, satisfied with the answer for the moment. The kid was a replacement, a backfill they'd picked up on Titan to fill the gaps from the Serpentis campaign.

Thorun finished what he was working on and looked up in time to see Private Rhodes walk up to Sergeant Jake Manu. He couldn't hear his question, but judging by the broad smile he saw spreading across Jake's face, he knew Private Rhodes would be taken care of when Cannon paused in checking his own gear to help square away the new guy.

Jake Manu, call sign Cannon, was a giant Samoan. Once he'd finished helping the new guy, he fell back into his premission ritual—slamming protein drinks and making sure he had enough of his signature protein bars he was always eating to get him through him the next few days. He'd picked up the call sign Cannon on account of his massive biceps, honed by years of rigorous weightlifting and too much time in the gym. During the final years of the Zodark war, and this past campaign on Serpentis, he'd continued to prove he was a force of nature on the battlefield, a leader among his peers and a valuable asset to Demon Company.

Thorun knew something else about the man. Lurking behind the intimidating exterior of this giant was a man with a heart of gold. A friend who was always willing to help. But God help you if he was in a dour mood and you pushed him one too many times. While he'd refrained from striking a fellow platoonmate, he had no such qualms with outsiders when in port at one of the local pubs or dive joints they liked to frequent as friends.

Just then, the door to the troop bay opened and Lieutenant Grubich walked in, spotting him and heading his way.

Great, let's see what Psycho has for us now, he thought to himself.

It was a little atypical to pick your own call sign. Then again, there was nothing typical about the LT. In fact, he was about as atypical an officer as they came. Thorun had been a staff sergeant the first time they had met. Back then, Grubich had been a young private first class when he'd shown up to Third Platoon, two months prior to the start of the Sumer Campaign. While some of the OADs had left for Primord space to participate in the Alfheim campaign, their division was going to Sumer—to liberate the Sumerian people from their Zodark overlords. It was during that campaign that the LT had acquired his call sign, or rather, had self-appointed it.

The Sumer campaign hadn't gone the way they had hoped. When they'd arrived in system, the Zodarks had apparently decided to cut bait and run. Opting to abandon the place rather than make a stand, they'd relocated as much of the population as they could, liquidating the ones they couldn't. For many, the sight of so many corpses—men and women of varying ages, usually above forty—was too much. Bodies had been strewn about the cities, towns, villages, and anywhere and everywhere you would normally find people. Having fought the Zodarks for years at this point, Thorun, like many others in the company, felt there was little that could shock him. He was proven wrong when they arrived on Sumer. It was a reminder of the savagery that awaited the people at home should they fail out here among the stars.

It had been eight days and three firefights since they'd arrived on the surface. While the first couple of engagements hadn't been too serious of an affair, the third battle had been a slugfest. They'd encountered a serious opposition force, drawing in the four platoons of the company until eventually four out of the sixteen companies in the regiment had been drawn into battle. The fighting had lasted for nearly nineteen hours, leading to dozens of casualties across the platoons. One of those casualties had been Grubich.

Somewhere during the middle of the battle, a few soldiers in Grubich's squad had gotten injured and were being pinned down by a few Zodarks. Try as they might to get to the wounded, the enemy had kept them from retrieving them. Accounts of what had happened next differed a bit. One of the wounded soldiers said that when a pair of Zodarks had swarmed their position and were about to hack them to pieces, a soldier he identified as Grubich had charged the enemy, firing his rifle into one of their chests as he unleashed a primal yell of rage.

As the first Zodark had gone down, his comrade had reacted to the situation, swinging an object that threw Grubich up in the air and into a tree before falling to the ground. Thinking he was dead, the Zodark returned to finish the wounded off. But he wasn't dead, and he wasn't about to let his wounded comrades die at the hands of this murderous beast. Crawling on his hands and knees, he saw what was about to happen and sprang into action. He grabbed for the pair of tomahawks Thorun made sure everyone in the platoon carried as a backup weapon and charged after the beast—their business still unsettled.

It heard him coming and turned just in time to see the human soldier leap into the air, both arms uncoiling like a spring, holding tightly to the tomahawks as they crashed into the base of its neck and its upper chest. As their bodies collided, they fell to the ground in a bloody heap. The blades of the tomahawks had sliced into the brute with such ferocity and force that they had decapitated the beast, its head rolling to a stop at the feet of the five wounded soldiers he'd just saved.

While Thorun hadn't seen the event and Grubich's helmet cam had sadly been destroyed when he'd slammed into the tree, the account of it by the wounded he'd saved was enough to ensure the private first class would eventually be awarded the Medal of Honor for having saved their lives from certain death at great personal risk to himself. Unbeknownst to them at the time, Thorun's insistence that he get checked by the medics had ultimately saved his life. They'd spotted a brain bleed and a hairline skull fracture from his impact against the tree.

Thorun figured after a lengthy recovery time, Grubich would have taken the disability pension the Army usually offered to soldiers with certain injuries or awards and gotten out. The war had just ended, a few days after he'd recovered from his injuries and returned to the platoon. Instead, to their surprise, he'd leveraged his MOH award to land himself a slot at the Space Command Academy to become an officer. As they say, after that, the past became legend and he'd eventually found his way back to the 327th, just in time to deploy to Serpentis.

When Lieutenant Grubich approached, he placed his Qpad on the table next to his kit, then commented, "The plan from the cap'n looks pretty straightforward, Master Sergeant. We should be on final approach to the planet. Let's load up in the Osprey and get ready to roll."

"Roger that, sir. You want me to do the honors, or you?"

"You can do it, Thor. You have a way of riling them up for a mission," the LT replied with a sly grin.

Thorun smirked as he grabbed his body armor, lifting it over his shoulders until it settled tightly against his body. As he cinched the straps in place, he closed his eyes for a moment, pressing a hand over the nametape stitched with his call sign—*Thor*. He pressed harder against the center of his chest, his fingers touching the chevrons of his master sergeant rank. He cleared his mind, letting his inner warlord take over.

Opening his eyes, he grabbed for his rifle and helmet, shouting, "Listen up, First Platoon! Who are we?"

"Savages!" roared the sixty soldiers of the platoon.

"What are we?"

"Savages!"

"That's right! Now grab your gear and let's load up. It's time to kill us some Zodarks!"

"Savages!" the platoon roared again as they grabbed for their rifles and the M48 tomahawks that had become the platoon's new calling card in battle.

Somewhere along the way, the platoon had started carrying the tomahawks in lieu of knives after seeing him wield a pair in more than one melee over the years. Now they'd become a staple weapon of choice to anyone assigned to the First Platoon "Savages" of Demon Company.

Climbing aboard one of the new Ospreys they'd picked up at Titan, Thorun had to admit, these new Charlie models were badass. They packed enough weapons to clear a drop zone and stick around to fight alongside the OATs they'd just delivered.

Wish we'd had these around for the last war…

Moments later, the hum of the engines grew a little louder, and suddenly they were off, making their way out of the hangar and toward the surface of the red planet.

Time to earn our pay…it's killing time, he thought, savoring the thrill of impending battle, a chance to satisfy this urge to kill…this desire he felt but couldn't explain…

****

FMT-161 "Greyhawks"

Once Scooby had cleared the *Wasp*, the other Ospreys and Scarabs under his command maneuvered closer to him. They flew in a loose formation while they waited for the escorts to fly ahead and clear 'em a path before descending to the surface.

"There's our escort," Lieutenant Shane "Buster" Gonad announced as the pair of Orion starfighters zoomed ahead.

"Let's hope the intel guys are right and they don't have any fighters down there."

"The only fighter I'm worried about running into is a Zeek. Not sure how well it would do on Mars, but I'd rather not find out," commented Buster.

Scooby felt his heart race at the mention of the dreaded Z-word. In space, the Zodarks relied heavily on the Vultures as their dominant starfighter, the Glaives as their bomber, and the Zeeks as a planetary-based fighter. The Zeeks, however, were tough little buggers and fast as hell. They were nimble beyond belief, and if you weren't careful, they'd slice your Osprey up before you had a chance to react or try and get out of the way.

He and Buster had only encountered them once, over Alfheim. They'd lost a friend from their squadron who'd gotten nailed by one just hours before the war had ended. It had been a punch to the gut for Scooby, losing a friend on the final day of the war. If he'd survived just a few hours more—he'd still be with them today.

"Well, if there's any Zeeks down there, then they'll probably go for the Dogs. You can see 'em heading in now," Buster commented. He pointed in the direction of the squadron of Reapers beginning their descent. The Fleet Attack Squadron 223 Bulldogs was going to start flying over the colony looking for targets of opportunity while a handful would loiter nearby in case the ground force requested some help.

"Yeah, I guess we'll see. Let's run through our checks and get ready to begin our descent," Scooby replied, pushing aside the thought of a few Zeeks looking to score a kill or two against a pack of fat, juicy transports.

******

First Platoon, Demon Company

As the Osprey continued towards the landing zone, Master Sergeant Thorun could feel the tension in the air. The reality of the Zodarks' attack on Sol was all the more intense now as they continued their descent into battle. They were not on a foreign planet in some obscure star system—this was Mars—this was home. Despite how they felt, Thorun knew they had to stay focused on their mission: supporting a Delta team in retrieving the package and ensuring their safe extraction.

He listened as the LT outlined the plan for deploying the platoon in support of Second and Third Platoons, who were deploying with eight of the Regiment's DF-12 Cougars. Fourth Platoon was arriving with Baker Company and the four other Cougars that would pick them up before the column of sixteen infantry fighting vehicles would begin their journey to the rally point to link up with the Deltas for pickup and get them back to the LZ for extraction.

With no idea how many Zodarks were on the ground or what the conditions were like, the brass who'd cooked up the mission hoped the added firepower of the infantry fighting vehicles would give them an edge. Having fought the Zodarks before, Thorun knew they were a formidable enemy and that anything could happen once they hit the ground. He still remembered what his drill sergeant had told him right before graduation more than twenty years ago: "The enemy always gets a vote—don't expect it to be in your favor."

No truer words have been said…

"You approve?" Lieutenant Grubich asked, his voice tense.

"Yeah, this'll work," Thorun replied, trying to keep his own anxiety in check. "Let me send it to the squad and fire team leaders. Do you want to brief the platoon on the specifics?"

"Sure. Ah, crap. Never mind, go ahead and brief them. Captain Fern just pinged me. I gotta see what she wants," the LT replied, his frustration palpable. Thorun knew that the constant changes to the plan were taking a toll on all of them, but he couldn't let it distract him from the mission at hand.

Standing at the front of the troop bay, Thorun shouted to gain everyone's attention. "Savages, eyes on me! The LT just sent the squad and fire team leaders a copy of the battle plan. I'm going to review it with you now, so everyone knows the plan and what's expected." He quickly outlined the roles for each squad and fire team, noticing the anger and determination in the eyes of his soldiers. He could tell they were ready to take on the Zodarks; now he just had to keep their emotions in check.

"Once the bird hits the dirt, First Squad is going to provide dismount infantry support to the IFVs transporting Second Platoon. Second Squad, you're supporting the IFVs carrying Third Platoon while we establish an initial perimeter until the Baker Boys arrive in the second wave. Third Squad, you're in reserve with the LT. Dread Squad, my LMG gunners, you're with me," Thorun explained, trying to keep his voice steady.

As the Osprey neared the LZ, Thorun could feel the adrenaline pumping through his veins. The Zodarks were out there, and they were ready for a fight. He knew it wouldn't be long before they made contact, and they were nearing the LZ. He had to wrap this up. "Listen, once the shooting starts, Staff Sergeant Deimos and I will get the LMGs running to support First and Second, while the IFVs work the line and hopefully won't need to dismount their pax. Remember the mission—we're supposed to aid a Delta team already on the ground. Once Baker Company arrives, they'll have the IFVs that'll pick us up and then we're off."

Thorun's voice was heavy with the weight of the mission. "We don't have a lot of time to make it to the rally point before we're supposed to link up with the Deltas and pick 'em up. We may have to fight our way to the pickup point or fight our way back to the LZ for extraction. I need everyone to stay focused and stay on mission. I know this last part is going to be hard to accept, but we aren't here to liberate. That's what the rest of the regiment is doing. We're here to support the Deltas—nothing more, nothing less. Got it?"

"Hooah!"

****

ODA 915
Gemini District

Royce advanced slowly, steadily moving into the building that would lead them towards the casino. Once the team was inside, they waited a moment, observing where they'd come from and making sure no one was following them.

Knowing Lieutenant Rogers would have led the mission had Royce not come along, he opted to pull rear security with Sergeant Danes and let Rogers and Tanner clear the promenade and secure the package. Taking a defensive position near the entrance, he and Danes settled in to make sure no Zodarks would sneak in behind them.

"Danes, keep an eye on the entrance. I'm going to tap into Rogers's HUD and track their progress."

Danes just gave a nod, keeping his eyes on the door.

Syncing with Lieutenant Rogers's HUD, Royce was able to watch the team stealthily move through the promenade towards the casino near the end. Many of the shops, bars, and restaurants were damaged in one way or another. Some had blaster burns to the walls. Others had shattered windows and merchandise strewn about the floor, intermixed with the bodies of dead civilians. It pissed him off seeing how many bodies were scattered around, some of them beginning to bloat, having been dead for many days now.

Considering how many bodies they had encountered on their way to the building, he was surprised they hadn't seen any Zodarks up to this point, but he was also glad they hadn't. Fortunately, the Gemini District's dome hadn't been one of the domes destroyed during the invasion. At least half of the districts still had pressurized, breathable air, which meant there might be survivors if they had been able to seal themselves off from the invaders or beat them back.

Tactically speaking, the challenge with infiltrating Gemini was that they had to cross through an airlock, a perfect location for an ambush if the Zodarks had any tactical sense behind what they did. Once they'd made their way through the airlocks and hadn't been ambushed, they moved further into the district, still not encountering any enemy resistance.

I guess our little diversion plan is working, Royce thought. They knew the Zodarks were heavily engaged around the Mattis Facility, where DARPA was located, but they had no idea how many were still operating around the districts that comprised the population centers on the surface and near the spaceport and space elevator.

The deployment of the 327th, however, seemed to have succeeded in drawing whatever local forces were in the area to them. Now he hoped he'd given the Zodarks long enough to focus their efforts on the 327th that they would leave the Gemini District free of any nearby enemy force. Still, the further they moved through the district towards the mall where the casino was, the more he had a gnawing feeling like they were walking into a trap.

We should have brought a few Synths for this… Royce wasn't sure what the deal was with the Synths lately, but they hadn't been able to replace their losses from the Serpentis campaign when they had stopped for a few days at the Titan facility. The limited number of Synths meant they were being held in reserve for the time being to support the OATs and not his Deltas.

Watching Rogers observe his soldiers stealthily move along the sides of the promenade, he'd nearly jumped out of his skin when he heard over the comms, "Freeze, don't move, Lee!"

The warning jolted Royce's senses the moment he heard it, his hands gripping his rifle tighter as his body and muscles prepared to react to whatever was about to happen next.

I need to see what's going on…

Royce tapped into Staff Sergeant Lee's helmet cam, hoping he might see what Sergeant Major Tanner spotted that had led to the warning.

"Hang tight, Lee. I'm sending a drone to check around that corner before you enter the casino. I swear I saw a shadow or something near the entrance," Tanner explained, barely above a whisper.

Then one of his microdrones detached itself from the surveillance kit mounted along the rear shoulder of his Dragon Skin suit.

Royce switched from Lee's helmet cam to sync with the drone's camera feed. He watched the drone's video as it approached the entrance to the casino. The image flashed—gone before he had a chance to see around the corner. Then the audio receivers to their helmets detected a noise. A *pop* sound like a gunshot, only this sound was distinct in nature, and Royce knew exactly what it was.

We got Zodarks in the casino…it's an ambush. No sooner had he thought the words than all hell broke loose.

"It's an ambush! Go, go, go!" Tanner shouted as the operators sprang into action—their counterambush training taking over as a deluge of fire erupted within the mall.

Crap, I need to get up there, Royce thought as he bolted in the direction of his team. Sergeant Danes raced to keep up.

They sprinted through the promenade leading to the casino, the sounds of blaster fire and yelling filling the place as the shooting intensified.

"Contact to your three o'clock!"

"Covering fire!"

"Lookout to your right!"

"Frag out!"

BAM.

"You got two moving on your right!"

"I see 'em! Moving now!"

"Rogers! They're going for their swords!"

"Here they come!"

Yells and screams in English and Zodark filled the air as Royce heard the battle devolve into a melee of hand-to-hand combat and close-quarter battle in the confined space.

"Take that, you bastard!"

"Die, you piece of—"

Then the shooting stopped and so did the yelling. A moment later, someone shouted, "All clear."

Then another voice shouted, "Ah hell, man—they got the lieutenant."

"What?! Someone talk to me," Royce yelled as he neared the casino, the entrance in sight.

"Rogers is dead, Colonel. Freaking severed his head." Royce heard the anger in the voice of Sergeant Major Tanner as he spat the words out.

When he and Danes rounded the corner into the casino, they saw Tanner standing near the bodies of several dead Zodarks. As they approached, they saw it. The body of their comrade. His severed head was still strapped to his helmet—detached from the rest of his body.

Royce stopped what he was doing, shaking his head slowly in disbelief. In that moment, all he wanted to do was scream in frustration. To punch a wall, to kill a Zodark, to do something. But there was nothing he could do. Rogers was dead. No amount of nanites or advanced medical treatment was going to repair this kind of injury.

"We should have held back. When they zapped our drone, we should have held back until we had a better idea of how many of them we were dealing with and where they were at," Tanner commented, clearly upset at the situation.

Taking a breath in, Royce shook his head. This was on him. Not his senior NCO. He was the boss and the buck stopped with him.

"No, Sergeant Major, you made the right call. You acted on instinct and training, just as we've been taught. This wasn't your fault or anyone else's. Sometimes you just lose."

Letting his words hang there for a moment, he finally instructed, "Let's get his body taken care of and get ready to move. Sergeant Danes, on me. Let's find the package, get back to the rally point, and hope the IFVs are ready to pick us up."
****

First Platoon, Demon Company
Mercury District

"That's it. Everyone's in the truck. Now let's move out. We're running late and our dates are already waiting in the limo," said Lieutenant Grubich as he shut the door to the Cougar.

"Hang on back there. It's about to get bumpy and we've got some lost time we need to make up along the way," announced the vehicle commander as the Cougar got underway.

"Well, that couldn't have gone worse if we'd tried, LT. What the hell was all that?" Thorun said over a private channel.

"What do you mean, Thor? You thought we wouldn't encounter any resistance down here?" the LT countered in annoyance.

"Oh, I expected resistance, LT. What I didn't expect was losing air support. We're running late to pick those Deltas up because we couldn't disengage from the fight and not lose control of the LZ. What the heck happened?" he answered, frustrated with the LT, whose laissez-faire attitude towards the situation wasn't instilling a lot of confidence in his ability to lead the platoon or aggressively obtain support when needed.

"All right, Master Sergeant, I'll tell you what happened. When the rest of the regiment had landed on the far side of Mercury and Apollo Districts, the Zodarks attacked. Our CAS got reassigned to another company in greater need of it than us. I know you're annoyed at being late to pick up some SF operators on a secret squirrel mission—they can wait. If we had lost control of the LZ…well, you know how that would work out. Let's just move on, Thor. How are the rest of the guys dealing with all this?" asked the LT, waving his hand about.

From the time they'd landed next to the Mercury District, it had been one attack after another from the Zodarks. At times, the fighting had gotten so intense, so overwhelming, they had considered calling for an extraction and attempting to relocate to a new LZ to which they could exfil the Deltas. Fortunately, the presence of twelve infantry fighting vehicles had been enough to change the tide of the fight, and they'd managed to hold the line.

Feeling better about the situation after the LT had clued him in, Thor assured him, "They'll be all right, LT, and thank you for letting me know about the other attacks drawing away our air support." He paused for a second, then added, "Sir, even you have to admit the situation out there—so many—"

"I know, you don't need to say more. These Zodarks…they're animals. This is what they do. They invade systems and either subjugate the people or kill 'em. I had hoped the peace would hold, but now that it hasn't, I hope they let us finish them off. No more peace treaties if you ask me," the LT replied, then ended the conversation.

The Cougar continued to jostle and bumped around a bit as they sped through the district—racing to make up time on their way to the customs office near the spaceport.
****

ODA 915
Customs Office

Colonel Royce stood in the doorway as he stared at Ashurina and the man seated next to her, the package they'd been sent to retrieve. *To think this is the guy we've been after all these years…* His brain stewed on the number of times they had almost had him. Each time Royce thought they'd got him, he'd slip out of their clutches at the last second—disappearing again for months or even years.

Then the man staring at Royce commented, almost apologetically, "It may surprise you to hear this, but you almost caught me once."

Royce grunted, dismissively shaking his head. "Let me guess. Rio, fall of 2109, right?"

The man nodded slowly. "Yeah, that's the one. Your people are good, Colonel, really good."

Then the man hesitated for a moment. "I know this won't make a difference to you now, Colonel, but I see it—I wish I had seen it sooner. But I see it now—I will atone for what I've done."

Royce stared at him for a moment, lost in his thoughts and the memories of what this man had done to his people. How he'd just aided the Zodarks in their invasion of Sol, of Earth and its colonies. Taking a breath in, he asked, "So you think you've seen it? What is this epiphany you think you've had that's led us to this moment?"

Before he'd left the ship for this mission, his friend Drew from Republic Intelligence had shared during the mission brief that Dakkuri, the Karaff of the Mukhabarat for Sol, had apparently come to the realization that he'd sided with the wrong team. Following his apparent come-to-Jesus moment, he now wanted to change sides, to make things right. Royce wanted that to be true; he wanted to put an end to this perpetual threat from the Zodarks and their proxy, the Mukhabarat. He'd also spent enough time working intel ops to know an operative might flip if they felt it could better position them with the winning side. The problem for Royce was the winning side today wasn't always the winning side next year, or the year after.

Just as the man was about to respond to his question, the comms channel he'd been casually listening to lit up with a series of urgent warnings. Sensing something was wrong, Royce held a hand up, exiting the doorway as he jumped on the comms. "Badger One, Badger Six. Someone give me a sitrep."

"Badger Five, Badger Two. Five tangos approaching from the south. Hundred meters and closing quick," reported the soldier observing the southern approach to the building they were in.

Damn it, where the hell is our ride? We're minutes away from having to engage the enemy and our extraction team is nowhere to be found, Royce cursed to himself. He fumed over what should have been a simple pickup as it steadily moved towards turning into a hot mess they'd have to fight their way out of.

"Badger Four, watch your seven o'clock—oh crap, those are charges he's attaching to the door. Stand by for contact!"

Badger Four...that's the west side of the building. Royce tried to recall the location of the door when the blast occurred.

BOOM!

The nearby explosion knocked him to the ground as the concussive wave slammed into the armor of his Dragon Skin. He shrugged off the worst of the effects, scrambling to his feet just in time to see the first Zodark charge through the hole where a door had previously been.

Royce saw the Zodark firing his blaster at him and leaped to the right as a few blaster bolts zipped through the air where he'd been moments earlier.

Firing from the hip, he jinked to the left before diving into a rolling position as blaster shots continued to dance around him. As Royce came out of the rolling position, rifle tucked in his shoulder, he squeezed the trigger, sending a few blaster shots into the center mass of the Zodark trying to shoot him.

No sooner had he taken the first alien down than two more rushed through the door, blasters firing as they did.

Royce ducked behind a pile of crates—firing his rifle at the attackers who'd barely missed him moments earlier. He cursed when one of the Zodarks broke to the right, the other to the left as they sought to split his attention, one of them firing at him while the other moved. It was a classic cover-and-move tactic he'd trained countless soldiers in over the years.

Hearing the roar of blaster fire, shouts in English and angrier shouts in Zodark, Royce knew they were in trouble if they allowed the Zodarks to pin 'em down while they waited for their buddies to arrive before the Zodarks could overrun their position. As he reached for one of his grenades, a Zodark had sprinted towards him from the door, closing the distance between them in seconds. Knowing he had seconds to move before the knife-wielding Zodark was upon him, he leaped through the air and out of the reach of the beast that'd almost grabbed him, landing some twenty feet further away.

Wow, how have I not used the power of this exoskeleton suit built into our Dragon Skin armor before... The thought raced through his mind as he fired at the Zodark still trying to shoot at him. Still holding the grenade in hand, he activated the device, tossing it through the hole in the door they'd just created before shooting at the last Zodark he hadn't engaged yet.

Bam!

The grenade had gone off just in time, injuring a pair of Zodarks moments before they could enter the warehouse. While the shooting between the two sides continued, he heard the sound of a weapon steadily getting closer. *Oh sure, now our ride's here...after we've eliminated the threat.*

With fighting now happening on the other side of the warehouse, Royce made his way to the office where he'd stowed Ashurina and the spymaster he'd been sent to retrieve. He sighed in relief to see that they were OK. He held his hand out to Ashurina. "Come on, you two. This side of the warehouse is clear. It looks like our rides have finally arrived. It's time to get out of here."

Chapter Twenty-Two
Why Now? Why Gurista?

Viceroy's Personal Quarters
RNS *Freedom*
Near Earth, Sol System

It had taken Miles a little more than a day to get everyone here for the meeting. With the Chancellor dead and most of the Senate wiped out, there had been a bit of a tussle about who was technically next in the line of succession. The six people that should have assumed the role had been killed during the first twelve hours of the invasion. Near the end of the first day, still without a clear picture of who was the new Chancellor, Admiral Bailey used a lesser-known clause of the Martial Law Act. When the lines of succession were unclear and the position of Chancellor had been empty for more than twelve hours, the head of Space Command could assume control of the civilian government until combat operations to secure the system were over. A new election could be held no later than thirty days after the end of combat operations.

As Miles sat at the table, observing the reactions of the others to the information Drew from Republic Intelligence continued to brief, he could see the emotional conflict playing out in the expressions on their faces and in the way their bodies squirmed. This was why he had wanted them here—why he needed them here. Decisions needed to be made—decisions that shouldn't come from him. But the challenges he'd gone through just to get them aboard the *Freedom* were making him question whether they were even capable of deciding such important matters of state when they couldn't be bothered to venture outside the bunker long after it was safe to do so.

While military operations were still happening on Mars and across pockets of Zodark resistance on Earth, who were still battling Republic forces a week after the invasion, it had been like pulling teeth to convince them to come aboard the *Freedom* for this critically important meeting—decisions had to be made, and their input was needed whether they wanted to provide it or not.

"And that concludes the intelligence summary and assessment of the Mukhabarat Kafarr, Dakkuri Canaan. If you have further questions, now is the time to ask. Once the briefing has ended, everything you heard and saw will be classified under a Special Access Program. Discussing this material outside approved locations will result in criminal prosecution for willful disclosure of classified information," Drew concluded.

For a brief moment, no one spoke. Miles suspected they had questions—they just didn't want to be the first to speak.

"Fine, I'll be the one to ask the question. Why haven't we thrown this man out an airlock and watched him die yet?" Ambassador Nina Chapman spat the words out of her mouth with venom and hate. Then she doubled down. "If he's this Karaff character that he claims to be—and your double agent says he is—then that means he's the Mukhabarat spymaster for the Republic."

Then, before anyone could respond, she held a hand up. "No, not yet, Reinhard, I know you all are going to try and justify why we should accept this man's proposal—*his* offer. But I want to remind everyone that if this is true, then that means he's the one responsible for the years of terrorist attacks, dozens of political and military assassinations, industrial sabotage, and now, the invasion of Earth, our home world. He's responsible for the deaths of untold millions—no, likely tens if not hundreds of millions. Pardon me if I appear to have a problem with this idea of allowing him to change sides now that his is the one that's losing. This bastard has no right to live after what he has done to our great Republic!"

Miles had seen the rage and frustration building beneath the surface of the usually calm diplomat. The more Drew explained Dakkuri's desire to change sides, the more questions it raised about his seemingly well-timed epiphany about who the Zodarks really were, which wasn't exactly winning her over or doing him any favors.

Director Gehlen then tried to intercede. "I understand your hesitation, Ambassador. I, too, share your desire to see this man held accountable for his actions. But if what he says is true, then how could we possibly say no—"

"You mean how can we turn down some carefully designed lure to save his ass and potentially deliver him home to his own people while serving us up on a silver platter for his Zodark pals? No, Reinhard, we just tell him no deal and then eject him out the airlock. That's how we handle this," Nina interrupted.

"Please, Nina, everyone understands who this man is and what he's been responsible for. We also have to take into consideration the kind of information he can provide us about his organization, the Mukhabarat, and the Zodark intelligence agency—I believe it's called the Groff. As you can see, we know little if anything about the Zodark organizations or anything more about their worlds, or anything at all," countered Director Gehlen from the Interstellar Marshall Service.

That was when Viceroy Hunt stepped in before Nina could derail the conversations further.

"Enough. I have heard the opinions and thoughts of each of you. You've made your cases for why we should or shouldn't accept this man's offer to flip to our side in this renewed war we now find ourselves in." Hunt turned to face Nina as he explained, "You make a compelling case, Ambassador, and on an emotional level I agree with you. But I'm going to accept his offer, just not on the terms he thinks."

She was about to launch into another protest when he more forcefully explained, "I am the Viceroy—the head of the alliance. Not you or anyone else. While I am also a uniformed member of the Republic, and Earth is my home, I now have a greater responsibility than just to Earth—you know this, so don't try and twist things around on me or guilt me into making a nationalistic decision. If this Karaff can provide us actionable intelligence that can thwart future attacks, and aid in a counteroffensive I intend to launch in the future, then I want to pursue that option with him. Not see him spaced from an airlock to satisfy an urge for instant justice. Now, if everyone but Drew could leave the room, I have some final questions that need to be asked in private. Tomorrow, we will resume our conversation and begin assessing how badly the Zodarks hurt us and what kind of recovery effort it's going to take to restore the Republic to preinvasion levels."

As the group stood to leave the room, Drew walked over to the wet bar and poured himself a drink. Miles stood and joined him, pouring himself a healthy portion of Tennessee whiskey. Motioning with a nod of the head, he led Drew towards the pair of chairs placed at an angle that allowed their occupants to enjoy the view from the floor-to-ceiling windows when the blast shield wasn't down.

"You handled yourself well back there," Miles complimented him.

"They're right to be emotional. We've been violently attacked—some of this is even our own fault," Drew commented as he stared at the brown liquid swirling in the glass as he gently played with it.

"Not every plan works the way you intend, Drew."

"I've spent enough time in Special Forces and intelligence to accept that, Viceroy. Still, I feel as if some of this is our fault."

Miles stared at Drew for a moment. The intelligence operative had come a long way since their first meeting. He saw great potential in the man, but there was a weakness to him, a vulnerability—Miles wasn't sure if it was an asset...or a liability.

"Drew, do you remember what I told you about the burden of command?"

Drew stopped twirling the liquid in the glass as he answered, "Heavy is the burden of command—"

"And heavy are the shoulders of those who bear it," Miles added.

"How do you do it, Viceroy? Decide the fate of worlds, of hundreds of millions—billions, even—and not drown in the knowledge that you chose their fate? To live—to die. It was never a choice they had but one chosen for by those in positions of power they've never met and never even knew had such power over them," asked Drew as he fought to maintain the emotionless facade required of him.

Miles could see Drew was conflicted, struggling with the weight of the decisions they had made. They had spent years orchestrating and baiting the Zodarks to invade the system of their choosing, to fall into their trap. Instead, Sol had been invaded utilizing the discovery of Humtar technology and the false intelligence they had leaked to the Zodarks of the Republic's perceived strengths and weaknesses.

Miles placed his glass on the table between them, leaning forward to look Drew in the eyes as he began to explain. "Drew, you played a persuasive role in our convincing the Zodarks we were weak when we were strong—that we were few when we were many. Lives, ships—they were always going to be lost in baiting the Zodarks to invade our territory. To remove them as a long-term strategic threat, to buy time for me to transform our Republic and the alliance into the kind of fighting force necessary to achieve final victory, risks had to be accepted, losses endured.

"Drew, I need something from you that cannot be ordered or demanded of you but is vital to our continued working relationship—"

"Let me guess, loyalty?" Drew interrupted, an unsure look in his eyes.

"Loyalty?" Miles raised an eyebrow. "Drew, that's never been in doubt. I know I have your loyalty to the Republic and to our people as a species. What I need from you is more than loyalty—it's trust. Unwavering trust that what I'm doing is in the best interests of the Republic, our people as humans, and the alliance writ large. I need you to trust me without question, without hesitation—to execute orders in the knowledge that they are but one part of a grander scheme of things that I may or may not have shared with you.

"Drew, you asked me how I live with the decisions I make— especially ones like this. I do so with a heavy heart because…I must." Softening his tone, Miles continued, "This is not something I take lightly—or gleefully enjoy or relish. I make the tough calls because men of lesser character, insight, and moral integrity would be chosen to make them in my stead should I not carry not this burden of command that has been chosen for me.

"While having good intentions, the Altairian King, Grigdolly, while also holding the rank of admiral, lacked the ability to rally the alliance and lead it to victory. The Altairians are a mighty people, technologically advanced, vast in number, and they control a sprawling empire that many species within and outside our alliance envy. While they are many things, good and wonderful warriors, they are not. They have expanded and grown throughout the centuries by having a technological advantage over those they encountered—until they met the Orbots and, by proxy, the Zodarks—"

"And this is why the Gallentines interceded and chose you over King Grigdolly. To turn the war back in our favor—and the Gallentines'," Drew interrupted, beginning to piece together how Miles calculated his decisions.

Miles gave a curt nod, downing the last of the whiskey in his glass before pouring another.

"Drew, this war is bigger than you know. It's more than just the Zodarks and the Orbots. They're just pawns, proxies of the true masters of the universe who are pulling the strings. We are but pieces on the board—moved about with little regard for our futures," Miles explained, then poured Drew another whiskey as he continued. "I need your professional opinion on Dakkuri, and Ashurina. Can they be trusted? Are they playing us as part of some greater Mukhabarat or Groff intelligence operation? What are the chances of them truly looking to defect—to change sides?"

The question hung there for a moment, Miles observing Drew as he appeared deep in thought. Not jumping rashly to a conclusion. Miles valued that aspect of the man. He sometimes came off as a less-than-thoughtful operative because of his southern accent or the way he spoke. Miles had caught on to that facade when they'd first met. It was clever, a way to ingratiate himself, placing potential adversaries, sources, and assets at ease with his charm or lack of sophistication. He was a chameleon, a man who faded into the background of his environment and became whatever was necessary to stay hidden in plain sight.

Drew raised his refilled glass, taking two gulps before looking him in the eye. "Here's what I know, Viceroy. As fleeting as life is—people want to live. They want to grow old, even if they say they don't—they do. I'm willing to die for my cause, for my country, but that doesn't mean I don't want to live. I do. But that desire just beneath the surface, that desire to live—that's something I see in the eyes of both Ashurina and this man Dakkuri. They're willing to die for the causes they believe in. They're willing to die so their loved ones may live. However, given the choice to live in peace with their families and grow old—they'll choose to live every time."

"So you believe Dakkuri's desire to change sides is sincere, then?"

"I do."

Miles thought about that for a moment. *If Drew thinks he's sincere…then I guess I should speak with him…*

"I want to talk to him. To see into his eyes. To ask him something only I can. Bring him here, to my quarters, in two hours. Dismissed."

Chapter Twenty-Three
Infestation

Second Spear, Blood Raider Clan
Palácio da Pena
Sintra, Portugal
Earth, Sol System

Otro snarled as another of the tiny flying insects landed on his exposed flesh, feasting on him again. He cursed as he swatted at the bug. His anger was growing with each passing moment as he waited to receive the report on the success or failure of the attack. In the meantime, he stood in what had once been the formal dining room of a bygone palace, with tiles that ran up the walls and all the way onto the ceiling, where an intricate pattern of interlocking stone arches remained. Now the space was filled with tables and maps, and he cursed this planet's infestation with these damn biting flies.

As Otro studied the digital map displaying the locations of the advancing units of the Blood Raiders, his mind raced with strategy, with the options that could have been pursued if he had brought with him a proper invasion force—instead of a raiding force. Still, the Republic was putting up a fierce resistance, fighting house to house and street to street across a line of contact that stretched from the river Tagus in the south to the hilltop fortress in Belas to the north, with Amadora in the middle.

His finger tapped the Monsanto Forest Park. If they were to break through the enemy defenses, the high ground of Monsanto would need to be captured. He had ordered the Fourth and Fifth Shrictars to use their speeders and storm the park, in hopes of taking control of the high ground and opening the way into Lisbon and the surrounding areas. It had been hours since the two Shrictars had initiated their attack. With three more in reserve, he felt he should hold them back until the point where the elite warriors would be able to make their impact most felt.

We need to get past this line. To break out into the rear guard...then we can defeat the cities with ease and without fear of being encircled... Otro still couldn't shake the feeling that time was running out—that soon, the enemy would rally, and their encirclement and destruction would be complete.

Taking a step back as he looked at the map, he nodded in approval before changing to another section. In some locations, his forces were doing quite well, rampaging with almost no resistance. In others, they were routed, slaughtered in some cases by overwhelming enemy forces. He knew it wouldn't be long before the Republic had rallied. For now, they still controlled the high ground above them—space. Once that was gone, time would be short.

Otro was still stewing over the failures of Vak'Atioth and the Groff. It was their failures, after all, that had led to the *Nefantar* being destroyed. Yet at least one element of their electronic chicanery had worked better than others. When the ground invasion had begun, an error message had popped up across the operating systems of the Republic's synthetic combat soldier program. Just as the Republic had during their initial encounter with the Orbots, they had shut the synthetics down until they could purge the systems and ensure they hadn't been compromised. It hadn't been designed to be a permanent solution, but it should give his force a few precious days to cause havoc before the machines returned and their impact on the battlefield was felt once more.

NOS Griglag stood next to Otro as he continued to scan the map. Then Griglag mused, "Mavkah, when you see the big picture like that, I bet it makes you wish we had brought an invasion force instead of a raiding one." He laughed in both frustration and pride. "With what we have achieved with just the Spears, can you imagine if we had brought Hammers? We would have this planet conquered and a new world of slaves to serve the empire," he boasted arrogantly—or maybe it was confidence Otro heard in his voice.

He snorted in response, the map still the focus of his attention.

The NOS commander continued, "Mavkah, I have come to inform you that the Third and Fourth Spears have broken through at Amadora. In fact, they have linked up with your Shrictars and succeeded in capturing the high ground."

"Ah, yes, Griglag! This is wonderful news you bring," Otro exclaimed as the elation of the moment washed over him. He had been waiting hours for definitive news and to hear if his Shrictars had succeeded in overcoming the enemy on the high ground.

Griglag typed on the terminal near the map, bringing an image up for them to review. Pointing to the location, he said, "This point here, the Humberto spaceport. It is going to be a problem. Republic forces have reinforced it and are even now expanding into the city towards their units that are falling back just south and west along the edges of central Lisbon, creating another line of control. To the north, here, Malveira—First Spear just reported their first encounter against the machines. Those machines they call Synths." He spat the word out of his mouth like spoiled milk.

"How many have they encountered?" Otro wasn't ready to panic yet. It was only a matter of time until the machines eventually showed up.

Shaking his head dismissively, Griglag commented, "No, Mavkah, you misunderstand. They have not encountered dozens or even hundreds of them. It is much smaller than that—three or four attacking right now."

Now Otro was confused. Why would the Spear commander make note of just a small number of machines attacking his force? They had destroyed many times that number of them in the last war. Why was this a problem now?

Griglag must have seen his confusion as he further explained, "I, too, was confused, Mavkah. When I inquired why he was reporting a problem with just a few of these synthetics, he explained to me that these machines…they are not the same machines we had encountered in the last war. He said the machines are different—they appear to be stronger, faster, and far more powerful than the ones we encountered in the last war."

"What? You and your commander are surprised the Republic has some new killer robot? I would be shocked if they had not improved upon those machines from the last war. We are just lucky some of the Groff's trickery has worked and delayed their appearance till now," Otro said, mocking his commander's concern, unconvinced this was something to worry about just yet.

Griglag caught on and dropped the subject. Otro motioned for the two of them to walk outside, away from the others in the command center. When he was sure they were out of earshot of the others, he paused, stretching his back as he cracked a few bones and inhaled deeply.

Turning to the military commander of the Blood Raider Clan, Otro explained, "Griglag, now that it is just you and me, there is something I wanted to say. This was a smart decision, heading north like this. When our landing force had to settle on the African continent to avoid those remaining orbital sentry towers, I was unsure at first if we were going to be able to disperse across the planet before the Republic was able to respond. Your quick thinking to use the transports to skim above the ground and the oceans to disperse our Spears rather than having the ships stay parked on the ground or return to orbit with nothing to do was a brilliant idea. I only wish we had a way off this planet, a way to return to our people one day so that I might tell of your exploits here and give you a proper reward."

Griglag replied, "That is most kind of you, Mavkah. Perhaps Lindow will show us favor somehow, and a way for us to return to the empire will be made possible. If that is not his will, then we shall die a warrior's death here, on this planet, and know that this was where he had ordained for us to join him in paradise, to dine with the warriors of our past and present while we await those of the future."

As Otro listened to Griglag speak, he felt honored to fight alongside someone so devoutly loyal to Lindow. Their god and creator had led the formation of their empire and guided it to become what it was today. He was confident that even if he did not survive this battle, the empire would live on, as Lindow lived on in each of them.

Chapter Twenty-Four
The Guristas

Viceroy's Personal Quarters
RNS *Freedom*

When Dakkuri entered the living room of his quarters, Miles stood there, staring at the man responsible for so much death, so much chaos and carnage. He had half a mind to strangle him where he stood, to have the two Delta operators dismember his body slowly and painfully as penance for his crimes.

I suppose we shall learn soon enough if we're going to allow you to live. You best sell your abilities, Dakkuri...or this might be a short meeting...

"Remove his restraints," Miles directed, then motioned with his head for them to join the four Gallentines Admiral Wiyrkomi had arranged to join this meeting.

As the restraints came off, the soldiers complied, joining the Gallentines to stand watch over the prisoner and ensure no harm befell the Viceroy or the admiral.

"Walk with me. I'll fix us a drink, then we can talk," Miles said to Dakkuri as he made his way over to the wet bar near the chairs he and Drew had sat in earlier. He still had them positioned in a way that allowed them to have a spectacular view out the floor-to-ceiling windows when the blast doors were down.

Dakkuri seemed unsure of the situation. The room he'd entered was lavishly furnished, unlike any warship he had previously seen. There was also the presence of another race he hadn't encountered yet, causing him to hesitate as he approached the bar. Dakkuri eventually asked, "I appreciate the drink. But I am unsure who I am drinking with. How should I address you?"

Miles heard the question but ignored it as he pulled a bottle of Pappy Van Winkle from beneath the bar. "Wiyrkomi, will you join me and our guest in a drink?" he asked his Gallentine friend.

"Yes, of course, Viceroy," said the Gallentine dressed in the military attire of someone important.

Miles poured three glasses of the expensive whiskey, then gestured for Dakkuri to grab one as he walked towards the chairs.

"Come, there is much to discuss," Miles said flatly, handing a glass to Wiyrkomi. "I hope you enjoy this. I felt this conversation deserved the good stuff. Figured that bottle of Old Van Rip Lilly had bought for my birthday would do just fine." Miles took a sip after settling into the chair, motioning for Dakkuri to do the same.

As the Mukhabarat spy chief took his seat, Miles observed the man, noting the operative's calm demeanor and sharp eyes that missed nothing. The man sitting before him was a killer, of that Miles was certain. But there was more to this man…much more.

"You asked who I am, but I believe you already know the answer to that question, don't you?"

Dakkuri stared at him, the two locking eyes for a moment before he looked away. "You are the Viceroy—Miles Hunt."

"Correct. I am the Supreme Commander of the Galactic Empire, the Viceroy of the Milky Way Galaxy. The man seated to my right, his name is Wiyrkomi. You probably haven't met his species yet, have you?"

Dakkuri shook his head.

"That's OK, few have in our galaxy. You see, Wiyrkomi is an admiral. In fact, he is the captain of this vessel you find yourself aboard. Perhaps you have heard of it—the RNS *Freedom*."

Miles saw a look of acknowledgment on Dakkuri's face as he realized where he was— aboard the Gallentine warship that had been seen by few but was feared by all.

"In case you hadn't pieced it together yet, Wiyrkomi and those soldiers sitting across the room are Gallentines. A race of people nearly as old as the Humtars, the ones who gifted us the stargate before disappearing into the sands of time. But that's not what we're here to discuss. So let's get down to the reason you're here and determine if your life shall extend beyond the next hour."

Miles observed how this last comment seemed to have caught Dakkuri off guard, unnerving him to a degree. Just as he had hoped it would. Pressing on, Miles continued, "Let's start with the basics, shall we? What is your true name?"

"As you wish. I have nothing to hide, and my intentions are true, and I hope through this conversation to prove that to you. My given name is the name you know—Dakkuri. My surname, as I've learned your

225

people call it, is Canaan. I am of the Clan Akkad," he answered, then appeared to wait for the next question.

Then Wiyrkomi posed one of his own, asking, "Tell us, what planet are you from and what constellation is this planet within?"

Dakkuri seemed puzzled by the question, countering with one of his own. "Do you not know what planet our people are from? I believe you debriefed Ashurina on these details, yes?"

"We know where you are from, Dakkuri—that is not the point. This conversation is to ascertain if you are sincere in wanting to change sides. I suggest you stick to answering our questions truthfully, as if the days, hours, and minutes of your life depend on it," Miles politely commented.

The operative seemed to have caught on to the gravity of the situation, explaining, "Apologies, Viceroy, what I meant to say was I come from a planet called Tanian, in a star system called Valencia. It's part of the Yanis Constellation. There are two habitable planets in Valencia—Tanian and Lagash, both populated by our people. In the neighboring system, Orinda, that is where the majority of our people live. Most reside on Gurista Prime, where Ashurina and her clan are from. There are three other planets, however, that also have colonies of our people on them."

He's speaking the truth, Viceroy. This corroborates what Ashurina has told us, and what our surveillance has verified, Wiyrkomi confirmed via the neurolink.

Miles took a sip of the aged whiskey, doing his best to admire its taste, savor the experience of the specialty drink his wife had purchased for his birthday. He had intended on saving it—perhaps this meeting, depending on its outcome, could qualify as an important enough occasion.

"Dakkuri, you mentioned to Ashurina and then to Drew that you wanted to defect. I find it hard to believe a man of your stature, of your placement and access within your organization, is suddenly wanting to change sides. Convince Wiyrkomi and me that you're sincere and we'll determine if you'll be allowed to leave this room alive. So talk, share your come-to-Jesus moment, your road to Damascus epiphany that has changed your heart."

"I am not sure I follow what you mean by those last two statements, but I will share why I believe my people are on the wrong side of history. Prior to our encountering the Republic, the only species I had known were the Zodarks, and our own. I was never a Sumerian; I was a native-born Gurista. It is all I have known. What I know of Sumerians is that those taken in tributes are the ones that sow chaos, confusion, and disorder among our people. They are the ones the Mukhabarat have been trained to deal with.

"When I joined the Mukhabarat, I had only known our planets, our people. I had only known the Zodarks as benevolent, the ones who gave us the technology to travel the stars, to cure diseases, and all but eliminate poverty and hunger. They were like demigods among us. When I had been with the Mukhabarat for a while, a senior post came available on Sumer. This posting—it began to open my eyes to who the Zodarks really are. It wasn't until I became the Karaff on Sumer, a position that required me to work closely with NOS Heltet, that I learned something more about Sumerians and Guristas. Something that caused me to question not just my own actions but those of our organization. I believe your people, Viceroy, have a saying for this. 'You can't unsee what you saw, you can't unhear what you heard,'" explained Dakkuri, his mood taking a dour turn.

"What might that be? What you saw and heard that can't be undone?" the Gallentine asked, posing only his second of the meeting.

Miles observed Dakkuri's discomfort with the question, or perhaps its answer. *Now we're getting somewhere...*

"Um, the word does not translate into English. I believe you have a similar word or meaning I had found in the histories of your species. I believe the term is called janissary. It was used extensively by an ancient society called the Ottomans. When they conquered parts of Europe, they imposed a form of service through a child tribute. The child taken in tribute would be groomed, mentored into becoming a soldier in service to the Sultan or ruler of the Ottoman Empire. This tribute system, it required the firstborn son of largely Christian families to be handed over in a form of blood tax. The child would be converted to Islam and then trained to become either an administrator in service to the state or a soldier, a warrior for Islam and protector of the empire.

"Essentially, that is what we are. Sumer being the Christians forced into giving a blood tax annually, and us Guristas, we are the army being grown, cultivated like cattle to one day be culled in the slaughterhouse."

As Dakkuri continued to speak, Miles found himself being drawn in. The parallels between the Ottoman janissary and the tributes imposed by the Zodarks were strikingly similarly. *My God, the Zodarks have been grooming and cultivating a completely separate society of humans to be the ultimate foot soldiers for them…*

"Viceroy, you asked what caused me to change my perception of the Zodarks and, ultimately, my faith in and allegiance to them. I cannot say with certainty that it was one particular thing, so much as it was an accumulation. There were, however, a few specific events I can point to as to when I realized I needed to begin figuring out an exit strategy. At some point it clicked with me that to the Zodarks, we are but cattle, foot soldiers to be used to expand their empire through sheer numbers and force of will, without any regard for our futures or well-being. I came to this realization early on after I infiltrated the Republic.

"It was here inside the Republic where I saw for the first time what a functioning society looked like—one that didn't live in fear of the Zodarks. People were legitimately free to go about their lives, to build businesses, to write books, to paint paintings. It was here that I realized it was us, the Guristas, who are the ones being used. Then a few years back, I encountered the final straw for me—and, yes, several years went by after this final realization, but you have to understand, we have an intricate counterintelligence apparatus across the Republic that keeps an eye on each of us—the Watchers. It's these Watchers that make it almost impossible for us to defect. If I was going to make this happen, then I was going to need an event to cover my exit and allow me to safely cross over without my own people killing me—"

"Yes, we've heard about your Watchers. They are challenging, to say the least. You said there was a final straw that pushed you over the edge. What was it?" Miles asked, unsure if Dakkuri had accidentally gotten sidetracked.

"Ah, yes. As I was saying, a few years back we had a group of Ani pass through the safe house I ran. Among the new group was a man by the name of Sargon. At first, I didn't catch the man's surname, but then I realized who he was. He was one of Ashurina's half brothers, and the son of Tammuz Zidan—the effective leader of our people. When I saw he had been sent forward as an Ani for the mission he'd been chosen for…that's when I knew I needed to devise a way out," Dakkuri explained, going on to recount the mission Sargon had been selected to be a part of.

Miles recalled the event well. The Mukhabarat had carried out an attack on the moon during the annual naval symposium, a yearly gathering where the vendors and shipbuilders displayed the latest in technology in hopes of luring a procurement officer into giving them a further look. Because the symposium was held on Luna, the security around the place had been tight. Thus, the only way an attack like this was going to succeed was if the Ani was willing to sacrifice their own life in the process.

"So a suicide attack was the incident that finally crossed the line for you?" Wiyrkomi asked. His tone told Miles he wasn't convinced.

Dakkuri shook his head. "No, not the attack," he replied. "In our minds, we were at war. An attack like this was justifiable. What crossed the line, however, was using Sargon for a mission like this. He may have been Ani, but he had been specially trained for far greater tasks. His father was also the leader of our people and his half-sister is a pivotal spy in the organization. You don't assign someone with connections like that to a suicide squad. You choose someone of lesser value. What changed my mind was the message that came along with his orders. Sargon had been selected by Heltet to remind us Guristas that none of us are too important for such tasks.

"It made no tactical or strategical sense. The only reason it was being done was to send a message to their father—to remind him of who was still in charge, who he reported to. I realized we were never going to be treated even remotely like equals by the Zodarks. That was when I knew I had to get a plan set into motion, which is what I did."

"OK, I can buy what you're saying so far, Dakkuri," said Miles. "However, you still went along with this invasion, providing intelligence that would ultimately lead to the death of our people. You had no idea if we would prevail and they would lose. How do you square that?" pressed Miles, wanting to believe he was sincere but still not fully sure just yet.

Dakkuri didn't respond right away. He looked out the window for a moment, collecting his thoughts before he explained. "What you say is true. I did continue on like normal all the way up until the invasion. What I would like to point out, however, is the Zodarks did not succeed—"

"And that's because of you?" Miles cut in.

"No, not entirely. A lot of it has to do with the false intelligence you provided Ashurina for me to pass on. But there was something I didn't pass on, someone I allowed to slide that ultimately changed the outcome of this battle. You see, I found out about that parallel operation network you guys switched over to when you flipped Ashurina. I wasn't totally sure if she had truly flipped or if she was playing the role of double agent, something we had gone over with all our operatives in case they were to be captured. But what I found out was the specs she gave for the sentry towers…they had been altered. They were made to look weaker than they were. In fact, many of the specs of your warships, weapons, defensive systems, etcetera, had been made to look weaker than they were."

Miles snorted. "So you *knew* we were onto you, but you let it slide because you knew it was going to create a false sense of superiority with the Zodarks and it would only fuel the bait I was laying for them to invade?" Miles queried, impressed with the spymaster.

"Exactly. I wasn't sure when the invasion was going to come, or where it was going to happen. But I knew once it did, that would be my chance to defect—and that's what I did." Dakkuri paused for a moment before continuing, "Viceroy, I cannot take back what I have done or what my operatives and agency have done. Nothing will change that. But what I can offer you is my insight, my knowledge of how the Mukhabarat operate, how we interact with Zodark intelligence, a group called the Groff, and anything else you or I believe can be of value to aid in your defeat of the Zodarks. I'll be able to earn my own redemption for what I have done."

Wiyrkomi leaned forward in his chair, his voice barely above a whisper. "How can you possibly earn redemption for the lives lost to the plans you created for your masters, who just used them? Who savagely attacked this star system, killing untold tens of millions of your fellow humans?"

As the Gallentine sat back in his chair, Miles observed Dakkuri sit there for a moment, frozen by the question. When he sat back, he looked at him. "Perhaps the Gallentine is right. Redemption is out of the question for me. But what about my people? The Guristas have done the Republic and your alliance no harm—yet. If they could be cleaved from the Zodarks, shown who they really are, how they are being used by them, maybe with the help of Ashurina, I might be able to help you pull off the defection of my people. To bring the Guristas into the Republic."

Miles reached for his glass, draining the remains before realizing he'd left the bottle sitting on the bar. Standing, he motioned for them to stay seated as he walked the short distance to the bar, his mind racing with thoughts. *We've thought about trying to peel off the Guristas before...but we never had the support of a Kafarr...*

Refilling their glasses, Miles asked the obvious question. "Why don't you tell us a little about how you think this could work—how Ashurina factors into it?"

For the next hour, Dakkuri explained how the political structure of the Gurista society worked. He shared how the Zodarks had cultivated their society into becoming the clan-based society they were. Most importantly, he explained how Ashurina's clan, the Clan Zidan, was currently the clan in power on Gurista Prime, the capital planet and city for the Gurista people.

Miles had known Ashurina came from a politically connected family back on her home world. Until now, he'd had no idea just how connected. *If we arrange for Ashurina to see her father—to share with him the designs the Zodarks have for his people—then, yes, the Guristas could be pulled away from the Zodarks—maybe even brought into the fold of the Republic.*

Looking at Dakkuri, he smiled for the first time that evening. "I think we may have found a use for you after all. Time will tell, Dakkuri, and you're going to be on a short leash, but we'll play this out. You'll be working with Drew for now. He has my full faith and trust. If he determines you're lying, that you intend to betray us, he doesn't need my permission to eliminate you. Understand?"

The spymaster nodded, then held his hand out to shake on it. "I believe your people shake hands when a deal has been agreed to."

Miles reached for his hand. "We do. Welcome to the team, Dakkuri. Now let's focus on how we're going to cleave the Guristas from the clutches of the Zodarks and bring them into the fold of the Republic."

Chapter Twenty-Five
State of the Republic

RNS *Freedom*
Kita Wardroom

"I got to tell you, Chuck, I'm glad you weren't caught up in that mess in Portugal. That last-minute change of plans to stay an extra day in Havana likely saved your life," Miles greeted Senator Chuck Walhoon warmly as he shook his hand, and the two of them made their way to the large table where the others were seated.

"Thank you, Viceroy. I, uh—I didn't think we were going to make it for a little while," said Walhoon, who was a bit haggard and definitely worse for the wear. "When the attack happened, it all went so fast. I told my security to just get out of Havana. We ended up in some remote place in Guira National Park. The head of my detail suggested we keep our electronic equipment off and just lie low the first day or so."

Miles couldn't imagine what it must have been like to be on the ground when the Zodarks had attacked. He'd never admit it publicly, but he still had nightmares from that evening on New Eden when the *Rook* had been destroyed. The sound of those Zodarks, the taunting, the growls, his crew members being snatched one and two at a time only to be brutally tortured by the enemy for them to hear.

Admiral Bailey stood as they approached the table. "There's the man of the hour. See, Viceroy, I told you he'd survive. The senator didn't survive the AI war just to die at the hands of a Zodark," exclaimed the fleet admiral as he praised the tough, gritty nature of the senator and his will to survive.

"Yes, well, let's get to the matter at hand, shall we?" Miles commented as he moved to his seat and motioned for the others to sit. Surveying the room before he started, he could see it in their faces and their body language—the exhaustion and even confusion at why he had forced this meeting to happen now, before they'd even had a chance to bury the dead, to grieve for those lost and process emotionally what had happened.

There will be a time to grieve…but now is not that time, he told himself before realizing it might help them and his cause if he were to share that.

"I want to say something before we start, something I should have said during our meeting this morning. What happened eight days ago is a tragedy beyond words. In spite of our efforts to protect Sol, to safeguard the seat of the Republic—Earth. We failed—I failed. I have spent my whole life in service to my nation, to its preservation, to its survival, and to allow our people to live happy, prosperous lives with their families. You have devoted your lives to serving our nation as I have. You may even feel this attack was somehow your fault, or that you could have done something more. I want to tell you, every one of you— I rebuke that idea. It's simply not true, and I will not let you carry that kind of guilt.

"This attack on our home world, on Sol, it was not the fault of any singular person. Nor is it a failure to plan or properly defend Earth and Sol. In fact, it is because of our planning, our relentless pursuit to grow and expand humanity across the stars, that we have allies to call upon in need and a military that prevented the Zodarks from destroying Earth. To that end, we owe it to ourselves, our people, and the allies who have suffered losses coming to our aid to stay strong, even now, in the midst of our pain, of our need to mourn for those we have lost.

"There will be a time for those things. But as our allies come to our aid, as they shed blood with our blood in the final battles against the remaining Zodark holdouts, now is the time to stay strong, to stay united in our common cause to live, to grow, and to expand. So I ask of you for the next few days and weeks to stay strong, to stay focused and committed to our cause and know that in time, when the threat of extinction no longer hangs over our heads as a Sword of Damocles, we will mourn for those lost and will honor their lives through the preservation of our species as we seek to eliminate this Zodark threat once and for all," Miles exclaimed. For just a moment, he felt as if he'd given a commencement address at the Academy when someone near the back of the room began to clap. Then Senator Walhoon joined, standing to his feet as he did.

Admiral Bailey then commented as they took their seats, "Miles, that was exactly what I, and likely everyone else, needed to hear right now. Bravo, my friend," Bailey thanked him, then faced his staff and the officers present. "The Viceroy is right. The lives of billions are relying on us to pull it together, to work as one, now with a singular purpose—putting an end to this Zodark threat once and for all. Now let's get to work and put our nation back together."

****

Four Hours Later

Admiral Fran McKee felt like her head was swimming in data as the meeting came to a close. They'd covered a lot of material during the brief, and still it seemed like they'd only scratched the surface. For eight days, her singular focus had been trying to keep her fleet alive, protecting the Republic Naval Shipyard, and doing whatever she could to keep the remaining Zodark fleet focused on her and not wrecking the cities of Earth. When Miles had started the meeting, he had made a point of saying the events of the last eight days weren't the fault of any one person, let alone any of them in particular. That was an odd way to start the meeting. As it continued to grind on and each person briefed their piece of the puzzle, she came to understand why he'd pointed that out at the beginning. When the totality of the damages was laid bare for them to see, she'd have had half a mind to reach for her sidearm once she got back to her room.

He was right...and he knew exactly how we'd feel by the end of today. Damn you, Miles. So why did they invade now? She doubted she'd ever know the real reason why the Zodarks had chosen now to attack.

"I think that's enough for today. We'll resume tomorrow at 0800 hours and look to wrap things up by noon. Get some sleep, people. Dismissed," said Admiral Bailey.

As McKee reached for her Qpad, she felt a tap on her shoulder. "Fran, I know it's getting late. Care to join us for a nightcap?" Miles asked, a look of concern on his face.

"Um, OK. Little side meeting after the main meeting?"

Miles cracked a slight smile. "Oh, you thought this was the main meeting?"

McKee canted her head slightly. "It wasn't?"

Snorting at the question, he turned and made for the door, followed by Senator Walhoon, Ambassador Chapman, and Admiral Bailey. *I guess not*, she thought, following them down the hall in the direction of the senior officers' quarters. She continued to marvel at the size and awesome power this singular vessel brought to the field of battle. On more than one occasion, it had turned the tide in their favor as its superior weapons and capabilities were unmatched by even the best ships the Orbots could field.

As they made their way further into the birthing section of the vessel, she was reminded of why this aspect of the ship stood out to her the most. A warship was typically designed around the weapons it carried and the systems necessary to keep those weapons going for as long as possible during a battle. This often meant that the quarters for the crews that manned these weapons and often lived in for a year or more were usually an afterthought if they were given any thought at all. But that wasn't how the Gallentines viewed the construction of their warships. They placed an emphasis on caring for the crew that had to operate and maintain the vessel, that fired its guns and would brave through damaged sections in the heat of battle to reach its most vital parts. This was in sharp contrast to the somewhat utilitarian approach she'd seen aboard the Primord, Altairian, and to a lesser degree, Republic warships.

These spacers have no idea how good they have it aboard a ship like this..., she thought as they approached the Viceroy's quarters.

"Miles, it should be criminal how palatial these quarters are—have I stepped aboard a luxury cruise liner?"

McKee chuckled at Bailey's joke as they entered the private quarters. That was when she realized they weren't alone.

A figure stood to greet them as they walked in, and she wished she hadn't laughed a moment earlier as the Gallentine admiral, Wiyrkomi, replied to Bailey's attempt at humor.

"I should hope these quarters are more comfortable than those of a luxury cruise liner. The Emperor believes it a point of pride when a navy can afford to look after the needs of its crew without sacrificing the lethality or survivability of its warships," the Gallentine intoned, an opinion she shared, though the shipbuilders of the Republic had yet to fully embrace it.

McKee saw Bailey's cheeks flush and knew he'd embarrassed himself. Then Senator Walhoon swooped in, gracefully sliding between the embarrassed fleet admiral and the Gallentine like a politician looking to shore up a vote before the roll was called. She hadn't spent much time around the senator as she despised politics—in or out of the military. But she did have to respect the smoothness with which the senator could turn a potentially embarrassing moment into one they could all laugh at together or simply forget and move on from.

As she followed Miles into the large living room, she realized that the importance of this meeting had just gone up a few notches.

Miles had walked over to greet Admiral Pandolly, then introduced the rest of them to a Tully general named Muhammadu and a Primord senator named Aguard. She'd heard of the latter via her Primord friend, Admiral Bjork Stavanger, but she had yet to meet the man. As Miles made the introductions, a thought continued to race through her mind. *This is the kind of meeting that decides the fate of empires...*

As people took their seats, McKee noticed that Miles continued to stand, a worried look overtaking the look of exhaustion she had seen throughout much of the previous meeting. Then her stomach tightened as he explained, "I want to thank our allied representatives for meeting on such short notice as we have a lot to discuss. A little more than six years ago, the war between the Galactic Empire and the Dominion Alliance had come to a head in perhaps one of the largest fleet battles in known history in the Sirius system over the planet Alfheim. The costs in lives and ships during that multiday battle were unprecedented and something I had hoped would never be repeated during my lifetime. But it was during that battle that we achieved something we had been unable to achieve previously—an end to the war—or so we thought.

"Sometime after the signing of the treaty to end that bloody war, the Zodark intelligence service, known as the Groff, initiated a plan that ultimately led to the invasion of Sol and the attack against our home world, Earth. We had sought peace while we prepared for war—a war I had hoped to avoid. Unfortunately, now that hostilities between our alliances have resumed, the enemy is making their opening moves."

As McKee listened to Miles speak, she felt her heart race. Her palms grew moist with sweat, and her stomach tightened further. They had fought so hard, so long to achieve peace, only to have it all taken away now. It angered her that more of their people were going to die in a war that seemed to have no end. *We have to finish the job this time...we have to eliminate the Zodarks...no survivors this time...*

"—new intelligence. This means time is not our friend. In fact, we may be out of time entirely. But I will step aside now and let Admiral Pandolly brief you on what the Kraxmer have uncovered, and then Admiral Wiyrkomi will share a recent message he received from their

Lord of the Fleet, the head of their naval force," Miles shared before taking his seat.

What did I miss? I can't believe I allowed my mind to drift like that, McKee thought angrily as the Altairian stepped forward to speak.

"During the past few weeks, Kraxmer operatives have uncovered a series of ship deployments to known logistical bases near the neutral zone in Sector One-Echo," Pandolly began to explain. The briefing tool he was using projected a copy of itself in front of each person so they could follow along as he spoke.

McKee stared at the holographic display and marveled at this neat piece of technology. She'd heard rumors that Space Command might soon integrate it into the Fleet. For now, she stared at a star map that showed the division of territory between their two alliances. As it floated a few feet in front of her, like a personalized display that adjusted its focal point to what Pandolly was speaking about at the moment, a pair of highlighted sections moved to the foreground.

"Of particular concern are these two points here," Pandolly indicated. McKee recognized one of the points. It was the likeliest system the Orbots had used to aid the Pharaonis in capturing the Tully star system—Serpentis. By creating a wormhole connecting the two systems, the Pharaonis were able to bypass the stargate connecting their territory to the Tully system—avoiding the sentry towers entirely. Then McKee saw the other system he'd highlighted, which came forward in greater as the Altairian continued to speak.

"The Kraxmer, however, believe this system is the one we should be most concerned with. The star system contains a relatively large fleet logistical support base. During previous operations when the Orbots were assisting the Zodarks, this outpost was heavily used to keep their forces supplied. Since the war ended, however, the outpost has been largely devoid of activity. Then, around six days ago, something changed. Ships began to arrive at the outpost. At first it was a handful of support ships. Then large numbers of warships began arriving— battleships, cruisers, frigates and corvettes. Then, two days ago, our operatives began noticing the arrival of Zodark ships. The number quickly rose to forty-six. While the number of ships is concerning, it is the type of ships arriving that are the cause for alarm," explained Pandolly as images of the various Zodark vessels began to appear in place of the holographic map.

As she stared at the images of the vessels, it dawned on her that she'd seen them before. Then it hit her what she was staring at. *Those are troopships...those others look to be lander ships...oh God, it's another invasion—but where this time...*

"—we strongly believe Sol is the target for this next operation. However, this is where things start to get tricky."

Snapping herself out of her own head as Pandolly continued to speak, she found herself momentarily confused when it was now Admiral Wiyrkomi speaking, not Pandolly. *Am I so tired that I'm practically asleep while they discuss the pending battle that may decide the fate of the Republic?* She reached into her pocket, her fingers finding what she was after—a stim pill. Slipping it into her mouth, she felt it dissolve almost immediately. In seconds, she felt its effect as the tiredness fell away and the sleepy fog that clouded her head turned to clarity of mind.

She returned her attention to Admiral Wiyrkomi, who said, "Our assessment of the situation is this. The Zodark force doesn't appear large enough to be considered a credible invasion force. Rather, it almost looks as if it's actually some sort of recovery or rescue force. The Orbots, on the other hand, appear to be playing along with the Zodarks, assisting via establishing a bridge—connecting the two systems. After further analysis of the composition of the Orbot fleet, however, we believe they are facilitating this Zodark operation with an ulterior motive. In fact, it would appear, given the composition of their fleet, that their intent is to destroy something specific. Something that requires an immense amount of firepower rapidly brought to bear against it—"

"It's the *Freedom*. Has to be," interrupted Admiral Bailey. "Think about it. What ship in our entire alliance poses the greatest threat to the Orbots and the Dominion Alliance itself?"

"He's right. It has to be the *Freedom*," McKee blurted, the words escaping her mouth before her brain had time to think about it.

McKee saw Admiral Wiyrkomi and Miles share a pensive look as they began to accept the most likely option as probably right. Then Miles spoke confidently, explaining, "OK, then. If we believe this is what they're planning to do, then let's use that to our advantage. Let's prepare a trap. Let's lure them, get them decisively engaged, then destroy them."

****

Miles realized it was almost two in the morning by the time everyone had left. With just him and Wiyrkomi alone and able to speak privately, Miles confided, "I'm concerned about this battle."

"You should be concerned," Wiyrkomi said as he continued to stare out the window—the Earth continuing to rotate nearby while a cluster of warships held station around the *Freedom*.

"Is this a battle we can win?" asked Miles, concerned with Wiyrkomi's response.

After a moment of silence, the question still hanging unanswered between them, Wiyrkomi turned to face him. "You asked if we can—I cannot say. I do not know. This ship—it is powerful, yes. But its true power is derived from its ability to fight with a combined force that is able to complement its strengths and protect against its weaknesses. We have not fully built the kind of support fleet necessary to truly realize this vessel's potential. I had hoped we would have more time to prepare for a final showdown with the Orbots. I feel the Zodarks have unwittingly given the Orbots what they have been seeking for some time—"

"Oh, what's that?" interrupted Miles.

"The location of the *Freedom*. Prior to the Zodark invasion, they did not have a definitive location where the *Freedom* was or was likely to be for an extended period of time. Given the actions of the Zodarks, wittingly or not, now they know where the *Freedom* is and where we will be for some time while your people recover from this attack," Wiyrkomi explained. "The situation, Viceroy, is not looking good right now. Perhaps the Collective has given the Orbots some insights or intelligence assistance as we have to the Republic. What is clear is that the Orbots have decided to make their move. To ensure they are the dominant power not just in their alliance but in ours as well. This is not something that can be allowed to happen. Not if you are to consolidate these alliances for the greater war—the war against the Collective.

"Viceroy, I need to tell you something—something you may not want to hear," Wiyrkomi said as he held him in his gaze before continuing. "The situation we find ourselves in has been shared with the Emperor—he is not pleased, Miles."

Miles felt a stab of genuine concern and fear as Wiyrkomi spoke. His last comment, dropping the title he had always insisted on using in favor of his given name, was not lost on him either. Wiyrkomi was concerned for him if he fell out of favor with the Emperor.

"Thank you, Wiyrkomi, for this insight. It has been most helpful, and I share the Emperor's frustrations right now as well. We have strived to scale our industrial capabilities to produce the necessary warships to turn the tide of the war in our favor and consolidate the alliances as he has requested. Time, however, is something I cannot create more of or find a way to slow down. If the Emperor is able to assist us in creating the necessary time needed to accomplish his goal, then I'm confident that it will be us humans who will achieve it for him. We haven't had the luxury of hundreds of years of development and spacefaring growth and expansion as the Altairians and others in the alliance have. Given what we have accomplished in our short period in space, I'd argue we have proven beyond doubt that we are the ones he has sought," Miles explained. He wasn't sure if his words were being delivered to the Emperor, but on the off chance they were, he wanted to make sure he continued to project confidence and competence regardless of the situation.

As Wiyrkomi stood, he looked at him. "Miles, you can be disappointed in someone and still believe they are the right person for the position. That opinion can, in time, be proven false—you haven't proven him false yet. He is a perceptive man. He sees in others what they fail to see in themselves, but given the right circumstances and the opportunity, they transform like a cicada into what he always knew they were capable of.

"I do not have more details to share with you now, but know that help has been sent. When I said earlier that I did not know the outcome of this battle, I meant that if we had to fight right now, should our help arrive prior to the battle, then the outcome is certain—we win."

Chapter Twenty-Six
Gurista Prep

Titan Military Complex
Site 42
Saturn VI, Sol System

Shortly after their meeting with the Viceroy aboard the *Freedom*, Admiral Wiyrkomi had given Hunt access to one of the highly secretive Gallentine reconnaissance shuttles to assist them in infiltrating Gurista Prime. With the mission to make contact officially a go, Drew had tasked Ashurina and Dakkuri separately with coming up with a plan for how they would infiltrate the planet without being detected by the Zodarks or Mukhabarat and how they would establish contact with Ashurina's father. It was a unique challenge, and he wanted to see how similar their approaches to solving it would be.

While he'd tasked them with a project that should keep them busy for the remainder of the trip, Drew decided to check in with the pilot. Just prior to leaving the *Freedom*, Wiyrkomi had given him a set of orders, placing the pilot flying the ship and the two soldiers who were last-minute additions assigned to protect it nominally under his control.

Having served in the Deltas for most of his career, Drew was used to the kinds of orders he'd been given and likely the kinds of soldiers, whom he suspected were Special Forces of some sort like him. Still, he questioned the utility of sending only two. There was only so much a pair of operators could handle before things got away from them. Then again, he'd never seen a Gallentine soldier in battle, so he was unsure of what their true capabilities were and how well they could handle themselves in a fight.

As Drew made his way past the Gallentine soldiers on his way to the flight deck, he walked past the six C300s the Viceroy had insisted he bring along. It wasn't that Drew didn't see the value in having them. He just didn't trust the psychotic killing machines, especially in light of their recent upgrades. The thought of the Orbots, Zodarks or someone else gaining access to the machines' operating system to redirect the C300s to attack them was the stuff of nightmares. He shuttered at the idea of having to fight one, even in the new Dragon Skin armor.

When they'd added the same Bronkis5 material used in the armor of the new warships, it had increased the strength of previous armor used by a factor of ten. As if that wasn't enough, the newly upgraded combat AIs now included the shared experience of hundreds of battles the C100s had fought in. While he wouldn't deny the impact the combat Synths had had on the war, it just didn't seem like a great idea to create a machine that was stronger, smarter, and faster than even their best soldiers.

Drew sat near the pilot for the remainder of the flight to Titan. He asked questions about the ship's capabilities and how the pilot would handle everything from the infiltration of the system to landing on a planet while avoiding detection. While the pilot seemed guarded at first, the more scenarios Drew asked him about, the more subtle clues he revealed about the ship's capabilities and how it could overcome the various challenges they might encounter. By the time they had reached the Titan facility and landed at Site 42, he had a good understanding of what made the ship good at reconnaissance work and why Admiral Wiyrkomi had offered it for the mission—it was a ghost. It was as close to stealth or invisible as possible while still having a physical form. While he had no idea or understanding of how the technology worked, what he did know was that its outer skin was built to absorb electronic signatures that hit the outer hull and then mimic the signature return to appear as if nothing was there.

While it sounded all neat and cool to him, he was a Special Forces operator turned spy. His interests now were in spy craft and finding tools to better help him accomplish whatever tasks he had been given.

When the shuttle had docked at the hangar used exclusively by Republic Intelligence, they headed into the building, where they were greeted and given a section of the facility to use as they saw fit. After getting the lodging sorted and dismissing the team to let them settle in, he told them they'd link back up after dinner to start figuring out what was possible, what wasn't, and what they should try and do first.

Infiltrating a hostile planet was challenging even when you had access to any and all pertinent information about the planet, help should you get in trouble, and an exit plan in case things went sideways and you needed to bug out. However, in their case, they had next to nothing to work with, and the information they had about the planet itself and the kind of environment they were about to land in was mostly dated or irrelevant. In short, it was a blank canvas to work with, but while it wasn't ideal, he hadn't failed a mission yet, and he was determined to make sure this wasn't the first.

****

One Hour Later

As Drew approached the housing section of the building now that the Gallentines and their ship were taken care of, it was time to settle into his room and enjoy a few hours of the silence and alone time he craved as part of his process to recharge his mind.

Spotting the room he'd claimed for the time they were on Titan, he neared the door. As he did, he heard the magnetic lock deactivate and the door open. Making his way into the room, he smiled with delight. A friend had told him to angle for this room if possible and to trust him on why.

Standing briefly near the entrance, he made a mental note to send his friend a bottle of his favorite bourbon. He stared at what should have been a wall but was instead a window that stretched from floor to ceiling, giving the room's occupant an unobstructed view of the surface of Titan.

Drew tossed the go bag containing a few articles of clothing onto the bed as he approached the window. Extending his hand, he touched the glass, and for the briefest of moments, he thought it might crack or his hand might extend through it. He chuckled at the idea when all of a sudden, his hand felt cold. Holding it against the glass, he felt the cold from the outside transfer itself to him. He told himself that the cold was the absence of heat and oxygen, a reminder of their status on Titan— outsider. While he wasn't a particularly philosophical man, it was easy to understand his place among the stars. He was a foreigner—a traveler from another world. He was mindful of the constraints placed upon him as his eyes did the exploring of Titan—the planet Saturn visible in the distance.

Grabbing a chair from the table nearby, Drew took a seat and opened the proposals from Ashurina and Dakkuri. He was curious to see how each would approach the same problem. Would they identify the same risks? What variables would each consider addressing or ignoring?

Most of all, he was curious to see if they independently generated the same solutions to the problem or provided different ways to address them. He suspected neither of them was aware they were being tested, vetted to see if they operated independently of each other or if their training was so ingrained and entrenched that no matter what challenge they faced, they'd invariably arrive at something close to the same answer.

While Drew had come to the espionage world via his time in Special Force, he'd found some skills between the two professions were heavily intertwined and interdependent. The most obvious thing to look for when trying to uncover the identity of a foreign operative or someone from within was patterns. The sequencing of everyday events, if looked at in a particular manner, almost always revealed a hidden pattern you could now track. What Drew had to figure out from the problem he'd asked them to solve was whether the training Ashurina and Dakkuri had received resulted in a problem-solving process that left a discernable pattern as both attempted to solve the problem in almost identical ways. It was kind of like how a person was taught in school how to use a math formula to solve a problem. No matter what the problem was, the formula you used to solve it was the same—only the inputs changed.

Starting with Ashurina, Drew looked at the ways she addressed the problem, noting specific markers he thought might be of importance. Once he'd gone through Ashurina's, he reached for Dakkuri's next and started over. Halfway into the review, he breathed a sigh of relief. By the time he made it to the end, he felt reasonably confident they'd be able to hold their cover, hopefully for long enough to finish the mission and report back a success.

Now comes the fun part...figuring out how we're going to do this.

Chapter Twenty-Seven
Clearing the Districts

RNS *Wasp*
TF Silver Fox

Brian lifted the coffee to his lips, taking a moment to breathe in the rich aroma of the fresh cup of liquid caffeine his aide had brought him. He glanced briefly at the clock, noting it had been forty-seven minutes since the meeting had started. If there was one thing he'd learned from working with Major General Crow, it was that the man had his fingers in everything. He wasn't sure if the general just didn't trust his commanders or if he thought he was teaching them something by continually inserting himself into the planning minutiae of his regimental commanders.

In Brian's experience, what separated the average commanders from the great ones was that the latter knew how to give their subordinates a clear objective, a timeline for when to have it completed, the resources to accomplish it—and the trust to get it done. From his perspective, if you couldn't trust your commanders to achieve the objective you'd given them without inserting yourself into the minutiae of the unit, then that was a result of poor leadership at the top, a failure to properly mentor junior officers to become the competent commanders they needed to grow into.

Having now sat through nearly fifty minutes of the briefing and only making it through three of the sixteen regimental commanders' briefs, Brian felt more and more like the general's aura of greatness had more to do with timing on the battlefield than his strategic brilliance. Sometimes, the difference between strategic brilliance and sheer incompetence was timing. Arriving at the right place but at the wrong time could have disastrous results. Conversely, arriving at the wrong place but at the right time could discover an enemy fleet or a ground force unprepared to fight, allowing you to score a quick victory.

"Colonel Royce, you still there?"

Damn it, the moment I checked my Qpad, he finally decided to call on me, he thought, annoyed. "Yes, sir, standing by," he rattled off, hoping to appear busy but ready to update the group.

"OK, why don't you bring us up to speed on where things stand with clearing the subterranean levels? We've got a lot of civilians I'd like to get relocated to the lower levels until we can get the biodomes resealed," the general asked.

Brian leaned forward in as he stared into the camera. "It's been a bit of a fight the last few days, especially once we cleared the surface habitats of the districts. At this point, the remaining Zodark force has taken refuge in the subterranean levels. We've managed to clear the bottom three. In another hour, the final operation to clear the fourth and final level will begin."

"Good, good, that's reassuring. Originally you had thought you could have had this wrapped up a day ago. What changed that caused the delay?" the general probed.

"Lack of C100 support and casualties. We ran into some heavily fortified positions in a couple of the districts. Particularly the Artemis and Gemini Districts. We chewed through most of the C100s we had left from the Serpentis campaign—"

"Colonel, I understand the situation with the C100s and I have seen how your Deltas make use of them in your operations. But if we're short Synths, then you gotta just make do with what you have. You do it the old-fashioned way, brute force and numbers," interrupted the general in a not-so-subtle jab.

Brian stared at the general for a moment before speaking, making sure to shoot him a glare. That wasn't how Special Forces worked. They were a scalpel, not a broadsword. He had to remind himself the general was confusing Deltas with regular soldiers, something he seemed to do more often than he liked. The two did not operate the same way and their approaches to overcoming an enemy position were wildly different. But then, an idea came to mind. *OK, you want the brute force route, then let's see if you're willing to support it...*

"Sir, you bring up a good point. If you'd like us to push harder the old-fashioned way, with brute force as you said, then I'd like to request that the 327th supporting us be moved to the top of the priority list for receiving replacements or, if necessary, transferring some bodies from another regiment to the 327th to bring them back up to strength. They've taken a twenty-one percent casualty rate during the last three days, clearing the districts we already have. They'll take a lot more if we go the brute force route. I'd just like to make sure the regiment that's supporting us is getting the support they need and isn't out of sight, out of mind when it comes to replacements."

Brian watched the general talk to someone off camera for a moment before looking back at him. "That's a good point, Colonel. Sometimes when a unit gets orphaned off from the main family, they can be forgotten; thank you for speaking up for them and making sure that didn't happen. They'll be plussed up to a hundred percent before you start the next push. In the meantime, push hard and finish securing the last level. We've got to get the civilians out of harm's way and into the safety of these subterranean levels. I hate to do this, but if we've got to lose a few more soldiers to expedite that process, then I'm sorry, some people are going to have to die to make it happen."

Damn, that is one cold bastard, Brian thought to himself, confirming with the general they'd have the place cleared by the end of the day.

****

First Platoon, Demon Company
327th OAR, Artemis District
Mars, Sol System

Descending the stairs to sublevel four, Thor had taken point, leading the soldiers of First Squad down into the darkness—into the enemy's redoubt—its last stand. For days they had been battling across the districts, fighting an enemy that knew it was trapped—knew it had nowhere to go. When they encountered a fortified position—a habitat building turned into a fortified death trap—the C100s would go in first, using their speed and agility to take a hit, to keep going until they were destroyed or the enemy was. Following behind the C100s, the assault teams would advance, finishing where the machines had left off or been destroyed.

As the districts were cleared, the enemy fell back, eventually ceding the surface entirely—moving the fight underground, to the subterranean levels.

"I'm approaching the door now," Thor whispered to Psycho.

"That's a good copy. See if the thermals will work. We might get lucky," the LT offered.

Thor wasn't going to hold his breath on that. The stairwell access points were more or less controlled lockout rooms. Should a containment breach occur in the district, the safety protocol would initiate a lockdown of the buildings and the subterranean levels to contain the breach. It also meant the pressurized doors connecting the buildings and the sublevels were incredibly thick, making it difficult at best to detect thermal readings opposite the door.

"Thor, why not give the spectral nods a chance? We haven't tried those yet," proffered Cannon, his team behind him, ready to move.

"Yeah, what the hell—why not?"

Thor fiddled with the settings on his HUD until he found the spectrometer scanner and activated it. It took a moment of him staring at the door and the wall next to it before it finally gave him an image. It certainly wasn't perfect, but it was able to confirm there wasn't a Zodark waiting for them on the other side—at least not within a short distance from the door.

"The door's clear. Moving to enter and secure the other side," he announced as he entered the override code to unlock the chamber. A moment later, the lockout panel confirmed the code and measured the pressure difference between the two spaces. "Nominal" was the response on the display moments before the door unlocked.

"We got this, Thor. Let me and Young clear the chamber and advance to the end of the room," Cannon offered, motioning for Alpha and Bravo Teams to get first crack at the enemy. With a slight nod of the head, Thor pulled the door open—and their descent into chaos began.

Cannon led Alpha Team into the darkness, his LMG ready to lay waste to anything that got in his way. Then Sergeant Logan Young and Bravo Team followed hot on their heels as the squad rapidly entered the chamber, clearing a path for the rest of the platoon.

When Thor followed them in moments later, he saw Alpha and Bravo had swept through the chamber, advancing into the hallway that led to a T-intersection, each side leading down a different path. Making his way to the right as the rest of the platoon filtered in, Thor saw signs of past fighting. There was blood smeared on the wall, pools of it on the floor, but strangely, no bodies.

"There's drag marks. Can't see where it goes, but they dragged away whoever was hit," Cannon said, using his IR marker on the NVGs to point to what he was talking about. The subterranean level was still pitch black, requiring them to leverage the HUD's built-in night vision goggles.

"Hang tight. Let's see how the LT wants to clear this."

After consulting the map and reviewing the layout, they opted to run with the drones. Let the scouts go ahead and take the risk of them being detected and giving away their presence rather than going in blindly and stumbling into an ambush. As the drones moved slowly ahead in opposite directions, the platoon split up. Thor took First and Second Squads, the LT Third and Fourth.

The two halves advanced in opposite directions, relying on the HUDs' night vision ability that turned the darkness into light.

Moving stealthily on point, Thor lurked in the shadows as he steadily moved deep into the unknown, his heart pounding in his chest as he inched forward. He hadn't expected the mission to be easy, but it didn't have to be this hard either. They should have had some C100s for this mission. Apparently they'd lost a few too many in earlier battles, the short supply now hurting them most. It seemed the deeper they went into the subterranean levels, the more the Zodarks were entrenched, and the more radical their defenses became.

As they moved forward, keeping to the shadows, he was thankful for the darkness, and their ability to see through it. But even in the darkness, he could still hear the faint sounds of battle echoing in the distance, reports of Third Squad reacting to contact.

The Zodarks knew they were trapped. This was the final floor, the last place they could descend. It was now a fight to the end, a fight to see how many of them they could kill before it was over. As the fighting intensified with the LT, Thor thought about doubling back, coming to their aid or at least bolstering their numbers. Then something happened—an object was tossed from a room, the door closing swiftly before the object turned into a mini-sun in the pitch-black corridor they had been moving through.

In an instant, the HUDs whited out, their ears were assaulted, and the dissociation hit as the stun grenade blew and half the soldiers fell to the ground. Thor barely had time to think as he realized they'd tossed a stun grenade into the blackened hall as soon as First Squad had walked past the door. He blinked hard, trying to clear the white spots flooding his vision with each blink, knowing the enemy was about to burst through the door and he'd need to be able to see or he was dead.

Then he heard the door swing open with a loud squealing noise. Next came the ominous growls and howls from the Zodarks as they roared into the corridor. In an instant, they ran into their ranks, slashing and stabbing with guttural shouts of excitement and rage as their bloodlust took hold.

Thor rolled over to the side, shaking off the effects of the grenade as he lifted his body to his hands and knees. Then, out of the corner of his eye, he saw the kick moments before it slammed into his body. Unable to avoid the blow he knew he was about to take, he tucked his torso down, placing more of the body armor and magazine pouches between his ribs and the kick he was about to receive.

Then he felt the blow, wincing as the pain shot through the right side of his rib cage, his body thrown into the wall nearby like a rag doll before collapsing in a heap.

Mother—

He cursed in pain, gasping for air as his vision tunneled. Then he heard that voice, that oh-so-familiar voice he heard in moments of great distress, in moments when he thought he was going to die. Blinking away the tears of pain, he saw the figure behind the voice, the warrior representation that haunted his dreams, calling out a command he felt no power to resist. *Snap out of it before you die! Give me control and I will end this!*

"Now you die, human, like the slaves your species are," growled the Zodark as it closed the distance between them.

As he blinked away the pain, he saw a strange light from the room they'd emerged from casting an eerie shadow across the figure approaching him and the swords it playfully twirled.

Give me control now so I may end this! the voice in his head commanded, louder and more forcefully this time than any other before. Relenting, he whispered, "I give you control, Thor. Take charge and use me as you will…"

No sooner had he whispered the words to the Norse god than he felt as if something had come over him. It was as if he had been watching the situation from afar before suddenly remerging with his body. Instantly, he felt his strength return as his hands reached for the tomahawks on his vest, his fingers tightening his grip against the reinforced fiberglass handles. Then, like a coiled viper, he launched into action, his body arching through the air as he raised the weapons to attack.

The burst of movement and the ferocity of the attack had caught the Zodark by surprise as the blades of the tomahawk crashed into the base of its neck. Thor felt the bones collapse, crushed by the force of the blow and the sharpness of the blades as they cut through muscle, tendons and tissue in a slashing motion that nearly severed its head—eyes still wide in shock.

Thor yanked the tomahawks out of the beast as a geyser of blood erupted into the air around them. The beast's head barely held to its body as it collapsed to the floor. With blood pooling around his feet, Thor felt a sense of rage, of pure hate-filled fury overtake him. He arched his head as he screamed a war cry of his own and charged the nearest Zodark.

In the midst of the battle, power had been restored, the lights turned on, and fighting continued. Swinging the tomahawks like a Viking of ancient times, Thor hammered the beast, his blades cutting deep into exposed and unarmored flesh as he battered and slashed like a man possessed.

The brawl lasted minutes, but the damage was done. As the survivors collected their wits and took stock of themselves, the cries for medic began to rise.

Soon they heard footsteps, calls of support, offers of help. As reinforcements arrived and assessed the situation, someone pointed to him. "Holy Mother of God, would you look at that. Thor is that you?"

Hearing his name, Thor looked up, staring at the faces of the soldiers looking back at him. He stood alone, covered in the Zodarks' bluish blood, the pair of tomahawks now held by his side—blood dripping down his blades and from his armor.

Then a figure stepped forward, calling to him. "It's OK, Thor, the fight's over. It's all right."

Then in the distance, further down the corridor, a Zodark howled in anger, urging them to fight. Thor looked at the lieutenant, a crazy grin spreading across his face. "This fight ain't over yet, Lieutenant." Looking past the officer to the men behind him, he shouted, "There's killing to be had, and I ain't done yet. Let's roll, Savages!"

Thor gripped the tomahawks as he turned and raced down the corridor towards the Zodarks, yelling a battle cry that even sent a chill down his own spine. Somehow, he was sure his ancestors would approve as he quickened his pace towards the enemy—his hunger for killing still not satisfied.

Chapter Twenty-Eight
Staging Grounds

GN Vraxerian's Mind
Kepler-67

Commander Rintuas sat at the controls of the *Vraxerian's Mind*, observing the formation of warships near an outpost in the orbit of Kepler-67b, an exoplanet his sensor told him was somewhere around the same size as the planet Venus in the star system he'd been directed to relay his intelligence to and warn once the fleet initiated their wormhole bridge and began to cross. When Rintuas saw the name Admiral Wiyrkomi and realized that the ship he'd be communicating with was none other than the *SuVee*-class Titan *Emperor Triantis SuVee*, named for the current emperor's grandfather, he understood why his ship had been chosen for this mission.

The *Vraxerian's Mind* was the first of ten *Vraxerian*-class stealth corvettes to enter service. Two more were also in service, and the final seven were in various stages of completion. What made the ship special, however, was something they had discovered long ago. When a survey team had been exploring a system for potential colonization, during one of their many survey scans of the planets and moons in the system, they'd detected a structure in orbit around a moon near a Jovian planet.

As they'd gotten closer to the structure, they'd detected a derelict ship still docked to it. Eventually, it was determined to be a Humtar vessel of unknown class or purpose, so it was brought back for further analysis. It wasn't until years later that they had realized the ship was coated in some sort of biological material that seemed to come to life once they found a way to restart the ship's power. It didn't take them long to figure out that this coating, whatever it was, absorbed electronic signals directed at the ship, making it virtually invisible to current detection systems. Once the scientists and engineers figured out how to replicate it, the designs for the *Vraxerian* had come into existence. With twelve reconnaissance missions and not a single detection by Legion, Rintuas didn't really care how the organo-synthetic material worked. He just cared that it did.

Like every other officer in the navy, he knew the war against the Collective was not a war that could be won on their own or by magically stumbling upon some ancient weapon that was going to save them all. This was a war that would be won by uniting other species to fight alongside them for the good of them all. That meant finding allies and then cultivating those allies into partners that could provide meaningful support and help. That made their mission to sit quietly, observing the vessels arriving in Kepler-67, important. This alliance he'd been told was called Dominion had allied itself with Legion. Now that that alliance, a proxy for Legion, had gone to war with an extension of their alliance, the Galactic Empire, he and his crew would do their best to alert Admiral Wiyrkomi when this force looked to be headed their way.

****

Nayi Akat
Kepler-67b

NOS Damavik placed the tablet down. Having finished reading the report, he was satisfied with the analysis and battle plan for how his ground commander was going to use the Gurgorra. In fact, it was a brilliant plan. *I should have thought of this.* Taking a breath in, he turned to his ground commander. "NOS Izal, this is a brilliant and cunning plan you have devised. I approve." Then Damavik laughed, slapping Izal's shoulder. "I should have been the one to come up with this idea and not you!"

Izal and his lieutenants laughed with him. They were happy he approved of how they were going to make use of the Gurgorra once they started deploying to the surface.

Once they had had their laughs, Damavik turned serious again. "Once we have arrived in Sol, I will activate the blue star. It will take a moment once it has been turned on. The pulse it emits has a range of two million kilometers. Whether he is alive or has gone ahead to prepare a seat for us with Lindow, the blue star will guide you to him."

"What if those jackals use their electronic trickery on us? Will the blue star be able to get through the jamming?" one of Izal's warriors asked.

Damavik nodded. "Their jamming should have no effect. The blue star operates on a unique subfrequency. We have tested it during periods of intense jamming in battle. It was never jammed, even when we intentionally tried to—we couldn't. It will work."

"Damavik, is it true the Mavkah needs to respond? Will it work if he does not respond and send the confirmation code?" Izal probed.

Damavik placed his hands on his fellow warrior, looking him in the eyes. "NOS Izal, it will work. The confirmation only hastens the identification of where the Mavkah is. The blue star will lead us to him whether he confirms receipt of the message or not. It was built to recover the body of the Mavkah should Lindow choose to dine with him rather than allow us the pleasure. It will work. You will do fine. Now go, prepare your warriors. Prepare the Gurgorra. We have much to do."

****

Vortex of Oblivion

Captain Narkeh' looked at the admiral, saying, "The last of the ships have arrived. We are ready to begin when you give the order."

Admiral Garkeh looked across the bridge of the *Tikiona*-class supercarrier and saw they were ready. At least, the Orbots were ready. Turning to Captain Narkeh', he replied, "NOS Damavik says his forces are ready to begin?"

"They are, Admiral."

Garkeh gave him a slight nod, a gesture he felt his biological side compelled him to perform for some reason. He brushed aside those thoughts. The time for rational thought, for war, was upon them. Nothing more mattered; nothing more would consume his thoughts. Today there would be a great victory, the day they put an end to this warship—*Freedom*.

"The order is given. Let us begin."

With the command given, the spatial anomaly that would create the bridge between Kepler-67 and Sol began to form.

****

GN Vraxerian's Mind
Kepler-67

"Here you go, Commander. Fresh pot of raztitle," First Soldier Landuzo offered as he handed him the cup of steaming liquid.

Rintuas accepted the cup, lifting the hot drink to his lips. He held it there for a moment, breathing the steam into his nostrils, savoring the aroma before he lifted the liquid into his mouth. Suddenly the alarm blared on the bridge, nearly causing him to spill his drink as he sat forward in his chair.

"Get me a status update! What's going on?" He started barking orders to the crew as they snapped into motion.

"Sir, it's the fleet. They're starting to open a bridge," announced one of the officers.

"OK, that's it. That's the signal. Get a message sent to Admiral Wiyrkomi. Tell him the fleet is the on the move. Make sure you pass along the final composition of the fleet. Let's make sure they know what's headed their way."

With their initial warning sent, Rintuas sent a message to the other fleet he'd been told to keep informed. He had no idea how big it was or who was leading it, just that the orders to keep them apprised came from the admiralty.

"All right, guys, now it's time for us to have some fun." He smiled as they waited for the fleet to empty out. Once the system was empty apart from the outpost, they'd send a pair of Shockers to the outpost and then jump out of system and back to Sol. See what kind of help they could provide without placing the ship at risk. It was time to get into the action.

Chapter Twenty-Nine
Deliverance

Second Spear, Blood Raider Clan
Palácio da Pena
Sintra, Portugal
Earth, Sol System

The sounds of war, explosions and the ever-growing presence of aircraft and drones continued to close in on the hilltop of Palácio da Pena or Pena Palace atop the high ground of the Sintra-Cascais Natural Park.

Mavkah Otro studied the digital battlefield before him, examining the disposition of forces, his own and the enemies. It was clear the final battle was nearing—the moment his god had prepared for him. The time when his tribe had chosen him to become NOS, then leader of the tribe, then later the clan. As his reputation on the fields of battle and his tactical acumen had grown, he had caught the eye of the politically powerful NOS Utulf, whose selection to serve on the Council had led to his ascension to the Malvari—eventually becoming Mavkah. Yet something in all of this wasn't right. His rise through the ranks, his survival of countless battles—political and military. All had led to this culminating moment—his selection to the Council by Zon Utulf, and ultimately to replace his mentor, his benefactor and patron, all seemed doomed right now. Yet somehow he felt a strange calm, a peace about the situation. Almost as if Lindow was standing beside him now, whispering to him, "Trust me. Have faith that I am not done with you."

When the door leading into the operation center opened, NOS Griglag approached Otro. "Mavkah, the enemy has reached the final perimeter. It will not be long now until our remaining warriors collapse the lines to the grounds of the palace for the final battle."

Otro acknowledged the report, then placed a hand on Griglag's shoulder. "Have faith, Griglag—the Great Lindow is not done with us yet."

No sooner had Otro finished speaking the words than Griglag's eyes widened. He took a step back as he pointed to Otro's chest. To the blue star that hung around the neck of the Mavkah—pulsating like the beat of a heart.

Otro grabbed the chain, holding the vibrating blue star in his hand. He looked at Griglag as he pressed tightly, holding it until the throbbing light changed colors from blue to crimson red—burning brightly for all to see.

"Our faith has been rewarded—help has arrived."

NOS Griglag beamed with joy, shock and surprise as he shouted, "Lindow has saved us! I must tell the others. We must hold as our deliverance is at hand."

Chapter Thirty
Vanguard Makes a Stand

RNS *Vanguard*
IVO Republic Naval Shipyard

As Commodore Dobbs studied the image of the tactical action map, she was glad the XO had recommended they move it to the bridge's main monitor. The expanse of it spread across the front of the bridge gave her bridge crew an incredible level of 360-degree situational awareness as far out as one million, one hundred kilometers in all directions. When the map refreshed, a message appeared letting them know it hadn't detected any new or unknown contacts.

Seeing the negative contact report should have put her at ease—but it didn't. With each passing hour, the flagship of the Fleet, the RNS *Freedom*, disseminated the Dominion contact report to the captains and CICs of the ships across the Fleet. The hourly updates were a result of the combined efforts of the Altairian and Gallentine reconnaissance assets deep behind enemy lines as they tracked the movements of the enemy fleet. When she'd learned how the information was being acquired, she hadn't been sure if it was a joke or if they were serious. Then a friend of hers in the CIC section aboard the *Freedom* had shared an image of a Gallentine reconnaissance shuttle. While her friend couldn't share how it worked, the fact that it could slip across the neutral zone undetected was incredible. She hoped the Gallentines would be open to sharing the technology used to make it possible with them one of these days.

"Commodore, we just received the squadron's hourly status report. All ships report status green. The captain of the *Rass* said to inform you he's moved the status of reactor four from yellow to green. His engineering officer said it was a faulty sensor that was reporting the energy spike. He said it's been taken care of and they're green across the board now," informed Commander Wright. She'd placed him in charge of following up with the *Rass* and staying on top of any issues being reported by the ships in the squadron.

"That's good to hear, Commander. Thanks for keeping this under control. Lord only knows when the Dominion will begin to arrive.

Once they do—we're going to need every ship we can get," she opined, trying not to sound unsure of herself or the situation.

Smiling confidently, Wright replied, "I'm sure the Fleet will do just fine should the Dominion try to invade us again. This time the *Freedom* is already here. Plus the Primords sent an expedition with another forty-two ships, the Altairians have beefed up Admiral Pandolly's fleet, bringing his warships up to eighty-one, and even the Tully, as weak as they are, sent a squadron of nine ships to help us. When you factor in that most of Third Fleet came with the *Freedom* and you add in what we had there at the end, that gives us one hundred and thirty-one allied warships on top of our eighty-four. I'd say we have a pretty solid fleet here."

Dobbs nodded along, admiring his optimism and wishing some of it would rub off on her. Still, she needed to stay positive for the crew and the officers, who looked to her to be the stoically calm captain who was always in control of the situation around them. *If only that were true...*

"XO, don't ever lose that optimism. It's easy to lose—hard to regain."

"Wise words, Captain. If there's nothing else—"

"No, we're good. Let me know if things change. I'm going to take you up on that offer from earlier. I'm going to my quarters for a little—take the opportunity to catch a short nap while we're still in the clear." Standing, she announced, "XO has the bridge. I'll be in my quarters if I'm needed. If anything changes out here, come get me."

"Aye, Captain, XO has the bridge," Commander Wright confirmed as he gave her a slight nod.

As she made her way off the bridge towards her quarters nearby, she was glad her XO had been hounding her to get some shut-eye before the action started. She'd been running on pots of black coffee and stims for twenty-seven hours. At some point she needed to crash, to let her mind rest and her body stop. Entering the captain's quarters, she sat on the bed, pulling her boots off. She fell asleep before finishing the job as one foot hung from the edge of the bed in a sock and the other in a boot.
****

As Commander Wright sat in the captain's chair, he could see by the looks on people's faces that they were nervous, maybe even a little concerned about what might or might not happen in the coming hours. They knew based on the reports they'd been receiving from the *Freedom* that an enemy fleet was preparing to invade—they just didn't know when. One thing was certain: you could only keep people at a high state of readiness for so long. Eventually they became exhausted, and their brains turned to mush. Once that started to happen, it became hard to keep your people sharp and ready for battle. He was glad Dobbs had taken his advice to catch up on a few hours of sleep. She commanded the squadron, and it was important that she try to rest to keep her mind sharp; if she wasn't going to do it herself, then as her XO, he'd try to prod her into it.

"Ops, let's take advantage of the lack of activity and go ahead and do the crew changeover now. I'd like to get a fresh set of eyes on the stations and get the crew coming off duty into crew rest," Commander Wright directed, amending the captain's original orders.

"Aye, Commander. I'll alert the department chiefs and the crew chiefs of the changes."

Returning his gaze to the TAM on the main screen of the bridge, he privately marveled at the size of the fleet that had been assembled on such short notice. The sheer power it represented was hard to comprehend, yet he knew an even more powerful fleet was on its way to do battle.

How could a fleet this large—this powerful—be defeated?

The last time he had seen a fleet of this size was during the final battle of the last war, the Second Battle of Sirius during the second invasion of Alfheim. That battle had been intense, terrifying if he was being honest. But it had also ended the war—or so they had thought. Now, as he sat once more in the captain's chair on the eve of battle, he hoped that their luck would hold and this might be the battle that finally ended the dominance of the Zodarks and their cyborg overlords, the Orbots.

As the minutes turned to hours, he was glad he had rotated the crews when he had. He needed them sharp, just like they needed their commander to be sharp. When he glanced over to one of the clocks on the bridge, he saw it was time to wake the captain, so he sent a message to her neurolink that it was time for her to wake up.

A moment later, she messaged him. *You were right, XO, I desperately needed that sleep. Anything I need to know about, or am I good to grab a shower and a coffee?*

See? I told you you'd feel like a new person if you took a few-hour nap. No, it's been quiet, nothing to report. I did go ahead and move up the crew rotations by two hours. A few of the crew on the bridge were starting to look a little worse for wear, and I don't want to force stims right now, not until the enemy shows up or we absolutely need to.

Good call, XO. Thanks for taking the initiative on that and being perceptive enough to see it was time. See? We're going to make a captain out of you yet. I'll see you in twenty.

Damn straight I'm going to get my own command after all this, he thought excitedly to himself. Dobbs was a good officer and leader. He'd learned everything he could from her, and she'd been willing to teach it.

Another five minutes had gone by when he felt the need to stand and stretch his back. As the XO, and sometimes filling in as the captain, he was often inundated with reports from the numerous department chiefs aboard the ship. The Navy loved its reports and God help you if you failed to properly fill one out or submit it on time. The admin gods would strike you dead with a nastygram warning you that if you didn't handle it immediately, it would be referred to your superiors for disciplinary action.

Damn REMFs...always got to make it hard on us.

As he twisted his torso, cracking a few joints along the way, a warning flashed across the top of the TAM. *Warning—Anomaly Detected...Warning—Anomaly Detected...*

"TAO, zero in on that location now! Comms, set condition one across the ship and bring us to full alert. Then send the order to the rest of the squadron while the commodore makes her way to the bridge," ordered Commander Wright, bringing the ship and squadron to battle stations. If the anomaly turned out to be nothing, then he might be accused of being overzealous or jumpy. But if it was the fleet they'd been waiting on...then they'd be ready to act during those crucial opening minutes when a vessel crossed the bridge and their sensors took a few moments to recalibrate.

"Aye, Commander, redirecting the TAM to the anomaly now," the deputy TAO announced. *Damn, I knew I shouldn't have let Maggie talk me into having her check on turret three. I need her here now!* Wright chided himself. Commander Little's deputy would have to run the section until she returned.

The crew manning the bridge had kicked into overdrive, issuing orders to the departments they ran and preparing the *Vanguard* for battle.

As Commander Wright waited impatiently for the TAM to report on the anomaly it had detected, he glanced briefly to the weapons screen and saw the green color code across the primary and secondary turrets change to a brighter green, confirming they were ready to fire. He was about to look away when turret three changed its status from yellow—functional but limited—to red—inoperable.

You have got to be kidding me...we've got a primary turret down on the eve of battle?

"What the hell, TAO? I need a status on turret three ASAP, and where the hell is Commander Little?" he barked angrily.

"XO, Comms, incoming message from the fleet commander to all ship commanders," announced Commander Waldman.

"Comms, patch it through to the bridge. Best everyone hears it at once."

"Good call, XO. I've got the bridge now," Commodore Dobbs announced as she entered the bridge.

"Captain has the bridge," echoed Commander Wright as he moved from the captain's chair to his own.

Then the link to the *Freedom* came to life as the Viceroy, Miles Hunt, began to speak.

"This is Viceroy Hunt speaking to you aboard the *Freedom*. The moment we had hoped to avoid is happening. A bridge is being opened from Dominion space and a fleet is beginning to cross. As our fleet prepares to go into battle—a battle that will determine the fate of the Republic and that of our alliance—I want each of you to remember that we are warriors, forged in battle and united in our fight for freedom and survival against this dastardly race of Zodarks and their insidious cyborg patrons—the Orbots."

As the Viceroy continued to speak, the TAM began to populate enemy contacts near the anomaly. Fifty-two ships, then eighty-one...one hundred and nineteen...one hundred and eighty-two...

"While the enemy fleet may be fierce and may be numerous, we have something they do not. An alliance willing to stand shoulder to shoulder, united in our shared cause for freedom. As the battle begins in the coming moments, I ask you to dig deep. To find that inner strength and to remember why we fight. Remember your allies and comrades in arms, who stand beside you now, who have chosen to fight with you, and who will die beside you if necessary. Now get to the fight! And let's kill 'em all!"

A raucous cheer erupted on the bridge, the spacers coming alive as the adrenaline of the moment kicked in and the Fleet's orders to attack were given.

Commodore Dobbs turned to her XO. "Commander, you've got the bridge. Score me some kills while I handle the squadron. Let's do this."

Commander Wright stood from his seat as the commodore moved to her station. As he looked at the TAM, he saw that the number of warships had now risen beyond what he'd thought possible. But then he saw it—a cluster of transports—and suddenly the numbers didn't seem so daunting. Not when twenty percent of the fleet was transports. *I think those will make nice trophies in the wardroom*, he thought devilishly at the prospect of them getting in range of their guns.

"Helm, unless the commodore disagrees, set a course that'll put us in range of those transports. It's time to hunt—and I'm hungry."
****

From the Author

Miranda and I hope you have enjoyed this book. If you are ready to continue the action, the preorder for the next book in the series, *Into the Uncertain*, is already live. Simply sign up on Amazon and receive the next book in the Rise of the Republic series as soon as it becomes available.

As most of you know, Miranda and I have been writing books in two genres at the same time for a little more than two years. Unfortunately, trying to make this work has reached a breaking point and is not something that we can continue to do at the same breakneck pace. I set the pre-order for *Into the Uncertain* far enough into the future that I should now have enough time to finish the final two books in our Monroe Doctrine series first, so I can devote one hundred percent of my writing time and effort into a single series at a time. I want to get back to focusing on one series at a time, so I can more efficiently write them and take less time and not hit a wall.

I hope you will bear with me as I endeavor to focus on finishing the Monroe Doctrine series so I can devote all my energies and attention to the final two books left in *this* series. As always, we try to release our pre-order books early, so grab your copy today. With no other series or books to get in the way, these final books to this series are going to be amazing.

If you would like to stay up-to-date on new releases and receive emails about any special pricing deals we may make available, please sign up for our email distribution list. Simply go to https://www.frontlinepublishinginc.com/ and sign up.

If you enjoy audiobooks, we have a great selection that has been created for your listening pleasure. Our entire Red Storm series and our Falling Empire series have been recorded, and several books in our Rise of the Republic series and our Monroe Doctrine series are now available. Please see below for a complete listing.

As independent authors, reviews are very important to us and make a huge difference to other prospective readers. If you enjoyed this book, we humbly ask you to write up a positive review on Amazon and Goodreads. We sincerely appreciate each person that takes the time to write one.

We have really valued connecting with our readers via social media, especially on our Facebook page https://www.facebook.com/RosoneandWatson/. Sometimes we ask for help from our readers as we write future books—we love to draw upon all your different areas of expertise. We also have a group of beta readers who get to look at the books before they are officially published and help us fine-tune last-minute adjustments. If you would like to be a part of this team, please go to our author website, and send us a message through the "Contact" tab.

You may also enjoy some of our other works. A full list can be found below:

Nonfiction:
Iraq Memoir 2006–2007 Troop Surge
Interview with a Terrorist (audiobook available)

Fiction:

The Monroe Doctrine Series
Volume One (audiobook available)
Volume Two (audiobook available)
Volume Three (audiobook available)
Volume Four (audiobook available)
Volume Five (audiobook available)
Volume Six (audiobook still in production)
Volume Seven (available for preorder)

Rise of the Republic Series
Into the Stars (audiobook available)
Into the Battle (audiobook available)
Into the War (audiobook available)
Into the Chaos (audiobook available)
Into the Fire (audiobook available)
Into the Calm (audiobook still in production)
Into the Breach
Into the Terror
Into the Uncertain (available for preorder)

Apollo's Arrows Series (co-authored with T.C. Manning)
Cherubim's Call

Crisis in the Desert Series (co-authored with Matt Jackson)
Project 19 (audiobook available)
Desert Shield
Desert Storm

Falling Empires Series
Rigged (audiobook available)
Peacekeepers (audiobook available)
Invasion (audiobook available)
Vengeance (audiobook available)
Retribution (audiobook available)

Red Storm Series

Battlefield Ukraine (audiobook available)
Battlefield Korea (audiobook available)
Battlefield Taiwan (audiobook available)
Battlefield Pacific (audiobook available)
Battlefield Russia (audiobook available)
Battlefield China (audiobook available)

Michael Stone Series

Traitors Within (audiobook available)

World War III Series

Prelude to World War III: The Rise of the Islamic Republic and the Rebirth of America (audiobook available)
Operation Red Dragon and the Unthinkable (audiobook available)
Operation Red Dawn and the Siege of Europe (audiobook available)
Cyber Warfare and the New World Order (audiobook available)

Children's Books:

My Daddy has PTSD
My Mommy has PTSD

The End

Abbreviation Key

AI	Artificial Intelligence
AO	Area of Operations
AT	Assault Transports
ATK	Akron Thornberry Kinetics (Company Name)
BLUF	Bottom Line Up Front
CAS	Close Air Support
C-FLO	Chief of Flight Operations
CIC	Combat Information Center
DARPA	Defense Advanced Research Projects Agency
DZ	Drop Zone
ETA	Estimated Time of Arrival
EW	Electronic Warfare
FTL	Faster-Than-Light
HQ	Headquarters
HUD	Heads-Up Display
HVAC	Heating, Ventilation, and Air Conditioning
HVI	High Value Individual
IFF	Identification Friend or Foe
IMS	Interstellar Marshall Service
JATM	Joint Advanced Tactical Missile
JSOC	Joint Special Operations Command
LMG	Light Machine Gun
LT	Lieutenant
LZ	Landing Zone
MOH	Medal of Honor
MOS	Mars Orbital Station
NCO	Non-commissioned Officer
NFL	National Football League
NIP	Neuro-integrated Processors
NOS	Zodark leadership
OAD	Orbital Assault Division
OAT	Orbital Assault Troop
ODA	Operational Delta Attachment (Special Forces)
ORD	Orbital Ranger Division
PDA	Public Displays of Affection
PDG	Point Defense Gun

PSD	Protective Security Detail
RPC	Remotely Piloted Craft
SF	Special Forces
SIGACT	Significant Activities
SITREP	Situation Report
SOF	Special Operations Forces
SWAT	Special Weapons and Tactics
TAM	Tactical Action Map
TAO	Tactical Action Officer
TF	Task Force
UP	Unknown Person
VLS	Vertical Launch System
XO	Executive Officer

Made in United States
North Haven, CT
28 May 2023

37093132R00147